The
KINGLESS LAND

A Tale of the Band of Four

ED GREENWOOD

TOR®
fantasy

A TOM DOHERTY ASSOCIATES BOOK
NEW YORK

To Brian, for a dream shared
True friend, superb editor, fellow fan

This is a work of fiction. All the characters and events portrayed in this book are either products of the author's imagination or are used fictitiously.

THE KINGLESS LAND

Copyright © 2000 by Ed Greenwood

All rights reserved, including the right to reproduce this book, or portions thereof, in any form.

A Tor Book
Published by Tom Doherty Associates, LLC
175 Fifth Avenue
New York, NY 10010

www.tor.com

Tor® is a registered trademark of Tom Doherty Associates, LLC.

ISBN-13: 978-0812-58014-3
ISBN-10: 0-812-58014-1
Library of Congress Catalog Card Number: 99-089056

First edition: March 2000
First mass market edition: February 2001

Printed in the United States of America

0 9 8 7 6 5

All we can boast about
All we hold proud
Comes to us drenched in blood:
The spilled lives of those who won it
For us all. Revere them.
Forget not their names.
In time of need,
Over the flames of fires,
We call to them
To come again.
For no land ever has heroes enough.

Especially not this one.

——Whisper-chant of Kurgrimmon,
Master Bard of Aglirta,
in the elder days, when there was a King

ONDBLAS

N G S

LIRTA

River Silverflow

LOAURIMM
FOREST

BARONY
OF
VERLANDA

Veralk

BARONY
OF
BLACKGULT

BARONY
OF
SILVERTREE

LAKE
LASMERAL

BARONY
OF
PNELNEDDAR

BARONY
OF
NAERLIN

DARPANNEN

ALAGLATLAD

River Sheiryn

TELSHEIRYN

Map of
a part of

ASMARAND

Continent of Darsar

Prologue

The tavern sighed again.

*Flaeros frowned across the warm room. Jacks
of burnished copper hung on a forest of stout pillars
flashed fireflicker back at him. Long-whiskered men
hefted pipes and tankards unconcernedly, as if none
heard the mournful wail but a would-be bard visiting
from oversea.*

*He covered his darting glances with a sip of wine. A
shiver trailed cold fingers down his back as the wailing
ghosted past to his left. Peering that way, he caught the
eye of a lion-maned old man two tables away: an eye
that was keen, hawk-gold—and amused.*

*"You'll get used to it," the man told him, scratching
his nose with a thoughtful thumb. "Truly."*

*Flaeros Delcamper drew in a deep breath. Arching
his brow in a failing attempt to look unconcerned, he
asked as quietly as possible, "Is—is it a haunting,
then?"*

*The old man chuckled. "Came in the back door, did
you? From over the wave?"*

*Flaeros flushed. "From Ragalar," he said shortly,
"for the Moot. Landed at dusk, on the Storm Bird."*

Bristling brows rose. "Costs a pearl or two for that

swift a passage." *Flaeros found himself measured, that golden gaze flicking up and down like a thrusting sword. He squirmed, suddenly more uncomfortable under scrutiny than he'd been since childhood.*

Those golden eyes saw a man excited, young, and with a little too much wine aboard. From a prosperous Ragalan house, by his garb, eyes bright with all the wonders of the world on his first venture away from stern, gray Ragalar. Lilting voice, plenty of coins—a romantic, dreaming of being a master bard, probably sped hence with the blessings of parents beginning to think hopes of their youngling becoming anything were but wispy dreams.

Nettled by that knowing gaze, Flaeros opened his mouth to say something rude—but the moaning died as the old man glided soundlessly to a seat beside him.

"What you heard is why this house is less crowded than most, with the Moot coming down swift upon us." Old lips curved in a wry smile. "Sirl folk come here to avoid being jostled by the ballad-hungry . . . or just to spare their ears."

The severe wine matron who'd begun ignoring the beckonings of the youngest Delcamper appeared like a silent shadow to set down a generous platter of hot herbed woodwings tarts and a decanter of decidedly finer vintage than Flaeros had yet tasted. He turned to look at her in surprise, only to find a tapestry rippling back into place in her wake—an instant too late for him to miss the flashing smile she gave the old man over her shoulder. Who was he?

By then, the dry old voice was telling Flaeros that he was sitting in the Sighing Gargoyle. When breezes blew just so through the sculpted stone ears and many-fanged mouth of the archmount gargoyle out front, a sigh arose that was loud and lifelike.

Flaeros nodded and then stiffened at a warm touch against his hand. The old man had pushed the heated platter his way. He looked up warily as the delicious *smell of heartgaer and roast woodwings rose around him.*

"Eat," the old man said simply. "You have to give the wine something to work on, down below. Maershee's tarts are as good as you'll taste in all Sirlptar."

Flaeros was suddenly so hungry that his mouth filled with juices. He bit into a tart like a starving man and found it as good as it smelled.

Hot gravy was running off his chin, and the old man was grinning at him. The youngest Delcamper suddenly found that he didn't care. He grinned back, and the old man promptly pressed another tart into his hand.

Flaeros had come to the fabled Glittering City to behold the Moot of the master bards. Every two years they gathered at Sirlptar to exchange news, decide which towns and baronies were to go "under the ban" and hear no tales or harping for a time, and consider which bans should be lifted. For a score of nights they bought and sold instruments, sang to crowds who paid far too much to cram shoulder-close into taverns, took on or exchanged students, confirmed a few new bards . . . and in rare years, named a precious handful of harpists to the maroon mantle of Mastery.

Flaeros Delcamper was years away from such a wondrous fate, and he knew it. Yet he was giddy with the sheer joy of his venture, sitting in a tavern in fabled Sirlptar with wonders on all sides. Small, but more worldly than the best tavern in Ragalar, filled with folk from far sailings . . . folk more confident than the anxious coin-pinching merchants of Ragalar the Stern. Aye, he was alone and far from home, in a city of ready swords and, the tales ran, expert thieves . . . but was he not near invincible, with the Vodal on his finger?

He looked down at it—a twisted and battered nail spotted with black tar, roughly banged into a finger ring long ago. It looked as worthless as the seaman's bauble it had been before the best mages the Delcampers of old could hire laid a score of enchantments on it and made it . . . the Vodal. He glanced away quickly, afraid he'd drawn attention to it. It had done the Delcampers much service and was worth (he'd been told, sharply) ten younger sons of the blood, and more. He casually closed his hand over it, feeling its familiar tingle. The Vodal could do many things, but Flaeros had been properly shown only one of its powers: when he stared at a person or a thing and set his will just so, he could see through all magical guises and gaze on the truth. Not that he expected to encounter many spell-cloaked mages . . . but why else waste a truly powerful heirloom on a wayward son?

Suddenly impatient with kin and home, Flaeros heard himself asking, "So where exactly did Aglirta lie, and how fare its remnants? I've heard tales of its fall, and I'm sure I'll hear them told better and broader in the nights ahead, but merchants are fond of wild gossip, and I'd rather hear some truth."

The lion-maned old man slowly lost his smile. "You honor me, lad, to think my words hold truth. Know, then: all the mountain-girt vale of the Silverflow that comes down to the sea here, cutting Sirlptar in two, was once proud Aglirta. You probably know the water better as the River Coiling. Somewhere in the depths of green Loaurimm it rises. No baron ever ruled those silences, but from where the woodcutters left off, down its windings through a dozen baronies, was Aglirta. All between the Windfangs to the north, and the Talaglatlad—the peaks you see from Ragalar—to the south, is now the Kingless Land: a lawless string of battling baronies. A good place to stay out of until the Sleeping King wakes."

Flaeros raised an eyebrow. "That's more than a child's tale?"

The old man shrugged. "You know how such things are . . . yet it's curious; with bards spinning new words for centuries, that tale never changes: the last true king *of Aglirta will awaken when the Dwaerindim are set just so, at the right place."*

"Yes," Flaeros recalled eagerly. "The enchanted stones—are they just, well, stones? I was told they were gems: huge jewels that could each fill a man's palm!"

The old man spread his hands. "Four old stones, he who saw them said . . . and being a bard, Elloch would have embroidered his tale if what he'd seen left him room to do so."

"But that was but a dream," Flaeros protested.

Golden eyes flashed sudden fire. "'But a dream'? Lad, what do you think bards—and mages—and lovers high and low feast on? What do you think barons and kings heed and hunger for? Dreams drive us all!"

"But I want to hear truth. Dreams aren't truth!"

"They can be the goblet that holds it."

The young Delcamper frowned at that. Raking the air as if waving the thought aside to consider later—or never—he asked fiercely, "But you believe all that? The Sleeping King, and Aglirta rising again?"

Golden eyes met his steadily. "Aye. I do. I doubt I'll live to see it happen, and I scoff at the notion his rising will at one magic stroke restore peace and bounty to the land—I think it'll bring us a war leader who'll have to swing his blade mightily for years to hammer Aglirta together again. But there is a Sleeping King, waiting to be awakened. Somewhere."

The young bard-to-be muttered, "Yet I'm hardly apt to go tripping over him outside the gates, am I?"

Old lips twisted wryly. "True enough, young lion. The corpse of a brigand, or the farmer he knifed, perhaps, but not a snoring monarch."

Flaeros stared at him, eyes growing large. "What? Just how dangerous is the Kingless Land? Should I buy a sword on the way back to my room?"

The old man's smile thinned. "Oh, it's safe enough here in Sirlptar. Life's not bad upriver, either, if you belong—firmly under the gauntlet of this or that whim-ridden baron or Tersept. Wolves and worse roam the fallen baronies. I'd not head into the forest without a blade, no—but then, were I you, alone and new to Aglirta, I'd not go out into the forest at all. A blade stops no arrows."

Flaeros shook his head. "I'd heard Aglirta was beautiful but dangerous; one had to be careful. You make it sound as if 'careful' means bring your own armed host, loyal mages and all!"

The old man smiled and propped one battered boot up on a chair. A flourish of his arms seemed no more than a stretching of old limbs, but Maershee appeared before Flaeros could draw breath, as if summoned up out of the empty floor by a spell. Setting sparkling goblets of sweet-smelling wine before them both, she vanished again without a sound.

"These are interesting days in Aglirta," the old man replied calmly, "what with the fall of the Golden Griffon—Baron Blackgult, that is, who ruled the barony of Blackgult—and the rise of his old rival Silvertree."

"Another baron?" Flaeros hazarded, sipping. This new wine was like the juiciest berries he'd ever tasted, drowned in liquid fire.

The old man nodded. "There's an Aglirtan saying you'd do well to remember: 'Never trust a Silvertree.' He's made swift work of pillaging Blackgult and almost built himself into a new king of the Kingless Land, with at least three barons on the verge of kneeling to him."

"Almost? Will he rule it all?"

The lionlike mane of air shook in a firm no. "Faerod Silvertree's cruelty has ever clouded his long sight. He's made foes of a thousand men by declaring them outlaw. With a price on their heads they'll have no choice but to take to the woods and raid farms for food. Much blood will smoke on the snow, come the cold."

"I never knew Aglirta had 'thousands of warriors.'"

"Men whelmed from all over Asmarand who fought

in vain to conquer the Isles of Ieirembor for Blackgult,"
the old voice explained. "Now they're trickling home—
to find homes and farms gone, and friends turned
against them. Aye, the wolves'll be busy this winter."

Flaeros looked across the room. Through a diamond-
shaped window, he could see the darkness of full night,
hiding the river Silverflow endlessly sliding past behind
tall, crowded houses. Somewhere out there in the dark,
not so far off, desperate men with drawn swords were
creeping. . . .

"Why do that?" he asked suddenly. "Why turn so
many battle-ready warriors into your foes? Is this
Baron Silvertree mad?"

Heads turned. With a kind of cold thrill Flaeros realized his words had come out a trifle more loudly than
they should have done.

The old man, however, smiled easily. "Some have
claimed so, but I find it does a man better to use the
word 'cunning' instead, and act accordingly."

As their eyes met over raised goblets, he added, "If a
baron began hiring armaragors without warning,
rulers up and down the Coiling would rise in alarm and
do the same. All would be thrust closer to bloodshed,
all would have to spend coins in plenty—and coins are
something that barons never do seem to want to part
with."

Flaeros snorted. As if other folk liked to see coins roll
away from them, either . . .

"Yet consider," the old man went on, "how it seems if
you loudly trumpet the perils outlying folk suffer from a
few raiders and make a show of the diligence with
which you rush to defend them. And lo—some of these
foes are renegade wizards; your patrols suffer under
dark spells! To keep Silvertree safe you need fresh
swords, and put out the call, urging friendly barons to
do the same, proclaiming a blood price on this dark
legacy of darker Blackgult, come down on fair Aglirta
like thieves in the night. None cry out at the strength

you build against a phantom foe. Those who do come raiding taste your strength and turn to harry other baronies, weakening your rivals—and hastening the day you'll reach out and snatch them down, one by one. Cunning."

Flaeros looked wonderingly out the window at the night and a single twinkling light he could now see, and protested, *"You speak of scheming that rushes lands to war and cares not for lives shed in the doing!"*

"Ah," the old man whispered over his goblet, *"that's where the madness comes in."*

Eyeball to eyeball young man and old stared at each other, until Flaeros asked almost despairingly, *"How is it that you know all this?"*

Old lips laughed without a sound. *"I am Inderos Stormharp."*

Flaeros gasped, thrust his chair back as if he'd strayed too close to a hot fire, and gaped at the old man—who raised his glass in an almost mocking salute.

Inderos Stormharp! Most famous of the master bards!

The oldest and most respected weaver of ballads in all Asmarand, the seldom-seen master of enchanted harps who could call forth the strains of a dozen instruments out of empty air to dance with his voice. The man who'd wooed the sensuous Nuesressa of Teln, only to unmask her as a dragon using shape-shiftings to lure men as a spider catches flies. The man who'd called forth unicorns with his singing and danced with dryads in mushroom groves to learn their secrets.

Flaeros knew he was staring like a man brain-smitten and searched for something intelligent to say. It was a doomed quest. *"I—I—ahhh . . . ,"* he began.

Stormharp waved him to silence. *"Gabbling is not needful, nor the fawning I find myself in constant oversupply of,"* he said lightly, and then cocked his head

*and asked, "You looked at me strangely when first I
spoke to you . . . have you seen me before?"*

Flaeros blinked. "Ah, no," he said truthfully, "I know
I haven't. Heard of the great Stormharp, yes, but . . .
bards come seldom to Ragalar, and respected merchants look ill on their sons learning ballads when they
could—should—be mastering a trade."

The old man nodded silently. There was something of
danger removed in that gaze, like a dagger being slid
back into a sheath. Out of habit Flaeros called on the
Vodal then, letting it govern his right eye, while he kept
his left gazing unchanged on the old man with the
golden eyes.

His right eye regarded a rather different man looking
back at him over a goblet. A younger man, though no
youth—a man of weathered features, piercing black
eyes, and the lionlike build and manner of a warlord
who rides into battle rather than lounging on a baron's
throne. A man who was holding a hand-length deadly
firelance wand trained at the breast of Flaeros Delcamper.

The hairy-knuckled hand that held that wand so patiently and steadily bore a large gold ring, and its large
head in turn bore the device of a golden griffon.

Flaeros drew in a tense breath and devoted himself to
looking innocent. It would have been more difficult if
he'd known what, by the Three, was going on—yet
thanks to those same gods, truth had always been in
short supply in Darsar.

"So," he asked, with a joviality he did not feel, "what
should a man visiting Sirlptar do to stay out of trouble?"

Inderos Stormharp chuckled. "Too late, lad," he
added, waving to Maershee for more wine with a hand
that—without the Vodal—seemed empty of both ring
and wand. "You'll just have to settle down to enjoying
yourself instead."

1

The Lady of Jewels

The River Coiling is cold at night. It slid endlessly and restlessly past Hawkril's shoulders as he swam steadily closer to the solid stone darkness of the castle walls, hoping no alert guard would hear Craer's teeth chattering beside him—and that they'd not meet with a watersnake.

But then, what was one more pair of hungry fangs now? They were outlaws, every man's hand raised against them. As a ripple slapped his face with chilling water, Hawkril recalled their desperate scheming, over a meager fire high in the Wildrocks.

It had been cold then, too, and he'd challenged his clever-tongued, spiderlike comrade to find them a warm lair before the winter snows.

"With *what?*" Craer had snarled.

"Your wits, Longfingers," the armaragor had told him, almost merrily, knowing they hadn't even coins enough between them to buy an ax to hew firewood. Craer Delnbone *was* quick-witted, too (no army procurer prospered for long who wasn't). After all, "procurer" was just a handsome title for a word most folk knew rather better: thief.

"The only places that seem to have coins to spare are

Sirlptar," Craer had reasoned, "which holds far too many prying mages for my liking—and Silvertree, which already regards us as foes to be slain."

"I knew we were going to end up charging right at the throat of the strongest foe you could find," Hawkril had answered. "How are we going to find out where Faerod keeps his gold? His castle fills an entire island! He's got that wizard Gadaster, too!"

Craer had smiled, and shared his one good bit of news: "I heard two merchants in Dranmaer hawing on about how important they were and how much they'd make off of Silvertree. One of them said old Mulkyn died whilst we were away at war. They wondered about his replacements—and if Aglirta has heard nothing of them, they can't be powerful mages hired from someone else in the Vale—and so can only be more feeble at magic than Gadaster was . . . and thus hopefully less likely to find and track down two gown thieves."

"'Gown thieves'?" Hawkril had asked patiently, as he'd known he was supposed to.

"Who's the richest woman in the baronies?" Craer had asked briskly.

He hadn't had to frown for long. "The Lady of Jewels," he'd replied, "or so rumor has it."

"Exactly," the procurer had agreed, proceeding to make a show of leisurely taking a tiny bite of the stolen lamb they were sharing.

The armaragor had put the toe of one of his boots into Craer's thigh, not ungently, and the procurer had added hastily, "A tall, beautiful thing, or so we're told, whom no one ever sees these days—not that many folk have ever been welcome to step into Castle Silvertree, or wanted to. She wears gowns festooned with gems; everyone still agrees on that, and she certainly did when she was a wisp of a girl; I saw her . . . *and* her forty-three guards."

"Not a pleasant memory?"

Craer had shrugged, licking grease from his fingertips. "I'm sitting here talking to you with all of my limbs intact, am I not?"

Hawkril had given him a grin. "Yet I'd not be mistaken in thinking she lost no gems that day?"

The procurer had sighed theatrically, and told his fingernails, "I thought that if I let the girl be, she'd grow much larger . . . and of course, her gowns would grow with her, so I'd have more and bigger gems to harvest, some day. . . ."

"We set off to conquer the Isles," Hawkril had growled slowly, "and now we're talking about stealing a lady's *dress.*"

"Not just any lady," Craer had reminded him. "And recluse or not, this one can hardly be innocent or even nice—after all, she's Baron Faerod's *daughter!* The Lady of Jewels, famous for her life of indolent luxury. She probably has forty gowns festooned with gems— and only one body to wear them. Why, she probably has wardrobes and even whole robing chambers full of gowns she's tired of and won't wear. We'll be doing her a favor by taking one off her hands—and one, just *one* should be good for five or six seasons of guzzling wine and searching for just the right woman in Sirlptar, or even fabled Renshoun across the Spellgirt Sea."

Hawkril had shrugged. Craer had done it again. "Well, if you put it that way . . . ," he'd said slowly.

"Yes, we may well die in the trying," the procurer had hissed in his ear, "but why not go splendidly, fighting and striving, instead of shivering away cold winter nights of hunger, waiting for the wolves to end it all?"

Water slapped his face again, jolting Hawkril out of his memories of warm dripping lamb. If he'd dared to speak at all, he'd have dared the procurer swimming at his elbow to justify stealing a gown—*a lady's gown, sargh and bebolt it!*—again.

But they were close in under the grim gray walls now, and he dared not say a word. The icy breeze ghosting past could well be carrying the ears of a listening wizard. A mage whose boredom would die swiftly in the glee of slaughtering two outlaws daring to intrude on the island that was Castle Silvertree.

Why, oh why, did he let Longfingers talk him into such madnesses? They'd agreed to get in, steal a gown or whatever else of substantial worth they could easily carry off that didn't look magical, and get out without tarrying to explore or get greedy.

Castle Silvertree occupied an entire island in the Silverflow . . . or at least its walls enclosed the isle. Walls that now towered up into the night like a black hand raised against them—a black gauntlet waiting to close down and crush what it grasped.

It was well known that a forested garden grew at the heart of the island, between the palace wherein dwelt the Lady Embra Silvertree—the tall, beautiful, never-seen Lady of Jewels—at its downstream end, and a dock and fortress, the true Castle Silvertree, at the "prow," or eastern end. Walls as steep and crenellated as any bold baron's linked them, rising from the rocky roots of the isle like a huge shield to wall out unwanted intruders. Two desperate outlaws from the ruin of Ezendor Blackgult's army, for instance.

The Golden Griffon badge they'd been so proud to wear would now mean their deaths—and a ruthless man somewhere on the island ahead seemed a few swift battles away from claiming the kingdom Blackgult had fallen short of, with the baronies of Brostos, Maerlin, and Ornentar bowing to his writ and wishes. A greater snake than anything the Silverflow might hold.

The river rippled again, carrying away most of Hawkril's deep growl of anger.

Craer had led the way, striking out from shore the moment full night was down and the river mists had risen, hopefully cloaking them from any watchers on the frowning battlements. Their only hope of reaching the isle without tiring was to swim for the dock and let the river carry them down the length of the fortified island, to the rough outcropping in the otherwise sheer castle walls, where a jetty had been torn away at the orders of Faerod Silvertree—to keep unwanted visitors far from his daughter.

Their only hope of even reaching the castle alive was to get to it before the moon rose and transformed the river into a sheet of rippling silver. Even a yawning guard could hardly miss two heads moving steadily nearer.

Tarry, old moon . . . for once. . . .

"Close, now," Craer gasped, so quietly that Hawkril only just caught the words. As their fingertips brushed wet and slimy stone at about the same time, the procurer added in an almost soundless breath, "Seems like we've been in this bebolten river all night!"

He shivered like a swift-wriggling eel as he clawed himself up the broken face of rock, a dark and glistening shadow in front of Hawkril's nose. They both wore carry-sacks and bore their weapons lashed into goose-greased scabbards . . . and they were both cold, wet, and having second thoughts about this bold—ah, by the Three, call it true and call it "foolish"—plan.

"Ready?" Craer asked in Hawkril's ear, as the armaragor clambered up onto a rock shelf beside him and tugged off one boot to let far too much river water spill out.

"No, but if we meet a guard, I can always drown him," the swordmaster muttered, carefully working his boot back on. They both wore their light fighting-leathers without the battle padding that, when wet, would have made it too heavy to climb in. At least the walls here were rough set and easy to scale. No doubt the Lords Silvertree, down the years, hadn't given much thought to the steadily diminishing ranks of thieves idiotic enough to try to drop in on a succession of barons known for their cruelty, slave-dealings, and love of torture. It seemed that the latest flowering of the line, Baron Faerod, was no more vigilant.

"Well, that's it: he's doomed now, the fool," Craer told himself in silent sarcasm, as he wiped his fingertips on the stone walls until he judged them dry enough and reached up to find his first fingerholds.

The palace was somewhere on the far side of the island, with a Silvertree riverboat—according to local gossip, the home of restless Silvertree soldiery set there to intercept attempts by enemies of the baron to use his ferry—anchored not far off its walls.

Hopefully no one and nothing dwelt or guarded the walls just here, where the pavilion and jetty had been torn down, and two desperate men were now making their way up. "Desperate, or just foolish," Craer grunted, not realizing he'd spoken aloud until he heard Hawkril answer from below.

"Master it, Longfingers: you're desperate. *I'm* just foolish, look you?"

Craer grinned into the darkness and climbed on without answering. The going was easy—too easy, old instincts were shrieking at him—and they were almost at the crenellations that topped the wall already. He'd heard and seen no sign of sentries, but . . .

Straining to make no sound, and to hear even the slight whistle of sliced air a stealthily swung weapon might make, the procurer hauled himself up onto smooth stone strewn with bird droppings—a thankful sign of neglect—between two merlons. The wall was thick and showed not the slightest signs of weathering, here at its top. Not the slightest signs . . .

The hair rose on the back of his neck. A frowning Craer unlaced the ties on two of his daggers. Then, swallowing, he crawled forward to make room for Hawkril. The armaragor was patting his leg impatiently, wanting to get clear of the danger of a killing fall back down to the cold, waiting river.

A simple, railless walkway ran along the inside of the walls for as far as the lastalan's eyes could see in either direction, without stair or tower or platform to break its run. It seemed deserted, silent trees standing in thick ranks right in front of them. The walkway was perhaps the height of three men aboveground. It didn't seem to bear any traps or pitfalls but was in truth largely lost in darkness.

Some spells give off a faint, high singing, an endless keening of aroused magic . . . but there was no such sound here. The trees had been trimmed to keep ambitious boughs from reaching out to overhang the walkway. Craer looked up and down the deserted curve of the wall, frowning, but could see nothing amiss. Behind him, he could feel more than hear Hawkril's heavy breathing on his shoulder. Something was *wrong*. . . .

He reached back and tapped the armaragor's arm deliberately, twice—the Blackgultan signal to wait silently until bidden otherwise—and then eased himself forward, keeping low and inching with infinite care, looking for a tripwire that might bring death out of that close and dark foliage. He found nothing.

Unlacing the cords that secured his needle-thin whipblade shortsword, Craer thrust it out before him and waved it around. Its blade was black and dull finished, but the grease that might keep it from rusting glistened in the first light of the rising moon. Nothing happened, even when he touched the walkway and pressed down hard. Then he sighed, shrugged, and stepped forward and down, knowing this was going to be a mistake.

It was, but Hawkril had joined him before something brushed Craer's leg. He spun away, and felt leather tear. Looking down, he stared at a humanlike arm that had sprouted out of the stones to clutch at him. Another was reaching for Hawkril—and a third!

"'Ware!" he snarled, shoving the armaragor away from him. His skin crawled as he saw a forest of fingertips growing out of the stones, now. "Jump!" he hissed. "We've got to get gone before—"

Cruel stone fingers clutched them from all sides.

"Horns!" Hawkril swore, and put his whole body behind a swing of his war sword. Craer heard stone shatter and shards clack and clatter off the stones around the swordmaster, an instant before he bent to hammer with the pommel of his own blade at the stony hands now tightening with crushing force around his own ankles.

"Get off the wall!" he snarled in Hawkril's direction, twisting and stamping his feet as he whacked aside stabbing fingers of stone.

He heard the tall armaragor grunt with effort, and something struck his leg a numbing blow. Craer felt wetness in his boot—and sudden freedom. He spun away into space, drawing up his knees to land in what he hoped was earth and not spikes or the waiting jaws of some guardian beast.

His heels found soft earth and leaves that tore under him—and then he was rolling desperately out of the way, as an off-balance armaragor, arms flailing, toppled down out of the night almost on top of him. The procurer felt another blow on his leg . . . and then silence fell. He drew in a deep breath and sprang to his feet, tugging at Hawkril.

"There may be a warning spell! *Come!*"

The armaragor answered him with a groan and then a curse. As he rolled over to find his feet almost reluctantly, what was left of some spiny, berry-bedecked shrub fell from his back and shoulders. Hawkril looked down, found that he'd crushed whatever it was thoroughly, and waded rather stiffly out of its shattered ruin onto what must be a moss path. The garden ahead was a maze of moon-silvered tree trunks, winding paths, and beds of half-seen, shadowed flowers and shrubs. It seemed to be a succession of gentle hills.

Craer was already a few paces down the path, crouching and peering intently as he drew on soft (and sopping) leather gloves. "They say the baron hunts stags here," he murmured, "and that his daughter wanders idly about in floral gardens that are probably *that* way."

Without another word the procurer set off in the direction he'd pointed, in a sort of crouching run. He seemed to be limping. Ignoring his own pains, Hawkril dug in his heels and lumbered along in pursuit, grumbling, "If she's wandering around a garden right now, in the dark, it won't be for idle purposes . . . not unless she's a deal less sane than most of us."

Neither of the intruders saw the wall behind them ripple and bulge, for all the world as if it was pudding being mixed vigorously and not old and massive stone.

One of the crenellations toppled suddenly, and seemed to *flow* through the walkway and downward rather than crashing and shattering. When it reached the torn flowerbed where the two men had landed, it stopped, and its shape seemed to shift subtly. When it moved again, it walked like a man—a lumbering knight in full armor, visor down and stony blade raised to slay, its free hand wearing a massive spiked war gauntlet.

It moved stiffly, as if a little uncertain of its surroundings, but its course was clear: it was following the intruders, sword raised and ready to slay.

Hawkril thrust his head forward, listening intently. Faint crashings of disturbed foliage could be heard far back along the way they'd come. He frowned. "Dogs?" he asked, puzzled. "No, something that moves more slowly . . ."

"Come," Craer said, moving on at a trot. He *was* limping, and his smile was tight and mirthless. "No doubt we'll learn what it is soon enough." A few paces on, he changed direction. "Formal plantings!"

"Whence this sudden fancy for flowers?" Hawkril growled. "'Tis a bit dark, surely, to be admiring blooms!"

The procurer gave him a pity-the-poor-dullard look and explained. "If the Lady Embra wanders idly in floral gardens from time to time, said floral gardens are therefore probably free of sentries or guardian beasts. Through the thick helm yet, Tall Post?"

The rustlings and crashings were growing steadily nearer. "Getting there," Hawkril told his brother-in-arms dryly, and joined the gasping procurer in a last sprint toward flowers and open moonlit spaces. The moon was very bright now; the open space ahead shone like a row of candlelit swords in a swordsmith's shop. Against that shining rose a dark bulk: a rampant watch-wyvern, its fearsome beak poised and its glittering gaze bent upon them.

"Graul," Hawkril gasped, losing his breath for the first time. "What's this, friend Craer? Rush to thy doom evening?"

"What?"

"Yon—look! The wyvern!"

"A statue, thick helm . . . see? There's another, there, and—"

"In this place, they're probably all real wyverns, made statues by magic until we try to walk past them," Hawkril complained.

Craer asked mockingly, "Want to be an adventurer, laddy, and use that sword?"

The armaragor noticed, however, that as they ran the procurer shook his strangling wire out of his glove and let it dangle ready in his hand—and that the point of the short sword he bore in his other hand never dipped in the direction of its sheath.

The garden glades were lovely by moonlight; 'twas a pity something was chasing them and that they dared not linger for even a single look into each bower they passed. Ahead, the silver light touched stone balconies and gleamed back from windows. . . .

That were blotted out an instant later by something large and furred and silent, springing through the air with its gaping jaws agleam!

"*Horns!*" Hawkril swore, driving his blade at the thing as it plunged past. "'Tis a wolf!"

His steel met the leaping form solidly and tore along its ribs with a rattling impact that sent blood spraying and nearly tore the sword from his grasp. The wolf made no sound of rage or pain—only the snap of its jaws as it pounced on Craer and drove him over backward, biting viciously at his face.

The armaragor swallowed a curse and chopped at the wolf's head. Its jaws were caught on Craer's strangling-wire, which the procurer had hastily stretched from hand to hand to bar the way to his throat. The beast was ignoring the long, jagged wound Hawkril's blade had opened in its side—a rent out of which much dark liquid was pouring—but it couldn't ignore the blows that nearly severed its head from its body.

Craer was making wet choking sounds under all the gore, and Hawkril bent to snatch the wolf off of his . . .

The sudden blow to his ribs drove the wind from him and tore both hot and cold; Hawkril cried out despite himself as he went to the ground, sword flailing the air in futility. There was a second wolf.

Gore burst from the jaws and cloven throat of the wolf atop Craer, half drowning him in a hot, wet, blinding flood; he spat and coughed and tried to keep breathing, smashing at lolling jaws with his elbow in an attempt to get out from under. These must be a pair of the legendary smoke wolves, who always kept silence as they slew . . . at least, he hoped there were only two.

Hawkril was gasping in pain, the sound almost drowned out by horrible gnawing noises. Craer struggled desperately to roll away from the wet and dead weight on top of him. He had to get to his friend in time.

He was free! Rolling to his feet, Craer stumbled and fell onto his knees as the ground shook, and something large and dark blotted out the moonlight. It loomed over the struggling forms of Hawkril and the wolf, now rolling and kicking, and a massive stone sword swung ponderously up—by the Three, a knight of stone!—and then down, ringing sparks from ornamental stones set in a floral planting. Hawkril was a hand's width away from that descending blade, but the wolf that had savaged him was thrashing and sagging on the ground, cut cleanly in two.

Craer was sprinting by then, dodging past the rising stone sword to pluck at his groaning friend. "Up! Up and *run!*" he gasped. "Run, you thick-headed sword swinger!"

Hawkril swayed to his feet, made a sort of a sob, and stumbled out of the floral bed into a staggering, lumbering run, the procurer at his elbow urging and tugging.

"Come on, come on, hurry, come *on.*" Craer glanced back at the approaching stone guardian and saw it striding after them, sword raised, staring stone eyes blank. If he was wrong about the magic that moved it, the lives and careers of Craer Delnbone and Hawkril Anharu bid fair to be soon over. The open moonlight of the gardens was close ahead, now, and he'd find out soon enough.

Was it ever soon enough to die?

The ground shook beneath their desperate boots; the stone knight was gaining on them. Just a stride or two more, though, and . . .

They were out, gasping, into the moonlight, with the tattered leaves of a last bush whirling around them, and a tranquil fountain ahead. Craer caught at Hawkril's arm as the armaragor staggered sideways, cursing, and risked a look back—just as the knight took a step out into the open.

It did not freeze, as he'd hoped it would. Soon they'd be close enough to the palace for even snoring servant-maids to hear its lumbering progress, and then it really wouldn't matter if that heavy stone sword chopped them down—or if they died by guards' blades or wizards' spells.

Dead was dead.

"And not a gown to show for it," he muttered, as the stone knight loomed up over them and swept its blade up, heedless of snapping, dancing branches.

"Hawkril," he hissed, "there's a statue yonder! Get around the other side of it—use it as a shield!"

The armaragor lifted a face that was tight with pain, and nodded. "And you?"

"I'll be busy doing something clever," Craer told him, and was rewarded with the ghost of a smile. It vanished as the thundering fall of the stone blade turned into a scream of stone clawing stone, and an ornamental paving—it might have been a gravestone—burst up in shards from the ground . . .

Stone shards that kissed the heels of the staggering armaragor, goading him into a stumbling run, and almost beheaded a desperately diving procurer. Craer rolled, spitting out dirt and carefully groomed grasses, finding his feet again with the patiently striding stone knight close behind him.

He did a little dance for it, weaving away from the statue he'd seen—some Lord Silvertree waving his sword at the stars to make the stallion beneath him rear, a pose that by the looks of things vastly impressed all the incontinent birds on the island—to be sure it didn't follow Hawkril yet. The stone face never looked at him, and the stone eyes stayed blank, but its shoulders turned toward the procurer who hated to be called Longfingers, and its blade rose again to smite.

A seeking spell, then, and not some wizard awake in a room of the Castle directing it to smite thus and so . . . thank the Three at least for that!

Craer caught his breath, watching it loom up over him, and cast another glance at the statue. Yes, 'twas tall enough, and Hawkril was safely in its shadow, gasping loudly enough to be heard from here.

This would be a slim, deadly chance—but slim, deadly chances were all they had just now . . . were all they'd had for some time.

"Come on, then," he murmured. "Hew down the hero."

The stone knight's blade rose again and fell. It didn't have to be fast, if a foe couldn't flee. One strike of that stone sword—as large and as heavy as a horse—would kill even someone as large as Hawkril. It would probably reduce Craer Delnbone to bloody pulp, not even worth the bother of burial.

Stone whistled down, and Craer leaped for his life.

The ground trembled dully behind him—very close behind him—and then he was sprinting through the moonlight, racing across the neatly trimmed sward as if there were more wolves plunging after him.

Perhaps there were, in some distant glade of the garden. A worry for later; he had worries enough to keep him busy now. The procurer swarmed up the stone statue, his wet hands slipping all too often, and thanked the Three for sculptors whose flowing tails and high-backed saddles made easy footholds for desperate climbers. He saw Hawkril peering up at him as he reached the horse's head, kicked a bird nest from its mouth, and saw the stone knight bearing down on him.

Its sword was rising, and its head was tilting back as if it could see him. If there wasn't some way to knock its head off, they were probably doomed—unless Craer could get it to fall over the statue somehow. He stood above it on his sculpted perch, waiting tensely. He'd have only one chance to leap.

Its sword swept around in a chop that rang off the statue's sword, turning the knight slightly, and would have missed Craer by inches. He let the stone sword go past, and then leaped almost delicately onto the knight's shoulder, clawing at its head.

No, there was no seam here, and no wobbling weakness. It might have been a living man, it felt so alive. Alive, and as solid as stone, and he was going to die, here and now, as the stone sword swept back again to shear him off the knight's head.

At the last instant Craer swung himself around the far side of the head and dropped, clinging by his fingertips. The knight smote itself hard on the head, and Craer's world rocked.

Brief lightnings crackled through his fingertips, raging over the curved stone, and the procurer fell away, pain stabbing through him in a rush that left him unable to even cry out. He bounced on the damp grass, and far above him, the dark bulk of the knight swayed, blotting out the moon, and then started to fall, in a dark and looming rush he knew he could not escape. . . .

A strong arm snatched him by one elbow and threw him into a flowerbed.

"Can't you keep out of tr—," Hawkril snarled, before the deep, ground-shaking crashes began, drowning out whatever else the swordmaster was trying to say. The knight's fall threw Hawkril helplessly up into the air, and in the moonlight Craer saw his tumbling friend arch in silent agony before a different part of the flowerbed swallowed him.

And silence, after ponderous pieces of stone stopped rolling, finally fell.

Craer rose into a low, tense crouch, keeping his eyes on the shattered knight, but its parts did not move again, and he let out his breath in silent thanks as he peered all around, seeking running wolves or armored figures or other guardians and finding blessed nothing.

"Hawk," the procurer hissed, "it's down. How badly?"

"Do I look like a master healer to you? How the horns should I know?" the armaragor snarled, from not far away. "My ribs . . . gone. Everything . . . wet and open . . ."

Craer scrambled through floral displays to pluck Hawkril's arm away from his side and look at the wounds, but the armaragor shook him away, wincing and gasping, and staggered to his feet, stumping off across the grass toward the fountain.

The procurer frowned at the wounded warrior's back for a moment, and then slowly sat down on the smooth turf and took off his left boot. It held about as much water as Hawkril's had—but it also held something else: a flat glass vial that Craer unstrapped, held in his hand for a moment as if reluctant to let it go, and then sprang up, bootless, to offer to the swordmaster.

Hawkril sank down on the stone lip of the fountain and swallowed the healing draught without query or hesitation. Craer held him firmly by one arm as the usual brief, teeth-chattering seizure wracked the armaragor.

When it was done, Hawkril looked up, the creases of pain gone from his face, and said softly, "Have my thanks. That's a very large thing I owe you, Craer."

"We'll be wed come morning," the procurer joked, stepping into the fountain. The waters were cold and the stone beneath his boots slimy with greencreep, but he had to get rid of the wolf blood, or there wouldn't be a blind hound in all the Vale that wouldn't be able to follow him.

As Craer crouched down and watched dark threads of blood drift away from him across the water, Hawkril followed him in. He growled, deep in his throat, at the water's chill, and then sank down as the procurer had done, wincing as the slimy wet touched his ravaged side. He touched himself there rather gingerly, then looked up and asked, "Well, shall we press on? By now she's either up and waiting for us, or she's deaf."

Craer lifted his lip in a mirthless grin and led the way through a still and coldly beautiful succession of paths, lawns, bowers, and little arched bridges over ponds. It was a surprisingly long way; if the Lady of Jewels had only her ears to rouse her, and not the promptings of magic, Hawkril might be wrong . . . and they just might live to see another morning. Beyond that, the procurer wasn't willing to entertain any bets.

The westernmost outcropping of the castle stretched

away along the wall out of sight, in a series of towers and buttresses and balconies that looked for all the world like some great and many-legged stone beast sprawling asleep along the ground. In front of them, though, its grim gray stone launched out into space in a trio of slender hanging bridges, covered and windowed walkways that led to the Lady Turret, built of ivory stone to house the many wives of a long-dead Lord Silvertree . . . and now the home, it was said, of the Lady of Jewels. The balconies and arched windows they'd seen from afar were, of course, larger than they'd thought, but the two intruders reached their shadows at last and held still for a long time, looking and listening for any sign of sentries or something stirring. Only in bards' tales had wizards so much magic to waste that they cast field upon field of nightly watchings and wardings—but, as the old saying went, it took only one.

Craer threw back his head and drew in a deep, soundless breath, shaking his shoulders and fingers to relax. Then he plunged his hands to his belt, drew his sodden tunic up to his armpits, and began to unwind what looked like ridged armor from around his midriff. It was a long, dark waxed cord, and it piled up in a coil by his feet with only the faintest of wet slitherings. As Hawkril watched, the procurer adjusted his wet gloves and went up the wall with the slow, deliberate ease of a master climber. He'd chosen a fluted column that ascended beside three tiers of balconies, and he moved up it like a slow shadow, as silent as Hawkril's held breath—past one balcony, then the second, onto the third. After a moment or two came the ripple along the cord that told the armaragor to start climbing.

Hawkril set booted feet against fluted stone, gathered a winding of rope around his arm, and grimly hauled himself toward the stars.

It was a long way in the bright moonlight to that third balcony, and Hawkril was breathing heavily when he crouched down beside Craer and made the double finger-tap that told his brother-in-arms that he was ready to proceed. The procurer put his mouth to Hawkril's ear and breathed, "I mislike the look of all these doors. A simple cord-and-bells would serve as a night alarm, with never a spell needed."

Hawkril looked at the row of balcony doors. They were little more than ornate metal frames set with glass, with closed draperies behind them forming an endless dark wall veiling all view of any treasures—or guards—within. He shrugged and muttered, "You're the procurer. Whither on, then?"

Craer pointed at a small, shuttered window along the wall, a good way out above a sheer drop. Hawkril rolled his eyes and then smiled, shrugged, and made a be-my-guest gesture. The thief surged along the balcony like a shadow in a hurry, bent double to keep below the height of its parapet, and without hesitation swarmed along the wall, finding holds with uncanny ease and in eerie silence.

Clinging to the wall with his fingertips, Craer reached the shutters and pulled ever so gently, first on one and then the other, only to find them both fastened firm. He glanced down for the first time, checking on what lay below, and then reached for the top of the shutters, clung, and slowly shifted his weight onto them.

If Hawkril hadn't been straining to hear the faint groan of protest from wood and hinges, he wouldn't have heard it. The procurer hung there like a patient spider for a moment, drawing a knife from a sheath along his forearm. Hawkril watched him run it up the crack where the shutters met with slow care—and then, as it lifted an unseen hook fastening within, saw the shutter Craer was still holding onto swing open under his weight, heading for a crash against the wall.

The procurer shifted during that brief journey so that his shoulders took the impact with waiting stones. Shutter and procurer shuddered together—the silence was uncanny—and Hawkril saw Craer grimace in pain before the procurer heaved, swung his legs up, and vanished into the tower.

In a torn and ravaged flowerbed that lay in full, bright and cold moonlight, a stone larger than a man shuddered—and then slowly rolled over.

There was no one there to push it, no monster thrusting up from beneath it to break the earth and send the stone rolling, but it was rolling, now, slowly and in eerie silence.

Rolling out of the flowerbed, to clack against another stone it had been attached to, not so long ago. A stone shaped like a giant human hand.

A stone that rose on its fingertips like a dark, dog-sized spider to creep tentatively through shadows to touch a shattered row of stones that had been its arm. Stones that shuddered and drew together, clacking like stones bowled by gamblers that strike each other in a long, rippling line.

A line that rippled, surged, and suddenly rose into the air, the hand atop the line questing into the moonlit sky like the head of an ungainly snake. The arm swayed upright atop a strange cairn of unbalanced stones and then swooped like a striking hawk to pounce on the stone that had first rolled out of the flowerbed. A brief fire of darting sparks laced from one stone to another, and suddenly stones everywhere in the moonlight and the shadows were shifting and stirring, rolling together with sepulchral gratings. A toppled head settled onto shoulders, a fallen sword rose, and a stone knight raised its head and stood up in the moonlight once more. Like a beast sniffling for scent it stood turning its head slightly this way and that. It was seeking something. Something it had failed to slay.

* * *

No lamps were lit, but the procurer could see enough to tell there was a table in front of him, in a long and narrow chamber whose walls all held curtained archways. Spindles of thread stood on shelves to his left; shears hung on a wallboard to his right. This must be a sewing and fitting room—and that shape across the room was no guard, but a dressmaker's wooden lady.

Well and good. A gentle, spicy aroma of mingled scents was already telling Craer he'd entered the chambers of a lady of high station. He perched on the sill, listening and looking and deducing, until he'd decided where best to proceed. First, secure and quiet footing—so—and then to draw the shutters closed behind him.

Craer crouched in the shadows beside the table for another silent eternity, listening, and then crept catlike toward one of the archways. Parting the curtain with his knife, he peered. Ah, he'd guessed right: beyond lay a robing room. And *what* a robing room!

Fanlights above the draperies allowed faint moonlight into the chamber he was looking into, and by its blue-white glow he could see a low, ornate wardrobe whose glossy top displayed a row of wooden heads—all of them sporting sparkling tiaras, dangling clusters of gleaming earrings, or finely graven metal masks. Hooks on the walls and harnesses hanging on chains from the ceiling all held gowns. Scores—nay, hundreds—of vivid and stylish garments, all of them glistening with the cold fire of gems!

Cascades of gems, clusters and swashes and swirls, thumb-size here and larger there, never lone stones or paltry trios . . . zelosters and blackamarls and even a starburst brooch as big as his hand, adorned with the rarest gems of all: the rainbow-hued, glistening teardrops known as scarmareenes. By the Lady's Horns, what riches! More than he'd ever dreamed Aglirta or even all Asmarand held! Why—but no, tarry gawking no longer. Take and flee, before any doom could awaken. . . .

Craer took a handful of gowns, wrapped them around his arm, and turned with infinite care, careful not to make a sound that might bring—

Blue fire snapped out of the darkness without warning, the fire of a spell that smashed into him, searing and piercing, and drove him reeling across the room in a numbed, gasping dance of agony.

Wreathed in lightnings, the procurer staggered through a row of gowns and another curtained archway beyond, into a chamber Hawkril must be crouching outside. With his last sobbing strength Craer ran into the curtains and tore at them, bringing them down.

Hawkril rose out of his crouch, sword in hand, and gaped through the glass at his writhing friend and the crawling, flickering radiance that was killing him. He snarled and swung his sword with all his might at the balcony doors, leaping from his feet to put all his weight behind the blow.

Glass sang and screamed into shards, guardian spells shattered in sighing silver smoke and sparkling dust, and the armaragor charged through the ruin into the room, to snatch at the convulsing procurer with a snarl.

The lightning was silver and green this time. It struck the swordmaster like a ram, plucking him from his feet and smashing him back against a wall. In his wake, the procurer was whirled along like a leaf and tumbled against the stones beside him, to be held there as helpless and breathless as Hawkril in the roiling, risen force.

He stared at its source, a room away but striding toward them as terrible as any angry baron shouldering through archways. Tall and terrible she came in her nightgown, with the witchlights of her risen power sparkling and swirling around her. The Lady of Jewels, it seemed, was a powerful sorceress.

The gray and slab-sided peaks known as the Windfangs stood like a shield between Coiling Vale and the worst of the winter winds that seared the rolling plains of Dalondblas to the north, piling up glittering snows there in drifts as high as tall castle towers.

Winter in the Windfangs meant mist-tattered gales howling down the clefts over the glittering corpses of frozen crag sheep, but in summer heavy carts groaned down from quarries through the prosperous barony of Loushoond, whose fat and wine-loving Tersept blinked pale, watery eyes at anyone complaining of brigands and sent armaragors in gilded armor to riding the roads in glittering display. Above the quarries rose tortured knobs and shoulders of rock called the Wildrocks. The frowning mountains rose behind them and betimes sent huge sheets of rock crashing down upon them. They were home to monsters and lawless, desperate men, wherefore law-abiding folk shunned the Wildrocks but spoke much of them, at night in taverns.

On the night when Flaeros set foot in Sirlptar, a tongue of flame rose in the Wildrocks. Crouching around it, cursing at how long it had taken them to bring down a sheep so their cookfire burned in darkness, visible from afar, were two of those lawless, desperate men.

"Oh, sargh!" Craer Delnbone snarled, as flame roared up the dry bough with which he was prodding the fire, scorching his fingertips. "Sargh, sargh, sargh!"

As he shook his hand in pain, the tall, mighty-shouldered man across the fire asked, "Need some help with words, there? Can I offer you a 'bebolt,' or perhaps a 'by the Three!'?"

Craer sent his companion a glare that seared as hot as the flames snapping between them, and hissed, "Graul you, Hawkril! Graul you!"

"Repetition is good, yes," the deep-voiced armaragor agreed, not quite smiling. "Helps us battered helms understand your drift."

"If you're quite finished being clever, Hawk," Craer

hissed, *"set meat cooking before a wolf has it—perhaps after it's made us its first two feasts!"*

"I'll spread the last of the sauce on you, if you'd like to go first."

"We haven't even coins enough to buy another bottle of that," Craer said bitterly.

Hawkril shrugged. *"As we don't dare go down to Loushoond to buy one, what boots it?"*

Craer sighed as he watched the armaragor set two bloody slabs of lamb to cook, nod, and lounge back against the rocks, unconcerned by the grease and gore of the sheep he'd butchered—or the flies now buzzing around in enthusiastic profusion.

Hawkril Anharu was as good-natured with a price on their heads and no home to return to as he'd been swinging a sword in Ibrelm or peering his way through the brothels of Sirlptar with that same easy grin on his face. A tall, red-skinned mountain of an armaragor, better muscled than most, he wore the scarred bracers of a veteran swordmaster. His only traces of desperation were the words spilling out of him; usually Craer gabbled glibly while Hawkril saved his words, offering a quiet handful only when absolutely necessary.

Feeling Craer's gaze, he looked up, flashed that grin, and used the back edge of his sword blade to scratch an itch between his shoulderblades. *"How fared you in Dranmaer, swordbrother?"*

"No better than in Sirlptar," the short, spiderlike man replied. *"Everyone remembers an overclever procurer who snatched a haunch or a handful of coins from them a season ago, it seems."*

"Well, if you didn't taunt and sing and play jugglers' pranks when you stole things," Hawkril said calmly, *"folk might not be so swift to remember your face."*

"When I want you to slap my face with simple facts, Tall Post of an armaragor," Craer told him wearily, *"I'll be sure to bid you to do so. Until then . . ."*

"Oho, a threat looms before me," Hawkril rumbled.

"*Unfurl it, pray, Master Clevertongue; quaking, I await the bright blade of your wit.*"

"*As I suffer under the spiked bludgeon of yours,*" Craer snapped, snatching at his belt. A black-bladed knife spun from his fingers to find firewood with a solid thunk—pinning slowly sliding lamb instants before it would have fallen into the flames.

Memory flared: a man of the Isle choking on that same knife and falling; a fate shared with many. Yet for all the deadly skill of Craer Delnbone, veteran procurer, the Isles of Ieirembor stood unconquered yet, and it was Hawkril and Craer who'd come scrambling home on leaking, overladen ships—to instant outlawry.

Baron Ezendor Blackgult had been a proud and handsome man with a swordarm of iron, a wit sharp enough to hew foes with, and a ready laugh. Under him, Blackgult had risen to become the largest and mightiest of the River Holds, richer than Ornentar and even Silvertree, with coins to spare for folk to hire bards to craft new songs . . . coins enough almost to rival the Glittering City itself.

Perhaps that had been Blackgult's downfall. The rich merchants of Sirlptar had grown to fear the baron's rise, war wisdom, and reach. A prosperous barony up-river was one thing—but a barony with the stomach to snatch at the Isles of Ieirembor was quite another.

The Isles rose out of the sea like a wall sheltering the mouth of the Silverflow, five shoulders of forest-girt rock that were both Sirlptar's treasure garden and its rear battlements. The most populous, Ibrelm, rivaled only the smallest barony, but all five held rich stands of the timber that made the Glittering City's close-packed buildings soar, and the copper that gleamed as pots and pans in its every third shop. Perhaps those shopowners had hired wizards and swordmasters enough to break the warriors of the Golden Griffon.

Craer and Hawkril had never seen such endless, tireless foes before. The Baron's bold stroke had failed, and *his few surviving loyal warriors fled home from bloody defeats to find their Lord Baron dead or fled and Blackgult conquered by his old rival Faerod Silvertree. The Golden Griffon badge now meant not only slim hopes of honest coin but also a price on the heads of its wearers—and the long-mythical throne of Aglirta seemed very close to feeling the backside of proud and ruthless Baron Silvertree.*

Hawkril stretched. "It's good to be back with you, Craer," he said slowly, squatting by the meat with his belt knife flashing bright in one hairy hand. "Shall we hunt together?"

The procurer shrugged, not wanting his brother-in-arms to see eager tears in his eyes. "I can think of no better road than one we share," he said awkwardly. "Meat done yet?"

The armaragor chuckled. "I'd miss that tongue of yours, if I wasn't around to hear it."

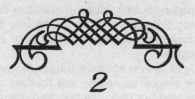

2

The Trembling Flight of the Castle

Slender fingers and lips that were thin with anger wove a spell that might well hold their deaths. Eyes that blazed raked them up and down. Craer and Hawkril could do nothing but watch.

Numbing, searing lightnings held them hard against the wall, pressed against the cold curves of gems and wire bodice-snakes and harnesses; their greatest strainings left them gasping, sweating, and shuddering, muscles burning in protest—and won them, amid soft tinklings of metal, only a few feeble shiftings of their limbs.

Helpless in their prisons, the two men did the only thing left to them. They stared.

Not that the looking was hard. Long, flowing hair cascaded in a dark flood over slender shoulders, framing eyes that glittered with fury in a face whose cheeks and chin shaped more beauty than either of them had ever seen.

Barefooted, Embra Silvertree stood as tall as Hawkril, or taller, and moved more gracefully than any tavern dancer, a smooth shifting of softnesses that was all the more alluring because it was but herself, and no deliberate lure for men. Her hair might be blue black, her eyes might be dark blue—it was too dim to tell, with the only light in the room raging like fire around them and flickering fitfully on the ends of those long, graceful fingers.

The Lady of Jewels spun the fingers of one hand in a gesture that shaped an ending and then sat down on a lounge to regard her two prisoners with eyes that were dark and dangerous. The thousands of glistening gems on garments hanging behind her seemed to add their weight to her grim gaze, like so many dark and disapproving eyes.

No magic occurred that the procurer or the armaragor could see or feel—but when the lightnings slowly flickered and died, much of the tinglings and pain fading with them, the two men found that an unseen force held them against the wall as securely as before.

"Why are you here?" the Lady Silvertree asked, as calmly as if she'd been discussing what hue of garments would best go with their hair. Her gauzy gown did nothing to hide a figure that was sleek and beautiful. The severe expression she wore stole nothing from the beauty of dark eyes and brows and a face that would have been breathtaking on a corpse.

On a corpse . . .

Craer licked his lips in the hanging, slowly lengthening silence, tried not to look at a swan wing, made of diamonds clustered as thick as his closed fist, that hung not four inches from his nose, and said, "Lady, you will find this hard to believe, I know, but we were hired by your father to test the defenses of the Lady Turret, to—"

Slender fingers moved slightly, and the procurer gasped as sudden pain arose in him again, raging along his limbs like fire. He could feel his limbs twitching uncontrollably as fell power surged through him, and—thank the Three!—faded.

"*Very* hard to believe, sir," Embra Silvertree replied

coldly, "and your claim makes it quite clear to me that you're unfamiliar with . . . this household. My patience is limited. Honest and direct answers are desired of you, good sirs."

Her other hand lifted from her lap, fingers wriggling in a silent reminder of the power she commanded. Emeralds flashed green fire here and there along the walls, as if in eagerness to acknowledge the power their mistress wielded.

Craer banished all pain from his face, gave the Silvertree heiress a smile, and said smoothly, "Of course. My apologies, Lady. You'll appreciate that we were given several tales to tell, in place of the truth. In the time before he served your father, the wizard Gadaster Mulkyn had several apprentices, and one of them—you'll understand that I'd rather avoid names at the moment—was promised something by Gadaster that he was to inherit at that great mage's passing. We've been sent to find and fetch that something, and—"

His gasp was almost a sob, this time, and became a low, wet moaning as the procurer writhed against the wall, limbs trembling. Craer watched in wide-eyed horror as his own right hand rose stiffly from his side and awkwardly swept sideways to strike his face so hard that tears swam and his ears boomed. She'd made him slap his own mouth.

The armaragor snarled and thrust himself away from the wall, teeth set and veins quivering in his throat. He got perhaps half a pace forward before being slammed back so hard that the thud of his head against the wall shook several ropes of pearls off their stand, to hiss smoothly to the tabletop beneath.

Beautiful lips tightened once more before they coldly spoke the words, "The limits of my patience fast approach, good sirs. Choose your utterances carefully, for you choose your fates with them."

Craer nodded and opened his mouth to speak again, but Hawkril rumbled, "Enough lies. Lady, I am Hawkril

Anharu, armaragor; this is my friend Craer Delnbone, a procurer by trade; your father uses the title 'lastalan,' I believe. We both served the Golden Griffon, and are but lately returned from defeat in the Isles to find the Vale much changed. Our bellies growl emptiness, our purses hang slack, and we've long heard of a lady whose gowns drip with gems . . . are those blunt truths enough to win our swift deaths, or more patience of you?"

He thought the Lady Silvertree almost smiled before her eyes flickered and she asked, "Have you any other friends, allies, or hirelings here on Isle Silvertree?"

"No," Hawkril answered simply.

The Lady of Jewels turned her eyes to Craer, and said softly, "There—see you how it's done, Sir Procurer? Simple truth is a rare treasure in Aglirta, I've found. I value it." She looked back at Hawkril, and asked gently, "And your future plans?"

She raised a slender hand, cupping empty air as if she held a fire of leaping flames that caused her no pain.

Craer saw a short and dark future ahead, undertaking some deadly task as an expendable pawn of this slender, dark-eyed lady, and blurted, "Oh, no. Nay, Lady . . . slay us here and now if you must, but—"

An irritated, imperious hand waved him to silence. They saw the glitter of anger in Lady Silvertree's eyes again as she leaned forward to stare at them both. Anger, and something else . . . rising excitement? Then, almost impulsively, she commanded, "Sit. Sit and listen."

Her hand waved again, and the force pinning the two men was suddenly gone. They barely had time to stagger and find balanced stances again when the Lady Embra wove another quick spell.

Two gilt-trimmed stools thumped behind them, as if in greeting, and decanters rose in a stately parabola from a nearby side table to hang in the air beside their hands. The two men eyed these uneasily; even after the ornately curved vessels bobbed beckoningly in midair, neither moved to touch them.

Exasperation and disgust chased each other across the fine-boned face of the Lady of Jewels, and she crooked two fingers in a come-hither gesture as she snapped, "Sit *down,* horns to you!"

One decanter sped to her waiting hand like a bird fleeing a hunter's bow; she snatched it, pulled the stopper like a thirsty warrior, and took a swig. Then she did the same with the other. They watched her throat move in tense silence, and in like manner they received the glare that followed.

"See you? Safe, 'tis—now drink and be seated, gentle sirs! I grow weary of watching you peer at exits and tense to snatch at weapons. In case you hadn't noticed, it's late. Sleep beckons; I'd probably be able to enjoy slumber even with the riven bodies of two idiots sprawled bloodily at the foot of my bed."

She let silence fall and stared at them both, a clear challenge in her eyes. Hawkril answered it by sitting down heavily on his stool and taking hold of the decanter that was drifting smoothly back to him. He raised it, said roughly, "We mean you no harm. Your health, lady," and drank.

Craer stared at the armaragor as if he'd just grown a second head—and then sighed, shrugged, and followed suit. He was still wiping his lips with the back of one hand when he saw a little smile almost rise to her lips and her fingers trace a gentle weaving in the air.

The procurer sprang to his feet, choking as he tried to spit out what he'd taken in and at the same time swallow it so he could find breath to curse, but a strange, roiling tingling rose in his mouth before he could manage to snarl out a single word.

Craer froze, fingers not quite to the hilt of his nearest dagger, as he saw golden flames snarl out past his nose, flames coming from his own mouth, and mirrored by those spilling from the parted lips of Lady Silvertree. Gold flickerings curled past her chin, and he looked quickly at Hawkril, to see an identical conflagration—and look of astonishment—there.

"Be at ease, Craer," the sorceress said gently. "Even the fire down within you . . ." A rising warmth was suddenly racing and roiling in the procurer's belly. He swallowed as his fingers closed on the hilt of his dagger . . . and tightened.

". . . harms not. 'Tis but a shielding, to keep magical spying at bay. Now for the love of the Lady sit back down and *listen*. We haven't much time."

"Oh? How so?"

Embra Silvertree leaned forward, resting her elbows on her thighs like any gossiping warrior, and said in a voice that was low and swift with urgency, "I'm a prisoner here as surely as if all these windows and doors were made of armor, and thrice barred. My father and his three mages—who'd lose no contests in cruelty, believe me—have bound me here to become, in the end, part of this castle."

"What? Lady, I don't understand," Hawkril said, and meant it.

"In time soon to come, I will lose this body," the dark-eyed lady told him, "and breath, to become a spirit bound into the stones and timbers and all of Castle Silvertree. A 'living castle,' they call it: aware and rooted here forever, given magic enough to repair their hurts and the crumblings that even stout stone suffers with the passing ages and to open or shut gates and doors and the like to defend this place . . . forever."

Craer frowned. "And what of your own magic? You can't flee or withstand them?"

Dark eyes looked sadly, almost pleadingly into his. "I've been taught only magic enough to serve well, not wage war on my teachers. I was but a child when the first bindings were laid on me—and some of them have lasted from that day until your blunderings this night."

"We?" Hawkril rumbled, still suspicious.

The Lady Silvertree looked at the armaragor. "The two of you broke some of the bindings that hold me, yes, meddling with one of the guardians of the wall. I've been watching you since then. Hoping. For the first time in my life, I *can* hope . . . to be free."

"You want us to help you flee this place?" Craer asked, discovering that his fingertips had gone numb on his dagger hilt. He let go of it and wriggled them to bring them back to usefulness.

The sorceress swallowed, lifted her head a little, and replied, "I offer you a choice. Break the last few bindings as I bid you and then flee with me, with all haste, accepting me as your equal and as a companion in your adventurings . . . or refuse me and be turned over to my father's justice."

"Cruel deaths, after spells worm at our minds," Craer almost whispered. "Lady, that's no choice at all."

She spread her hands and said bitterly, "I'm in no position to offer you anything more, Sir Procurer, and if we tarry tongue-wagging overlong, your choice—and my chance at freedom—will be swept away together. All it takes is one wizard to notice the bindings gone or even to idly decide to spy on the charms of a sleeping maid—as they often do, not bothering to hide their floating eyes if I awaken—and . . ." She made a snatching gesture, let her hand fall, and stared at them both.

The challenge was back in that dark gaze. "Gentle sirs," she said flatly, "I am desperate."

Craer watched the dying motes of the golden flames her words had made drift into oblivion and then looked at Hawkril. They both had good cause to hate magic. Bitter battlefield memories rose, flashed and flared. The faces of dying comrades, blasted by spells, hung like ghosts between their grim gazes as the two comrades regarded each other.

After a little silence, the armaragor rumbled, "A sorcerer of any accomplishment is a rare and precious thing." He spread his own hands in a shrug, and added, "And who in all Darsar would not want their freedom?"

Craer frowned at Hawkril, and slowly looked back at the Lady of Jewels. Soft curves sheathed in silk were far from the cruel, hard-riding battle mages he'd known, but . . .

"How dare we trust you?" he murmured, shaking his head in disbelief and despair.

Embra Silvertree rose in a soft whispering of silks and walked to him slowly, keeping her hands down by her sides. Kneeling in front of the procurer, she drew the dagger he'd gripped so tightly moments ago out of its scabbard, put it into his hand, and then guided its point to her throat.

Kneeling in front of him, she looked along its keen length and whispered, "The same way I dare trust you."

"Claws of the Dark One!" Hawkril swore disbelievingly.

Craer snatched an excited, almost desperate look at his friend and then stared down into the dark eyes so close to his, his dagger trembling in his hand. He could feel the warmth of her breath, and the flesh of her throat against his blade. Her face was calm as she lifted that beautiful chin to let him better see the throat his point was pricking.

Glancing down at his war steel and then slowly up into dark eyes that held pleading and hope, but no fear, the procurer swallowed and said tightly, "Lady, it seems we have agreement."

The Lady of Jewels closed her eyes and let out a deep breath, freeing Craer from her gaze as if she'd snapped away shackles. Against the point of his blade, the procurer could feel her start to tremble, almost shivering. "Then," she said unsteadily, "take away your blade and let me rise."

Craer did so with speed and care. Hawkril dared to offer her his hand; with the first trace of a real smile she took it, saying crisply, "Leave my gowns lie. Yonder lies one of the laundry sacks; empty it and bring it into the next room. Procurer, have you any blades you can spare?"

"All of them, Lady, if the price is my life," Craer told her rather grimly. As they strode into the next room together, his hands were busy at wrist and thigh and collar. They held six fangs ready when she stopped, swept a hand across an opening to part another sighing spell, as if it were a cobweb, and said, "Hawkril—fill your sack from that little chest at the back. Touch nothing else, if you'd live longer."

She turned, pointed at a sideboard and at a wardrobe, and asked, "Craer, do you think the two of you can move those to stand under the two hanging lamps—and climb them, when I bid you?"

The procurer nodded. Shifting the wardrobe might take all their strength, but if they were otherwise to die . . .

"My hands must take no part in this, or all will fail," Embra Silvertree explained. "Fetch those two bowls. Put one on the floor, here . . ." She touched the smooth marble pave with one bare foot, and then pointed again. Her hand, Craer saw, trembled with excitement. ". . . and set the other down here."

The procurer put his daggers down on the floor in a glittering heap and hastened to obey. As he bent to position the second bowl, he heard her hiss, "Hawkril, not done *yet?* Just dump the chest into the sack—we've no time for marveling and peering!"

Craer looked up. Hawkril's face was pale with wonder. The sack in his hand bulged, and his other hand rather unsteadily held out a glistening mountain of gems—bezrim, amblaers, starglisters, and peldoons enough to buy many a barony, more than either of them had ever seen before. The procurer nodded hastily, and Hawkril shook himself, as if coming awake, and spilled the glassy rain of great fortune into the sack. "That was the last," the armaragor said, awe plain in his voice. "I'm done."

"Then drop the sack and help shift the wardrobe," the sorceress said impatiently. "We don't want to see the six guards who put it there in here now, do we?"

Hawkril hastened. The wardrobe was heavy—by the Three, it was heavy!—but by hurling their shoulders against it in unison and running as if charging a ram through a door, the procurer and the armaragor managed to scrape it across the floor to stand under one of the lamps. Craer frowned at it, swung its doors wide, pulled an interior drawer out enough to serve as a foothold, and nodded in satisfaction. "And now?"

"Get another sack," Embra told him, and followed her words with a sudden grin, like a child delighting in a prank going well. "And water—there's a spigot behind that third door down, and a bucket—enough to fill that bowl."

Craer and Hawkril hastened. In short order the sack held a dozen fat and impressive-looking books from a bed-foot chest, covered over with high boots, breeches, and a dark tunic the Lady Silvertree had pointed out, and the bowl was full. She stepped into it, directed Craer to set one of his daggers on the floor beside it, and then ordered, "Take a dagger each, and climb the furniture."

Hawkril lifted an eyebrow and one restraining hand in unison. "It was my remembrance," he said in level tones that held only a faint rumble of warning, "that we agreed to take on a companion—not an officer in full authority over us."

The Lady Silvertree met his eyes and said, "Granted, friend Hawkril—but in this I know how to proceed, and mistakes will get us all slain. Trust me in this, please."

The armaragor held her eyes for a long moment after she let silence fall.

Then, slowly, he nodded, took up a dagger, and

vaulted up onto the sideboard. It groaned under his boots, swayed as he shifted his feet—and held. Craer was already atop the wardrobe, dagger in hand.

The sorceress looked at them both, drew in a deep breath, and then said, "I'll ask you to strike in unison. At the metal bosses, where the lamp chains reach the ceiling; be sure to cut across some part of the runes there. Strike hard and—by the Three!—miss not, and then close your eyes and let go your blades without delay. There will be . . . an impressive reaction. In what follows, each of you must pluck up a sack: fix in your minds now just where they are. It may be dark, and we'll need to move very swiftly. Strike only when I give the word."

The two friends exchanged glances and then nodded to her. Embra knelt to take up the dagger, tore something on a fine chain from around one ankle and set it in the dry bowl, then stood, turned to look at them, and deliberately drew Craer's knife down the outside of her arm.

The blood welled out dark and fast. The Lady Silvertree held out her arm so that it would run from her fingertips into the dry bowl, watched it race for a moment, and then snapped, "Strike *now!*" At that last word, the first dark drops fell toward the bowl.

Daggers struck sparks from rune-graven metal—and in the wake of where they touched, lightnings burst forth into the night.

White and furious, these, leaping lances hot against the very air.

Craer swore and snatched his hand away. His dagger exploded into droplets of metal, smoking spatters that headed past his cheek into the night. A howling was rising from all around, and *something* surged through the very air around him, rolling as ponderously as a wave smashing into a small boat of grimly clinging warriors off the rocky Ieiremboran shores.

Another surge of force moaned through the room,

awakening many small radiances in its wake, and in their fading flashes Craer saw the sideboard toppling, and Hawkril leaping away.

Its crash shook the room, and was echoed by a dozen smaller disasters in nearby chambers. In one of the bursts of lightning-touched fire—spells dying, these must be—the procurer saw the sorceress silhouetted, still standing in the bowl, tearing off the last of the skirts of her nightgown with a triumphant jerk and reaching to wrap the silk around her arm.

The floor shuddered in an abrupt wave of its own— and the wardrobe began its own slow and mighty journey to a thunderous meeting with the floor.

Craer sprang from tilting wood toward where his sack must be, winced as something falling from the ceiling smashed against his shoulder, and spun helplessly in the air to land hard and rolling, his bootheels crashing against the sack. Books and not gems, thank the Three . . . as he stood, the entire tower shuddered under and around him, sending him staggering. The bindings had been broken, all right—and the baron, his three mages, and half Coiling Vale could hardly help but notice!

A firm hand took hold of his elbow in the darkness. "Hold to this," Embra Silvertree said, guiding one of his hands to a fold of cloth on one of her slender hips. "And if your fingers begin to wander, I'll give you back the three knives you left on the floor—one at a time, and point first."

Craer answered her with a sound that was more snort than chuckle, and moved with her through trembling, littered gloom, running up against her soft limbs only once, when Hawkril loomed out of the darkness with a low growl to identify himself. The Lady of Jewels never faltered, but gave him back a hum of reassurance and caught at his forearm to guide him. Together they traced a path around chairs and through beaded curtains that rattled and clacked like bones on an alchemist's slab, to a narrow, steep unseen stair that Embra led them down, sighing more than once in relief—as she found spell barriers she'd feared would still rise before her gone, Craer guessed—ere she slid two somethings aside and thrust open a door that let in silver moonlight and laid open the gardens before them.

The shoulder that shook itself free of the procurer's hand was trembling with fear and excitement, but Lady Silvertree's voice was calm and level as she turned to face them and said, "For all our fates, I hope you have a secure lair and some swift way to reach it." Without waiting for a reply, she waved her hand in a haughty noblewoman's flourish, bidding them lead the way.

Craer looked at her, tried not to think of stone statues waiting to crush and maim, then turned and raced into the trees, shifting the sack on his shoulders to keep from falling in his rush. Hawkril broke into a lumbering run in his wake, and as the trees flashed past, the procurer was surprised to see the sorceress sprinting along barefooted at his shoulder, hair streaming behind her and bosom heaving as her gasps began.

No wolves came at them out of the nighted woods, but all too soon there came the dull shuddering of the ground that marked the strides of the stone knight.

"I thought you broke it apart," Hawkril growled, hauling out his sword and glaring back at the guardian of the wall as if his anger could lay it low.

"I did," Craer gasped. "Do they heal, Lady?"

"Unless someone breaks enchantments I dare not, lest I face my father's mages here and now," the sorceress told him in a level voice. "Nor have I governance over that one any longer. Ambelter's weavings lie over and beneath my work, to guard against independence on my part."

"He trusts you so little?" the procurer muttered, stepping away from Embra to force the advancing knight to choose a target.

"He trusts no one," Embra said, in a voice that was

little louder than a whisper but as bitter as a winter wind. "He is *proud* to entertain no such weaknesses."

"How do you suggest we fell this thing, then, Lady?" Hawkril called, hefting his blade and moving forward to draw the guardian to him. Anger rang clear in his voice.

"Craer, you run at it, and then draw it off that way," she said, rousing herself into briskness. "Hawkril, be ready to carry me clear if it comes at me—like a grain sack, just scoop me without speaking or slapping me or suchlike. We've one chance left."

The armaragor's reply was an angry growl, but he fell back as Craer caught his eye, nodded—and rushed forward.

The stone blade swept down, and the procurer sprang into the air, looking for all the world like an oversize spider, landed on all fours, and leaped away, rolling through bushes as the guardian turned to pursue, hacking with more speed than accuracy.

Hawkril took a stand beside the sorceress, his eyes narrow with suspicion and his blade not far from her breast. He glanced quickly around in search of wolves, armsmen, or wizards, but the greatest foe just might be this beautiful statue of a lass right in front of his blade.

The Lady Silvertree stood with her eyes closed, swaying a little. A low murmuring, almost a drone, was coming from her slightly parted lips, and as Hawkril watched, she slowly put her head back until she was looking—had her eyes been open—right up at the starry sky.

Then she shivered, suddenly huddling down like a woman scuttling down a storm-lashed street, and said roughly, "There. 'Tis done. Hawkril, put away your sword."

"That, Lady," the armaragor growled, "is something *I'll* decide. I have a mistrust of wizards telling me to do anything, and if half the things you've let slip about your father's mages are true, so should you."

He stiffened as something thundered out of the night behind her other shoulder. It was another stone knight, marching swiftly off through the trees whence Craer and the other knight had gone. "Lady Embra," Hawkril growled, "if you've played us false—"

The sorceress turned a weary face up to his furious one and murmured, "Then kill me. Here and now. It might give you some small satisfaction before my father's mages have you screaming. I think we both want—and, by the gods, *need*—trust between us. My control over the guardians of the wall, I fear, is now gone. I can compel only that one."

"And?" Hawkril barked, the point of his sword still drawn back to thrust up into her throat.

"I'm sending it to battle the one chasing your—our—friend," she told him, dark eyes very steady on his, and then added with a fierce anger to match his own, "Hawkril, *trust me!*"

The ground shook then, and the armaragor whirled away from her with a growl, lifting his war sword to face what he knew must be coming. He glanced at two stone heads, crashing through the trees, and then back at the sorceress, clearly wondering if slaying the Lady of Jewels would bring both statues toppling into ruin.

"Wait and watch," Embra snapped, her voice wavering. "You'll see. . . ."

Branches crackled and Craer Delnbone whirled out of the night, tumbling between them and gasping, "Sorry I led them back. . . ."

Hawkril stared at him and then back up at the stone titans looming over them. He lifted a sword that might as well have been a blade of grass, for all the good it would do against either of those huge stone swords—and then gasped.

The guardian whose stony skin was covered with cracks swept its sword up to smite him—and the other knight struck it from behind and one side, swinging its blade around like a woodsman's ax with all the ponderous force of its shoulders behind the blow. Its stone sword struck the raised sword arm and crashed on through, in a crash of sundering stone that deafened the sorceress and the two men of the Griffon. Shards of stone and smaller rubble flew in all directions as the knight's attack carried it into the disarmed guardian.

Stone shrieked against stone, the ground seemed to groan, and the two titans toppled slowly, plunging together through a planting of white-bough trees with a crackling and booming that echoed back across the gardens from the unseen castle walls.

Hawkril gaped at the sight, but the Lady Silvertree plucked at his arm, crying out something his ringing ears couldn't hear. Craer was at her side, and she pointed as she pulled at him, urging him on.

The armaragor shook her grip free and gave her a fierce, excited smile as he sheathed his blade and gestured for her to proceed, like a court dandy indicating a lady should proceed him onto a dance floor.

Embra Silvertree rolled her eyes in the moonlight before breaking into a trot, Craer a half pace ahead of her. Grinning like an idiot, Hawkril followed, the thunder in his ears slowly fading until he could hear his own swift breathing again, and the rustle and whisper of their feet through the dark gardens.

No more guardians or wolves came at them out of the nighted woods, but when the dark shield of the wall rose before them to bar their path, it seemed alive, the stone teeth of its crenellations rippling and shifting. Hawkril almost fell in his haste to come to a halt and drag out his sword—and a moment later, they were all staggering as the ground shook again—a rolling thunder that went on and on, this time, raging up and down before the three fleeing humans.

All along the wall, knight after knight was bulging forward out of the stones, raising ponderous blades in slow menace.

"There were hands, too," Craer muttered, remembering the arms that had clutched at him. This was going to be less than pretty. . . .

The Lady of Jewels lifted her hands and murmured something firm and careful. Her eyes seemed to flash for an instant, and then glow—a glow that seemed to roll out from her through the air like a wave scudding across sand.

Where that glow struck stone, be it hulking knight or the massive wall, the stone seemed to smoke for an instant—and then burst apart with a roar, streaming away from the sorceress like so much dust.

A little grit eddied around the armaragor and the procurer, and then drifted past their ankles and was gone. The two men stared at the empty, trampled turf where the statues had been, and at the gap in the wall beyond, with moonlight dappling the river silver . . . and then back at their newfound companion.

Lady Embra Silvertree lifted an eyebrow as she met two dumbfounded gazes and announced crisply, "Now we must be swift indeed. *Hence,* sluggards!"

"So tell me, Spellmaster, what you think Silvertree's next move should be," Baron Faerod Silvertree bade, raising raven-dark brows. He looked like a sleek, handsome bird of prey as he set down his glass with almost silken delicacy, smiling at his most senior mage across the map graven in the table.

It was a familiar smile but not a nice one. The fat, softly sinister Ingryl Ambelter was deep in the last and most succulent mouthfuls of his spitted bustard's mushroom-and-butter sauce, but he knew better than to displease the rage-driven man who employed him. The master of Silvertree could storm hot or cold, but neither was comfortable to see, and both were humors better left slumberous—even by the mightiest wizard in three baronies.

So Ingryl wiped his chin and his pudgy, many-ringed

fingers with every evidence of eagerness, plucked back the full sleeves of his robe, and leaned forward to look up and down the winding course of the Silverflow on the table map for a moment before speaking. His words would have to be both sure and precise to sway his employer; madmen chafe under the steerage of others.

"Lord Baron," he said, catching what he judged was just the right note of restrained excitement, "I think we've a rare chance. . . ."

Across the room, a deep booming erupted, followed by the high, musical tinkling of falling glass.

Two heads snapped around to watch the shards of the spell telltale tinkle and scatter across the floor. The rightmost head was missing from the row of grinning glass gargoyles: something had breached the enchantments on the outer wall of Castle Silvertree.

A golden row of dragon heads was set into the baron's edge of the high table; he snatched and pulled two of them before the gonglike echoes of the riven telltale had faded, then reached for his glass with rather less delicacy than he'd set it down.

He'd scarce had time to drain it and sigh at the burning its contents left in his throat when two arched doors opened in the walls of the chamber. Armed guards issued from one, and two robed wizards hastened in the other. None of the arrivals was foolish enough to blurt out questions; the baron had rung for them and would issue his orders in his good time.

He did not disappoint their expectations or keep them waiting long—though they attended him with no particular eagerness. They'd all seen the scattered glass without making any show of looking at it and knew it betokened a night of hard work . . . and more than one of them still held sleep in his eyes.

"The Castle wall has been breached, probably at the far end of the Isle," the baron snapped. "Follow whoever has left us, and bring them back to me—without delay and as alive as possible."

Armaragors bowed their heads and hustled back out the door they'd entered by. Lord Silvertree raised his eyes to the three robed men still in the room and asked quietly, "And you're waiting for—?"

Nothing beyond those words, it seemed. In a swirling of sleeves, all three mages sped to their benches in respective corners of the room, to work magic.

It wasn't long before Ingryl Ambelter hissed, "There!" He spread his hands, leaving a glowing eyeball spinning and floating in the air before them. It darkened, rose, and burst into a mist that flowed up in iridescent chaos along the ceiling, a crawling carpet of magic.

Its colors winked, spiraled, and then abruptly twisted into a sharp and lifelike image of three dripping figures clambering up the far bank of the River Coiling.

"My daughter," the Baron said softly. "How interesting." He looked around at all three of them and added almost carelessly, "You know what to do."

The youngest mage was still eager and foolish enough to need to display his cleverness by answering aloud. "Keep her unharmed," Markoun Yarynd murmured, "and bring them all back. The condition of the two men matters not."

"Precisely," the baron purred. The three mages exchanged expressionless glances and returned to their corners to work magic anew.

The books—and Embra's clothes, atop them—hadn't fared well in the river, Craer feared, but the Lady Silvertree didn't seem to care. Nor did the wet nightgown clinging to her soaked body appear to bother her, or the drenched and clinging tail her long, unbound hair had become. Not that they had overmuch time to contemplate such fripperies as they stumbled through tangled trees in deepening darkness.

A pace ahead, Hawkril swore and plucked out his

blade. The branches they'd been breaking through or pushing past were *moving*—turning like questing snakes, reaching out to strangle or bind, and curling around them, now, in a gigantic, living cage.

Craer snatched out his shortsword to join in Hawkril's enthusiastic hewing, real fear rising in his throat with a chill as cold as the Silverflow. A bough snaked past his head, and he ducked away from its strangling return, almost impaling his throat on the spearlike tips of another reaching branch. "Claws!" he swore aloud, almost sobbing; how soon would it be before living wood brought them down, blinded them, or choked the life from them?

The Lady of Jewels chanted something imperious close by his ear, and abruptly an ale-brown radiance washed out of her and away into the dark trees ahead. Boughs shuddered and recoiled from it, shrinking away . . . no, *withering,* to dwindle and then break and hang, dangling lifeless and weightless. Craer hacked his way clear of the last two branches, stumbled over a third, and found himself in a long scar of lifeless trees, a path of ruin leading off into the night. Hawkril was waving at him impatiently to take the lead.

"You know the way, Longfingers," the armaragor growled. "I've never been all that welcome in Silvertree, remember?"

Craer and Embra found themselves looking at each other. The procurer lifted his sack. "Uh—you want your boots? And—"

"Later," the sorceress told him crisply. "When we reach whatever safe lair you're taking us to. My father has too many overclever mages for us to be standing around talking."

"Just how many overclever mages does he command?" Craer asked, a trifle grimly. By the Three, but it'd have been less foolish to walk into Castle Silvertree and start snatching the baron's silver in broad daylight than going after the wardrobe of the Lady of Jewels! It was more than likely that by dawn they'd—

Something clapped large wings behind them, and came through the trees in a dive of many small crashings and snappings. Something scaled and dark and bat-winged, with altogether too many snapping jaws.

"Horns! What's *that?*" Hawkril gasped, bringing up his blade.

"Run!" the Lady Silvertree snarled at the two men. "Run, and keep low!" She followed her own advice without delay, fleeing past them into the night like a damp, barefooted wraith. With one accord the two men raced after her, stumbling into many trees with numbing force, and rolling off without slowing to plunge onward, lurching and staggering over unseen roots and uneven ground. Ongoing splinterings behind them told that the flying horror was following with unbroken enthusiasm.

"You know . . ." Craer panted, when he finally caught up to the sorceress they were supposed to be guiding, or abducting, or taking far away from Castle Silvertree and the reach of its cruel baron, "what that thing is?"

"It's called a nightwyrm," Embra gasped, "conjured by one of my father's mages. It'll tear us apart if it catches us."

Neither Hawkril nor Craer had time to make any clever reply just then—the nightwyrm seemed to be able to fade in and out of solidity and was diving through trees that should have stopped it, plunging after them with frightening speed. It was only feet away, it was—

They flung themselves away, sprawling desperately, as teeth clashed only inches behind them, sinuous heads reached greedily, and—a gnarled tree intervened.

The crashing impact would have slain any normal beast. The trunk of the tree shivered and split, torn but still standing, boughs rained down all around, and Lady

Embra Silvertree somersaulted over backward among them in an undignified landing that bounced the breath out of her, spun her around, and thrust her dazedly up into a sitting position amid a tangle of riven wood.

She found herself staring into one open, many-toothed maw from inches away. Gurgling, the night-wyrm lunged to engulf her.

"Will you not eat, Lady?"

Mressa's voice was almost a sob. To see her young charge this desolate tore at her heart even more than the evil this girl's father had done to her mother. An evil that might yet stretch—such a little, little way—to claim the younger Lady Silvertree, too.

The girl turned away fiercely. Mressa watched her dwindle along the battlements, a black-robed wraith drifting . . . to her doom? Silent and bone white, waiting to be struck down as her mother had been. Or would Embra choose the moment of her dying, looking at the rocks in the river below—as she was now—before flinging herself out and down, down, in a brief and broken flight that could have only one ending?

Mressa brought the spurned platter back against her ample bosom, watched a still and silent Embra looking down at her own death, and shivered. She dared not go to the girl, now, lest her approach be the spur that made Embra end it all, screaming.

Screaming . . . as her mother Tlarinda had done all that long night, howling out her agonies strapped to a table under the tortures of her lord husband. Screams that had ended just before sunrise, when her mutilated body breathed its last and the gently smiling Baron Silvertree turned away, drenched in the blood of his wife, to ask calmly if his requested bath was ready and warm.

Mressa shivered at the memory—and then froze. High on the topmost tower a lone figure was standing, watching Embra even as she watched the Silverflow slide endlessly past. A vulture perched above prey he knows can't escape, the cold weight of his gaze a dagger pinning the maid in place.

Mressa could feel his cold smile. She tried to gasp but could find only breath enough to tremble. She kept her eyes on the silent girl she must call the Lady Silvertree henceforth, not daring to look up again. She was rooted here, fated to stand watching while Embra Silvertree decided whether or not to die.

Learning his error, he'd shrugged and smiled. Mressa would never forget that smile.

Still smiling, he'd drained his stirrup cup as always and ridden off to buy for his breeding stables, changing his plans not one jot. It was then the fourth morning since Tlarinda had died at his hands, butchered for the sin of faithlessness.

The baron had seen her talking with a man in a lane—a man the Lady Silvertree had seemed delighted to see; they'd kissed, embraced, and laughed together. A stranger, who was in irons in a cell when the bloody pieces of Tlarinda were delivered to him by the baron's order . . . and hauled out into the main square, before the morning was an hour older, to have his arms and legs hewn off, the wounds sealed by flame whilst the cruel spells of Gadaster Mulkyn kept him alive . . . and be left there, naked in the sun, to starve to a slow death.

The stranger who'd been Tlarinda's long-unseen brother.

That was the news that had made Faerod Silvertree shrug and smile. A smile of trifling regret, as if he'd worn the wrong cloak or lifted an empty decanter rather than the full one beside it. A passing error not worthy even of an oath, let alone remorse or amends. A stunned Mressa watched as the remains were fed to the castle hogs, and the matter was done. Leaving behind a quiet, dreamy girl, given to wearing gem-adorned gowns

*and reading alone in the gardens. A girl now silent and
shattered, who'd neither spoken nor taken off her black
mourning gown since the deaths.*

Something moved along the parapet, snatching Mressa's
attention back to the here and now. A stone had swung
open like a serving hatch, and the lass was lifting forth
books from a hiding niche behind it. They looked like
wizard's tomes, very like books she'd seen, twice or
thrice, in front of the baron's highest-ranking wizard,
Gadaster Mulkyn.

Something else moved, higher. She forced herself to
glance up, in time to see Gadaster join the baron. They
stood coldly smiling down at the young Lady Silvertree
as she paged through the books in wonderment. Oh,
horns of the Lady, was Mressa Calandue going to be the
only witness to one more dark deed? A tongue Faerod
would still the moment he thought of what it could say?

She was. There was a balcony below the battlements
where Embra stood: a round platform jutting from the
wall where the Lord and Lady Silvertree had been wont
to sit and watch the river slide by on pleasant evenings.
It was deserted, but Gadaster Mulkyn waved a hand,
the balcony air shimmered for a whirling instant—and
then Faerod Silvertree stood there looking out at the
Silverflow, a goblet in his hand. He leaned on the balcony rail, seemingly oblivious to the girl above. She noticed him and stiffened.

Mressa glanced up at the high parapet in time to see
the baron—the real baron—step back to stand just behind the wizard Gadaster. He watched as Embra stared
at his image below her, glanced quickly all around—her
eyes counted Mressa as a friend or as loyal furniture
and slid on past the aging maid without pause—to ensure that she was alone, then flipped pages furiously,
her head bobbing in frantic haste.

It seemed an eternity before she straightened, put out one slender arm like a sword to point at her father below, and said something sharp and clear.

The air above the balcony boiled and flashed, the entire castle shook, and baron and balcony were suddenly small, blackened fragments clawing at the air before plunging to the river below.

Guards shouted and came running, heads appeared at windows—and on the highest parapet a shining globe flashed into being around wizard and baron. Quivering, it drifted out into empty air, descending smoothly to where a young girl stood staring at the nothingness that had been a balcony. The voices of Gadaster and the baron came to Mressa as clearly as they did to Embra, spinning her around to stare up, her face as white as bone.

"A swift, vigorous, and natural aptitude for magic," the wizard murmured.

Faerod Silvertree smiled. "Good. She's going to be of more use to me—at last—than as a walking display of my jewels. Do what you will with her, Mulkyn, so long as she never dares disobedience. I can't abide faithlessness." And he smiled.

At his last word, Embra Silvertree's face changed. For a moment it held greater rage than Mressa had ever seen, a contorted flame of fury.

And then, because she was a Silvertree, it smoothed back into inscrutability, and the Lady Embra watched her doom come for her with her feelings hidden behind a mask.

3

Eluding Comprehension—and Worse

Of all the beasts that hunt humans, none is so widely feared as the nightwyrm. Darsar does hold more formidable monsters—and there are even a few thought to be more ruthless—but there is something about a glistening, eellike thing as long as ten men, that flies through the air like a giant bat and has jaws enough to devour an entire family at once, that makes men sob in terror.

There have always been nightwyrms in the valley of the Silverflow. They hang motionless in midair when the sun is high and bright, usually in the shade of deep forest thickets or floating above swamps where men do not go . . . and drift out to feed at dusk. A cow or several sheep or goats are better feeding than a human, but some nightwyrms love to hunt. Some delight in daylight snatchings. Some seem to love taunting and teasing humans by smashing traps set against them or repeatedly awakening humans in their beds—by plunges through windows, to upset the bed itself, and tumble occupants in all directions—to visit terror nights before they arrive to slay and feed.

A few develop the taste for the flesh of one family or

seem to develop an enmity for folk of a specific barony or town. All of them hate those can hurt them most: archers and wizards. Minstrels often tell the tale of Maerdantha, who lost an entire family—son after daughter after uncle—because they could all hurl spells at dark flying things who devoured their sheep. In the end, she spun the shape of a nightwyrm with her own spells and lurked in that shape among the fast-dwindling family flock.

When the hunter came, she clung to her life and slew him only because he reacted amorously to her form rather than deciding to rend her at the first sight.

The body the servants found, after carrying their sorely wounded mistress to shelter, was sixty feet long from the shoulders of its batlike wings to the tip of its barbed tail. Even torn in death, it lay sleek and sinuous, looking so graceful and so deadly that few dared approach it. Its pointed heads were many, and all of them had birdlike beaks as long as a man is tall, lined with many sharp, sharklike teeth. Its eyes were white shapes, without pupil or focus, and even priests were seen to shudder as they drew near.

This nightwyrm seemed smaller than most, but far more generously equipped with jaws. As they gaped open, snapping hungrily as it plunged down at Embra, the beast did not seem the slightest whit amorous.

Unless, that is, its love was for the blood-drenched, smokingly fresh corpses of sorceresses.

The Lady of Jewels spat into her hand and stammered a word of power she'd hoped not to have to use until she was years older than now. It echoed eerily around her as she thrust her arm forward, hurling her spittle down one of the wyrm's yawning gullets. The sick weakness born of using that word burst forth within her, and she moaned aloud.

The other head darted at her, dark-fanged jaws snapping. Embra kicked it away and threw herself up and over the tangled pile of tree limbs in one desperate, twisting motion. Branches raked her skin like tongues of fire, jolting her out of her nausea.

The nightwyrm began thrashing as her magic raged inside it, black coils whipping wildly. She rolled away, keeping one arm in front of her face, and hissed the word that would bring her spell to its fatal conclusion.

The night exploded in a wet, rending rain of angry magical fire and enchanted monster, shaking the dew-drenched ground. Somewhere near, men shouted in fear.

Gore slapped onto trees all around and splattered down through shuddering leaves. Wood and flesh alike hissed in the afterglow of the blast as the black droplets that had been the nightwyrm landed on the tangled branches and the three escapees. Tiny tendrils of smoke arose from where those droplets fell.

The Lady Silvertree scrubbed at the worst of her burning patches, just above her knee, with the smoking remnants of her nightgown. Sobbing for breath, she tried hard not to empty her swimming stomach . . . and managed it, somehow. "Serpent in the shadows!" she cursed, using the strongest oath known in the Vale almost wearily.

Tearing herself free of one last, daggerlike tree branch with a wrench that left a bloody gouge along her ribs, she gulped cold night air hungrily, blinked, and found herself staring into the eyes of Hawkril Anharu.

The armaragor's hair was smoldering here and there where the acidic ichor of the nightwyrm had struck home, and his wet, smoke-smudged face wore a look of awe. Craer rose into view beside him, as drenched with monster innards as his two companions, and wordlessly offered Embra a dark bundle that she recognized as the clothing she'd had him put in the sack.

"Later," she snapped, and pointed imperiously along the seared scar her earlier spell had cloven through the woods. When neither of the men moved, she snarled something wordless and stumbled past them. For heroes, these two were a prize pair of dazed idiots. . . .

"Is there something about the word *unharmed* that eludes your comprehension?" the Baron Silvertree asked mildly, lowering cold and level eyes from the scene floating near his ceiling. Three wizards stared at him, sweat and fear mingled together on their faces.

"I . . . crave pardon, Lord," Ingryl Ambelter mumbled, reading a certain look in the eyes of his employer. "The Lady Embra's sorceries—"

"Are mightier and more numerous than you expected," Baron Faerod cut in, his voice like the edge of a slow and deliberate sword blade. "She *is* my daughter, gentle mages. I expect your best efforts and that these strivings include, shall we say, rather more precision."

He lifted his eyebrows in the tense silence and added silkily, "Your magics will protect every hair on her head, gentle mages, and every inch of the skin she's so eager to display to passing swordsmen—won't they?"

They gave him only silence in reply. Baron Silvertree inclined his head and in like silence looked from one sweating face to the next until each mage, however reluctantly, had given him a nod of acquiescence. Then he turned his gaze again to the scene from afar hovering by the ceiling, ignoring the almost-audible mutterings and sidelong looks the three mages gave him as they retired to their corners again, to work more spells.

One of those three customarily spake but little and—as is the way in too many lands—was often forgotten and ignored in the rush and prattle of his more vocal fellows. His name was Klamantle Beirldoun, and for what seemed like sweating hours he'd been working a mighty magic unbeknownst to his fellow wizards and to the baron: a curse upon the Lady of Jewels. If her magic was the real problem here—for without it, how long could two vagabond Blackgult warriors last against the sorcery of Silvertree?—then let her magic be shattered until such time as she knelt to her father in heart and in limbs once more. If such a day ever came . . . which he doubted much. Until then, let the curse ride her: each time she worked a spell, the magic would steal some vitality from her, leaving her enfeebled and at the last but a walking skeleton, clinging to life only so long as she worked no magic.

Klamantle smiled a slow and soft smile and breathed the final word of the incantation in a whisper. Let it be done. Ah, yes, let it be done. Often forgotten, indeed.

"Silvertree seems not the safest place in Aglirta," Delvin of the Many Harps murmured to his companion, eyeing the dark forest around them. Night dew glistened in the fashionably curled brown hair that brushed the bard's slender shoulders as he spoke, darting wary glances at the night around.

Arching branches overhung the road where the two men stood, plunging everything into a gloom deep enough to hide prowling bears and nightcats or any number of dagger-wielding outlaws. Hastening down to Sirlptar on the night-cloaked roads of Silvertree seemed a far less sensible idea than it had yesternoon, in the full light of the beating sun.

"I am coming to think there *are* no safe places in Aglirta, anymore," Helgrym Castlecloaks replied quietly. Night dew glistened in the gray and white hairs of his short beard as he stopped to listen, his hand on the knife at his belt. "Hold!" He laid his other hand on Delvin's arm, and the two bards grew still together. There had been a sound . . .

There it was again: the rasp of armor. A full-armed warrior was somewhere near and moving nearer. No, several warriors . . .

Helgrym had seen war before. He drew his younger companion to the side of the road and crouched in a ditch that smelled strongly of rotting leaves. "Be *very* quiet," he breathed into Delvin's ear, and pointed.

Coming from the trees on the river side of the road were a band of warriors—hastening in grim determination and dripping from a recent swim. As they crossed the road, many with weapons drawn, there was much buckling and adjusting of armor. Spiked gauntlets and crested helms gleaming . . . Armor of the finest make, adorned with the arms of Silvertree. Wherever these armaragors were bound, they were in a hurry—a hurry to slay.

The Lady of Jewels clambered up a slippery ridge of moss-covered stones and found herself gasping for breath again. She clung to the nearest branch for balance, drew in the air she needed, and looked back along their trail. Moonlight flashed on the helms and blades of the foremost Silvertree soldiers; ah, but it was a beautiful moon-drenched night. Graul it!

"Our shared need for your secure lair is becoming quite pressing," Embra snarled at her two companions in a sarcastic parody of noble courtesy. "I don't carry the wherewithal to spell-battle half Aglirta when I take to bed, you know!"

Hawkril grunted in alarm, not the sound she'd been expecting, and she spun around to see the brawny armaragor stepping hastily back from something that had begun to arise from the stones they'd clambered over. Something ghostly that glowed a sickly green and was taking a vaguely manlike shape, looming up and over them . . . this must be the work of Markoun. He always did prefer impressing folk to actually getting a task done.

Wearily, Embra destroyed the thickening shape with a wash of conjured fire. The brief flare of her flames evoked shouts from the pursuing soldiers, who began to sprint toward them.

Winded again, the Lady Silvertree stared at them and shook her head. "Your turn to save *me*," she muttered grimly to Hawkril. His wordless reply was the spreading of his large, empty, and helpless hands in a shrug.

Craer darted out of the night at the hulking armaragor, slapped his arm, and hissed, "Take her up, and to flooting with her dignity! Hurry—this way, and through yon arch!"

"That must be a sorceress!" Delvin gasped excitedly, as fire burst into brief life up on the slope.

"Hist!" Helgrym whispered fiercely, thrusting Delvin down until his chin touched ditch water. "D'you want them to hear us? *I'd* rather live!"

He broke off his rebuke to gape in openmouthed astonishment at what he saw next. In unconscious unison the two bards rose from their knees to get a better view. The Silvertree soldiers were jostling and clanking into a charge, another green glowing figure was rising into view a little way down the slope—and out of the moonlit sky past that eerie, building light swooped something bat-winged and black-scaled, with two heads and long, rending claws. It led the chase after the sorceress and her two companions, who were busily vanishing through an archway in a crumbling stone wall atop a hill.

"By the Three," Helgrym hissed in awe, "they're heading for the haunted catacombs!"

"The Silent House?" Delvin gulped. "They say a longfangs lairs there!"

He gulped again when Helgrym nodded and said slowly, "You know what we must do."

"Yes," Delvin whispered, even more slowly. "We must see what passes, to sing of it later."

They drew in deep breaths, looked around at the dark trees of Aglirta as if saying farewell, and moved in reluctant unison, watching the flying thing, the ghost shape, and the hurrying armaragors all plunge through the arch into the walled burial ground of the Silent House. Resting place of sixteen Barons Silvertree and perhaps more, ran the ballad, and no less a minstrel than the Master Harper himself, Inderos Stormharp, had once told Delvin that it clove to the truth. One didn't have to be a veteran bard to know about the man-eating longfangs that lurked inside. Enough folk had been eaten, or disappeared trying to find tomb treasures buried with dead Silvertree nobility, to convince the most skeptical that *something* that dined on human flesh dwelled within.

The moss-girt stones were slippery but the way all too short. They reached the shattered archway in a matter of moments.

"Is this how bards get killed?" Delvin murmured, pausing beside the crumbling stone wall. His voice was not quite steady.

"Yes," Helgrym replied, in a bleak, weary whisper. "Yes, it is."

Together they stepped through the arch into the haunted darkness.

The foreyard of the Silent House had once been a park studded with small formal gardens and later a place where bastard family offspring, much-loved servants, and better-loved horses and hounds were buried by a long line of Lords Silvertree. For years, now, the tirelessly creeping forest had held sway, and within the crumbling stone walls it seemed to wrestle back the moonlight so that leaning burial markers and even cottage-size tombs loomed up out of the gloom with startling abruptness.

"Put me *down*," the damp bundle on the armaragor's shoulder hissed. "*Down,* bebolt you! I . . ."

Her words broke off in a little scream as something leathery flapped through a sodden tress of her hair, squeaking.

"I didn't catch that last comment," her carrier rumbled, sounding more angry than amused. "Now stop struggling, or I may have no choice about dropping you onto some tombstones."

His burden gave another little shriek as his boots slipped on wet stone, and Hawkril caught his balance with a jerk. That had been a true misstep, not a little lesson to the lady on his shoulder—and if she thought otherwise, what booted it?

They had *real* concerns to think dark and worried thoughts about. Behind them, down the hill, someone snapped orders, and they heard the creakings of men in armor hastening. A small army of men hurrying. Men of Silvertree, hunting to slay; Hawkril growled.

Bats swooped and flitted, trailing tiny squeakings. Craer moved on like a surefooted shadow, but the armaragor, laden by his wet and furious burden and a swinging sack of gems that bumped at his thigh with every step, stumbled and then stumbled again.

The inevitable time arrived when his boots came down on loose stone and slipped. In a moment, Hawkril's arms were empty, gems spilling in a clattering torrent into the darkness in one direction and the Lady Embra, with a startled gasp, in another.

She landed hard on a tablelike tomb and bounced on the slab, bruising both elbows and knocking her head on weathered stone. Her curses, once she'd drawn breath enough to utter them, were so hot and swift that the fearful armaragor fled into the night.

Embra Silvertree spun around to face her father's forces, scrambled to her scraped and bleeding knees, and lifted both hands. Well, graul if the stupid mages hadn't conjured *another* nightwyrm—and another leech spirit, too!

The spell that howled out of her then shattered the

stones of the arch, driving their shards right through the diving bulk of the nightwyrm in a deadly spray. It perished not even having time to scream.

Bubbling forth bloody froth, its rent, headless body flailed and spasmed in midair before tumbling to the ground, tearing apart the leech spirit it crashed through by overwhelming the leech with the very life essence the spirit sought.

Embra watched the glowing, thrashing deaths with her lips a tight white line of anger. Wincing and ducking through all she'd wrought, of course, the Silvertree armaragors came stumbling, loyal and determined, waving wet swords and looking grim. Whatever magic might roar and flash, it always came down to thick-headed warriors, didn't it?

Embra suddenly found herself trembling. She felt weak and sick again—and she was using up her magic much too fast. Three mages to defy, and defeat, all of them no doubt stronger than she . . . and certainly more ruthless and cunning. Time to run again, and—

She clambered down off the slab, slipped on her own unseen gems, and realized she stood alone. *Where* was that ox of an armaragor?

She was spitting curses too swiftly now to even recall his name, but his face came to mind easily enough, and that was all she needed.

The Lady of Jewels snarled a spell that jerked Hawkril Anharu around in midstride. He almost fell, but cruelly surging forces were burning and tugging at his thews. He could not even curse as unseen hands forced him to turn abruptly around. Fires seemed to rage inside him, and he found himself staggering back to where the sorceress stood, a sudden prisoner in his own body.

Embra glared at the trembling warrior. Hawkril's face was white with fear and tight with fury that only her iron control kept in check, but the ripplings of his muscles and his awkward stride told of his struggle against her magic. He extended his arms stiffly, and she sat into his grasp, not needing to look to know just how close the foremost soldiers were.

A moment later, the armaragor and his burden were crashing through the burial ground once more, gems forgotten, with the panting of the foremost, boldest Silvertree warriors loud and close in their ears.

"Here! Hurry!" Craer called from ahead, and Embra let her unwilling steed turn toward the voice. The procurer was standing before the dark and gaping doorway of a mansion-size tomb. In the moonlight, it looked like the empty, staring eyesocket of a gigantic, half-buried skull.

"The Silent House," Embra spat at him through clenched teeth. "*This* is your 'safe' lair?"

Craer nodded, urgently beckoning her to enter.

"You before me," she replied curtly. "A longfangs lairs here, and I haven't the magic left to blast it down. Show it your blade, and let's hope it flees. I'm tired; my control over Tall-and-Mighty here is starting to slip."

Craer gave her a look of mingled surprise, alarm, and warning before he darted into the darkness, knife drawn.

Embra slipped out of Hawkril's reach before the enraged, violently trembling armaragor could charge forward and smash her against the doorposts. Freed of her weight and much of her control, he raced forward the instant she was away from him. Well, he wasn't alone in carrying a load of fury through the forest this night. Her choice had been made, the slender chance taken . . . only death awaited if she faltered now.

She made herself turn despite the soldiers hastening toward her. Glaring at them, Embra Silvertree told the moonlight softly, "I know you can hear me, Father. Know this: I have had my fill of being used. Henceforth, watch for me—and fear my coming."

She ducked through the doorway as soldiers came clanking up to it.

Embra remembered the large, lofty chamber beyond the threshold. Its own fading enchantments lit it whenever there was movement within, and by their feeble glow she saw the vaulted stone ceiling still thick and furry with hanging cobwebs, the two rows of statues still standing as she'd first seen them so long ago, from within the shielding spell woven by old Gadaster Mulkyn. Armaragors of stone a head taller than living men, they stood in watchful ranks, their cold, sculpted eyes seeming somehow always upon you, wherever you might move or stand. . . .

Hawkril was standing in the center of the room, struggling against her magic. She drove him before her with a hot flare of her anger, seizing the last few moments of the spell to lash him like a herder goading a thickheaded beast, and danced after him. Shouts from behind Embra, as she neared the open archway in the far wall, told just how close the soldiers had come. Had her father's orders been different, she knew, knives and swords would be kissing her shoulders even now.

As her foot touched the threshold, she spun around with an anguished shout. The spell seemed to crack out of her this time, leaving a ringing headache in its wake, and Embra staggered and almost fell. Clinging to cold, unfeeling stone for support, she watched the ceiling of the chamber fall almost lazily onto the foremost rushing soldiers in a rain of tumbling stone that went on and on until the room, statues and all, was completely filled with fallen stone.

"Great laughter of the Three," she said sourly, in the ringing, dusty aftermath of that tumult, "now we're walled in with it: a hungry longfangs and me without a spell even to light a candle."

As the words left her, sparks struck off the wall by her hand with a furious snap, and tinder cupped in a hand glowed, crackled, and caught. As it flared around a wick, Embra saw the coldly furious face of Hawkril glaring at her above its rising light. His dark, blazing

eyes held hers like two dagger points as he deftly
snapped open a folding candle-lamp from his belt, and
used the wick to light it.

His hands were steady as he shuttered the lamp
against breezes and returned his flint to a belt pouch,
but his voice was like a sword being drawn when he
said, "You used your magic on me as if I were a mule—
or a slave under the lash. I don't recall that being part of
our bargain."

"You *dropped* me," Embra snarled, "and there was
no time—"

"And are those going to be your words whenever you
want to march us about like little stick dolls? No time
for what? To ask for our aid? Or will there always be
just time enough to take it, moving our limbs in thrall?"

"I was going to *die*," the sorceress stormed at him.
"If you hadn't run away, I—"

"Run away is the very *least* of the things I'll do if
you ever dare to enslave me with spells again, Lady! Be
glad I don't break your jaw and hands for you right
now, to stop you from such excesses in the near future!"

"And if you did, how long do you think you'd last
against my father's mages? Horns, but swordsmen are
so *stupid!* About all they're good for, it seems to me, is
to be ridden and bidden by those with wits enough to
guide them!"

The hand that slapped her jaw then snapped her head
back, stung forth a flood of tears, and hurled her bodily
back against a wall with a grunt of pain.

Embra found herself on the floor, with the taste of
blood in her mouth and her head singing a new tune.
She looked up through watery tears at the armaragor
standing over her, his jaw set and his face dark with
anger. He seemed to be waiting for her to rise so that he
could knock her down again. A man she'd kept alive
half a dozen times this night, thus far, and—ah, to horns
with it!

The Lady Silvertree struggled to her knees, discovering fresh aches—one elbow seemed to be on fire, or touched with ice—and looked up again at Hawkril, eyes blazing, to discover one of his hands waiting to take her by the throat and the other hovering above the hilt of his sword.

She brought her gaze back up from his weapon to the fear in his eyes that underlay the revulsion written all over his face, and fresh anger rose in her. Ah, so goading men with magic is such a great evil, but sticking sharpened steel through their guts is just fine and noble, hey?

Embra tore open the bodice of her sodden nightgown to lay bare her breast, and snarled up into the midst of his astonishment, "Right, then—plunge your blade in! I know you want to!"

Hawkril's face grew almost black with anger, and his blade grated out in an instant, scraping its way to freedom because his hand was trembling so with fury. Embra felt cold fear awaken deep in her throat as the hulking armaragor raised his steel to strike, but she met his eyes boldly, eyes still spitting fire of her own, and straightened herself to thrust her chest out toward him.

The sword drew back an inch or two—and then halted. Hawkril stared at her bared, curving flesh, and then up into the blazing eyes of the lady sorceress once more. Setting his jaw, he drew his sword back again . . .

And Craer darted between them hissing, "By the Three! You'll doom us all! Come *on!*"

He plucked and jostled as he swept past, bearing Hawkril's blade up over Embra's head and snatching the candle lamp from the armaragor's unsuspecting fingers.

The warrior turned to look at his old friend, and the procurer said, his voice high with warring fear and anger, "Pair of idiots! As if we've got time for quarrels! Put your blade away, Hawk! And—and put *those* away, too, Lady, and get up and get on! Or do your father's mages all stop work to catch up on their snoring at the

same time? Hey? Or have I interrupted some solemn
Silvertree ritual or other, wherein a warrior carves his
initials on a lady? . . . Well?"

By sheer force of personality, ridiculing and tugging
and cajoling, the procurer got his two companions moving again, though neither answered a word of his torrent
of nonsense. As he jabbered and danced around them,
they traded dark looks and fell into step shoulder to
shoulder, Embra not bothering to refasten her bodice—
and Hawkril not bothering to resheathe his sword.

The three had scarce traversed three rooms, all dust
and the rubble of fallen ceiling facings, when an eerie
howl echoed around the unseen passages ahead. The
longfangs. Embra sighed.

Craer seemed not to have heard the beast's cry. He
was calmly peering at small markings scratched on the
rock wall where their passage split into two identical-
seeming halls. After a moment, he nodded and chose
one of them.

Impulsively, Embra plucked a hand-size stone from
the rubble on the passage floor. Hawkril whirled to face
her, his blade up and eyes narrowed in suspicion, but
she gave him a glance of contempt and hurled the rock
down the passage Craer had rejected.

It landed with a clack and clatter that was promptly
lost in a roar of falling stone. The trap Embra had triggered dropped two rusty but still massive portculli from
the ceiling with a booming crash, then filled the space
between them shoulder high with loose stones.

"By the Three!" Delvin said suddenly, crouching down.
"What's that?"

A twinkling, spinning mote of light about the size of
Helgrym's fist flashed past the two staring bards,
through the riven arch of the Silent House gates, and
flew through the tombs beyond like a small, racing star.

"Quiet," Helgrym said in a low voice, far too late and

knowing it. "That was a seeking spell; it can see and hear you."

They watched it vanish into the skull-like front of the Silent House, whence all the Silvertree soldiers had gone, and shivered in unison. It's never comfortable to be too close to suddenly risen magic.

Embra stiffened in midstride and spun around. Hawkril almost jostled her in his haste to see what she was doing and turn his blade around, too—and was in time to see her tear a bauble from the girdle cords of her nightgown, clench her fist around it, and murmur a word as she stared at something small and winking that was drifting in the air behind them like a tiny star.

Radiance flared between her fingers, then died—and the little floating star exploded in a burst of light that made Hawkril roar in pain and clutch his eyes.

"If you'll see to your own tasks, armaragor," the Lady of Jewels told him coldly, as he struggled vainly to see, "I'll *try* to deal with the magic. Craer, I'll be needing those clothes now."

The procurer was firmly guiding Hawkril to a sitting position on the floor by holding onto the swordmaster's elbow and murmuring, "Down!" He looked up at the sound of his name and saw that the bright silk nightgown on Embra's shoulders was speedily shriveling and darkening. In moments it looked more like a shawl or a giant fold of spiderweb gray with dust than a garment, and it began to fall away in tatters from long legs and soft curves that were—were sagging against the wall. The sorceress seemed to be reeling, or slumping in pain.

"Lady!" Craer hissed. "Are you hurt?"

"My last magic," Embra muttered, as he helped her down to the floor, "is gone. Which is good, since castings seem to be . . . killing me."

Fresh flashes made them both look up. Craer was still

gaping at the words the Lady of Jewels had spoken. On her knees beside him, she moaned in despair, tore free of his hand, and gasped, "Keep away! I've no magic left to fight these, whatever they are!"

As they approached, the radiances slowed and unfolded into coils of silvery thread, tendrils of magic that both veered to rush down on Embra Silvertree.

She threw back her head with a sigh of despair, eyes bright with tears—and then choked back a sob.

On the ceiling above the sorceress, as silent as any shadow, hung the longfangs, its fur glistening with dew. Its barbed, hairy legs were spread wide, and its wolflike head was staring straight at her. As their eyes met, it snarled and sprang down on her, claws and jaws extended to slay!

4

Four Long Fangs

*S*ilvery tendrils were everywhere, falling on her inexorably from all directions in a tangled net she could not escape. Embra Silvertree barely noticed them; she was frantically kicking off from the wall and rolling across hard and uneven flagstones to avoid being crushed. Somewhere nearby, an awed Craer Delnbone was softly and swiftly giving the world an impressive stream of curses.

The longfangs brushed her boots as it landed, and she could smell damp, slightly moldy fur. She rolled over, wondering how she'd reach her dagger in time—and then there was no more time.

Long, hairy limbs that felt like iron bars fell on her, slapping across her mouth and entwining around her arms. Dirty brown fur prickled and stung. Cruel barbs rose like teeth before her eyes, and she heard the clapping of the little rending jaws on its longest forelimbs, but no mandibles tore at her. Yet.

The furry, wolf-headed spider rolled Embra onto her stomach and shifted its weight onto her, pinning her until her breath whistled through her nose. Its scent, like soured apples or wine gone to vinegar, was strong about her. Its limbs never left her mouth, enfolding her throat and jaws so tightly that she could not have spoken no matter how dire the need. The other limbs of the long-fangs forced her arms slowly together; she could see that they sported thornlike barbs at the joints and ended in gripping pads, like the feet of snails she'd seen along the river shore. Pads that were now wrapped around her hands so tightly that she could not move a finger, as her arms came together and the limbs of the longfangs spiraled around them like ropes, in eerie silence.

It's as if it knows I can cast spells, she thought, *and is determined to prevent me.* Then she stiffened as the first spell threads settled upon her, and a tingling began. It went on, lessening slightly, as the longfangs shifted its grip on her and freed two of its long, spidery limbs. They reared back like daggers waiting to stab down, and by peering as far to her right as possible, Embra could see why: the still-blind armaragor Hawkril had smelled or heard the longfangs and was now hacking wildly but heartily at the air with his sword.

With the last wisps of her gown melting away from her as she lay helplessly pinned to the cold stone floor, Embra for the first time found the warm, furry weight of the longfangs reassuring: there was a lot of monster between her and that wicked blade—unless, of course, he was stupid enough to thrust at it right along the floor.

Nothing more than the ever-present tingling seemed to happen within her, and Embra dared to hope the tendrils had been some sort of spying or even shielding magics. Then she reminded herself wryly that she was in the grip of a beast that habitually tore men limb from limb and feasted on them. With no one to rescue her but a pair of incompetent thieves and her father's tender wizards . . .

Hawkril's blade cut at the air rather nearer. He seemed to be listening for sounds of a foe now, rather than snarling in wordless rage. Embra tried to buck upward suddenly and shift the longfangs off her; the armaragor heard the futile scraping of her knees and elbows on the stone floor and turned directly toward her, his blade sweeping out.

The longfangs shrank back, dragging Embra with it, as that long sword reached out again and again in great arcs. Hawkril advanced behind his sweeping steel, step by cautious step—until something sprang past the wolfspider to roll under the swordmaster's feet, sending him crashing to the floor with his blade clanging out of his hand.

Hawkril came to his feet slowly, shaking his head to clear it and cursing weakly. His vision was coming back, it seemed, as he peered this way and that.

The cause of Hawkril's fall was crouching warily not an arm's-reach distant from the helpless Embra, facing the longfangs. Staring into its golden eyes, Craer asked hesitantly, "Sarasper? Is that you?"

The tension in the ornate chamber suddenly eased. Three wizards sighed their relief in unison, traded glances, and sat down.

At the gleaming table in the center of the room, the darkly handsome baron of Silvertree calmly poured himself more wine and raised an eyebrow. "Well?"

Ingryl Ambelter managed a smile. "The protective magics have reached the Lady Embra, Lord, and settled on her."

His employer nodded. "I was unfamiliar with your embellishments, Spellmaster, whereas I recognized all of Beirldoun's casting. Pray unfold for me *all* the details of your combined enchantments."

Ingryl bowed his head and replied, "Lord Baron, the shieldings now active upon your daughter will keep her safe against almost all spells except personal curses and will staunch any bleeding from wounds, though the magic can neither prevent nor mitigate the actual puncture or cut made by, say, a blade."

Faerod Silvertree raised his other eyebrow. "If wounded, will she suffer?"

"Lord," Ingryl said carefully, "an unavoidable property of such magic is that any wounds keep the shielded one in constant pain."

"Good," the baron replied gently. "I don't want her getting *too* comfortable."

"One last property," Ambelter added. "Any mage of accomplishment who knows she is thus shielded can employ spells to trace her—or rather, trace the shield upon her—henceforth."

The baron grew a slow and evil smile, his dark eyes flashing almost green. Lifting his glass in salute to the three mages, he told it almost playfully, "'Tis well done. These three will be my swords where hitherto I've not been able to reach; rebels who unwittingly serve me. Grow strong in magic, my daughter—to be my dagger in the backs of those barons who stand against me."

Craer looked at the longfangs, and the longfangs looked back at Craer.

Silence hung heavy in the Silent House until there came a faint, wordless sound of pain from the Lady Embra as she twisted under the wolf-spider's furry bulk. Hawkril rubbed still-smarting eyes and beheld the monster clearly at last.

A longfangs, it seemed, looked like a spider cloaked in the pelt and lean, rippling muscles of a wolf. It had the jawed head of a giant wolf, and two of its spiderlike forelimbs also sported little rending jaws; the others were barbed at the joints.

As Hawkril watched, those barbs were the first things to melt away. Gradually the limbs followed, receding in slow and ghostly silence like mist stealing away before bright sunlight, until a sad-eyed and thin elderly man was kneeling, naked, on Embra's back.

Hawkril caught sight of his sword and retrieved it. Then he looked at Craer. "You called him 'Sarasper.' *Who* is Sarasper?"

The old man shuffled back from Embra on bony knees, leaving her gasping on the floor. She found breath enough to turn her head and say, "Yes, Craer, introduce us. And when you've done that, I'd like my clothes!"

The procurer smiled and turned to where his sack lay fallen. "Friends," he said over his shoulder, "meet Sarasper Codelmer, one of my elder friends. I lost track of him years back and only learned he was here not long ago, from another old friend."

"So it was Thalver who betrayed me, hey?" Sarasper growled almost wearily, running a mottled, dark-veined hand over his stubbled, jutting chin. "Old Thundersword . . . no better than all the others." His voice was thick and grating from long disuse, but he managed to make bitterness ring clear in its tones.

"He was dying on a Brightscar beach with three arrows through him," Craer said gently. "In the arms of a friend. Someone to spill his secrets to, and so find a little ease ere he died. Remember him not harshly."

"Hmmph," Sarasper replied gruffly, hunching his head down between his shoulders and shuffling away from them along the wall, eyes darting around the room ceaselessly. "How much did he tell you?"

"That you slew the real longfangs years ago and have dwelt in the catacombs here ever since, hiding from men . . . as a bat, a ground snake, or as the man-eating longfangs of the Silent House."

"Hiding from all men or just my father?" Embra asked, through tangled hair.

"From all barons, lass," the old man said shortly, darting a glance at her that strayed along her body for a longing instant before he looked away. "And who would your father be?" he asked the wall beside him.

"Faerod Silvertree," she said simply.

The old man looked at her sharply, and for an instant fur seemed to grow along his forearms. "He sent you to find me, sorceress?" he asked coldly.

Hawkril hefted the sword in his hand, but the old man never looked at it. His eyes glittered as he stared at Embra, hunching himself as if to pounce on her.

She shook her head, chin scraping the flagstones. "We three are fleeing his wrath and reach—or rather, that of his three mages."

The old man seemed to shrink a trifle and shuffled a little farther away. "So what of your spells, Lady of Jewels?" he asked, fetching up against a more distant stretch of wall. His words were sharp, almost a challenge.

"Gone in getting us here," Embra told him, and turned her head to glare at Craer. "My *clothes?*" she reminded him.

The procurer held out boots and a bundle to her and then held up the sack they'd come from in front of her, as a screen. It hid almost nothing, and she gave him a sour look as she sat up and started to draw on the wet breeches. They watched her shiver, and Hawkril suddenly rose and strode to the candle lamp. Setting it down close beside her, he stepped away to sit down against the wall with his sword across his knees, keeping his eyes always on the man who'd been a monster not so long ago . . . not long enough ago.

"So we've an old man with magic enough to take the shapes of three beasts, perhaps more," the armaragor rumbled. "He hides in his most fearsome form and eats folk raw when they come calling . . . why?"

"He's a healer," Embra said suddenly, the tunic in her hands momentarily forgotten as she whirled around to look at the old man hunched against the wall.

Sarasper stiffened but did not look at the half-naked sorceress. His nod was so brief that they almost missed it. "Secrets, it seems," he told the ceiling above him with a sigh, "never last quite long enough."

"He can heal wounds?" Hawkril asked. "With magic? *That* drives a man to eat human flesh for years?"

"Traditionally," Embra told her tunic flatly, as she shrugged it into place and tugged at its wet sleeves, "barons have kept healers as chained slaves, to heal on command. As the healing flows through such a one's body, it ages and wears out the flesh. A healer without the freedom to limit the use of his powers will probably die young, bent and broken like an old man."

Silence fell. The three companions stared at the figure hunched against the wall.

"You were afraid of being captured by Baron Silvertree," Hawkril said to him, but received no reply.

"And rightly so," Embra added into the silence, pulling on her boots. She kicked at the flagstones to settle her feet inside them, then got up.

Sarasper lifted his head to watch her walk toward him, but they could read no thoughts on his tired face.

"You hid behind the traps in the catacombs whenever my father's forces—or adventurers, seeking tomb coins—came calling, and you hunted outside these walls only at night . . . and only as a longfangs," she said slowly, reasoning aloud. Her thoughts brought her to a halt a few paces away from the old man.

Sarasper nodded again. "I've grown very tired of raw meat," he told her, something that might almost have been pleading in his rough voice. He raised an eyebrow in what might have been a challenge and then looked away again.

"Then stop hiding," Craer said with sudden urgency, almost pleading, "and live again! Once we rode together for Blackgult—remember, Sarasper? Now, we need healing; Hawk and the Lady both. She was as much the baron's prisoner as any chained healer. Will you aid us . . . please?"

For a long and silent time the old man looked at them out of his sunken eyes, his face expressionless. Then he said heavily, "I will. But there will be a price."

* * *

Delvin of the Many Harps and Helgrym Castlecloaks had retreated behind a row of tombs to decide what to do next. They could hear the groans of a few Silvertree soldiers, but the doorway into the Silent House seemed entirely blocked with a massive flow of loose stone. "It's probably filled the room inside that doorway," Helgrym judged grimly, "if so much has been spilled outside. I've walked all around this place in younger years—from a distance, I'll grant—and I don't remember any other way in. It seems not so much for a ballad, after all."

"Just turn around and go, you mean? After risking our necks creeping up here?" Delvin protested, with the disappointment of youth fresh from the victory of excitement over fear and unwilling to soon taste empty-handed defeat.

"Know you a wiser course ahead for us?" Helgrym asked, "or . . ."

Something large and dark swooped out of the night and snapped Delvin's head off with one bite. The headless corpse staggered, blood fountaining in all directions, and did not reply.

Helgrym cursed and turned to run, knowing as he did so that doom was upon him. As he sprinted through the uneven darkness, he started to sing his favorite ballad. If one had to die, 'twould be nice to hear it, just one more time. . . .

When dark wings swooped and the song abruptly ended in a wet, gnawing sound, eyes peering out of the doorway of a nearby tomb blazed golden with anger. A hand stroked the curves of a harp whose strings it did not touch, and a low voice told the night, "Stupid mages—may you all boil in the bile of your own arrogance! I had plans for those two!"

* * *

Sarasper did something to one of the stones in the wall, and it swung inward to reveal a niche, out of which he pulled a fist-size wooden box. He slid one side of it open, and light spilled out: bright radiance centered on a pebble, which he set on the floor before pinching out Hawkril's candle lamp with steady fingers.

"My price," he told the smoking candle gruffly, "is your aid in a matter that rides me day and night."

"A debt? A quest?" Craer demanded. "Something lost that must be found?"

"Four things to be recovered," Sarasper said shortly. "The quest may last longer than the life remaining to me."

"I don't know if I'm hurt that badly," Hawkril rumbled, and looked at the pale, pain-lined face of Lady Silvertree.

"I fear I am," she whispered, so softly that the armaragor had to lean forward to hear her. She raised her voice to add calmly, "Say more of this quest, healer."

The old man was busy at another place on the wall. The stone that opened this time yielded a robe that was more tatters and varicolored patches than whatever garment it had started out as. He shrugged his way into it, ignoring a strong smell of mildew, and said in his rough voice, "The patron of all healers is Forefather Oak, mightiest of the Three, and betimes he speaks to we who heal by sending us visions in our dreams."

Hawkril shrugged. "I often have dreams that blaze bright—or dark—enough to recall when I'm awake . . . most of them of blood, and battle, and friends gone down fighting. Does the Old One's face appear, or do you just do as most priests do and sort out the dreams that are to your liking and deem them the ones sent you by the Forefather?"

Sarasper stiffened. Slowly he drew himself erect, as grandly as if he were himself a baron, and said slowly and coldly, each word dropping forth like a stone, "Were the Forefather to send you a vision, you'd know it and not speak so. With gold fire he laces about his scenes, and they burn forever, fading not. Trust me in this, swordmaster, as I would trust you to correct me in weapon work."

Hawkril nodded, a little abashed. "Say on," he bade, waving a hand.

The old man inclined his head, as if dispensing royal justice, and said roughly, "Steep this price may be, but this quest gnaws at me."

He stopped and glared around at them all. "It should gnaw at all folk up and down the Silverflow. It should snarl and prowl at the hearts of every warrior and wizard in what was once Aglirta—and must be again!"

His voice lost its imperious edge and became a rough mumble once more. "It has worked on my thoughts these last few years, the visions coming again and again until I prowl these ways endlessly, never able to rest. The Worldstones must be recovered. The Dwaerindim must then be placed correctly to awaken the Sleeping King . . . who will rise, as the tales say, to restore peace and bounty to the land."

"Ah, horns and bebolt!" Hawkril burst out in disgust. "That's but a legend, a fancy tale to make children's eyes bright! 'But find the Four Lost Stones, and the castles will rise, the mountains fall, and golden age come upon the land, and everyone will grow fat and happy on endless plenty, as the perilous beasts flee afar!' *Nursemaids* prattle suchlike!"

Embra Silvertree nodded. "My shelves back at the castle still hold three tellings of the saga of the Dwaerindim that tutors read to me until I could read the words for myself. Those books are *old*. If the Sleeping King ever existed, he'll be but bones and dust by now! Tell me, Sarasper: just how would you tell if you'd made some dust come awake?"

Sarasper's voice was more tired than patient as he growled, "I'm neither mad nor minstrel-witted. I can tell you only that I speak of truth, not empty legend. I suppose you think the Serpent in the Shadows is just another pretty tale, too?"

"Some evil mage now worshiped by dabblers in poison and the like?" Hawkril rumbled.

"A wizard—," the old healer and the sorceress began, together. They fell silent and looked at each other. Sarasper gestured like a courtier to Embra, indicating she should continue. She gave him a narrow-eyed look and then nodded and said softly, "A wizard who had a hand in the enchanting of the Stones but went mad, or was mad, and murdered several rival mages to strengthen the enchantments he was placing on a Dwaer. When his deeds were discovered, the other mages of the Shaping confronted him. He fled into serpent form to try to fight his way free of their spells— and they imprisoned him in a serpent shape. He wears it still."

"He's still alive, too?" the armaragor asked, voice heavy with disbelief.

"Swordmaster," the healer asked in return, "is there *anything* in all Darsar you believe in, beyond that sword in your hand and the next meal heading for your belly? Or is it all coins and wenches, better armor and a good bed to sleep in?"

"Old man," Hawkril Anharu replied, fixing Sarasper with a level eye, "*I* often think all Darsar would be a better world to dwell in if more folk concerned themselves with such things and less about following gods and raising kingdoms and slaughtering their neighbors. Oh, yes—and dreaming clever dreams, too."

Armaragors with guttering torches held high cast towering shadows on the stone walls. Wordlessly they led the cloaked and cowled figures up secret stairs into a room dark with tapestries, somewhere high in the castle of Baron Ornentar.

A shimmering occurred in the air as each visitor

parted tapestries and stepped within. Most of them knew it as a shielding against spying magics, and welcomed its small reassurance. If the barony of Ornentar was to escape the yoke of Silvertree, Baron Eldagh was at least taking basic precautions against Faerod's Dark Three.

None of the visitors was particularly surprised to see magical wands in the hands of the hooded figure who stood behind the baron or armaragors seated on either side of him with loaded crossbows in their laps and swords naked and ready on benches before them . . . but then, none of the visitors had themselves come unprepared. Dark deeds—and plotting them—demand desperate measures. Doubtless armaragors stood ready behind every tapestry around the room: armaragors who served the desperate man who sat facing them all.

They all knew him, at least by face and repute. The Baron Ornentar was a fat, stone-faced man. His dark, lidded eyes were both cold and sinister. A man who thought himself subtle but was no more so than a descending ax—once one realized he was ruled always by his hunger for power.

His visitors did not recognize the wizard with the wands behind the baron, but had taken care that any mage traveling out of Silvertree would be observed, and any spying magic blocked. Whoever this masked stranger was, he was no tool of Faerod. His was probably the backbone that had made the baron bold enough to take this open step against Silvertree.

More visitors were arriving: tall and broad-shouldered warriors, the faint rattle of armor beneath their cloaks, and heavy war swords at their sides. There were even a few more sly and slight men; procurers, perhaps.

"The count is complete," the baron said at last. "Let the full guard be mounted." Tapestries swirled as armaragors behind them gave salutes and left for their posts. "Be seated, if you will, and unmask," the master of Ornentar added. "We are all here, I think, for the same reason, and need know no strife within these walls."

The same whispered word had indeed brought all of these visitors to Ornentar Castle, and that word was *Dwaer.*

"Word has spread up and down Coiling Vale as swift as a sunrise, it seems," the baron began, "and yet I've heard wild embellishments growing about the tale even within my own halls. Have patience, then, as Urdras—a scribe out of Sirlptar—recounts what little is known, for certain."

A slight, nervously restless man with gray, receding hair, who wore plain, worn robes and a worried expression, arose from a chair near to the baron, sketched a bow, and hugged himself, keeping his hands within his crossed sleeves. "I—ah—yes," he began uneasily.

Within a few words, he was pacing, his nervousness lending urgency to his steps. "A matter of days ago, a wizard died: the mage Yezund of Elmerna. He claimed to have deduced the present location of one of the Dwaerindim: Candalath, the Stone of Life. He did this, he reported, both through his own far-seeking spells and examination of old texts, and by the reports of hireswords whom he sent exploring. He places it somewhere in the library of the dead wizard Ehrluth, in the ruined city of Indraevyn."

Urdras paused to look around the room. The silence was as heavy as the dark tapestries on all sides, and with a nervous cough the scribe continued: "Yezund reported all this triumphantly to wizards gathered at the House of the Raised Hand in Sirlptar, where followed both derision and excited discussion. This house is a private club for mages, where Yezund was a member of no particular rank or regard."

The scribe paused again for dramatic emphasis, felt the cold eyes of the baron on his back, and hurriedly added, "Yezund swept out of the house immediately after making his pronouncements and walked home. He reached the Street of Lamps—and there was torn apart by unseen magics—perhaps wielded by the same sinister mage or mages who pillaged and then burned Yezund's house, within an hour of his death. The slayer remains unknown, but something or someone ruthless and magically powerful is obviously after the Dwaer."

The scribe bowed again and sat down without delay. Before anyone else could speak, the baron said, "Have my thanks, Urdras. You appreciate the importance of this news, gentles: if this Dwaer is found, it can be used to devastating effect. If it falls into the hands of Silvertree, none of us in all Aglirta is safe. Wherefore we are here, to speak freely. Sing out, if you will."

There was a general stir, and at least three voices started to speak at once. The baron lifted a hand to cry order, but a deep, thunderous voice cut through them all to say, "I—and many who swing swords, I daresay—know the Dwaerindim from mothers' tales. Let our scribe stand again, and tell us plainly what power these Stones have, without all the grand mystery that mages like to wield like swords against us lesser wits!" The speaker was a large and scarred warrior, seated near the back and wrapped in a dark green cloak that could have smothered three scrawny scribes out of Sirlptar.

"Claws of the Dark One!" one of the cowled mages snarled. "Must we sit through endless explanations for idiots?"

"*Yes,*" a warrior sitting near snapped, and then added in words slow, clear, and cold: "We idiots appreciate it."

There were chuckles and "ayes" of agreement from around the chamber, and at a nod from the baron the scribe arose once more, almost stammering in his nervousness now.

"This Stone is said to be able to raise the dead to life once more and to have many other powers besides. The Dwaerindim each have magics, and when used together, by one who knows how to place and command them, can unleash yet more spells."

"So what, beyond the death to life, makes them any better than a dozen hired wizards?" the deep-voiced warrior demanded.

Urdras smiled weakly, and said, "Forgive me, all here who know already, but it must be plainly said: magical control, creativity, and ability to shape and work forces comes from within a wizard, but the raw power that brings any spell into being is always called forth from enchanted items. Most items—pebbles that give forth light, for instance, or yonder gauntlets. . ."

Many eyes turned to look at the table where the scribe pointed. A pair of war gauntlets drawn off by one of the warriors was crawling restlessly around on their fingertips like aroused spiders. Their owner shrugged and said, "Whenever strong magic is at work, nearby. Here: the shielding spell, no doubt."

The scribe nodded vigorously. "Precisely. These items show us magic because spells are cast upon them, or stored within them, to issue forth. The time will come when their magic is gone, exhausted. All items of lasting enchantment—whose magic lasts more than our lifetimes, and which can be drawn on to power spell after spell, without being extinguished—are created by spells that involve sacrificing the life of an accomplished wizard. Most mages will do anything to acquire such an item. This Dwaer, like its fellows, is of this rare, lasting sort of item."

"You have just spoken," one hooded mage said softly, "secrets I will slay you for revealing, when I can. There is no place you can hide from our spells, master scribe."

Cowering and white-faced, Urdras sat down—and promptly slumped to the floor in a faint. It could be seen that he'd soiled himself.

"Your spells work swiftly," someone commented sardonically.

"Yet the words cannot be unspoken," a warrior countered the hooded mage, "and I see no crime in unfolding truths to better us all."

"In arming you," another mage snarled, "he has disarmed us!"

The baron brought the flat of his hand down on the table with a crack that brought silence. He rushed into it with the words, "No secret stands forever, and we speak of something more important than daily concerns of power. All our lives, gentles, are forfeit should this Stone fall into the wrong hands."

"I think we are all agreed that the hands of Faerod Silvertree are the wrong hands," another warrior said, "but I doubt me if any three of us here could agree for long on whose hands are the *right* ones, to wield such power. Would any of you trust me, while I held such a blade at your throat?"

Suddenly everyone was speaking, raising their voices over one another to be heard; the baron stood and bellowed, *"Be still!"* in a roar that shocked echoes back from the walls even through the tapestries.

In the head-turning silence that followed, he said, "This is the one point upon which we all know, I think, that our converse must needs fall apart into dissension. So let it be agreed, here and now, that we not wrangle over it. The time for such dispute must needs come if the Stone is ever held by any of us. Here, tonight, let us consider the threat, and benefits, of the Stone, so that no matter who comes to hold it, the most able men in Aglirta—we who are here tonight—know what it can be used for and won't act out of ignorance. Isn't 'not knowing' what we fear most?"

"As in, 'not knowing when the husband will return'?" someone commented, and after a moment of startled silence, there was a roar of shouted laughter, almost of relief that someone had found a jest. When it died away, a hush came over the room unbidden, born of the excitement—the peril—all who were present felt.

"We are all ambitious," the baron added, "but some of us are rightly fearful. Unhood, mages of Ornentar, and speak as plainly as this brave scribe dared to. My fear is that we've no time to spare for threatening each other or speaking cryptically."

"You speak truth as usual, Lord Baron," one of the mages replied. "The lure of this Dwaer is almost irresistible to any mage—but out of habit, many wizards are as fearful as they are ambitious." His hands drew back his hood, and most in the room recognized the calm countenance of Huldaerus, the Master of Bats, whose interests included using magic to give human warriors bat wings, taloned hands, and utter obedience to him. He was known up and down the River Coiling, and feared. A minstrel had once said at a Moot that "Aglirta's worst nightmare would be Huldaerus and Silvertree, working together—a terror for Silverflow Vale one year and all Darsar, the next." That minstrel had not been seen for some time.

The mage sitting next to him also unhooded, to reveal the handsome, faintly smiling countenance of Nynter of the Nine Daggers, who habitually defended himself with winged flying daggers and collected gemstone statuettes and pretty slave girls. His curls were dyed the hue of old honey, and his dancing eyes were merry with excitement. He was feared in Ornentar, but not so much beyond its borders as the Master of Bats . . . perhaps because he traveled less.

Seated some distance away, a third mage also drew back his hood, revealing the more forbidding features of Phalagh, who was known to collect coins and the severed heads of those who dared to cross him. His usual suspicious frown sat heavily under his high-domed forehead, and his huddled pose gave him the look of an irritated perched vulture.

"So, Huldaerus," the baron said almost jovially, "I bid you begin the converse—if not with your own plans and thoughts, then with a point we can dispute and debate."

Huldaerus inclined his head in a nod of acquiescence, and said, "Think, all: we could bring great mages back from the grave to fight for us!"

"Oh?" the deep-voiced warrior shot back. "And control them how? And when we're done, and all Darsar lies at our feet, who will rule—them, or us? How do you kill something that's already dusty bones, eh? Magic? Well, who'll be the masters of that—them, or us?"

"Well," a masked mage responded, "we can use the Stone to keep ourselves alive no matter what the Silvertree mages hurl at us!"

"Oh? Alive as their slaves forever? And what's to keep them from just taking the Stone from us—*your* spells?"

The masked mage stiffened in evident anger, but the baron lifted a warning hand to forestall any reply.

One of the procurers asked then, "Are the whereabouts of any of the other Dwaerindim known for certain? I would know more of these magics awakened only when two or more of the Stones are used together."

"To your first question: no, so far as I know and any will admit," Huldaerus answered. "To your second: legends and wild tales and dusty records all wrestle with the truth as to just what powers can be unleashed, but 'tis fairly certain that the Stones work together only when placed in particular patterns and, moreover, when specific incantations are uttered."

"*What* powers, mage?" a gravel-voiced armaragor asked. "Or are these more of your secrets that all nonwizards who learn must be slain out of hand?"

Huldaerus smiled thinly. "As I said," he replied, "there is much disagreement over these powers. Best known among them, for instance—told of in all nursemaids' tales—are the summonings. Use all four Stones one way, and you awaken, free, and call forth the Sleeping King!"

There were snorts and wordless sneers of derision, but the mage merely smiled and added, "Use them another way, and you call up instead his age-old foe, the Serpent in the Shadows."

"Empty bards' babble," one warrior sneered. "You waste our time, wizard!"

The cowled figure standing behind the baron raised both of its wands to draw attention—most effectively—and hissed in reply, "Not ssso. I have studied the Ssserpent all my life and have mastered the spells to control its sssavagery, to make it ssslay only those I choose. The Ssserpent is very real; at least three cities lie forgotten and overgrown today because their folk thought it empty legend, or sssomething they might easily master. It devoured them all—and it gleans sssomething from every mind it eats. Bring me the Ssserpent, and I ssshall win all Darsssar with it!"

A wizard who was still masked tapped the table before him with a wand of his own, and demanded, "I hear talk of serving the Serpent, if I hear aright—and I want to see who speaks such words!"

There was a stir of agreement—a stir that died to tense silence as the figure at the baron's elbow set down its wands, reached up slowly, and drew back its hood.

The face that had been hidden in the cowl belonged to no man, but was green and scaled and slit-eyed, with the fangs and darting forked tongue of a snake. "I have the pleasssure to be a priest of the Serpent."

Another masked mage sneered, "Oh? There are no gods but the Three!"

The serpent head turned to regard him and seemed to smile. "I agree, sssir. Oh, yesss. By serving the Ssserpent, I ssserve the Dark One. One of his tentacles gave me these scales and biting fangs and eternity to use them in. Can any of you say the same?"

In the fearful silence that followed, an eye whose presence would have surprised the baron and his three mages very much drew back thoughtfully behind a tapestry and watched that assembly of conspirators no more.

* * *

"Well, we've traded clever words," Sarasper growled, looking slowly around at the three adventurers, "and we know your need . . . and my price. You run from a known peril, and fear a known foe. I offer you a dream to follow, in years to come. A dream that shows us a road out of the death and tyranny that now rules what was once Aglirta, wherein outlaws, tyrants, and monsters outnumber farmers, and even honest folk outnumber those who are happy and bereft of fear."

He lifted his shoulders in a shrug. "Perhaps you care nothing for a brighter future or the land that birthed you. Perhaps you care only for the next meal and a way clear of all this. If so, know that I can show you other ways out of this House—or devour you one by one, if you offer me violence. I should do so anyway, to keep my secret safe . . . but I've little heart for that when there's a chance to follow the Forefather's will."

He shrugged, lifted his hands, and let them fall. "The choice remains to you. I cannot make it for you."

The healer let silence stretch; Craer was the first to speak, looking quickly to the armaragor. "Hawk? I dragged you into this. . . ."

The armaragor shrugged. "My will is to stand with you, little man, whatever road you choose. I think this man follows crazed dreams—but we all have to follow something or drift to our graves having done nothing. Stay or go; you decide."

Craer shook his head and said heavily, "I like none of our choices." Reluctantly, far more slowly than he'd sought out the gaze of his friend, he turned to look into the eyes of Embra Silvertree.

She looked back at them all and then at the floor, saying nothing.

"Speak," the armaragor rumbled, finally.

His bidding caused her head to snap up and her eyes to flash with anger. She held his gaze wordlessly for some time before she said softly, "I find in myself no stomach for seeking revenge on my father and naught else. I know not if I dare ever use magic again or what has befallen me, with the bindings broken."

Her lips twisted, as if to utter a warrior's curse, but when she spoke again it was to say almost calmly, "You dared to aid me, men of Blackgult. I think we should—must—all dare to aid this lonely man. I could not rest easy if we walked away and left him here alone, and I think we dare not fight him . . . nor would I take any pride in doing so, even if by some grace of the gods we defeated him. We cannot treat everyone we meet as a foe to be fought."

Sarasper abruptly turned his back. It was not until they saw the droplets on the stones in front of him that they realized he was weeping.

Embarrassed, Hawkril said heartily, "Well, if we're agreed, then we must be a band of adventurers, we four—and we'll have to choose a name, before bards hang something ridiculous on us. Anyone feel clever?"

"Always," Craer and Embra said in dry unison—and then, slowly, snorted in reluctant mirth. They glanced at each other, and snorts became chuckles . . . chuckles that grew slowly into laughter—roars of laughter, from four throats that rang around the room.

Four trapped and desperate folk . . .

"We must be," Sarasper the healer announced almost shyly, "until that cleverness smites us all with something better: the Band of Four."

"Let us be so," Craer nodded, sounding a trifle reluctant. It was his turn for lips to twist on the edge of a curse, before he said mockingly, "Embra, start working on the ballad!"

"You'll be sorry," the woman at his elbow purred in a voice that held equal parts mirth and warning, "and that's *Lady* Embra to you."

The three men all made sounds of mockery, but when she reached out her hand, their own hands stretched forth—slowly and reluctantly but without roughness or clever gestures—to clasp hers in a common grasp.

Four pairs of eyes met, sharing a little fear. No one cheered . . . but no one hastened to draw their hand back, either.

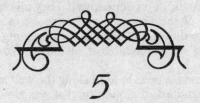

5

Spells and Secrets

H awkril watched the healer's hands touch his ribs and realized he'd been holding his breath until he could do so no longer. He let it out in a long, shuddering sigh, just as the icy and yet somehow warm tingling began to wash out from his ribs, spreading slowly. . . .

"Ohhh," he moaned, at the sheer pleasure of feeling all pain swept away. "Sargh, but it's good to be free of that!"

The armaragor breathed deeply, truly free of hurting, and after a moment looked down at the graying head bent over him and asked, "So why is it that mages hurl lightnings and bring castles crashing down and walk away all nonchalant . . . and healers die if they heal too much?"

"Healing comes from within. The Three grant the gift to a rare few," Sarasper growled, without looking up. His hands were trembling slightly. "Wizards take power from other enchantments to do their work."

"Oh? So who cast the first enchantment that a wizard drew on?"

"Ah," said Craer from where he sat against the wall, "now *that* question is one that sets priests at each

other's throats, in proper earnest! They all claim it was
their own of the Three . . . and there are even wizards
who revere this or that elder mage for giving his life to
fashion an enchantment that all other wizards could
draw on."

He turned his head to look along the wall at the Lady
of Jewels and asked a question that was almost a challenge. "Do your books say anything different?"

Embra gave him a bitter smile that faded quickly
from her face. "So many different things that I can believe none of them." She let her head fall back against
the wall she was leaning on, and sighed.

Craer's eyes narrowed. "When did you start to feel
worn out?"

She shrugged. "Not long ago."

Her eyes closed. The procurer watched her for a moment and then stirred himself to reach the healer. Touching Sarasper's shoulder, he pointed at the sorceress.

The healer looked at Embra's face and nodded
slowly. "I'm almost done here. The organs within were
well torn, beyond the power of your potion, but this
warrior is a right bear."

He glanced up at Hawkril and said gruffly, "Now just
lie still, for once, until I'm done with the lady. The
longer you lie quiet, the swifter the healing finds every
last little ache."

Sarasper did not wait for a reply but rose and crossed
the chamber with the stiffness and unsteadiness of one
who has seen many years—but also with the haste of a
warrior scrambling about in a battle. He came to a
clumsy collision with the wall beside the sorceress,
grunted in pain, and laid the backs of his fingers against
Embra's cheek.

She opened her eyes for just a moment, then leaned
her weight against his hand, seeming to fall into full
slumber. Sarasper frowned.

"There are spells upon her," he told the other men.

"Her own—or some dark work of the Silvertree mages, I wonder?"

"All my magic is gone," Embra murmured, against his hand. "These two broke the bindings set by my father's command, earlier this night. I know nothing of what these spells may be."

"Your father never ordered spells laid on you to keep you young, or . . . change your beauty?"

A faint smile touched Embra's lips. "No," she told the healer, her eyes still closed. "All you see is mine own."

"They're the work of Silvertree's pet mages, no doubt," Hawkril growled.

"Then I'll break them," Sarasper said.

"You can do that?" the armaragor asked, rolling up onto one elbow to get a better look. He was in time to see Embra's body jump under the healer's hands, like a horse kicked awake, and begin to shudder uncontrollably. She arched her back, her eyes opened to show only whites, and then closed again as she sagged, suddenly as limp as an empty cloak.

The armaragor could hear the chatter of her teeth as Sarasper put his arms around her and snarled, "Of course. Anyone can break a spell . . . if they know how. Unless the spell is on them." There was sweat on the old healer's face, now, and his skin was growing dark.

"You mean," Hawkril asked slowly, "that anyone who learns enough can be a wizard?"

"Almost," the healer snapped, as the shuddering sorceress in his arms shook him along the wall. Veins stood out on his flushed forehead as he wrestled with her. "It requires more patience than most folk have, an iron will to hold to a purpose—and a certain ruthlessness. That's why most mages act so grand or mysterious or sinister. They want others to think only special folk can become wizards so that few will pester them to become their apprentices."

The healer's growl broke off in a grunt of pain as Embra's thrashings bumped one of his elbows solidly against the stone floor, and he gasped out some curses and rolled away from her.

She twisted, like a dog scratching its back on a mat, and then fell still, leaving him the only one shuddering. Hawkril watched him hug himself in pain, like many a wounded warrior huddled around a campfire after a battle . . . but he was not clutching his bruised elbow.

"Sarasper?" he asked. "Are you—?"

The healer lifted a sweat-drenched face, looking as exhausted and gray as one of those wounded warriors Hawkril was remembering, and snarled, "Fine. Never been better. Must get up and frolic!"

He coughed, then, doubling over uncontrollably, and the two men of Blackgult exchanged uncomfortable glances as the healer retched and spat and groaned. When at last his shoulders ceased to shake and his breath lost its rasp and rattle—it seemed a very long time—Sarasper looked up, glared at them both, and growled, "Neither of you have the slightest idea how healers work, do you?"

He did not wait for them to silently and grimly shake their heads but instead turned to Embra. Looking searchingly into her still face, Sarasper seemed to see something reassuring. He rolled her into a more restful position, gently tugged her tunic back into place where her convulsions had almost laid bare one shapely shoulder, and then sighed heavily and looked away.

"It seems harder than when she worked spells," Hawkril said reluctantly. After a silent moment or two he added the query, "Could I cast spells like a wizard?" His voice was at once hesitant and eager.

Sarasper looked up at him, his hands on Embra's shoulders. "Someday, perhaps, if the need was great enough. But you'll have to lose something first."

"Oh?"

"Aye. Your good sense. To be a wizard of any power, it helps a lot if you're crazed."

Hawkril made a disgusted sound and growled sarcastically, "Thanks. I'll try to remember that."

Under the healer's hands, they heard Embra make a weak sound. It was a chuckle.

In the chamber in Castle Silvertree that all of the baron's pet mages were growing rather weary of, Ingryl Ambelter and Klamantle Beirldoun stiffened, exchanged glances, and shook their heads. Then they turned in unison to face the table where Faerod Silvertree sat, wine glass in hand, staring into its depths . . . doubtless on the verge of dozing. For that matter, Markoun had retired to his chambers; no matter what exacting private researches he'd claimed to be pursuing, by now he was assuredly snoring.

"Lord Baron," Klamantle said tentatively, and then cleared his throat and halted in confusion. His employer had responded not a whit. The baron's eyes were still seeing nothing, somewhere in the ruby depths of the wine, and he sat unmoving.

Ingryl strode forward and said firmly, "My Lord, we have, just now, both felt the shielding spell on the Lady Embra shatter and fade away. This leaves us not knowing her location or condition, henceforth."

With no change of expression, Faerod Silvertree told his glass almost delicately, "Graul the Horned Lady! Graul and rend her and all who stand in my way!"

He looked up, as suddenly as a falcon, and his glare was like a sword of fire.

"You will hunt down and capture my daughter right away, with no more gentle spells nor leisure for her," he snarled. "Use any magic that won't slay her or maim or disfigure her irrevocably . . . level Silvertree House if you have to."

* * *

"I feel better, yes," Embra told them quietly. "But I also feel . . . empty. As if something within me is gone, or torn away." She shrugged. "I just don't know. Perhaps Hawkril had better learn to be a mighty mage after all."

Craer winced. "I don't think we've years enough to spare for that. We've probably tarried here too long already; I can't believe the baron will just sit and brood over the loss of his daughter when he knows where we fled."

"If they want to come in through that door chamber," Hawkril growled, "it'll take a lot of digging."

"Not if the right spells are used," Sarasper told him sharply. "Every stone could be lifted and hurled in here at us like a missile, breaking joints until we're helpless, if the wizards are skilled enough." He turned back to the Lady of Jewels, the snap of anger back in his voice. "Just who works magic for your father?"

"Ingryl Ambelter, once apprentice to Gadaster Mulkyn, and the most dangerous; Klamantle Beirldoun—a quiet, cold man of whom I know almost nothing; and a young, ambitious man from somewhere outside the Vale, who fancies himself handsome: Markoun Yarynd. His eyes are hot on me, that one. Cruel, calculating men, all."

"Gadaster I remember," the healer said slowly, "and hearing of his death. The apprentice Ambelter I may have laid eyes on, once or twice, but in truth, they're all unknown to me. Capable and ruthless cold-hearts, I assume. What plots has your father set them to?"

Embra shrugged. "Finding ways to rule all Aglirta, of course. Slaughtering any folk of Blackgult and wizards they may find, along the way. They were trying to fashion me into a 'Living Castle.' I'm not sure if you know the term, but it's—"

"A scheme Gadaster boasted of perfecting," Sarasper said almost smugly, nodding. "It starts with the bindings. Once your mind had been shaped to their will with the proper spells—that takes a long time—they'd have severed both your arms at the shoulders . . . to turn your hands into little fetch-and-carry enchantments to fly around the castle at their bidding. Then the bloodletting starts . . . years of it, because they have to work a few drops of your flesh and blood into the mortar or plaster slather on every stone in the place." He grimaced, and looked away. "I read too much."

Embra merely nodded, but Hawkril shuddered, waved his arms as if to sweep away all thought of vicious mages and armless women, and then flourished his sword at the walls and ceiling around them. "But what of *this* place? Once the seat of the Silvertrees, aye, but why was it abandoned? How did it get haunted? Why was sh— Embra so angry when we came here?"

Craer sighed, and Embra and Sarasper both chuckled.

"Where to start?" the healer asked of the room in general and then shrugged and pointed at Embra. "The house belongs most to you, Lady: the tale is yours."

Embra shook her head. "We haven't days to waste, but . . . well, this is 'the Silent House' because its owners can't live here, so it—the high-minded bards presumed—stands empty. More properly, it is Silvertree House, once the mansion of the Barons Silvertree."

She looked at the ceiling, sighed, and adopted the cultured voice of an aged tutor: "The house was abandoned to the role of being the burial ground to the family when a powerful curse was laid on it by the wizard Harabrentar, long ago. To whit: any of the blood Silvertree to dwell herein for more than a month slowly but irreversibly change into a loathsome, dangerous beast—akin to the nightwyrms conjured by my father's mages, but flightless—and end their days hunted and mad. The efficacy of this curse has been demonstrated several times, down the years . . . usually when a partic-

ularly arrogant baron decided to reoccupy the house, or
a desperate rebellious son ran away to hide here."

Embra slowly got to her feet and strolled across the
room. Hawkril watched her every step, his sword tight
in his grasp. "The house has become a feared place,"
she continued, "shunned by outlaws and wanderers
alike because of its hauntings and its traps: pitfalls,
rockfalls from above, and walls that thrust out blades
into the unwary. These charming features were added
centuries ago on the orders of the Baron Suldaskes Silvertree, who didn't want a rival family to occupy the
mansion as a hostile fortress in the heart of his own
land."

She looked at the armaragor, smiled crookedly, and
added, "So there you have it; the just-the-flourishes
tour. I always wanted to explore this place when I was
young, but my tutors would never let me. They said
they weren't sure if the curse worked when one stays a
month at a stretch or if a few days here and a few there,
over the years, adding up to a month, would cause the
beast madness to come."

"What did you say about hauntings?" Hawkril asked
quietly, his eyes very large. "Are there ghosts in this
place?" The swordmaster glanced quickly at some of
the six or so dark passages leading off the room, as if
expecting a sudden parade of apparitions. He did not
look disappointed when nothing appeared.

"Many," Embra told him sweetly. "Most are harm-
less and silent; they startle the eyes but do no more."

"Most," Hawkril echoed, rather grimly.

"One thing I should add, Lady," Sarasper put in. "The
house is full of things that bear small magics, hidden
away by Silvertrees long ago—or by me, rather more
recently, to keep them out of the hands of the more daring intruders. If they'll be of use to fuel your spells . . ."

Embra looked up. "Yes! Can we collect a few of
those and get down to the catacombs? There are old

ward-spells on this house, but my father's mages won't be denied for—"

The floor shook, and there was a sudden roar and booming of rending stone. In its wake, the floor seemed to heave and roll under their feet, like a long wave lifting a boat.

"—ever!" Embra shouted. "Whither, healer?"

"Take *none* of these passages," the healer said warningly. "They're all—"

The passage behind Craer was suddenly gone, lost in a great cone of whirling wind and stones, and the roaring suddenly became deafening.

Hawkril grabbed the procurer, who was having trouble keeping his feet, and dragged him across the room to where Sarasper was frantically busy at the stones of the nearest wall. Embra stared at the magical whirlwind, seeing pieces of what could only be a shattered pillar tumbling around like chaff above a threshing floor. As she watched, the ceiling of the passage fell and was whirled away down the funnel of winds . . . a funnel that something was moving behind. Behind and above, on bat wings . . . another nightwyrm.

"These mages certainly have wild imaginations," she said bitterly, watching the ravening destruction come for her, right through the mansion that had stood for centuries. Across the stones it crept, shrieking.

"Lady!" She could just hear Sarasper's shout, and turned her head in time to see him tossing three small metal bowls, and as many statuettes, to her. "Defend yourself!" he cried, and then did something to the wall a few paces more distant. As he went, the healer left the wall behind him pockmarked with the niches he'd emptied, their little stone doors swinging crazily in the rising gale.

What opened under his hands this time was a little larger: a tall but narrow door, such as might be found in a servants' passage in Castle Silvertree. The healer hurled something small and glowing through its opening. Light burst into being, beyond.

"Through here!" Sarasper called, as Embra awkwardly fielded bowls and snatched at those that eluded her and bounced all around.

And then the floor obligingly whirled up to bring them to her, and she was tumbling helplessly in midair. Through a whirling chaos of dust and small stones she saw Sarasper spin through his opened door, cracking his head and his arm in the journey—as tapestries in another dark corner fell in a torrent of dust, burying a shouting Craer.

Then something large and heavy-booted smashed into her, snarling curses, and was whirled on toward the wall as she struck the floor, hard, and was suddenly deeper. Hawkril's vainly flailing sword was the last thing Embra saw before the snapping jaws of the nightwyrm blotted out her view of the room above.

She was falling, tumbling shoulders-first into heaving darkness, and landing with a crash, on a tangle of sharp points and things that crumpled under her.

There were grinning skulls and curving ribs and less identifiable bones bouncing up all around and collapsing under her like crushed eggs, with a queer sighing sound. Bone dust swirled up around Embra as she fell through what must have been several feet of piled bones, pulverizing them. Even after she shuddered to a stop, she could not seem to stop sneezing.

Through streaming eyes she saw stones whirling around the chamber far above. She was wedged into the narrowing pit, with her boots up in front of her face and a pile of bowls and statuettes on her throat and chest. Well, at least there'd been no killing spikes in the bottom of this pit . . . or had they turned to rust and collapsed, long ago?

This was no time for fanciful speculations; the whirlwind had moved on, and in its wake the nightwyrm had returned. A long, snakelike neck peered down the shaft at her, and dark-fanged jaws parted hungrily.

Bruised and winded, Embra juggled a statuette in her hands, frowning up at the conjured beast with mounting anger. She had no more spells stored ready in her mind—but with items to drain in her hands, she could call up any magic she could remember.

A firebolt, for instance. As the nightwyrm folded its wings back and thrust both of its heads down the shaft together, so as to use the full stretch of its snakelike body to reach her, the Lady of Jewels held up the statuette and carefully cast her spell.

The figurine crumbled to dust in her hands, its preservative magics gone, as ravening fire burst forth from its collapse and roared up the shaft. The flames beheaded the nightwyrm—twice, of course—broke the spell that gave it existence, and then faded away to nothing, in mere moments.

The gory black form wriggling down to crash lifeless upon her faded away just as it brushed her boots.

Embra let out a breath she hadn't known she was holding and started to cry.

Sarasper Codelmer clawed his way along a wall as the howling winds tugged and tore at the aging robes he wore. Stones and dust hissed and cracked around him, and for a terrifying moment it seemed the sucking whirlpool of spellwinds was coming in the door after him. "Graul, graul, *graul!*" he sobbed, clawing his way along the wall with bleeding fingers, heedless in his haste.

And then the fury of the spell-driven storm slammed the door shut with such force that the walls around him shook . . . and there was sudden stillness.

Tiny stones clattered to the floor here and there, and he could still hear a deep booming and roaring behind him, but a closed door now stood between him and the fury of whatever the baron's mages had sent after them.

The baron . . .

"Craer?" he called, apprehensively. "Anyone?"

There was no reply. He was alone again, his newfound friends swept away. His healing wasted, and worse. They must have been spying with their spells to know where to send this storm. They knew where he was, his name and likeness, and his long-hidden healing. They'd never stop coming after him now.

"Claws of the Dark One!" he hissed bitterly into the empty passage, watching dust swirl and settle. After all these years of hiding and lurking, more beast than man . . . his secret was out, in a few frantic hours, and the doom he'd long dreaded was here.

Or would be. He should have torn out her throat when first she burst into the house. Fled with her head deep into the catacombs, and eaten it down to a bare, gnawed skull so there'd be no wits to spellcall back.

He shivered, seeing her beauty again, and then snarled. "The baron's daughter—his *daughter!* Only heir, too, so *of course* he's reaching for her, and me too close. Too close. She could be after me and everything else here as weapons to wield against him or even to take back to him as his dutiful daughter."

Sitting himself against the wall, he added bitterly, "Who's to say she isn't serving him as wife by now? Silvertrees will do *anything.* Or compelling her with his mages to come in here to catch me? If they're good, she may not even know it! Gods, *gods,* but you're stupid, Sarasper! One glimpse of a pretty face and—and all, and you're fawning and talking and even *healing* them all, bebolt it!"

With a despairing groan he sank back against the wall and closed his eyes, suddenly shaking with weariness. He'd healed them, all right—and drained himself, an utter fool-head . . . oh, Sarasper, how could you forget the lesson that shaped your whole *life?*

Too weary to weep, the old man sagged down the wall, finding oblivion in the swirling dust even before his nose and cheek found cold, patiently waiting stone.

It was not tranquil slumber.

It was a bright morning when the soldiers of Brightpennant came for Qelder Waern.

The dirty-faced youth who answered to "Sarasper" or even the gruff shout "Pot boy!" was sweating over a dozen bubbling pots of herbal infusions and didn't even notice the armaragors until a long, dirty sword thrust through the tangle of pot chains and fire hooks to pierce the greasy leather of his only tunic. Too startled to shout, he slipped in the mud of many spilled brews. The blade laid open his shoulder on its way to thrust hard into the spongy wood of Qelder's old powders cabinet, and Sarasper made a sound that was half gasp and half sob and fell hard.

He had a confused glimpse of the blade drawing back over the pots, glistening with his own blood, and then it was cold and dark, and he was shivering, and old Skaunt was leaning over him and whispering hoarsely, "Boy? Sarasper! Wake, lad, and up! The wolves'll be here soon!"

Full night had not yet fallen, and the boy stood dazedly in Skaunt's rough grip, staring at the dark fingers of cloud in the westering sky, with the black spires of Brighttowers standing stark against them.

"What," he asked wearily, hardly daring to hear the answer, "befell? Does Qelder live?"

"I know not, lad. They've taken him; he's in the Towers right now!"

Sarasper stared hard at the castle, and his voice was thin and cold when he said, "Give me your knife, Skaunt."

"Wha—why, lad? You can't carve the armor of half a hundred armaragors with my little knife!"

"The baron," the boy said grimly, "only wears his armor on feast days. When he's grown so fat from feasting that it won't cover him, and they let the lacings so loose that its plates dangle. There'll be room in his guts for one little knife."

Skaunt looked into Sarasper's face, drew in his breath hard, and slapped the hilt of his knife—an old, broken war sword worn down to a wavering needle of a blade—into the boy's dirty hand. "May the Three watch over thee, lad," he whispered. "I dare not go with thee."

Sarasper nodded. "The knife is more than enough aid, old warrior." He clasped arms with the forester, and when Skaunt was gone, he turned to the cabinet, for the ten small glass bottles of acid in the upper drawers. He might need it to eat through chains . . . or the face of a guard. . . .

Qelder Waern was the most famous healer in all Aglirta Vale. Folk came for miles for his touch or his medicines, but always he refused to leave his hut by the brook and go to dwell in the baron's court at Brighttowers. They said in Sart that some upriver barons kept healers in cages, treating them less well than their dogs, and when the work of making others well drained them to withered husks in a summer or six, they tossed out the bones and sent their soldiers scouring Darsar for another. Sarasper had seen the Baron Authlin Brightpennant flogging his dogs after a failed hunt and was surprised it had taken him this long to just reach out and seize the healer dwelling on his doorstep.

The castle gates stood open, and it wasn't hard to see why. A steady stream of overpainted women in gowns side-slit right up to their waists was flocking into the castle, greeted by drunken shouts of enthusiasm from half-dressed armaragors. No one challenged or even noticed one small boy strolling among them as if he'd every right to be there. There were other boys, but this *one wore no rouge or perfume or lacy costume . . . ah, but the guards' shifts were changing, and it was a splendid summer evening, and no one had attacked Brightpennant in living memory. . . .*

It was a little harder finding an unguarded way upward, but once he realized that guards stood only on grand stairs, and the dark and narrow servants' flights were ignored, it was but the work of a few panting moments ere he found himself in a world of tapestries and soft murmurings and scented candles. He was, of course, hours too late.

"I'd not go in this night, were I you," a voice muttered warningly on the other side of a tapestry. "You just might find yourself with a sword through your guts or a table broken to kindling over your skull!"

"But the missive I carry is most urgent. The Baron of Tarlagar desires an answer by nightfall tomorrow! I—"

"Well," the first voice said heavily, "your most urgent baron's just going to have to wait. Saw you the corpse in the chair yonder?"

"Aye—what happened to him? Looks like a pig farmer, or some forest hermit, but dried up like the last barrel apples after a hard winter! And it looks like someone broke all his joints for him, throwing him around like a doll, too! Was it—magic?"

"It was, but not against him. That was the healer Waern."

"Qelder Waern? He saved my master's youngest— the Lady Athris—once, from the brownspots. Half Tarlagar sends word to him when folk fall ill!"

"Well, he won't be heeding words sent to him any more." The voice started moving away, and Sarasper scrambled along behind the tapestry to keep within hearing. "They brought him here this morn to bring the dead back to life."

"Healers can do that?"

"Well, you saw him; they can, and they can't. Our Lord Baron had more than a bit too much to drink last *night and saw things. He got down the Strongbow's Ax from the wall and started hewing his way from one end of this top floor to the other."*

"Serpent in the shadows! How many did he—?"

"Thirty-odd servants, though we're still finding more. You noticed how quiet it was, up here? Some of the servants who're supposed to be waiting behind the tapestries are waiting there right patiently, if you know what I mean. Oh, and he laid open both his sons and beheaded his wife, the Lady Rhildra."

"By the Three!"

"Aye. I had to pick up her head, down below—he threw it over the balcony rail, roaring that it was one less night serpent who'd come slithering up at him when he was asleep—and bring it back here. By dawn he was sitting weeping with his dead all around him, swearing to the Three that he was sorry and that the Serpent himself must have gotten into him and that he'd do anything to have them all back. I saw them; hacked like battlefield dog feed, they were, with flies buzzing all over them. When someone suggested the healer, he sent all the armsmen the castle can muster, with orders to sword anyone who got in their way or was around to see them take Waern . . . and they did."

"Horns! What happened?"

"The healer saw them, and started weeping worse than the baron. I think he knew it would make him a husk, but he was crying more for them and that he might fail. He seemed a gentle man."

Sarasper found something perilously close to a sob rising in his throat. He bit down hard on his knuckle, and trembled, straining to make no sound—and to hear every last word.

"Lord Dorn and Lord Bravyn, he brought back. I know they were dead; I helped lay them out, guts and splintered ribs and all—but he did it. They coughed a lot, and they stumble and tremble now and then, but . . . they're swaggering around with all their old bluster

and sneering, right now. The healer was near a husk by then, but he tried with the Lady Rhildra. He did. I guess even the best healer in Aglirta can't put a head back on."

"He died trying?"

"Aye, and after he'd collapsed, damned if the two lord sons didn't snatch him and shout at him and shake him, with their father crying and beating his breast not an arm's reach away, and then start hurling him about, clubbing him against the walls and the bed until he was as broken as you see. Then if they didn't march downstairs and call for the scribes and have a proclamation drawn up. Every kin and aide and pupil of Qelder Waern is to be brought back here and put to death under torture, while the two of them watch. I guess you and yours are going to have to send word elsewhere than Brightpennant for healing!"

The scream that burst out of Sarasper then set the two men on the other side of the tapestry to cursing in earnest. His frantic flight brought him through the bewildered guards before anyone recognized him, and down the stairs like a scared bolt of lightning, but he was still four sprinting strides from the doors when Lord Dorn's bellow rang out from the balcony.

"Let loose the dogs! Hunt him down, and bring what's left back here to feel Brightpennant vengeance! Hurry, you worthless whoresons!"

The doorguards spun to face the fleeing boy and block his way to freedom, swords flashing out. They grinned at his knife and moved in unison to swipe at his arms with their blades, and trip him. Sarasper threw Skaunt's old blade into the one guard's face and gave the eyes of the other the unstoppered contents of a bottle of acid.

It took only an instant for the screams to begin. Qelder had used it to melt away scar tissue and warts, but it seemed to work just as well on eyeballs.

The knife had only nicked the other guard's nose, but

Sarasper bestowed another bottle on his snarling features and then was out into the darkness, running hard.

It was hours later, just after dawn, when he heard them howling behind him. He'd been squelching his way wearily along the edge of a swamp, seeking a way around into the barony of Glarond. Thus far, he'd found far too many thorns and nettles, but no dry way east; the swamp seemed to go on forever. The barking and howling grew swiftly nearer, threading through every twist and turn he'd taken—until he could search no longer. Weeping in fear, he plunged into the cold, evil-smelling water and thrashed and flailed his way wildly east, trying not to think of watersnakes and scalyjaws and other things lurking under the black, bubbling waters. . . .

The war dogs were right behind him. Sarasper's prayers to the Three were lost in their triumphant howls and wet, hungry snarls; somehow he splashed onward into a place of tree-tall reeds and spiderwebs between them that glistened with dew like gems in the brightening morning.

A morning that held hunting arrows, humming through the reeds like hungry wasps to take the foremost dog through the head. Sarasper crouched chin deep in the chilly, stinking muck and tried to claw his way onward, as shaft after shaft tore through the reeds, and dog after dog died.

"Master of Arrows, fresh shafts!" came a cheerful command.

"At once, Lord. Ah, you realize these must be Brightpennant's dogs? They're hunting something, an outlaw perhaps. . . ."

"What of it? Any foe of Brightpennant is a friend of mine! Loose at will, all of you—if we can do my gentle neighbor out of every last one of his war dogs, all the better! Serves him right for hunting them onto my land! Taerlith, where're those shafts?"

Crouching in the blood-fouled water, Sarasper

Codelmer shivered, and he vowed silently to the Three that if no arrow found him this morn, he'd never serve any baron. . . .

The cowled figure leaned forward. "Ssso—you agree?"

A trembling breath was drawn, became a sob, and said, "Yes."

"Kneel."

When the gowned woman was on her knees before him, the cowled man tore open her bodice, baring her to the waist. His other hand came from behind his back, fingers cold and wet with glistening slime, to trace a design down her front.

As it touched her trembling flesh, the slime began to glow a dull green-white. By its light the kneeling woman saw something crawl out of the priest's sleeve.

A serpent, of course. It slithered along his arm toward her, tongue flickering.

"If you ssscream, you ssshall also perish," he promised calmly—and thrust his arm at her.

The serpent reared back and struck, biting her glowing breast.

The pain was fierce. She gasped raggedly, but forced herself to be silent and still. The snake watched her with glittering eyes as numbing fire washed slowly through her.

"Sssuch venom ssslays all but those who serve the Ssserpent," the cowled priest said formally, approval in his dry voice. "Rise, sssister, and join in the most sssacred service in all Darsar."

As the woman found her feet, the glow on her breast flared into white brilliance. Cowled figures were gliding silently to places all around her, forming a circle. Their faces were hidden under bent cowls, but she could feel their eyes upon her.

"Kisss the Initiator," the Priest of the Serpent commanded, extending his hand. The scaly head whose fangs had savaged her breast wavered in front of her, and she was seized by the sudden fear that its fangs would tear out her eyes or throat . . . but as she dared to bestow a kiss on those scales, the snake lifted its head a little to rub against her lips, like a purring cat.

At the dry, leathery contact, she was suddenly seeing not snake or priest, but a daylit field with a huge slab of rune-graven stone embedded in its trampled grasses, and robed, cowled figures standing around it. Live snakes slithered and coiled up and down their arms.

"Behold the tomb of the Ssserpent, in the backlands of Aglirta," the dry voice murmured in her ear, "watched over day and night by Ssserpent priests who await the time of the Rising. The vast body of the Ssserpent slumbers beneath it, invisible to any spell or digging shovel, awaiting the time of its Rising, when all Kingless Aglirta shall be devoured and made the realm of the Ssserpent. In that time, only the faithful shall survive the deadly feeding of the Coiled One—the faithful whose ranks you have just joined, sssister."

She felt his very human lips kiss her cheek, and then knew no more.

Her body did not bounce as it met the floor; many hands were waiting to catch her and cushion her fall.

Shattered bones shifted under her, and Embra found herself sliding helplessly back and down, following her left shoulder into darkness. Well, at least she wasn't staring up at her boots and the whirling storm far up the shaft above them any more, while struggling to breathe with all her own weight on top of her.

As if that made things any better. All she'd done was amuse her father and given his mages a little practice. She could have just given the two Blackgultans some gems and helped them back off the island as fast as they'd come. She should have asked them to make love to her—gods, how she ached for someone to just *hold*

her, with love and not for cruel sport!—and then kill
her, cheating her father out of his Living Castle by dis-
membering her and giving her parts to the river.

She should have killed herself years ago.

Not that she'd ever had the courage to do more than
pick up a knife and watch herself tremble in the mirror
as she thought about using it. Drenching her fine white
rugs with bright blood, staring at the ceiling until everything went dark . . .

She was no adventurer. Gods above, she wasn't even
a sorceress. And here she was, dragging men to their
deaths. Men whose hatred of her was only held back by
their fear, though they knew her not.

Well, they knew she could hurl spells, and they knew
she was a Silvertree. That was reason enough to hate
and fear her, was it not? All Coiling Vale hated and
feared the Silvertrees, with good reason in plenty.

"I will *not* be like my father," she told the darkness
around her fiercely. "I will not!"

As if the darkness was eager to answer, there came a
dry rattling sound off to her left. A clacking sound, as if
something old and dry was moving deliberately closer
to her.

Embra felt for the bowl that had struck her cheek earlier, hand grasping at empty air and tinder-dry bones in
the flood of debris between her legs. She needed magic
to call up magic; she needed a flame to see.

That dry clacking came again, a little closer, and she
was suddenly floundering around in bones, frantically
wallowing and rolling to try to find footing, and stand.
Her raking, darting hands found one of the little figurines Sarasper had thrown, closed thankfully around
its crumblingly reassuring curves, and spun her a flare
of flame as fast as she could shape her will.

Flame that danced wildly in the breezes roiling down
the shaft, but showed her enough to make her scream.

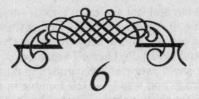

6

Odd Bottles and the Stone of Life

*E*mbra Silvertree was standing in a little chamber that opened off the bottom of the pit she'd fallen into. A half-height stone door had swung open to spill her and the bones of many, many intruders into a small stone chamber . . . a crypt. What were probably stone caskets stood on all sides, some of them cracked and discolored, and stains on the walls and floor told her waters had seeped into this place in vanished years.

The thing that had made the sound was perhaps seven running paces away, or a little more. It was the skeleton of a man, brown and gape-jawed and shuffling—and despite its eyes being empty sockets of darkness, it was moving toward her. When she stepped to one side, biting her lip, it turned its head as if it could hear the faint crunchings of whisper-dry bones under her boots and redirected its slow, patient advance.

Embra lifted the crumbling figurine and let her fear shape a slaying bolt of flame that snarled forth to smash into dry brown bones.

Bones that kept coming, that dangling jaw lifting for a moment in what seemed like a soundless laugh. When the figurine had quite crumbled away, Embra's flame died . . . and the skeleton was still advancing on her.

It was glowing slightly, now, as if it had stolen some of the radiance from her flames, and it seemed somehow taller. Less stooped—no, *larger.* Embra's eyes narrowed. Then she took two swift steps and plunged into the scattered chaos of old bones that had slid into this dark and secret chamber with her, clawing among the brittle brown and yellowed things again for one of those metal bowls.

Her fingers found the eye sockets of a skull, and she flinched back. There was a dry scrape behind her—too close—and she snatched up the skull, spun around, and threw it, as hard as she could.

The skeleton was a bare three strides away, its long brown fingers reaching. Her hurled skull smashed its jaw, the pieces tumbling away to clack and clatter down stone caskets to the floor, but it kept coming, as silent and patient as when she'd first laid eyes on it.

Gasping in sudden terror, Embra kicked and clawed her way through the bone rubble away from it, and—thank the Three!—heard the ringing sound of metal on the stones. A bowl! She snatched it up, whirled around, and danced three quick steps back and away, stumbling up against the cold stone of a wall. She could flee no more.

Not that the Lady of Jewels would have to. The enchantments on this bowl, whatever they'd been meant for, were strong, and she could give this shuffling skeleton more fire than dry bones should be able to withstand.

"Burn!" she shrieked at it, sudden rage boiling up in her. Was she fated to be fleeing and weeping in fear for the rest of her *life?*

"*Burn,* graul you!" And she gave it fire—white-hot and as furious as she was, flashing forth like a hurled spear, smashing into brown, advancing bones with force enough to hurl them back, shattered, against the far wall.

Fire that she let die away beneath her disbelieving

chin as the skeleton loomed up over her, blood red and glistening now, its bones covered with a webwork of stringy sinew. It stood a head taller than before, brown and dry no more, and the riven, dangling shards of its jaws were growing, lengthening as she gaped at it to re-shape, and join each other, and grow little gnarled bumps that would soon be teeth.

"*No!*" she protested, dancing away from its reaching hands. Her magic was *feeding* it!

Fingerbones clawed at her long, tangled hair, and she clutched the bowl to her breast and shrieked, tearing herself free in utter terror and darting away blindly, not slowing as she glanced bruisingly off caskets she could not see.

Far above her the spell-driven winds howled, swirling up dust from the bony rubble as they moaned down the shaft, and Embra found herself wishing an-other nightwyrm would come—come and smash this shuffling, silent horror to bone shards before it clawed or strangled her.

Gods, it was probably one of her own ancestors! Her father didn't have to slay her—one of his own forebears would quite capably accomplish the little task of tear-ing the head off his wayward heiress!

"Serpent in the Shadows!" she whispered in despair, watching the tall, smoothly striding bone man come for her. Shuffling no longer, it moved with alert and agile purpose, its hands spread wide so she could not hope to dodge past, here where the caskets stood close to-gether.

She almost screamed again when her hip fetched up against a casket that was open—and then saw that no skeleton lay within or was rising to menace her with its own dry clutches.

Of course; this must have held the thing that was coming for her. Something had shattered the stone slab that served as a lid long ago; its pieces, all of them larger than she could lift, lay tilted or fallen around the casket, and within—what was *that?*

Desperate, slender fingers closed on something cold and hard. Embra snatched it forth, found that she held a wand and that the skeleton was a bare pace away from its bony hands closing on her, and willed the magic in her hand into life. Magic might strengthen this skeleton, but perhaps its own magic could hurt it—and she had no other chance left.

Sharp, bony fingers caught at her throat, closed on her collarbone and shoulder as she twisted desperately away—and then shone with bright fire as the wand spat into life.

White sparks cascaded down its bony ribs and danced on the floor around them both; Embra didn't even know what she was awakening. The skeleton surged upward and seemed to grow more substantial, its glowing bones vanishing beneath a racing cloak of tissue, its hands growing more solid and fleshy, its—

As the heiress of House Silvertree sobbed in despair, bubbling laughter began, laughter that rolled around the crypt, gathering strength, and—

Broke off sharply, as something crashed into the ceiling. Something grated damply on stone, and then the grip that was bruising her was abruptly gone, and the body that now dwarfed her own toppled past her, crashing into the casket that had held it, its head lolling loosely.

Embra stared at that head, and then swung the bowl in her other hand with all her strength.

That skull shattered, and her hand was suddenly drenched in dark, thick wetness. She snarled in revulsion and swung again, smashing the cracked curve of a head. Again, and again until the thing that looked like an egg with its top shattered and gone broke free of the shoulders it was lolling on and fell, to roll away among the silent caskets.

The headless thing draped across the casket did not move, save to shrivel slightly, sagging down with a faint sound that might have been· a moan of disappointment . . . or might have just been escaping air.

Embra looked at the wand in her hand and suddenly flung it down. It struck the floor with a ringing sound that echoed loudly in the sudden silence.

Above her, the spell-born storm was gone.

The Lady of Jewels clutched the bowl to her breast and called, "Craer? Hawkril? Sarasper?"

"Lady?" a cry came back. It was the procurer, and he sounded anxious . . . truly scared for her. "Are you all right?"

Embra's face was suddenly wet with tears. She had to swallow twice before she could shape the words, "Yes. Yes, I think so. Now."

The trees they'd been walking through for most of the day gave way to swamp, and the stinging insects grew really fierce. Ornentarn hands slapped at cheeks and thumbed at eyes and nostrils, trying to keep the keening things away. Ornentarn boots slipped and slid in muck and evil-smelling water—and Ornentarn tempers smoldered.

The world stank, and even the reeds they rustled through were the color of sucking mud. By the smell, everything that had ever lived in Darsar had crawled here to die. All except the ever-present stinging flies.

Somewhere ahead lay the Loaurimm Forest, and deep in its vast, dark heart stood the ruined city of Indraevyn, no doubt overgrown and smothered by vines, trees, and brambles. Somewhere in all that would be the library of the dead wizard Ehrluth, where—if one crazed wizard was right and no one else had reached it first—might await Candalath, the Stone of Life. One of the four mighty Worldstones, the Dwaerindim of elder days. Power enough to rule Darsar or to reshape it.

Power enough to bring back the Sleeping King—or call up the Serpent in the Shadows.

The twenty-strong band of mages and warriors in the midst of the stinging, whining cloud understood power, wherefore they were here, far from the comforts of Ornentar—but far, too, it seemed, from lost Indraevyn.

"So if your spells can keep us going in one direction," the armaragor Rivryn of the Black Blade grunted sourly, "why can't they just whisk us to the library doorstep, hey?"

"In the days when Indraervyn stood proud and populous," the wizard Nynter of the Nine Daggers hissed in reply, "mages knew how to work spells to keep uninvited and unexpected neighbors from arriving anywhere nearby. A flying or spell-jumping trip to any long-settled place that old is likely to be a *final* journey. You generally burst into flames and burn like a torch in midair, at about the time you're breaching the wall wards. Along with anyone you're carrying with you, of course."

The conspirators trudged on in grim silence for a while after that.

"Do your father's mages ever sleep?" Craer called down the shaft, around the dangling chain. Its links had once been as thick as his forearm but were rusted away to a third of that, or less; Embra blinked as showers of red rust came down on her.

"I wouldn't rely on that," she spat, tasting iron, "if he thought by flogging them he could crush us right now." The chain tapped her knee and then her forehead; the Lady of Jewels caught hold of it, wrapped it around herself and then wound her ankles around it to keep from being curled over on herself and stuck against the walls of the shaft when Hawkril hauled on it. The armaragor nodded approvingly and pulled on the chain.

"Oh, really?" Craer replied, reaching down with a stick he'd found somewhere to keep her from bumping the sides of the shaft. "I thought he was too busy flogging *us*."

"Is this what passes for wit between you two?" she asked, over the rattle of chain.

"No," Hawkril growled. "Generally we do things like drop clever-tongued sorceresses back down shafts on their heads and then dance around chortling."

"I hope you're jesting," Embra told him, hearing a quaver in her voice that she'd hoped would not be there. An instant later, a strong hand took her by the waist and bodily turned her right side up in midair.

"I'm not sure," the armaragor told her levelly, staring into eyes that the sorceress had firmly closed. Shaking his head in mingled relief and contempt, he set her down gently on her feet.

There was a clink and then a clatter beside her, and Embra blinked her eyes open and looked down to see the chain on the floor, in several separate lengths, broken links still rocking gently around it amid the red dust of their dying. Hawkril kicked one aside. "Well," he growled with some satisfaction in his voice, "it held as long as we needed it to."

Embra shivered and looked away. "Is Sarasper all right?"

"My wits took another bruise or two," the healer grunted, from somewhere behind her. "But I don't suppose you'll notice the damage."

The other two men chuckled, and Embra shook her head. "The Band of Four Idiots, that's what we are," she told the nearest wall—and, for just a moment, it seemed to hold a half-skeletal face that grinned back at her.

Oh, yes. The ghosts. Settling the precious bowl she'd thrust into her bodice earlier so that it rode more comfortably over one of her breasts, Embra looked back at the channel of ruin through the house, and thought she could just see a glimmer of the day outside. "Are we agreed to move on now, before more spells come?" she asked.

Sarasper nodded. "I'll take us down into the catacombs."

"And then?"

"We head for Sirlptar, to talk to some bards—while cloaked in whatever magical disguises you can spin for us, Lady—about where legend places the Dwaerindim. The quest, remember?"

"Sirlptar?" Hawkril asked sharply. "Just how far do these catacombs go?"

The healer plucked up the glowing stone from the floor and held it aloft like a lantern. "A long way," he said softly. "You'll see."

Their eyes met in silence. It was a long moment before three pairs of shoulders lifted in shrugs, and their owners moved to follow the healer.

Sarasper turned with the stone held aloft like a priest bearing a relic toward an altar, and led them through the door he'd opened, along a passage that turned twice and ended in a blank wall.

After he did something to the stones in a certain spot beside that wall, it slid aside with a deep rumbling, revealing a large, dark space beyond.

Hawkril regarded it with deep suspicion before he shouldered through the opening. There were no signs of handles or pull-rings to move the wall again, and he glanced back along their trail twice as he followed Sarasper into the echoing gloom of a large, grand chamber.

In the center of the room beyond the sliding wall stood a massive but much-hacked stone chair. It had a high, ornate back, and—through thick dust and cobwebs—fist-size gems gleamed along its arms.

"And so the Band of Four set forth," Craer murmured, "unheralded—and into darkness."

* * *

Hawkril cast a swift glance around—at stairs going up, a table in a far corner, a stout support pillar, a rotting row of tapestries, closed doors here and there, and at the monster-bereft ceiling—and then peered at the chair. "That looks like a throne," he said slowly.

"It is," Embra said simply, walking around it with her arms folded.

Craer looked at the set of her jaw and told Hawkril in low tones, "Behold the Throne of Silvertree—which served the family until Baron Brungelth Silvertree died sitting in it, hacked to raw meat until his blood ran out all over the floor."

"Craer," Embra said plaintively, "*please*. I can see ghosts here that are hidden from the rest of you."

"You can?" Hawkril asked hesitantly.

"Yes," she snapped, and stalked past him without another word.

A man was sitting in the chair, his arms bloody stumps, his lap filled with a blood-drenched, glistening mass of organs, one leg a twisted ruin of protruding bone and the other a stump that ended at one dripping ankle. Only his noble face was unmarked by the blades of the helmed, plate-armored men who surrounded him in a grim ring of ready steel, and it was drawn with pain. Amulets flashed and dwindled at his throat and on the circlet that he wore about his brows, and as they faded, so did the life they struggled to preserve.

"I have no magic left to strike you down," he said almost wearily, "and it won't be long, now. You can put your swords away. The rings that could have slain you went with my arms."

One of the men facing him moved restlessly, but the ring of warriors said nothing.

"Well?" Brungelth Silvertree asked faintly. 'No taunts? No cries of 'Blackgult triumphs'?"

"We're not of Blackgult," the man who'd moved almost spat. "Father." He tore off his helm to reveal tangled black hair and eyes that were two dark coals of anger. Brungelth Silvertree tilted his head back and regarded that angry face with a faint air of puzzlement. "'Father'? An ambitious armaragor of mine, surely?" he asked. "Or—are you adventurers from outside the Vale, seeking to take a land of your own?"

Men were doffing helms all around the circle, now, their swords still in their hands. Their faces were different, but they all shared the same smoldering eyes.

"We're all your sons, Baron Silvertree," the first of his slayers snarled. "Your bastards, that is, the ones whose mothers you didn't strangle or hunt down with your dogs, when you discovered they carried your seed. The ones who've lived all their lives in hiding up and down the Vale, or farther—with mothers who cowered in fear at the very sight of the badge of Silvertree."

"We're the ones you missed," another man said bitterly. "O most brilliant butcher of the Vale."

He strode to a sideboard, caught up a decanter, flicked its stopper forth with the thumb of his gauntlet, and took a long swig, swallowing with a loud sigh of satisfaction. "Ah, but that's good!" he said with a smile. "Like sweet fire! All ours, now."

"Until you start to fight over it," the man in the chair said quietly, his head drooping forward.

"Hah!" the first man snarled. "I think not! And even if we do, at least we've lived long enough to taste some of your fine vintages!" He strode to the sideboard himself, snatching another decanter, and that started a general rush to take up slender silver and crystal.

"That you have," Brungelth Silvertree said softly. "That you have." His head settled lower, and the patter *of blood on the floor around the throne slowed to a gentle rhythm of drippings.*

"Your best amberfire, I believe, Father Baron?" another of his slayers asked tauntingly, waving a decanter in front of the dying man.

"And I have a fine stagblood, by the taste of it," another jeered, holding it up to catch the flickering firelight. "Most splendid."

The man on the throne asked wearily, "Have you all drunk, then?"

There was a general, rough roar to the affirmative, and the baron said faintly, his words slurred now, "Consider it a toast, then. If you've sipped, you're fit to hear the secrets of my hold before I die. Swift, now . . . I can feel the fading . . . bend close . . ."

One or two laggards hastily swigged and joined the wary, tightening ring around the bloody throne.

"Not too close," one of them warned. "He may have some last blasting magic."

"No," another said. "I wear a magequell ring—magic or no, there's nothing he can use in this room."

"I need no magic," Brungelth Silvertree said calmly, "to take you dogs down with me into darkness. All of the wines in this chamber are poisoned."

Decanters fell as faces paled, and amid the shatterings and oaths there was a general rush to the throne. "The antidotes, old man!" one son snarled, swordpoint raised to strike. "I know you'll have some! Speak, or lose an eye!"

"Take it," the Baron replied. "I'll not be needing it, soon. The antidotes are all in my bedchamber—not that you'll live to reach it. I had to take them for years to reach the dosages in those decanters you so heartily sampled. Farewell, idiots. Unworthy, all of you, of the name of Silvertree. Have my curses."

And with those words his eyes closed, and his head fell to one side. There was scarce time for the shouting and cursing to rise up again before men started to fall,

all around the throne, crashing to the floor in a limp,
helpless fellowship of death.

Embra Silvertree shuddered and drew her arms around
herself, her face bone white. Tears glistened on her
cheeks, and she threw back her head and drew in deep,
shuddering breaths as she glared at the ceiling. Her
whisper was so soft that they had to strain to hear it. "It
never changes, does it, House Silvertree? And you're
proud of it, all of you!"

The three men exchanged glances. Craer, who'd
reached forth his arm to touch Embra in reassurance, let
it fall back to his side, and kept silent. The sorceress
glared quickly around at their faces, her expression almost a challenge, and seemed to crumple into weary
sorrow when she saw that they'd heard and seen nothing at all of poisoned decanters and butchery and men
falling in heaps around a bloody throne. Her sigh, as
she turned away, was almost a sob.

"We'll move on very soon, Lady," Sarasper called to
her. The healer seemed almost a human whirlwind of
tapping on stones, pushing here, opening there, and
darting about.

As they watched, the wall yielded up hiding place after hiding place, and out of each the old man plucked
certain things, while leaving others behind. The table
swiftly grew a small mound of bracelets, candlesticks, a
candle snuffer, small metal serving bowls that stood on
taloned mock-dragon feet, belt buckles, and about a
dozen odd-sized wine and spirit bottles.

"For the thirsty traveler?" the Lady of Jewels asked,
picking up one bottle incredulously and peering at its
faded, crumbling label. Neither her voice nor her hand
was quite steady, and her face was still white to the lips.

"I wouldn't advise drinking any of that, after all this
time," Sarasper said, "but it still bears a few flickering
preservative magics. Enough to power a spell, I hope."

Embra looked around at the pile and pursed her lips. Wearing a lopsided smile, she sighed again, went to the tapestries, seized hold, closed her eyes firmly, and pulled.

The expected roar followed, and she let it take her to the floor.

When she could find her breath again, the Lady of Jewels crawled out from under the small mountain of dust and cloth that had fallen on her, triumphantly tore off a large piece to the audible amusement of Craer and Hawkril, and brought it back to the table. "Any chance of someone helping me rig this bundle to hang on my back?" she asked, stuffing knickknacks gingerly into disintegrating cloth.

"Just add them to the sack," Hawkril rumbled, swinging it off his shoulder. "If I can carry a dozen or so wet wizard's books, I can haul a few candlesticks, too."

Embra had forgotten the books. She could smell the mildew from here. She looked at the sack, sighed, and then held out a candlestick and a handful of bracelets.

Instead of taking them from her, the armaragor turned white and dropped the sack, hauling out his sword. "Claws of the Dark One!" he gasped.

"What—?" she asked in puzzlement, and then saw Craer crouching with dagger drawn, too. She spun around, snatching up another handful of bracelets.

The chamber seemed to be full of half-rotting, half-skeletal figures, floating in eerie silence in a tightening ring around the Band of Four. Three dozen pairs of glittering ghost eyes were fixed on her as she turned, slowly, hand on hip, and slid the bracelets onto her forearm. "We've disturbed something, healer," she said quietly, "but I see nothing here that can harm us."

"Some ghosts can harm, though, can't they?" Craer asked, his voice not quite steady.

"Yes," Embra replied in a soft voice, holding her bracelet-adorned arm up almost defiantly. The carrion-

apparitions seemed to fall back as she touched a finger
to the bowl in her bodice and made lights flicker up and
down the bracelets. "I met one, once. My father's idea
of strengthening my courage."

"Need we stay?" Hawkril asked abruptly, as, again,
the ghosts drifted nearer.

"I think we'd best move," Craer agreed. "What if the
baron's wizards slip some sort of menace against us—a
spell, a monster, or even one of them, in person—into
this room amid all of . . . these?"

Sarasper nodded. "That's why we must make haste to
leave." He looked at Embra and added darkly, "For the
first time in years of lurking in this house with ghosts
swirling all around me until they seem old friends, I've
begun to feel as if someone—or something—is always
watching us."

As the healer spoke those words, an eye silently
withdrew, unnoticed, from a tiny hole in the ceiling
above, hard by the place where pillar and ceiling met.

The sun came in through the highest arched window in
Castle Adeln and fell across the table at Baron Adeln's
elbow. He sipped thoughtfully at his wine and set it
down at the edge of the brightness to watch the play of
reflections while his mind roved elsewhere. He was
considering the implications of warriors returned from
Ieirembor wandering over the Dozen Baronies at will,
restless, hungry . . . and unpaid.

The servant standing silent and motionless in the corner saw the Baron's handsome face grow pale and acquire a tiny frown. Esculph Adeln reached up with a
finger to stroke his chin—a sign of decisions being
made and thoughts flying like striking falcons behind
that placid face—and then said to the servant, "Bring
the seneschal to us, and then withdraw until his depar-
ture."

Adeln rose and went to the window to look out over

the roofs of Adelnwater, and the river sparkling past, until he heard the familiar voice behind him say, "Lord, I am here."

He spun about and said crisply, "Send messengers to our eyes up and down the Silverflow, in haste. I want to know who's hiring swordsmen, how many, and what coin they're offering." He made the little flick of his thumb that signaled an end to things, with leave to depart granted.

The seneschal nodded and strode for the door, but Baron Adeln brought him to an attentive halt with a few more words. "Oh, Presgur—start hiring any warriors you find within our borders, forthwith. Rogues, cripples, unbiddable malcontents, thickheads—I want them all."

The seneschal stood still with his back to his lord for two long, eloquent breaths, but said nothing. Then he nodded and resumed walking.

Adeln listened to the receding thunder of his boots and gave the ceiling a smile that had no mirth in it.

The woman rose from the bed, her bare body beautiful in the soft candlelight, and drew in a breath that was tremulous with excitement and fear. "I could learn to call you master. Scales don't sicken me . . . as you now know."

"Then kneel," the serpent-headed man replied, settling his robe about his shoulders and pointing at the bed before him, "and know the power I promisssed you."

A serpent crawled out of his sleeve and along his arm as she hastened to obey. "If you ssscream, you ssshall also perish," he told her, tracing a symbol on her breast with cold, glistening slime that began to glow. He promptly thrust the serpent forward. It reared back, swayed—and struck.

The woman whimpered and trembled as the serpent reared back again, its eyes glittering, and numbing fire washed through her.

"Sssuch venom slays all who serve not the Ssserpent," the snake-man told her. "Rise, sssister, and join in the most sacred service in all Darsar."

As she stood, the glowing symbol she wore flared into white brilliance, exciting the serpent. It arched over her again.

"Kisss the Initiator," the priest commanded. She bent forward to kiss the dry, scaled head, and it nuzzled against her lips. Boldly she licked it—and it left the snake-man's arm to crawl onto her breast and shoulders, and thence down her body.

"You are favored indeed," the priest told her, sounding almost irritated. He watched the serpent slither over trembling skin and added, "Move not—and you may yet live."

"Are these the catacombs?" Craer asked, looking around at walls glistening with damp. The passage they stood in was cold and smelled of earth, and the only light came from the small stone in the healer's hand. When he closed his fingers over it, as he did now, the effect was eerie.

"No," Sarasper said. "We'll need money in Sirlptar."

"The Silvertrees have vaults down here?" Craer asked, brightening. "No wonder they didn't want others exploring the place!"

"We passed the vaults some time ago, when those ghosts stopped following us," the Lady Silvertree murmured. "They stand empty."

"We're in the tombs," Hawkril said suddenly. "You want us to rob the dead."

As if his words had been a greeting, an eyeless, skeletal figure in armor suddenly glowed in the darkness not far ahead. It raised a spectral sword, but Embra waved at it disgustedly. It seemed to rush at her, then fade away to nothingness as it did so.

"Hawkril," Embra said calmly, "I don't mind, and the riches here belong to me. My father—as a cruel joke, I think—gifted me with Silvertree House when I came of age . . . the day they laid the first bindings on me, and shut me away on the isle for good. Think of it this way: you'll be helping a Silvertree carry some coins she needs, taken from ancestors who left them here for her."

Sarasper's sigh of relief at her words came much faster than Hawkril's slow, doubtful one. "The gold I saw was along here," he said briskly, leading them around a corner, to a spot where the passage was broader, and several wall stones bore protruding coffins, beneath inscriptions surmounted by relief carvings of the Silvertree arms. A long crack ran down from the ceiling across one tomb, and the end of its coffin lay shattered on the ground, among a few yellowed scraps of bone, a shattered skull, and a flood of still-bright coins. The armaragor hung back until his distance from the healer's light became too great, and he took a few reluctant steps forward.

By then, Craer was already probing among the coins with his short sword, looking for traps or small biting and scuttling things. Finding none, he looked up over his shoulder at Embra, who nodded her approval.

Hawkril's sack shortly received a pile of seventy-odd gold coins—some so old that they bore the ax of the trading baronies that had preceded Aglirta—and Craer asked almost eagerly, "Will that be enough, or do we need more?"

A smile plucked at the corner of Embra's mouth, and she said, "I hesitate to counsel you to further danger, but I've heard that Sirlptar can be an expensive place."

"So whom do we . . . borrow from?" the procurer asked, waving at the row of inscriptions. "Vaedrym?"

"He was a mage who did much work with the dead," Embra replied. "Probably 'twould be better not to look therein." She took a few steps along the wall, and then said, "Try here."

"Chalance Silvertree," Craer said aloud, reading the inscription. "He died young. Hmm; 'Prince Royal'?"

The Lady of Jewels shrugged. "Silvertrees have thought themselves rulers of Aglirta before now."

The procurer sat down and tugged at the heels of his boots. Both came away in his hands, revealing themselves to be stubby daggers, with the boot heels as their hilts. Hawkril sniffed in amusement at the awkward weapons, but his mirth ended in amazement as Craer snapped a metal prying-wedge out of each heel and applied them to the edge of the casket lid, humming nonchalantly.

The armaragor held his sword tensely ready as his three companions huffed the lid askew, but nothing emerged from within.

Craer peered into the dust and bones, and smiled.

In a surprisingly short time their store of gold had more than doubled. By then the armaragor had seen several gliding apparitions—dark-eyed warriors and one gowned woman whose head was hidden within raging flames—and was anxious to move on. Sarasper obliged, leading them down hidden stairs and past a place where they could hear the murmur of moving water through the dripping walls.

"The underways," Sarasper said. "I came this way once, in another shape. I fear I remember little about what awaits us, other than that there *is* a way through."

There was a weird glow in the passage ahead, which proved to come from eerily pulsing glowworms crawling along muddy side ledges. Spiders as large as human hands danced and scurried aside as they went on, up a worn stone stair into another burial hall, where a row of stone plinths rose from the floor.

Hawkril eyed them dubiously. Helms and shields that had been hung on them long ago had rusted away to brown powder and crumbling shards.

Craer drifted closer, until Embra said quietly from behind him, "Things left undisturbed have a habit of not disturbing you. Words every procurer should live by."

The spiderlike man gave her a sour look. "And what words do Silvertree sorceresses live by, Lady?"

Embra closed her eyes, looking pained. "Craer," she said slowly, "I'm sorry if I've offended. None of this comes easily to me. I'm used to living alone, in caged luxury. I don't even know what I'll do when I have to relieve myself, in front of all of you."

The armaragor looked at her and said abruptly, "It's hard for us, too. We're afraid of you—and if your father can reach us, through you."

The Lady of Jewels turned slowly to meet all of their gazes. Her face was bleak. "So am I, Hawkril. So am I."

They stood looking at each other in awkward silence for a time, and then, wordlessly, Sarasper led them on.

Their way rose again, passing through chambers where many coffins lay under thick draperies of cobwebs, and into a place where the light from Sarasper's stone grew dim.

"Strong magic," he and Embra murmured in unison, and the sorceress laid hold of the bracelets on her arm. There were suddenly faint glows ahead of them, points of light flickering in a silent circle that stretched to the walls of the room, barring their way. There was a dark bulk—a casket, or stone block—at the center of that ring of radiance. Small glows were gathering atop it, quickening and brightening as they approached.

"Should we go back?" Hawkril rumbled.

"And fight our way through all Silvertree, with my father's mages hurling spells at our backsides with every step?" Embra replied. "I don't think so."

The glows atop the tomb suddenly coalesced into a ghostly figure—a bald man in robes, perhaps, though its hands looked barbed and scaled—which raised spectral arms to trace a glowing pattern in the air.

The Lady of Jewels stared thoughtfully at the floating symbol for a moment, and then lifted her fingers to shape a sign of her own.

The spectral figure responded by pointing at her—and lightnings spat blue-white from its fingers to strike her.

The bolts veered to one of Embra's upraised hands and then snapped to the other. Her companions saw her wince and waver, and there was pain in her face as the sorceress gathered the lightning in a nimbus around her shoulders, adding something of her own that put rosy flickerings into its blue-white coilings and then hurled it back.

In the roaring that followed, they saw the ghostly guardian become a faint shadow. Embra snapped quickly, "All of you—raise no weapon against it! Spread apart! Set down blades and other metal!"

Then she raised her hands and hurled something else at the figure—a soft, shimmering wave of force that seemed to drink the radiances ringing the casket as it swept over them. It passed over the ghostly figure and washed back from the far wall of the chamber, and when it receded again into Embra's hands, there was nothing atop the tomb but empty darkness.

The Lady of Jewels staggered and almost fell.

Before her companions could reach her, she'd stumbled forward to lean against the tomb where the guardian had been only moments before.

Embra clung to the worn stone for support and turned haunted eyes to meet their concerned gazes. "Whatever sign of recognition it was looking for, I guessed wrong," she gasped. "This tomb must be older than I thought."

Sarasper put his arms around her. She tried to shake him off, reeled, and almost fell. As she recovered, leaning against the tomb again, two of the bracelets on her arm crumbled away and fell. They were dust before they hit the floor.

Hawkril looked down at them and then at Craer and Sarasper. "Drained by Embra's magic," they said in unison, and lifted their gazes to look again at the pale-faced Silvertree heiress, leaning wearily against the tomb.

"Drained by Embra's magic," Hawkril repeated. Magic that also seemed to be draining *her*. . . .

Sarasper, looking troubled, stepped forward to put an arm around Embra, helping her to walk. After a few steps, she turned her face into his shoulder and shook silently; they knew she was weeping.

Wordlessly, Hawkril extended one hand, holding it out to Sarasper palm up and empty.

The healer looked at it, then at the sorceress shivering against his shoulder, and lifted his eyes to the armaragor's face.

Hawkril nodded slowly, and Sarasper reached out and took the proffered hand.

A moment later, the healer's skin began to glow as life energy flowed through it, from warrior to wizard. A few moments later, both of them gasped in ragged pain . . . but neither moved to break the flow.

Twice more they saw ghosts gliding in the ways before them, but none hurled spells at them—for which the white-faced and stumbling Lady of Jewels seemed grateful. It was a grim and weary Band of Four that halted in a chamber empty of all but dust and lacking any visible doors or side entrances. In their haste, they'd brought neither food nor water, but sleep was one thing they could find, and did.

The exhausted Embra fell asleep at once. Craer, Hawkril, and Sarasper stood over her for long enough to agree on watches, and the healer took the first one.

He was alone with sighing and snoring in a very

short time but knew better than to sit or lie down beside his companions. Leaving the glowstone in their midst, he strolled back and forth around the room, listening for distant sounds in the dark passages.

After a time, he cocked his head to one side, as if listening to something only he could hear. He nodded slightly, as if agreeing to words spoken in his head—and then looked over the other sleepers to where the Lady Silvertree lay. As his eyes dwelled upon open mouth and beauteous face, his own face slowly acquired a smile. A truly evil smile.

7

No Pressing Shortage of Mistakes

The Ornentarn warriors in the lead were veterans of the hunt, to say nothing of chases after outlaws and adventuring forays. They knew stonework when they saw it—even under a thick green cloak of creepers and thorny bushes. One of them held up a hand and called back, "Do we know of any other ruins in this forest?"

"None," two of the wizards replied sourly, more or less in unison. Neither paused in his enthusiastic slapping at stinging insects. Bright ribbons of sweat coursed down their faces, and dripped slowly from their chins. It had been a long time since either of those faces had worn anything that might be described as any sort of "pleasant" expression.

"Then we've found Indraevyn," the warrior announced calmly. "Or what's left of it."

The rest of the band crowded around him. Several of the wizards wore looks of open dismay, and one of them was even moved to ask, "Are you sure?"

No one bothered to answer. There were shapes among the trees—which stood more thinly here than elsewhere—that might have been buildings, and here and there stone showed through the clinging greenery. Ruined Indraevyn was no neat expanse of grand buildings untouched by time but a sea of vines and shrubs and saplings spreading out before them cloaked in trees. A bird whirred past, ignoring the cluster of men amid the busy flies.

Several of the mages were scrabbling in belt or breast pouches for maps, then looking around very slowly and gloomily. From where they stood, it was impossible to know *which* crumbling, overgrown mound was the library. Nothing seemed to match their fragmentary maps and descriptions. "Are you *sure* this is Indraevyn?" the querulous wizard asked again.

The warrior Rivryn gave him a look of contempt and said, "While we're exploring, bear in mind three things: those who split away to explore alone tend to die soon, we need to find drinking-water most urgently, and then a shelter we can defend, to sleep in. Libraries, right now, are optional."

"Explore?" one of the wizards asked in bewilderment. "How?"

"Take out your knife and start hacking and peeling back," another warrior grunted. "When and where one of us tells you to, and *only* where and when you're told. You'll be working with everyone else. You may find that last detail a novel experience."

The mages stared at him.

One or two of them slowly drew belt knives and joined the armaragors, who were pointing at one or two of the larger mounds and discussing whether it was best to find a brook or pond first—which was sure to have bestial visitors, after dark—and work outward from there on finding shelter or whether it would be best to get a shelter and then explore for water.

The others strolled off on their own, to stand and stare around and shake their heads. A few came back to join the band, which was slowly moving forward through the overgrown ruin, looking at everything but keeping together.

"Watch your feet," Rivryn told the mages behind

him. "We've stone underfoot, and that means easy ways to trip or break an ankle. It also means snakes."

"Snakes?" one of the wizards cried. "You didn't say anything in Ornentar about snakes!"

The dark-haired warrior shrugged. "You were sitting in a room full of them," he said in dry tones. "I thought you were used to them."

The wizard's eyes flashed angrily, but there were chuckles here and there among the band of slowly advancing men.

"The land seems to fall away yonder," another of the warriors said, pointing through the trees. "Water there, d'you think?"

Another armaragor nodded. "We could tr—"

There was a scream of terror, and a roaring, off to their right. "Find good footing!" Rivryn roared to the mages, as the warriors hefted weapons and spread out to give themselves room to fight.

One of the straying wizards burst into view over a mound of creeping greenery, sprinting hard. He promptly slipped, fell on his face with a cry of despair, slid a few stones down, rolled over frantically, and clawed his way on down the slippery green slope. Behind him loped a huge bear, yellowed teeth bared. It caught sight of the scattered band of men, roared a challenge, and came charging down the hill, clawing its way right over the shrieking wizard without stopping.

"Let it get into our midst," Rivryn called, "and surround it. If it comes at you, fade to one side. Watch your feet first, and the bear second!"

As the armaragor's shout ended, one of the other warriors could quite clearly be heard to say wearily, "Stupid, stupid mages . . ."

"Oh, by the Dark One!" said the wizard Huldaerus disgustedly. "Stop all this brave shouting, and stand aside!"

He took something from his belt, held it up, and wove a swift spell. Whatever was in his hand slumped into black powder and trickled away from between his fingers, to be lost in the faint breeze—and from his other hand streaked a dark bolt of force that sped into the chest of the bear. Black flames and a horrible screaming arose together, and the bear staggered a few strides, convulsed, and crashed to the ground, flames soaring up from its blackening body.

The warriors took a good look at it and then formed a watchful circle facing outward. The wizard who'd first fled from the bear shouted in triumph, as if he'd slain it himself. Clambering back up the mound he'd so recently sobbed his way down, to get a better look at the burning corpse, he adjusted his amber-hued robe with a flourish, repairing the damages of his fall.

Huldaerus and Nynter of the Nine Daggers exchanged sour glances. "Adventure, it seems," the bear slayer grunted, "is rather less glamorous than fireside bards have it."

Nynter opened his mouth to reply—and there came another roaring from the mound. They looked in that direction, in time to see the bear's mate tearing the head of the amber-robed mage clean off. Or rather, not so cleanly off.

Nynter plucked something from his belt, blew on it, snarled a word, and threw the tiny item at the bear. It dwindled to nothing, and he turned back to Huldaerus.

"Glamorous, no," Nynter said, acquiring the ghost of a smile, as his hastily hurled fire spell exploded inside the second bear, hurling it all over the surrounding trees in wet spatters, "but every bit as exciting."

"Bear stew, anyone?" Huldaerus grunted—and one of the nearby warriors bent forward and noisily began to be sick.

Silent servants conducted Markoun Yarynd into a room in the castle that he'd never seen before. A stately paneled chamber stretched out a long way before him, with sideboards ranged along its wall, surrounding a large, gleaming feasting table that seemed almost larger than the room could comfortably hold.

Yet the room also held Baron Silvertree, sitting at the head of the table with a glass in his hand. Steaming platters of food sat before him, a forest of slender bottles lay in an ice trench within easy reach, and an empty trencher was laid at the baron's right hand.

"Welcome!" the Baron said jovially. "Sit and eat, most able mage!"

Markoun knew better than to hesitate or look uncertain. "My thanks, Lord," he said, smiling broadly, and swept to the place set for him.

Faerod Silvertree passed him a platter the moment he was seated, and for a time they dined in easy silence, until the Baron sat back, glass in hand, and said, "I'm pleased with your plan, and I wonder if you have any other thoughts on . . . this matter of my daughter."

To cover the fact that his only thoughts on that matter thus far had been to keep this man from flying into a fury and ordering all their deaths, Markoun took a sip from his glass, sat back in turn, and said, "Wizards all too often fall into favorite tactics, Lord, and act accordingly. To use the old saying, 'To a horse tamer, all beasts are horses.' I dare not make any plans until I know more. Who are these men who came to our isle and left with your daughter? What plans are they pursuing? Where precisely are they right now, and where are they heading? All these things I would know before I set about making plans as to what to do."

The baron nodded briskly. "Wise enough. And how would you set about getting answers?"

"By scrying into the Silen—into Silvertree House. I took the liberty, when my fellow mages retired to sleep, of examining the records in your library of the wardings cast upon it. Many, of course, are unrecorded, but there is specific mention of a scrying key—that is to say, a spell that can slip tracelessly through the wards, without destroying or damaging them, to allow visual observation of what befalls within. By your leave, I would cast this key and learn more. I can, of course, so arrange the spell that what the 'eye' of the spell sees is shown to us both."

"Do so now, if possible," the baron bade his youngest wizard, in a deceptively mild voice that left Markoun in no doubt that he was being commanded. Yarynd bowed his head in acquiescence, moved two platters out of the way, and cast the spell with unhurried precision, avoiding any flourishes or attempts at a grand, mysterious manner. A floating oval of swirling hues, like a clouded mirror, appeared a few inches above the table, and Yarynd held his hands over and under it and spoke the secret words that he'd read in the records.

At once the scene cleared, and they were looking into a dark and empty room, with a square pit-shaft in one part of its floor and an open door in another corner. "This is the room inside the entry chamber, where— ah—"

"My armaragors lie crushed and entombed," Faerod Silvertree said gently. "Yes, go on."

Markoun cleared his throat nervously, and said, "By your leave, Lord, I shall attempt to move the spell-eye through that open door, investigating these various passages only if that route seems fruitless."

The baron waved a hand at him to do so, at about the same time that the ghostly shape of a high-helmed warrior drifted through the room, glaring about, and disappeared through a solid stone wall.

"Ah, the—"

"Silent House is haunted, yes," the baron said calmly. "You were about to scry beyond that door, as I recall."

"Yes, yes," Markoun said hastily, and then clamped his lips firmly shut to still further nervous gabbling, and moved the spell-eye. There was a short passage of several bends, and then another large room with a central pillar, a table, and a grand throne that looked to have been much hacked with large and heavy bladed instruments.

As they gazed at it, a part of the wall opened, and out of the hitherto-concealed door stepped a man with a short, neatly trimmed beard and a pleasant expression, dressed in the trail leathers of a vagabond or bard. His hair was brown, his age of the middle years, and his demeanor calm and assured; no man's servant.

"Do you know this man?" the baron asked. "I've not seen him before."

"No, Lord," Markoun said truthfully, watching the man approach another apparently solid wall and reach up to touch a particular stone.

"Move the eye to stay with him!" the baron said sharply. "Close, now, to see how he opens the wall!"

"Of course, Lord," the wizard replied, and added carefully, "he will be able to see the spell-eye if he turns his head."

"So he will," the baron agreed calmly.

They watched the man open a secret door, step through it as Markoun lifted the eye to hang directly above the man's head, and pull it closed. The man did not seem to notice their scrutiny as he strode along a dark, narrow passage, up a short flight of steps, and into a room where something gray and ever-coiling hung in the air.

"A veil of force, of the most powerful sort," Markoun identified it. The man reached through the magical field without hesitation or appearing to work any magic. No fires or lightnings destroyed him or severed his boldly reaching arm, and he drew forth a hand-size, mottled brown-and-gray stone sphere.

Markoun sensed rather than saw the baron leaning forward for a better view.

The bearded stranger hefted the stone in his hand for a moment, seemed to decide or realize something, and then turned and looked directly at them with an unpleasant smile.

"He's seen—"

The stone in the stranger's hand flashed—and the oval scrying-portal erupted in flames, flames that consumed it and roared at its creator.

The baron hurled himelf over backward, chair and all, and ducked beneath the table as his youngest wizard screamed, reeled back with his hair transformed into a torch, and spun around. Flesh sizzled, hair crackled away to ash, and one eye hissed and then burst, spattering Markoun's hand and cheek as he fell, howling in agony.

Under the table, the baron heard his bottle rolling along above him. He calmly swung himself around to catch it when it reached the edge and toppled.

"How long have we been walking, anyway?" Craer sighed, as something skeletal shrank back into the depths of the cavern they were crossing. What looked like human bones lay underfoot, and the Band of Four took care not to disturb any of the inky pools in the dimpled stone floor as they passed.

"Most of a day," Sarasper and Hawkril said together. The broad-shouldered armaragor ducked as the hundredth or so flight of bats whirred past his face, cast a glance at Embra, and frowned.

He felt sick and well, *empty*, from the vitality he'd given up to her, through Sarasper—and yet she was moving along as if in a dream, pale faced, listless, and silent. Was some dark magic eating the sorceress from within because they'd torn her away from the castle she was magically bound to? Or, as a Silvertree, was she falling victim to the curse of the mansion they'd passed through? Or—what?

Hawkril frowned again and peered into the darkness off to their right as he heard the small sounds made by yet another of the creeping, slithering things that took care to keep out of sight. He liked foes who faced him

with jaws and claws or weapons, that he could meet
face on in the fury of a fray—not all this skulking and
not knowing and lurking magic. May the Three blast all
wizards to ash, and leave Aglirta a happier place!

He glanced at the Lady Silvertree again. Well, perhaps all wizards but one. . . .

Yet no—for if she was the only one, what sort of
tyrant might she grow into? The armaragor frowned
again, and strode on, and was not happy.

"What's that smell?" Embra asked after a time, her
voice rough from disuse.

"Sewers," Craer said simply. "We must be under
Adeln."

"Food!" Hawkril said emphatically, and several
stomachs promptly growled in unison. The four companions chuckled.

Sarasper said gently, "We'll need disguises, Lady—
not yet, but before we go up where we can be seen."

"And once we're up," Craer added, "everyone cluster
around the sack Hawk's carrying. No one must see
those books . . . and we're going to need every last gold
coin, I'm thinking."

"May the Three save us!" Embra said suddenly, smiting her brow in mock horror. "He's thinking!"

There was a moment of startled silence before the
three men erupted into laughter—laughter that redou-
bled when Hawkril tapped Embra's shoulder with a finger and said reprovingly, "Lady, if you're going to walk
with us, I'm going to ask you not to steal my lines."

Embra gave him a weak smile, and then burst out,
"Oh, by the Horns of the Lady—take me somewhere
with a sky I can see, and wine, and something to *eat!*"

"Your tower in Castle Silvertree?" Craer suggested
slyly—and discovered that the sorceress still had
strength enough to launch a swift poke at his ribs.

Their way became damp, and the air reeked. No one
with a nose would have needed help in identifying the
sewers now.

Craer brought them to a halt and said, "It looks to run narrow from here on—we'll probably have to find a grating, or an alley dump that's washed down here by the bucket. Lady, if you need space to work magic, this had better be it."

"What do you want to look like?" Embra said teasingly, clutching her bowl.

Sarasper leaned forward, and said, "You'd best look less pretty, lass, and I younger. Make both of these rogues fatter, so their heights won't be so clear to a spy who's been told what four particular travelers look like."

The healer's words sobered them all. Embra went to Hawkril's sack for the bottles to fuel her casting and said, "It's not spies in Adeln I'm worried about—it's Father's mages, using magic. They must know, or be able to find out in our library, where the underways lead."

She reached up and laid her hands on either side of Hawkril's face, because he was nearest, and then with whispered words and little ceremony, went to each of the others. Each bottle she touched shivered and collapsed into shards and spilled vinegar as the faces seemed to change, and her bowl slumped into shavings of rust last of all.

Looking down at it, she leaned against Hawkril and murmured, "This spell leaves eyes untouched and alters only seeming, not flesh—so don't let any amorous wenches run their hands over you."

"Had *you* such plans?" he asked after a moment, sounding as much fearful as jesting.

The sorceress gave him a look. When she stepped away from the armaragor, she was shaking with weariness, and the three men exchanged worried glances.

"Lady—?" Craer asked, but Embra waved her hand sharply at him in dismissal.

"I'm all right," she said firmly, "or will be. Just get me food."

Craer smiled. "I know a tavern . . ."

"You would," she replied, raising an eyebrow. "Would you mind very much if we went to another one—one where I won't be expected to take my clothes off and dance on a table?"

"They *have* taverns like that in Adeln?" he asked, in mock astonishment. "Hawk, do you ever recall—?"

"No, I never do," the warrior rumbled. "I make a point of it. If someone's dancing on my table, they're putting their feet where I could be assembling a goodly pile of meat tarts!"

"Procurer," Embra said warningly, "don't make any jokes about 'meat tarts'—just don't."

"Lady," Craer said innocently, "the thought never crossed my pure, nay, pious, mind."

"He has a pure and pious mind?" Sarasper asked Hawkril.

The warrior snorted. "Aye. He cut it out of some priest in a brawl. It shriveled up into a little thing like a prune, and he carries it around and takes it out when he wants to impress ladies—*say,* Little Manyfingers, look! We've a lady with us now!"

"That's no lady, Lord Sword, that's a sorceress."

Embra winced. "That wasn't all that amusing."

"Lady," Sarasper murmured, "I don't think any of their jokes are. Just let the gabble wash over you, and the time passes."

Craer rolled his eyes. "Ready on?"

When they nodded, he led them up a slippery slope, into an incredible smell and a pile of rotting refuse, human waste, and bones.

"Behold—an alley dump," he explained cheerfully, "and unless I've forgotten all five of Adeln's streets, our tavern's right over there."

The procurer had dismissed perhaps forty or so laneways in Adeln in his reckoning, but he was right about the tavern.

* * *

It was hot, noisy, and crowded in The Ring of Adeln and smelled of unwashed bodies crammed close together, much spilled beer, and—other spilled things. The Four discovered just how ravenously hungry they were when they found themselves devouring three or four platters each of decidedly bad meat tarts and something called egg-and-greens scramble with hot sauces. The ale smelled like a gutter and was thin and sour, but one stopped noticing that after about seven tankards.

Folk were crushed in shoulder-to-shoulder, and the din of talk and drunken laughter was almost deafening. Someone had overturned a table, and there were several fights, but the four who'd come in together kept to the corner table they'd claimed and devoted themselves to listening and looking around rather more alertly than they pretended to.

Much of the talk seemed to be about trouble—trouble between barons, and the war that might soon bring to all the Vale. A Tersept had openly renounced all claim to his hold and taken a barge down to Sirlptar, wizards had been seen exploring back trails and wells, and armed men were riding into the Vale through every mountain pass, it seemed. . . .

There came a time, much later, when the Four were each on their eighth tankard. Embra was belching delicately as she idly pushed a dozen or so copper wheels—their change from just one gold falcon—around into patterns on the tabletop in front of her and wondering whether she should finish her ale and be sick or let one of the others have it and just feel uncomfortable for a while.

The wheels wouldn't stand on edge, she decided, after her third attempt—and her fingers were shaking just a trifle, mind you, no more—when a hush fell upon the place.

The four from the sewers glanced up in the stillness to see bright helms pushing through the suddenly shrinking crowd, accompanied by bright breastplates with the flame and crossed golden swords of Adeln large and splendid upon them. In between were grizzled faces that wore rather unpleasant grins, two of them belonging to men even larger than Hawkril.

"Ah, behold! Loyal citizens of Adeln who've shown their love for our brave baron by bringing their weapons into town so they can join the soldiery!" the largest of the warriors said jovially, around a mustache as large and as greasy as a butcher's slab. "Up, lads, and bring the wench with you! It's four falcons, and the barracks to spend them in, you'll be seeing this night!"

Even as they heard the rattle of manacles in one of his hands, the Band of Four found themselves staring down the sharp length of a dirty dagger he held in the other.

The recruiters were very good at their jobs. Hawkril and Craer had blades to their throats in a trice, even before their leader was properly started into his speech, and the pommels of daggers poised above their ears to strike them senseless, just for good measure.

No such rough measures had been used yet, though. The recruiters obviously expected a little fun—and some coins offered as desperate bribes, as well as unfinished tankards, to swig—before dragging their prizes away.

The large mustache reeked of old, bad stew and spilled beer as it bent forward over the Lady of Jewels, and its owner leered down at her, peering at all the flesh he could see and sliding his dirty blade forward to make the slice that would either scar Embra for life or lay her bare down to the waist.

Hawkril groaned, deep in his throat, and she saw the recruiter behind him tense to strike, just as Sarasper made a sudden movement, and—

"You are here," Baron Silvertree said simply, "because you are my best warriors. Succeed at this little task,

and you can both expect promotions and enough gold
to buy splendid houses, or a stable of horses, or anything of that sort you fancy. You have my word on
this."

The two burly armaragors kept as still as they could
and carefully avoided looking at each other. The
baron's word. They *were* Silvertree's best, and so they
knew very well that they'd not live to see their promised
rewards, one way or another. If it hadn't been for the
cursed mages who ruled everything in Silvertree, they
could simply fade from view after reaching Sirlptar.
But then, if it wasn't for those same thrice-cursed
mages, they'd not have this task in the first place. The
spells just cast on them had set their bodies tingling—
an endless thrumming that showed no signs of abating,
so as to let them, for example, sleep.

"Daerentar Jalith and Lharondar Laernsar," the baron
intoned grandly. "Two names that shall be heard in Silvertree often each day, as we await word of your success. You know the men all down the river to contact,
should you need aid—and they know to expect you and
to stint nothing in their efforts to make your venture a
success."

Daerentar and Lharondar smiled their thanks in unison. Both recalled the cold menace in Spellmaster Ambelter's voice as he'd explained that the shielding spell
they carried would do nothing to aid them and could be
discharged only by an enemy wizard using a spell de-
signed to shatter magic or by their touching the Lady
Embra Silvertree directly. The black looks the Spellmaster had given the wizard Markoun had made it clear
whose idea this magic was, but if the Baron, the other
mage, and Markoun himself gave no sign of noticing
that glare, neither warrior was going to be foolish
enough to do so, either.

The mages, the Spellmaster had proudly explained,
had used hair from her hairbrush to link the protective
enchantment specifically to the Lady Embra alone—

and they'd added "hooks" to the enchantment so they could fling a pain-inducing spell, such as bloodfire, onto it from afar, should "control of a wayward armaragor become necessary." No effort would be stinted, indeed.

"Go first to Sirlptar," the baron continued. "Fugitives and outlaws always run straight to Sirlptar, thinking they can hide from us amid the teeming folk. It's not all that large a place, really—just be sure they don't slip aboard a ship without you seeing them."

"Four falcons and the barracks? No, I don't think so," Embra said softly, looking up at the recruiter. He glared at her, peering to see if she held a weapon—but no, she was merely juggling a handful of copper coins in her hand.

The greasy mustache leaned closer, twisting in a leer. "What's that, wench? Not finished with these lads, yet?"

"Look into my hand," she murmured, ignoring the recruiter's foul, beery breath, "and tell me what you see there." And she opened her fingers.

There were four roundels of metal in her palm, but they weren't copper coins. Four miniature silver shields shone back the flickering candlelight, and each one proudly displayed the arms of Adeln.

"We serve the baron already," Embra murmured, "carrying secrets to him, and for him. For hampering us in our work, the penalty is—death. I know the baron *very* well; do you?"

The recruiter's face slowly turned the color of old, yellow cheese. "Uh—urrgh—uh, well . . ."

"I thought so," Embra continued, her voice acquiring a snap of steel. "Now leave this place, swiftly, and I'll probably manage to forget mentioning you in my report."

"I—ah—" the recruiter added, his eyes darting back and forth from face to face.

Craer and Sarasper gave him slow nods of equal parts menace and promise; Hawkril merely narrowed his eyes.

"Stand off, lads!" the recruiter snarled, and turned hastily away from their table, making a signal with his dagger that Craer resolved to remember for later use.

In moments, the brighthelms were gone from the tavern, and the Four were deafened by a roar of approval. Tankards clacked together, and beer struck the floors and tables in floods.

The procurer thrust his head against Embra's and shouted in the din, "*That* was well done! We'll have to come back here, next time we're into town!"

The Lady Silvertree gave him a sour look and the traditional withering reply: "When the land has a king again!"

Then she stiffened, laid a hand on his arm, and looked quickly down into his tankard.

"All gone, Lady," he said merrily, "but if you'd like anoth—"

"*Don't* call me that, fool!" she hissed into his ear. "Now keep smiling, look up and around at a lot of folks, and notice the man with the long nose and the cap, *without* staring at him!"

"One of your father's?" the procurer murmured, even before he did as he'd been bid.

Embra laughed and nodded enthusiastically, as if at a jest, and then leaned forward and said, "He was looking at us just now, trying to decide if we're the four he's been told to watch for. Pull open my bodice—and if you rip it, I'll cut you a new and smaller nose—and empty my tankard down my front; he'll stop thinking I might be the refined lady he's looking for then. Tell Hawkril to pick a fight with him and throw him in the river, but don't kill him. Be warned; he carries lots of knives."

Craer looked at her with respect in his twinkling eyes and said, "You've no idea how much I'm going to enjoy doing this!"

"Oh, yes," Embra replied, and let out a whoop that startled the procurer. As she reached out to pinch his cheek, she added joyfully, "I think I do!"

"Manyfingers," Hawkril rumbled, as Craer set enthusiastically to work, "have you gone *ma*—"

He broke off as Embra kicked him under the table, hard, and a moment later Sarasper was laughing a little unconvincingly into his face, and then hissing all he'd overheard said by Embra.

Hawkril scowled and grunted, "You're going to expect me to be subtle, aren't you?"

"I," Sarasper said grandly, sketching a formal bow, "have every confidence in your abilities, my good fellow."

"Afraid of that," was the growled reply.

"Just don't begin by overturning the table," Embra murmured. As the armaragor rose, looking somewhat like a small mountain deciding to relocate, he gave her what was known in refined Aglirtan circles as "a pointed look."

The Lady of Jewels smiled up at him and stuck out her tongue.

The healer's words were put to the test as the night drew on and the Four disposed of the Silvertree spy, changed taverns once or thrice, dealt with some would-be thieves, and found themselves, as approaching dawn made the eastern sky a little less dark, on the docks facing more than a dozen swaggering-drunk Adelnan soldiers.

"What d'you bet your spying friend put them up to this?" Craer whispered to Embra, as snarling warriors reeled toward them, blades and torn-off table legs in their hands.

Just in front of his friends, Hawkril growled like a bear and reluctantly backed away, step by step, awaiting the inevitable rush.

"Just keep me awake and unhurt," Embra hissed back, "or our disguises may fade." And she snatched the last old wine bottle from Hawkril's sack, did something intricate and very swift with her fingers, and narrowed her eyes.

A moment later, the Adelnans were joining in an enthusiastic chorus of startled shouts as their leather breeches blazed up in even more enthusiastic unison. The smell of burning hair and the thunder of frantically dancing boots both grew strong before first one warrior, and then another, sought the obvious relief, plunging into the icy harbor waters with roars of pain.

"That spy is sure to have been watching," Sarasper said, as the four trotted away down the street in the general direction of "away." "We dare not tarry here longer."

"I want to buy some food before we head out into the countryside," Hawkril said quickly.

"And some wine!" Craer added.

Embra shook her head. "You heard all the talk of war, this night!"

Indeed, the taverns had been full of little else, afire with the news that all the baronies were arming. War was in the air—but where, and with whom?

"I don't want to have to fight off an encamped army—or have my hands chopped off, tongue torn out, and eyes seared to ashes as an enemy mage somewhere," Embra added sourly. "It might be safest to be outside Aglirta for a while."

"What? One or more of the Dwaerindim are here— they felt *very* close to me, in Silvertree House!" Sarasper protested. "You owe me, all of you! I must find the Stones, not flee from them!"

"Let us at least go to Sirlptar," Craer said, poking his head up between them. "No baron to induce us to join his little army, out of the fray but not out of reach of all Aglirta—and if Embra's kindly, thoughtful father's sent agents, even mages, on our trail, they'll never find us there."

The Priest of the Serpent smiled grimly at her gasp— and so did the snake that had bitten her. The glow from her breast lit them from below with eerie fire as the woman swayed. Fire that numbed and yet burned was surging through her, as many cowled figures shuffled into view behind the priest.

"Sssuch venom slays all who serve not the Ssserpent," he said. "Rise sssister, and join our swelling ranks, in the most sacred service in all Darsar."

She knew what to do and was already bending forward to kiss the scaly head of the serpent.

The priest's smile broadened. "Word is ssspreading," he gloated, and the snake answered with a contented hiss.

8

More Mischances All Around

"We'll never find it," Nynter of the Nine Daggers groaned despairingly, waving out the archway at the overgrown stone mounds all around. The night now hid them from view, but everyone knew they were there. Knew all too well, after a back-rending day spent stooped over tugging and cutting away vines and thornbushes. "We could still be sitting here when the winter snows come, scratching our way into empty house after empty smithy after empty pigsty, and none the wi—"

"Oh no, we couldn't," the wizard Phalagh interrupted grimly, the lantern light gleaming on his high forehead. "We'll have visitors long before then, with murder in their eyes, spells in plenty up their sleeves, and a hunger to juggle enchanted stones in their hearts. We aren't the only seekers after Dwaerindim, you know— the tale let fall by Yezund's loose tongue has reached the ears of half the mages in Darsar by now! Watch out behind you, or something you dismiss as a tree is going to split your skull with an ax, or put a long sword right through you!"

"I've had both of those things happen to me," Huldaerus, the Master of Bats, agreed, stepping out of the darkness to join them. He sat himself on a rock beside their lantern, and pulled out a snuffbox. "'Twasn't pleasant."

The other two mages favored him with looks of open disbelief. Huldaerus met their gazes, shrugged, and added, "I was tutored in shape shifting by old Weslyn of Baerra. He believed in lessons underscored with pain—barbaric, but effective."

Outside, in the night, a wolf howled in the distance. As the mages glanced outside, seeing only dark trees silhouetted against the stars, it was answered by another, from very near at hand. They stiffened, traded wry looks, and sighed.

"It's time to start standing watches," Phalagh said wearily, reaching for the lantern shutters. "I'll take the first. . . ."

"Yes, four eccentric travelers," Craer purred. "Downriver, to Sirlptar—forthwith, under cover of darkness, yes, *this* late at night."

"Out of the question," the boatmaster snapped, eyes glaring out over dark pouches and heavily stubbled jowls. "I'm only up and awake, meself, on account of a deckload being delivered late. My crew have worked hard all day, an' it'd take the Sleeping King himself, risen with a bag of gold in either hand, walking up to me now to get me to . . ."

The man's eyes bulged as his voice died away, and his incredulous gaze locked on the heaping handful of gold coins the procurer was holding under his hooked red nose. He even stopped scratching at the undercurve of his ample belly, where tangled hair met the lacings of his patched and wrinkled sea breeches.

"Perhaps I'm one of the Sleeping King's courtiers, with a little from one of those bags, sent by the king to arrange a discreet little trip made for four of his special friends—a quiet, immediate sailing, helmed by the best boatmaster on all the river," Craer whispered.

The boatmaster licked his lips. There must be more coins there than he'd made in the last two summers, and . . .

The procurer's other arm moved forward to display another handful, just as heaping as the first. "And this much more to keep quiet for the rest of this season about ever having made such a trip," he added.

The boatmaster's hasty smile almost outshone Craer's own. "When did you say you wanted to leave, master?"

The clop and clotter of hooves, and a heavy rumbling, announced the arrival of a wagon. Craer glanced at it and tucked both handfuls of coins back into his girdle apron.

"The moment you're loaded, they've gone again, and I've put every last one of these good, solid gold coins in your hands," he whispered, and melted back into the shadows the pilings cast in the light of the boatmaster's pole lamp.

One of the men sprang down from the wagon and ran off into the night; the other climbed down more slowly, spat thoughtfully over the edge of the dock into the water, and said to the boatmaster, "The dungskulls back at the sheds went and hitched up the wrong wagon; Baerlus is gone to get the right one, and I've told him to bring you back four falcons extra for keeping you up later."

The boatmaster grunted. "Not the first time that's happened." He squinted up at the high load of lashed-down kegs on the wagon. "What's wrong with these, then?"

"There's nothing wrong with them," the wagon-driver said, settling bags over the noses of his beasts and clipping their reins to the dock rings, "but that they're kegs of beer and not long jugs of scented bathing oil."

"Bathing oil?" The boatmaster was incredulous. "Who'd want to bathe in something that stinks?"

The wagon-driver gave him a grin that split a straggly beard to show a few gaps where teeth should be and replied, "Folks who has money rot."

"Money rot?"

"Aye; them who think about coins and think more about 'em and finally go mad when they get enough. Their brains rot, and they get all sorts of funny ideas— some *always* to do with how to show everyone else how rich they are by spending money on things the rest of us've got too much sense to waste good coin on—like scented bathing oil."

The boatmaster let out a bark of laughter. "A clever mouth on you, Jorl!"

The wagon-driver struck a preening pose and then cocked his head, took a step along the dock and said, "Ah, that'll be our missing wagon. Baerlus can move when I tell him to."

"Tell him the right way, I'll bet," the boatmaster snorted. "Here, help me with the lashing-lines, in yon roof box. Hold's full, o' course."

"Aye," Jorl agreed good-naturedly, holding up his hands to catch the lines the boatmaster tossed. He hooked the well-used ropes down securely as they came; they held down the crockery long jugs in rows across the cabin roof, so that hopefully not more than a handful would crack on the voyage downriver. Baerlus had brought the proper coins and two sleepy-eyed jacks to help in the loading, so both wagons were rumbling away in a surprisingly short time.

Craer watched them turn a corner and disappear before he led his three companions to the boat's boarding plank, but he hadn't seen Jorl slip down off one wagon and step into an alley.

The wagon driver peered between two crazily stacked crates. Aye, these must be the four he'd been told to look out for, right enough: three men and an imperious woman—with one of the men short and weasel-like and another a muscular giant of a swordswinger—even if they didn't quite match the descriptions the wizard's voice had snarled at him out of his shaving-mirror this morn.

Jorl smiled. Scented bathing oil, indeed. Baerlus had wasted a little cheap perfume out of the warehouse stock by sprinkling a bottle's worth over the long jugs now festooning the cabin roof . . . but inside those jugs sloshed the usual old cooking oil. A right good thing he'd caught sight of the four before loading proper swig-worthy beer aboard; 'twould be a pity to lose that. After all, if one was to keep both neck and position—as Baron Silvertree's chief factor in Adeln, responsible for nigh twenty thousand falcons in profit this last summer, let the good baron not forget—intact, one had to watch where the copper wheels rolled to, hmm?

After all, these little unforeseen expenses kept arising. A trusty boatmaster and his boat, too, for instance. Ah, well. All lives and cozy arrangements must end sometime. . . .

Jorl smiled. The little weasel of a procurer—well, maybe he looked more like a spider, now that he was moving around a bit—was peering around to make sure no one had noticed that he'd hired a boat to slip out of Adeln before dawn. Clever dog.

But not, of course, clever enough to get ahead of the baron's best factor. Jorl's smile widened, in the instant before he turned and hurried off to do some hiring of his own.

He'd always liked the hangings in this part of Castle Silvertree. Klamantle waved to the perpetually aston-ished centauress in his favorite scene, winked at the saucy courtesan leaning out from her balcony in the next hanging, murmured "Temptress!" to the lady bard with the runes painted all up one bared thigh who featured in a third scene, and strode on to his chambers, humming his satisfaction aloud.

"A clever lad, our Klamantle," he told the door to his rooms grandly, and slipped through the faint tingling of the ward spell that ensured his privacy—even against such powerful mages as Spellmaster Ambelter. Its familiar chiming told him it had not been disturbed, which meant that it was safe to gloat at last!

Klamantle threw back his head and laughed aloud. He'd managed to slip a phrase into the shielding incantation that made him—and him alone, *not* Ingryl Ambelter—able to trace, when he cast the right seeking-spell, anyone using the shielding. His little trick also rendered the shield ineffective against spells cast by him, so Klamantle could prevail where the mighty Ingryl would be held at bay. All that remained was to get Ingryl or the baron to trust the shielding enough to use it on themselves. . . .

In a turret not so far off, Ingryl Ambelter sprawled in the soft grip of the huge, high-backed chair that was his greatest pleasure, dangling one foot over an arm of the chair and smiling faintly as he magically "read" all of Klamantle's thoughts. "A clever lad, our Klamantle," he echoed the unwitting wizard sardonically, and reached for his glass of ice-dark wine.

He'd not only seen what Klamantle was up to, he'd managed to subvert the incantation so *he* could tracelessly slip past any magics employing the phrase Klamantle had used to twist the shielding. That meant that Ingryl could slip through the shielding and trace a shield wearer just as well as clever Klamantle. It also meant that Ingryl could, if he cast the right magics, override anything Klamantle tried to do through such a shield.

Moreover, it allowed everyone's favorite Spellmaster to pass undetected through any other spells into which Klamantle chose to incorporate this personal phrase—

such as Klamantle's own shielding spell, and—of course—the wards on his rooms.

Klamantle's mind, however, was small and almost entirely consumed with schemes for domination, destroying foes, and gaining more power—quite dull to eavesdrop on. Ingryl took a long, lovely sip from his glass, and smiled grimly.

Controlling Klamantle would probably prove necessary someday, but in the meantime, there were more interesting and important minds in Aglirta to visit . . . such as that of Baron Faerod Silvertree.

"We're getting too far without stiff battle," Hawkril growled, peering around at the slowly brightening world. Huge cliffs towered above them as the boat rounded the bend that would hide Adeln from view. Mists hung thick above the murmuring water; Craer kept peering around as if he expected a dozen boats full of plate-armored Silvertree armaragors to loom up out of them at any moment. The water was running swiftly, carrying the boat along at impressive speed. Aside from a crewman slumped half asleep over the tiller, aft, the boat seemed deserted, sailing itself through the last wisps of night.

"Easy, Hawk. It's the magic, isn't it?" the procurer muttered, never ceasing his glances in all directions.

The armaragor gave his old friend a long look, and then admitted, "Aye. You're just as wary, I see."

Craer shrugged. "Like you, I'd not be unhappy if, one happy night not far from now, every wizard in Darsar got grabbed, trussed up, and drowned—all together, in the same vat of the blood they've caused to be shed. It'd have to be *every* wizard, though . . . if one is missed, that'll be the next tyrant to rise over all of us. They balance, see?"

"Over years and lands, yes," Hawkril said grimly. "But not if you're standing right beside one."

"Even if she's easy to look upon? She's just about your height, too," the procurer teased.

The armaragor gave him a dark look. "She hasn't used her magic to compel you yet. I'll never forget being marched along like a child's toy. Never. I might forgive her, some day, but I'll never be able to trust her the way I could, say, a swordsister."

"She has the tongue to be a swordsister!" Craer chuckled, hooking his fingers through his belt and looking at nothing for a moment, as if seeing something in his memory rather than out over the rushing water.

"They all have that," Hawkril grunted, "or so it seems. Perhaps I'm just good at getting them angry."

"Hawk," the procurer said quietly, "we're in it up to our necks now. It's my fault if anyone must be blamed, for thinking of her gowns adrip with jewels . . . but we're riding the storm now, and if we try to get off, we'll be like that Griffon trainer—Landaryn, was that his name?—who tried to jump off that runaway stallion."

"And broke his neck," Hawkril growled. "I know, you're right . . . but I still don't have to like it. What's to stop her father from sending spells through her at us, right now?"

Craer shrugged. "What's to stop his mages from sending spells through me against you—or through you, against me? We can't spare time worrying about our friends—the Three know our enemies are enough, even without wizards and their spells!"

"True," Hawkril Anharu admitted, "and I've seen enough of the Lady Embra now to know she isn't hiding some secret hatred of us and playing at being our friend until she can get us to the right place to be sacrifices in some dark scheme or other. She *does* hate her father, and she's not a veteran schemer or an adventurer. Yet still, Craer—something isn't right. I always know when something isn't right."

* * *

"Wait here, Anharu," said the Golden Griffon, handing the hulking armaragor his sword—belt, scabbard, and all.

"This is not wise, Lord," Hawkril murmured, as he received the baron's blade. His eyes were on the priestesses, down in the hollow.

"Meeting unarmed with servants of the gods is never wise, loyal sword," the Baron Blackgult said, his piercing black eyes flashing. "But then, wisdom is something I rarely have time for, these days. So—'tis time to be bold again. Wait here."

And the man Hawkril loved and admired more than any other strode away, weaponless, a toothless lion gone down to parley with priestesses armed for war. The high-horned helms on their heads crackled with magic, the black and creaking leather armor on their bodies bristled with weapons, and all six of them bore naked swords in their hands.

The mighty armaragor watched him go, shaking his head. "Something is not right," he murmured, though he knew very well what it was. For a summer and more the Priestesses of Sharaden had made verbal war on the baron, demanding larger temple lands, more powers to tithe, and recognition of the Horned Huntress as the supreme god in Blackgult.

The baron had told them he would readily agree to their first demand, grudgingly meet them in some wise on their second—and reject their third absolutely and forever. The Three ruled over Darsar, not "One." Even Dark Olym had his place—claws, tentacles, and all, and no mortal demand could change that or should try to.

The priestesses had cried that they, and they alone, knew the personal desires of the Lady, and that the baron must acquiesce—or be cast out, a godless man whom no man could serve or fight for, and receive any blessing of the gods.

The baron had replied that the words of priests were

not the words of gods, and no less than a dozen priests, of both other faiths, stood with him in Blackgult in repudiation of the demands made by the priestesses. Their response had been to request this parley in Telgil's Hollow, with the baron attending alone and unarmed.

The baron had boldly accepted, stunning his swordmasters and cortahars . . . and surprising even the clergy of the Lady, who'd obviously expected him to refuse such an obvious danger, so that they could cry his defiance of the Holy Horned Huntress, and call down war upon him.

And so it was that one bold lion of a man strode now down into the obvious danger, leaving Hawkril Anharu standing in tense unease. No man of Blackgult had been allowed to enter the hollow for six days now. The armaragor had risked much, some days before that, in making secretive preparations, but once he'd begun, others in the court of Blackgult had aided him willingly. None of it might be necessary, but somehow . . .

The limb of a nearby tree dipped once, deliberately, and Hawkril nodded his thanks for the signal. The wizards were at work, as well as one priest of the Forefather. No magic could have its birth in that hollow, or enter it, for the next little while, to aid or to harm. Which left the baron still alone and unarmed against six priestesses with drawn swords in their hands.

Hawkril saw him stop, and stand speaking. Horned heads moved, bodies shifted with insolent grace. Arms rose in florid gestures, as they sidled nearer, drifting to encircle the Golden Griffon.

The baron laughed, then, and said something, turning his head in time to see the blade thrusting at him from behind. He slapped it away, found another seeking his blood, and twisted it out of the hand of she who bore it.

All at once, the other raised their hands to smite him with spells, chanted in angry unison, and hurled— nothing.

Their looks of amazement were comical, and two of them even tried again. The baron said something stern—and in response one of the priestesses cried aloud for aid.

All over the hollow, brown-robed priestesses rose out of the bushes and ferns with long knives in their hands. Their horned superiors fell back swiftly, gesturing with their blades—and all of the lesser clergy surged forward, to slay, in a swiftly closing ring around one man with a sword in his hand.

Hawkril's horn was already to his lips, and his feet were already racing. He blew loud and long as he pounded down into the hollow, sprinting as hard as he'd ever run in his life, and on all sides of the hollow other armaragors in Blackgult armor were descending—into a crowd of fully armored priests erupting from trees and brush piles. By the Three, the clergy of Sharaden mustered eighty or more!

Hawkril threw his horn into the face of the first to stand in his way, cut down the second with a vicious chop, ran right over the third, trampling hard, and slashed open the face of a fourth. Then he was through the armored faithful, with others converging on him from all sides, and his Lord still a good sixty or seventy paces distant, in the heart of a surging mob of eager slayers.

Hawkril started to snatch and hurl the line of knives scabbarded across his chest, and across the hollow he could see other armaragors doing the same. Someone with a bow was seeking out horned helms and the ladies beneath them, with deadly accuracy; Hawkril cursed at that disobedience of orders, and vaulted over a priest who must have learned to lunge in some elegant school of arms somewhere. "Later!" he roared

*over his shoulder, as he sprinted on, waving his fists
wide to strike aside blades, knife-wielding priestesses,
and anyone else foolish enough to dispute the way.*

*A breath later, and he'd reached the tightening ring
around the baron. He plied his sword like a madman,
throwing knives at any face that turned his way,
screaming and spitting and seeking any way he could to
turn their attention from the man sinking down in the
center of the ring with blood glistening all over him,
and two blades at least protruding from his body.*

*He was still cutting his way forward, too, seeking to
stand over the baron if he could. Blood was everywhere, and a dozen armaragors, or more, were cutting
their way slowly—too slowly—toward the ring, from
other directions. The next few breaths would be crucial.
Hawkril cut open a snarling holy face, booted a holy
crotch as hard as he could, and the way was clear for a
desperate, twisting leap. He landed, swept his blade
around in a great circle that struck a few swords aside,
and hit at least one more solid obstacle, then slapped at
the vial at his breast, to make sure it was still there.*

*The eyes that stared up at him were darkening, but
the bloody lips beneath them framed a rueful smile.
"You . . . right, Hawk . . . but too late . . ."*

Hawkril shook himself, as if to drive off a chill, and
stared around, on a creaking boat on the dark Silverflow
once more, not in the midst of bloody butchery and dying priestesses. Some memories never stopped burning.

But then, what was a man's life but a bonfire of blazing memories?

Beside him, Craer Delnbone smiled and shrugged.
"We have the most powerful and cruel man in all Coiling Vale trying to catch and slay us, and using three evil
and formidable mages to do it—of *course* something
isn't right. I don't need a bard or an old sage to tell me
that."

"Something isn't right," the armaragor insisted. "Silvertree has some sort of trap waiting for us. . . ."

"You hardly think the Cold Baron would risk even one of his Dark Three in Adeln just now," Craer replied, "with everyone whispering 'war,' do you? Baron Adeln has archers enough to overwhelm any lone wizard . . . and he'd almost *have* to attack if Silvertree sent mages in to act openly in the very heart of his barony, or he'd be proving himself a weakling in the eyes of all."

"No, just sensible, to keep out of the way of a wizard," Hawkril grunted, "but I take your point: any Aglirtan ruler who doesn't react hard and swift to meddlings or invasions invites more such unwelcome intrusions. So Silvertree will strike once we're out of Adeln."

"Cheerful to be around, aren't you?" Craer replied, stretching. "Well, ther—"

Then the world exploded in thunder—thunder that came down out of the sky to crash on the foredeck.

The procurer and the armaragor stared openmouthed at the tumult of bouncing stones, splashing oil, and flying shards of crockery just long enough to realize that the sky itself wasn't raining stones—they were tumbling down onto the boat from the cliff overhanging the river, in a cloud of crushing destruction that was coming swiftly closer to two adventurers lounging on the afterdeck.

"Sargh!" Craer gasped, diving for the aft hatch.

"Graul, sargh, and be*bolt!*" Hawkril cursed, almost crushing the smaller man in his leap down the hatchway. Amid the dense rattle of stones bouncing on the cabin roof, they heard many shrill smashing sounds as long jugs perished and the smell of oil rose strongly in the air—cooking oil.

The hatch was locked . . . and, as the armaragor's first snarling pull on its handles proved, barred from within. Hawkril growled, set his shoulders, and pulled until the veins stood out along his arms and the wood literally bulged under the force of the armaragor's hauling.

Bulged, but did not break. Stone crashed crazily around the two adventurers, numbing the burly warrior's hands and shoulder enough to break his grip on the door. Hawkril fell back, hard, against the hatchway steps, and groaned at the pain of that landing, as the rain of stones fell away aft.

Craer risked his neck to peer up at the edge of the cliff above, where he saw nothing, and then along the length of the boat. Its decks were awash in glistening oil, with the shards of shattered long jugs everywhere, outnumbered only by the heaped stones.

"About a cartload," Hawkril grunted, gaining the decks with a gasp and putting a hand to his back with a wince. Craer was skidding and trotting down the unsteady boards to the forehatch; an instant later, he tore it open and bellowed into the boatmaster's angry and astonished face: "*Up* on deck while you've still got one! Someone's emptied a cart of stones all over the oil jugs, and they've probably got friends waiting to hurl torches at us at the next bend! You may not have a boat much longer!"

No crew beyond the dumbfounded boatmaster himself had made it up the steps by the time the boat came to the second bend—and received its first flaming visitations.

Hawkril, Craer, and the boatmaster cursed and crouched and burrowed under ropes and tarpaulins in unison as the arrows came humming. A fiery volley of fire shafts zipped hungrily into the decks all around, and oil caught light with a roar, flaring up into man-high flames in an instant.

Even before the blazing ship slid out of the bend and the last arrows fell harmlessly into the river, astern, Craer was down the hatchway and hauling a surly sailor up from a table strewn with cards and coins by the throat of his greasy smock. In the lantern light from a candle cage dancing on its ceiling-beam peg, five startled faces stared at him, brows drawing down in anger.

"Up above," the procurer snarled into the face of the man he held, "and hurl the jugs overboard, or this whole boat'll flare up like a torch, and us with it!"

"*You're* going to tell us what to do, little man?" another of the sailors sneered. "I think not."

"You can get up on decks and work—or snap and snarl at me down here and die in the flames," Craer told them hotly, "and right now I don't much care which. It's hero time, and this boat's sailing straight into a short, hot future as a pyre!"

He let the astonished man in his grip fall back into his seat with a crash, vaulted the table to pound on the door of the cabin where Embra and Sarasper were sleeping—and he and Hawk should have been snoring, too, if they'd had any sense—and roared, "Fire! Get out!" the moment he heard a snarl of reply, and then spun around and pounded back up on deck.

He was running into a sheet of roaring flame. Above the dancing shimmer of heat that made him choke, Craer saw Hawkril and the boatmaster plying boathooks like madmen, sweeping or kicking blazing crockery overboard as arrows hissed out of the brightness to thud into the deck or send fresh and glistening showers of shards into the air. Flames burst into being in midair around some of those shards, spinning up into the dark air in a beautiful—and deadly—cloud.

Craer cursed, emptied the nearest dipper of drinking water over his head to make his hair wet and slower to catch afire, and sprinted to the cabin roof, where he bent to snatch long jugs up from their smoldering ropes and hurl them overboard.

Crewmen were racing up on deck, now, and gaping in astonishment at the flames. A few made straight for the rail, to dive into the river, but Craer noticed that arrows came hissing in pairs and volleys to strike at anyone seeking to leave the ship.

Sailors spun around and fell, decorated with shafts, or staggered back amidships; not a one, so far as he could see, managed to strike the water unscathed.

All the while, arrows kept whistling out of the trees, in a deadly rain that made the sailors shout in fear as they danced amid the flames with water buckets or sawed with their knives at the net of ropes that held the oil jugs in place.

Hawkril took an arrow in the shoulder and staggered back, driven against the mast by the force of the striking shaft. He roared out his pain as Embra came hurrying up the hatch steps with Sarasper close behind.

Gaping, they saw flaming ropes dangling and swaying in the trembling air, Hawkril reeling—and atop the cabins, Craer, his brows singed away and the hair on his forearms crisped to ash, flopping about like some sort of fish, kicking and shoving away blazing cargo while arrows thudded home on all sides.

Embra cried out and rushed across the pitching deck. More arrows struck, long jugs bursting apart all around her. A jagged shard spun the Lady's way as she ran—and skipped across her scalp.

Blood fountained in all directions through long and tangled hair. The Lady Silvertree staggered blindly forward through a swelling inferno, mewing in startled pain, straight into a solid collision with the mast.

Sarasper stared at her, and at the blaze and whistling arrows, in openmouthed horror. Then he dashed toward the crumpling sorceress, only to lose all sight of her in bright conflagration, as the ship exploded in front of him with a mighty roar!

The tapestry fell back into place behind Maershee, and several of the bards leaned forward to resume the talk they'd let trail away as the wine matron served them. One took a long, slim clay pipe out of a mouth framed by amber-hued whiskers and said, "Well, it's my firm belief that no matter how they died, Silvertree had a hand in it. He hates all bards."

"And anyone else who's not cowering under his gauntlet," a young but white-haired bard agreed bitterly. "I had to run from his armaragors once. He told them to whip me—to give me, he said, good reason for the high, shrill noise I was making!"

There were grunts of anger and disgust . . . and a few sounds that might have been suppressed chuckles. Flaeros sat very still, still hardly daring to believe he'd been accepted as a fellow bard and allowed to sit in this private room with half a dozen veterans of minstrelsy. Outside its hushed and richly paneled privacy, the Gargoyle was crowded and noisy this night, but here, around a dying hearthfire, the men who made music all over Darsar were talking grimly of two dead colleagues.

"Helgrym taught me the thrumpipe," one of them said suddenly, "and introduced me to old Teshaera."

"By the Lady, but she could make strings!" another bard said sadly. "Gathered in and gone, like all the rest."

There were murmurs of sorrowful agreement, and nods, before someone asked, "I wonder what'll happen to all of Delvin's harps now?"

"Burned for firewood already, is my guess. His houselady hated having his room sit idle while he traveled. I heard she went up there and broke one, just for spite, whenever he went away."

"He never found an enchanted one, did he?" Heads turned, and the speaker added almost delightedly, in the lowered, excited tones of one who dispenses a juicy secret, "That's what he was hot for, all his days: to find a magical harp."

"There's not an endless supply of such things," the pipe-smoking bard said sourly. "He'd have been better off never to have known magic existed."

"Seeing as how magic slew him, that's a safe enough

declaration," another bard agreed, "but who among us can honestly claim not to know magic exists? Simpletons and madmen, that's who; and simpletons and madmen can't make good music."

"I know," one of the older bards grunted. "I've heard you sing."

There were chuckles and whistles of apprehension at that, and not a few rude gestures back and forth, before someone asked, "How exactly *did* they die?"

"Torn apart by something like a horse-sized dragon," a bard who'd been silent until now put in. "Something spellborn, sent out to slay by the Dark Three."

"Just how would they create something like that?" Flaeros heard himself asking. "Are wizards born knowing how to shape the winds and the forces of growing things, or . . ."

Heads turned to look at him, and Flaeros suddenly felt like an outsider again. He sat trying to look unconcerned while something cringed and died inside him. The silence lengthened until someone muttered, "What do they *teach* young bardlings today? Which end of a hunting horn to blow?"

"Easy, easy," an older voice said. "We all had to start learning somewhere—why shouldn't he learn here? Lad, hearken: mages work spells by draining things. Sometimes, if they want to curse someone more than they want to go on living, it's themselves. More often it's a foe, or slaves, or beasts . . . and sometimes it's things that already have magic cast on them."

"And it's not so mighty nor as reliable as the great mages would have you think," another voice put in. "You can be sure Baron Silvertree wouldn't be offering one hundred trade wagons full of gold for anything if magic could find him his daughter."

"Yet he has three of the mightiest mages Aglirta's yet seen to work it," an older bard said sourly. "Magic works best for things that can also be done by trickery—and I wonder why that is?"

"Hear that: he speaks of magic and wants answers. Now *there's* a simpleton and fool!"

"Enough," the pipe-smoking bard said loudly. "So the Lady of Jewels gets herself kidnapped—I hear she planned it all and hired a band of deadly swordslayers to rush in and seize her!—and we'd *all* love that much coin, every one of us here, to save us right now from ever having to travel and sing again."

"One hundred trade wagons full of gold offered by the baron for the Lady Embra Silvertree's safe recovery and restoration to him," someone murmured. "Wonder how much more she'd pay to be kept out of his reach, from now on?"

"*I* wonder how many folk up and down the Vale are foolish enough to try to find her and claim it . . . and think the baron'd ever allow them to live long enough to spend it!"

There were many nods and murmurs of rueful agreement to this, and amid them someone murmured, "First light," and pointed upward.

Flaeros hadn't even noticed the skylight in the ceiling. The first rosy fingers of dawn were touching the dying clouds of the night, high above the glass. The bards fell silent for a time to watch it grow brighter, and Maershee silently slipped into the room with fresh glasses and bottles for all. When she left again, it seemed to stir a dozen voices to talking. One of them said gloomily, "Plotting sorceress she may be, but I doubt the Lady Silvertree arranged her own kidnapping. If her father catches her, many floggings are the least she can expect to suffer!"

"You think a rival baron's behind this?" the pipe smoker asked. "To take Silvertree's mind off putting all Aglirta to the sword until he rules it?"

The older bard shrugged by way of an answer and turned to Flaeros. "You're very quiet, youngling. Feeling a ballad coming on?"

Flaeros shivered and said quietly, "Maybe. I was

thinking of Lady Silvertree as a captive, and where she might be right now—alone, no doubt helpless to defend herself against any horror or indignity life may now offer her."

Heads turned to regard him again, but they were wrapped in thoughtful silence this time, and something almost approaching respect was in their eyes.

"Well, lad," the older bard said, "when it's done, mind you sing it to us. The helpless Lady Silvertree, sad amid her small sorceries . . . hmmm."

The blast sent flames boiling up in balls and streamers of bright fury and shook the helpless Lady Silvertree back to consciousness. Embra was hurled against a blazing tangle of shrouds. Rebounding to her feet, she rose out of the flames in a fury. Under her feet the boat rushed on through the waters, shuddering now and seeming to settle lower.

Silently thanking the Three that she'd had sense enough last night to take some of the smallest Silent House knickknacks from Hawkril's sack to the various pouches and pockets of her own, Embra snatched out a few and wove a spell with careful, angry haste. Its final word made all the flames around her flicker in unison, rise straight up—and then, slowly, begin to move as one.

The Silvertree sorceress stood slender and silent, thin ribbons of smoke curling from her scorched and blackened garments, as the flames became a moving ring in the air above her, snarling faster and faster under her will. Their winds snatched arrows up to harmlessly menace the sky—and when sweat was stinging her eyes and running off her chin in a steady stream, Embra snarled out the last part of the spell and flung up her arms.

The deck was canted under her burned boots now, and water was snarling its own song somewhere close beneath its boards. She crouched to avoid arrows and watched through narrowed eyes as her magic sent the giant whirlwind of flames spinning into the trees that had been busily birthing arrows.

Flames crashed into the forest with a vicious crackling of branches. Embra heard a single ragged shout before that riverbank erupted into a blaze that outshone the dawn. She stared grimly at tree trunks standing like black fingers against an unbroken sheet of fire, then hauled herself to her feet again, looked down the creaking deck past the boatmaster staggering along with two arrows in him, and gathered in the rest of the Four with her eyes.

"Sail this thing!" she shouted imperiously, voice cracking on the last word, as long fingers of dark river water reached across the deck for the first time, and steam arose. Embra looked around at it, shivered, her eyes flickered, and then she slid to the decks in a loose flood of collapse.

Sarasper was nearest, and went stumbling along the flexing boards of the deck to where she lay. Parts of it were awash now, as the sinking ship rushed on; it would not be long before the river tugged her away. . . .

The healer reached her, hurled the top of a broken long jug aside, and took hold of her shoulders to drag her upright. He got the Lady Silvertree half-sitting, slipped, and caught hold of a smoldering shroud for support. Then he tried again.

Sarasper. The voice was back.

It was louder than it had been in the underways, when he'd stood alone on watch. The old healer stiffened, his hands on Embra's shoulders.

Inches from her throat, yes.

Sarasper went cold inside, and said in the silence of his own mind: *You call yourself Old Oak, and yet I feel no divine thunder. Who are you, really?*

YOU WOULD DEFY ME? The force of the shout sent Sarasper reeling, clawing vainly at his ears, as his body fairly thrummed to the force of the coercion now racing through it.

"I-I-I—," he sobbed, waving one futile hand as if to brush away a foe—and then the warm and angry tide rushing through him rose past his throat, and took hold of the back of his neck with fingers of steel, and he felt very cold.

Set her by the mast for now, the voice said, and Sarasper's limbs moved to obey without any bidding from him. The voice almost seemed to be speaking to someone else, someone not quite at hand. . . .

That keelpin. Turn thus, to hide it. Now take it up, into your sleeve.

The ship was canting over now, the right-hand rail dipping under the water. The body of one crewman, huddled around the three arrows that had slain him, suddenly rolled across the decks and left the ship with a splash. Sarasper had a brief glimpse of a mouth forever frozen open, and then the rushing boat left the dead man behind.

The healer's own body was moving under the bidding of the mysterious presence in his mind, climbing back along the dry side of the boat with a speed and deftness Sarasper could not have managed by himself. Old Oak brought him to where Craer and Hawkril were struggling with the sluggish tiller.

The procurer was cutting away a tangle of fallen shrouds as Sarasper came up behind him, waited until the sudden lolling of another sailor's body took Hawkril's attention in another direction, and then clubbed down with the keelpin, hard.

Craer's body danced under the impact, and for a moment the procurer started to turn, bringing the knife in his hand up . . . a blade that fell from opening fingers as Craer slumped to the deck. Sarasper was already moving, ducking along the aft rail behind the armaragor as Hawkril heard his friend's dagger clatter to the deck.

"Longfingers, *what?!* . . ." the warrior roared, reaching out an arm from the tiller to pluck at Craer's belt. "Ar—"

Sarasper sprang into the air, to make the force of his blow as numbingly heavy as possible, and brought the keelpin down.

The armaragor reeled, fell onto the tiller, and then struggled to rise. Sarasper struck him again, above one ear, and then a third time, and Hawkril fell on his face, leaving the tiller to swing.

The healer stood over him, swaying, as the irresistible voice of Old Oak thundered orders. He was to lash Embra to a rail to keep her safely aboard, and then hold the heads of his two unconscious companions underwater for a good long time before rolling their bodies off the listing ship into the river. Then he was . . .

Flying helplessly through the air in a tangle of ropes and rigging, as the boat crashed head-on into jagged rocks and tried to ride up over them. The deck buckled, erupting into deadly slivers as long as a man stands tall. Sarasper saw the boatmaster transfixed on one shard, clawing the air and wriggling vainly, before he struck something very hard, and everything rushed away on a roaring, echoing red tide, down into darkness. . . .

9

Chasing Stones and Starting Wars

*I*n a high, grand hall of white stone, two old men in robes that did not fit them sat stiffly side by side at a table, not looking at each other. Across the table from them stood an ornate chair whose lofty back bore the flame-winged crow of Cardassa; a chair that would soon hold the baron himself. At his request, it was early rising for both of them. An attentive eye—like the unseen one peering at the old men through a gap in the tapestry behind that empty chair—would readily, and several times, have noticed the tightening of jaw and throat, and flaring of nostrils, that marks a courtier's stifled yawn.

The rays of the rising sun chose that moment to touch the tops of the tall, narrow east windows, flooding the room with sudden light. As if that radiance had been a signal, the tapestry stirred, and from behind it strode a richly robed man with piercing dark eyes, glossy ringlets of black hair, and large red hands that bore many gleaming rings. They flashed back the rosy light as he took his high-backed seat, glanced at the open doors of the room, and nodded at the discreet hand signal of a man in mirror-bright armor who stood in the doorway. He made a sign of his own, in return.

The armored officer nodded and murmured something to the impassive cortahars behind him. Doors that soared almost to the ceiling slammed thunderously under their hands, and Baron Ithclammert Cardassa leaned forward in his ornate chair. "Well, Baerethos? It seems you'll burst if you have to keep silent any longer, so you may as well speak first."

Almost stammering in his hasty thanks, the thin old man in the faded blue-and-gold mage's robe plunged into eager speech. "Lord, my deductions are complete. Long have I labored, seeking the signs, casting divinations, and consulting elder lore, and their message have I here unraveled for you. One of the Dwaerindim—Hilimm, the Stone of Renewal—must now lie at Daern's Moot!"

The baron raised one eyebrow and glanced at the other old man, who sat listening in stony silence, thin lips pressed firmly together. "Daern's Moot" he mused. "Hmm."

"It's a crossroads in Felsheiryn, Lord," Baerethos added eagerly. "A ring of overgrown stones—once a wizard's tower, though long fallen in utter ruin—stands there, sometimes used as a camping place by passing peddl—"

"I'm familiar with the place," the baron said mildly, holding up a hand for silence, and took up his scepter from the table to rap a bell that sat beside it.

Its tones brought the bright-armored officer scurrying from the doors to stand at attention beside the baron.

"Orders," Ithclammert Cardassa said simply, not looking up. "Send two patrols in force, under Warblade Denetharl, to Daern's Moot. There they are to look for a mottled brown-and-gray stone—a smooth sphere about so big, with markings like a sun or star on it." The baron held up his hands, perhaps four finger widths apart, or a little more. "Tell them thus: it may be floating in the air by itself when found, or it may not. Turn over every stone of the ring and look beneath it. Use shovels. Bring back anything like that you may find at the crossroads, as fast as you can. Beware wizards seeking to take the stone from you."

The other old man at the table stirred and opened his mouth, but the baron gave him a stern look. He looked down at the tabletop, reddening, and kept silent.

The officer swept out his arm in the horizontal chopping motion that serves in Cardassa as a salute, and hurried away. Something that might almost have been a smile touched the baron's lips as he turned to the second old man and asked mildly, "You have other thoughts regarding the Dwaerindim, Ubunter?"

The old man in rather rumpled maroon silks shot his rival Baerethos a look of scorn, gathered himself upright in his seat, and said in stately, cultured tones, "Indeed I *do,* Great Lord. Rather than trusting the writings of the oft-drunken bard Haerlaer, as my colleague seated to the north of me has done, or mistaken the wizard Jhantilar's writings of 'the resting place of the sweetest master I have ever known' to mean the wizard Daern rather than the sorceress Skalaerla of Brostos, I have chosen to trust Hathparauntus of Sirlptar."

Ubunter leaned forward, seized by excitement, and almost chanted, "He writes that in the days before Skalaerla fell into disfavor, she planned for the fall she knew must come by walling up certain magics in a crypt under Castle Brostos—activities she was observed in by Delgaer the Halfwit, younger brother of the baron of the day. He—"

"You *believe* the incoherent writings of a halfwit?" Baerethos burst out. "*This* is scholarship?"

"The point," Ubunter said witheringly, "is not that Delgaer was as sound of wits as most men, but simply unable to speak—nor is it if he wrote the truth or not, or even if Hathparauntus reported it accurately! The point is that we know from other sources that the Baron Oldrus Brostos read Delgaer's diaries long after the halfwit's passing, investigated the crypt, and ordered it sealed after trap-spells bearing Skalaerla's warding runes slew three of his best armsmen! Something was there, and is there still; why should it not be what we know Skalaerla had but none could find after she was chained and her quarters searched? The something she would surely have used to end her captivity, or even prevent it, if it had been available to her hand! *I* say that Hilimm, the Stone of Renewal, lies hidden in the walls of that crypt under Castle Brostos, in the barony of the same name."

"Ridiculous!" Baerethos snapped, and a moment later both men were snarling at each other, fingers rising to wag in violent disagreement. The baron rang the bell once more, and then rapped both of his would-be mages on the hands and foreheads with his scepter, giving them cold looks when he had their attention. He added the terse words, "Be still" before the lancemaster reached the table. As calmly as before, the baron dispatched a second force to the barony of Brostos, with identical orders.

"But . . . but Thanglar Brostos will view your soldiers as an invading force! There'll be war!" Baerethos said in a strangled voice.

The baron smiled thinly. "Yes, no doubt he will. In fact, I'm counting on it."

As Baerethos gaped at him, face slowly going bone white, Baron Cardassa added, his mouth not quite twitching into a smile, "Cardassa is prepared."

Without pause the ruler of Cardassa turned to Ubunter. "I've heard a lot of grand words about 'ancient powers awakening' and these stones saving all Darsar or whelming all the dragons if they're placed just so— but I'd much rather hear some simple, definite, and true promises about what getting my hands on just this one Stone of Renewal can do for me *right now.*"

"Hilimm is the stone that renews," Ubunter said hastily, before his colleague could say anything. "If it is touched to things, it mends breaks, banishes rot and rust no matter how widespread, and banishes barrenness in soil or wombs."

Ithclammert Cardassa shrugged. "Nice enough, but I've smiths to forge new swords when I break old ones, and—"

"Lord," Baerethos burst out, "the Worldstones are mighty things, every one. With Hilimm in his hand, a wizard could cast spells he already knows from now until his dying day without need for study or sacrifices or the finding of fuel—you've seen us building bonfires to root our spells and how casting just one magic turns a man-high blaze to cold ashes in an instant. There'd be no need for that, ever, with a Dwaerindim."

The baron nodded, a half-smile on his face, and murmured, "Ah, that explains—something. . . . "

"He who holds a Dwaer can stand in hot sun, or the heart of a fire, unscathed, and laugh at most spells, too," Ubunter added quickly. "Nor need he drink nor fear taint or poison if he drinks of water the Stone has been immersed in."

"Hilimm can make an aged man young and vigorous for one day in every year," Baerethos added, "and all Dwaer can glow like torches, and if one gains more than one, they can be used together to command even greater powers."

"You describe wizards' toys," said the Baron Cardassa coldly. "Or something that could make the likes of you two into . . . something approaching a mage. Is this why you're both so hungry to get your hand on a Worldstone?"

The two old men stared at him nervously but did not speak. Baerethos licked his lips.

The baron smiled, and picked up his scepter again. Their silence gave him clear answer. He struck the bell on the table before him, and said, "Have my thanks, both of you. Now arise, and go to the kitchens, and eat.

Cardassa needs you healthy. In the days ahead, I may well have need even for bonfire wizards."

As Baerethos and Ubunter stared at him, swallowing the insult together even if they fiercely resisted doing anything else in unison, one of the doorguards hastened to the table in answer to the bell.

"Have them bring me the meal now," the baron said, "and tell Roeglar to have his men ready to ride as soon as he can. We've borders to inspect, and it's high time for an 'incident' with one of our neighbors."

As the armsman bowed, the baron tossed down his scepter and rose from his seat. The two old men bobbed up so swiftly to make their bows that Ubunter's chair went over with a crash. No one noticed the watching eye withdrawing thoughtfully from the gap in the tapestry that the baron had used earlier—and Ubunter's shrilly babbled apologies covered the faint sound of the door to the baron's private bedchamber-to-morn-meal passage opening and then closing again.

Two bleary-eyed merchants turned the same corner in Adeln just before the rays of the rising sun reached it. They were coming along narrow, barrel-strewn alleyways from opposite directions in the gloom, dusty boots quiet on wet and muddy flagstones, and nearly strode right into each other, brushing shoulders and clapping hands to blades with identical startled half-curses.

Two men, grizzled and thoughtful, clad in the breeches, vests, and overtunics favored by traders all over Darsar, wearing plain swords "hard at hand," and the expressions of men who knew how to use them, taking rather less time to measure each other than most merchants do, they smiled at each other rather tentatively. "A bright and pleasant morning," one of them offered, looking up and down the alley as if gathering evidence for this opinion.

"So it is," the other agreed heartily, peering up and down the other. "A fine morning to deal in fish, if you're interested."

"By the Three! I was just on my way to make some purchases at the docks!" was the delighted reply, and as they bent their heads together, one merchant muttered, "Is it time?"

The other replied even more quietly, "Not yet. They should get into the wine soon; I delivered it to all the barracks last night. Wait until you hear my horn."

As if his words had been a cue, the none-too-fragrant alleyway air was shattered by the deafening blast of a hunting horn. Both men froze in astonishment. "Wha—" one of them started to say, as the Seneschal of Adeln rose out of a barrel right behind them and swung a heavy mace with brutal force.

It takes very little time, and even less fuss, to dash out the brains of two men onto the cobbles, Presgur observed, vaulting out of his barrel. At his feet, the bodies stopped twitching, amid faint wet sounds.

"My thanks for leading us to all your friends, idiot Silvertree foxes," he told one sprawled corpse, in tones of satisfaction. Then he turned to the other, and added, "Next time, don't use almond root to poison wine—in Adeln, soldiers still have tongues to taste with!"

Men with drawn swords ready in their hands began to appear out of dark doorways up and down both alleyways. Presgur bent over to pluck a hunting horn from the belt of a Silvertree spy who'd be needing it no longer and ordered the nearest men, "Take these scum to Hawkroon House. Our Lord Wizard has a little surprise in store for overclever Silvertree mages—one involving fresh blood. . . . "

The bright light of full morning touching the trees around him improved Hawkril's mood not one bit. He went on grimly twisting dead tree limbs away from the trunks they'd grown from and hurling them onto a growing pile of gathered deadfalls. This was taking too bebolten *long*. . . .

It mattered little who heard him breaking branches or what unfriendly eyes might see the rising flame of the fire he planned; if he didn't warm his senseless companions soon, three of the Band of Four would be corpses. They lay in a little group of sodden bundles in the dell where he'd set them down, after three exhausting carries through the woods from the rocks where the boat had been wrecked, to the next bend of the river, here. All the Band of Four still owned was what they wore or he'd carried hence . . . and he hadn't the strength left to make another trip. The crows had been clustered thickly around the boatmaster, spitted on his spar and staring sightlessly at swarming flies, when last Hawkril left him, and the warrior from Blackgult didn't want any of them following him here.

The armaragor should have collapsed from weariness long ago, but sheer iron will was carrying him on through the gathering and stacking and flint-striking. His head swam as he knelt to blow on his tinder to get the smoldering going; someone had battered him but good with a club that had been small but quite hard enough.

He glanced over at the huddled body of his oldest surviving friend, and muttered, "Couldn't we have just hunted down deer for a season? Did you have to go after a lady sorceress because of her jewels? How far did we get with them, anyway? From one Silvertree mansion to another, across the river! Bah!" Hawkril turned grimly back to his work as the tinder caught and flared, and the critical time of introducing the right twigs began.

Behind him, the maligned procurer stirred. Craer's eyelids fluttered for a moment and then he came suddenly to full wakefulness. He lay still, listening to the snap and rising crackle of the fire and the scrapes of shifting boots and deep, slow breathing that had to belong to Hawkril. There were trees all around, and no rushing water or creak and groan of an old boat carried along by it. Where was he?

Would he live long enough for it to matter? The procurer explored the tender area at the back of his head gingerly, carefully felt the rest of his body with hands that still ached and smarted, and then unfolded his wet cloak from where Hawkril must have wrapped it around him, and rolled to his feet.

Hawkril's head snapped around at the sound; Craer gave him a rueful smile of gratitude, shook himself to make sure of his balance and that his aching limbs would obey him, and stepped forward to clap his friend's shoulder in silent thanks. Then he took off his dripping cloak and hung it on tree boughs to shield the light of the quickening fire from the view of anyone who might be looking across the river, or sailing along it under orders from the Baron Silvertree.

Grimacing at that thought, Craer stood for a moment listening to the forest sounds and then stalked off into the woods to relieve himself and gather more wood, moving as quietly as possible. He drew his knife as he went; his stomach would probably welcome a fire-roasted, juicy morn-meal.

Sarasper started groaning and murmuring things long before he awakened. Hawkril listened grimly, but the healer said nothing intelligible before suddenly sitting bolt upright, awake and staring.

There was dread on his face, and the sweat of remembered fear beaded his forehead and ran down his cheeks—but when Hawkril leaned close to look at him, Sarasper drew in a deep breath, waved the armaragor away, and insisted he was all right.

The weary warrior shot a suspicious glance or two in Sarasper's direction as the morning warmed. The dread never left the healer's eyes.

Once Hawkril was sure he heard the whispered word, "Overwhelmed!" but at least the healer was conscious, and walking about—even rooting among the rotting forest leaves for morn-meal roots and mushrooms.

When the armaragor lifted the last bundle to lay it close beside the fire, his mouth tightened. The Lady Embra Silvertree slept, no matter how much noise he made or how often he gently slapped or pinched her.

The time came when the smell of roasting rabbit and squirrel drifted strong around them, and three worried men washed the hair of a sleeping woman and cut the black dried blood out of it—while still she slept on, oblivious to gentle attempts to rouse her. They turned her, to dry all sides of the clothes she wore, and argued anew about what they should do now.

"We have an agreement," Sarasper reminded the procurer and the armaragor firmly. "If that still means anything to men who dwelt in Blackgult."

Hawkril's face grew dark. "I take rather more care with my mouth than you do, healer. Hard feelings are a poor reward for a man who pulled you from the river not all that long ago."

"Hey, now—easy there, the both of you," Craer said quickly. "Yes, we agreed—and yes, Sarasper, we'll hold to that agreement. But surely you must see that to succeed in . . . in what Forefather Oak wants you to do, you must stay *alive*."

Sarasper glared at him. "So much is obvious, Craer; what clever trickery is this?"

The procurer looked exasperated. "No trickery, Old and Suspicious, but a simple point: we none of us dare to devote our lives entirely and only to chasing the Dwaerindim. If we do, Baron Silvertree's mages, and other old foes we have who may turn up, and anyone else who's seeking the Stones—and that'd be half the mages and some of the bards and all of the barons here in Aglirta, now wouldn't it?—can expect our arrival in specific places and easily lay traps for us, time after time. All they have to do is spread word of a Dwaer in this spot or that, make their preparations, and wait. It won't take much; how well do you think you could heal of us, if a tenth of those arrows back on the boat had hit their marks? And all it takes is one, in the wrong place—eye or throat or heart—and the Horned Lady will be handing you to the Dark One, and your quest won't matter much anymore."

"I know this," the healer said in a small voice. "This fear kept me in hiding for far too long . . . until you came." His eyes were suddenly bright with tears, and he hung his head.

"Stop that," Hawkril told him roughly, "and look to the lass, here. What's *wrong* with her?"

"Nothing," Craer said brightly. "She sleeps, resting that sword-sharp tongue of hers, and that's fine. Let sleeping lady sorceresses lie, that's what I say."

Both Sarasper and Hawkril gave him sour looks and grunts of exasperation, united once more in their thoughts. Craer smiled at them, shrugged, and then plucked the tiniest knife either of them had ever seen out of his belt buckle, picked up one of Embra's limp hands, and started to do her nails. He ignored the glances of the other two men, even when they turned from irritated to incredulous.

A bright and pleasant morning, as the old saying went, was lighting the ruins of Indraevyn as Phalagh of Orentar stumbled sleepily out of the shattered chamber, which he'd shared with two other wizards, to relieve himself. One of them snored with a very loud, irregular boarlike snorting, and when he found out who . . .

Phalagh rounded a heap of loose stones in search of some trees to water and found the veteran warrior Rivryn standing in the stinking armor he'd not taken off for three days, one hand on the hilt of his blade and a sour expression on his battered face.

The wizard raised an eyebrow. "That's a stormy look," he said, wetting a helpless nearby sapling. "Wherefore?"

"A most vigilant watch you spellhurlers mount, I'm thinking," Rivryn replied with deadpan sarcasm, gesturing around at overgrown rocks and encircling trees.

"Hum?" Phalagh asked, shaking the last cobwebs of slumber out of his head. He looked where the warrior's out-flung arm indicated. "What're you pointing out?"

"Behold," the warrior said shortly. "Absence of wizard."

Phalagh looked around again, a little chill awakening in him. Rivryn was right; there was no sign of the wizard who should have been standing there on watch.

The mage frowned. "Nynter drew last watch," he said slowly, "and should have been right here—or over there, by yonder thrusting rock."

They clambered toward the rock together and then, exchanging grim glances, around it, peering this way and that . . . only to come to a halt in silent unison and stand staring.

Nynter was standing in the dark and doorless entrance of a nearby ruined building. Or rather, the lower half of him was standing there, facing them: legs and pelvis, still upright, but the body above them bitten clean off and devoured or carried away. Blood had flowed down the legs from those terrible gnaw marks to pool and dry around the mage's booted feet, and one of his winged daggers was orbiting the grisly remains, endlessly looping in a slow, lazy circle like a patient blowfly.

Phalagh swallowed and tried to speak. Finding his throat too dry, he swallowed again. "What could have done this?" he asked, his words coming out in a hoarse whisper.

The warrior shrugged. "Almost anything," he said shortly. "We haven't explored this place well enough, what with all your driving hunger and haste to find a floating stone, remember?"

The mage turned on him with a snarl. "Do you dare to mock me?"

"Oh, no," Rivryn replied calmly, hefting a dagger the wizard hadn't seen him draw in one hand, "I'd never be so foolish as to do that." The dagger rose with a little twirl and flash, to be deftly caught in callused fingertips and hefted again. "I need you too much; you're one of just two mages we've left, remember? And mages are *so* useful, and so vigilant. I sometimes wonder what we'd all do without them. . . . "

Glacial eyes met, expressionlessly, for a very long time. The dagger rose and fell in an easy rhythm, and the eyes belonging to the wizard looked away first.

Baron Silvertree preferred to keep his wizards out where he could see them—and they could keep an eye on each other—not off by themselves, free to work mischief. He also liked to keep them busy at his tasks . . . not pursuing little betrayals of him on their own. It was a source of some satisfaction, on mornings such as this one, to enter his audience chamber and see them hard at work. This required that he arrive at different times, to keep them attentive and respectful, never knowing when he'd appear.

So though he'd just as soon have dallied the morning away in his vast bed with his six maidens of chamber, this time he hurried them through satisfying and bathing him, let them dress him in a silken robe, and then strolled to his audience chamber in their company, to enjoy a lavish morn meal there.

His greeting, as the maidens knelt to serve him food, was jovial, but his wizards acknowledged it as briefly as bare civility allowed. The baron smiled thinly. All three mages were hard at work: Markoun on a way to heal his blinded eye or perhaps replace it with a copy of his good one; Ingryl on a means of hunting down the lost Lady Embra; and Klamantle eavesdropping on the minds of Silvertree agents in baronies up and down the River Coiling, to learn the latest news and confirm continued loyalty.

Of the three, Klamantle seemed the most oblivious; the spell he was employing involved its caster concentrating on distant thoughts by staring into the flame of an oil lamp.

Wherefore the baron was startled when the quietest of his wizards suddenly staggered back from his worktable with a raw-throated shriek and began stumbling about the room screaming and clawing at his eyes. Wisps of smoke seemed to lick out from between his fingers.

Ingryl didn't even look up, but everyone else in the room watched the agonized mage, and grew pale. The oil lamp was trailing smoke, its flame gone, and the baron caught the remaining eye of Markoun and snapped, "Where was he scrying?"

The youngest mage looked at the nut half-shells on Klamantle's map, and said grimly "Adeln. Someone there worked magic upon him." Then he looked at his stricken colleague and asked hesitantly, "Klamantle?"

The reply was a howl of pain and despair as Beirldoun whirled to look at him, dropping his hands away from his face.

Markoun shuddered. Klamantle's eyes looked to be gone—two holes, it seemed, out of which twin plumes of smoke were boiling. The wizard's mouth trembled, and then a fresh spasm of pain seized him, and the screaming began anew.

The maidens around the baron were wincing and shrinking away from the stricken mage, but Faerod Silvertree went on calmly eating. Markoun looked at him and then over at Spellmaster Ingryl, who was working on at his own spell without pause, and shook his head in disbelief. Then he turned back to his own worktable, drew in a deep breath, and reached for the clay he'd been using to craft himself the likeness of an eyeball. The sobbing and howling grew louder, and twice Markoun reached for a scroll and then drew his hand back. Finally he turned, frowning, and tersely cast a deeper slumber spell, stepping forward to catch Klamantle's suddenly limp and silent body and lower it to the floor.

The smoke was dying away now, and Markoun could see that his colleague still had eyeballs . . . seared white eyeballs. He shivered and looked up to discover the baron's gaze on him. There was something approaching contempt in Faerod Silvertree's eyes.

"I can't work with that noise going on," Markoun explained.

The baron shrugged. "One can learn to. Look yonder." He inclined his head toward Ingryl Ambelter, who was calmly and unhurriedly adjusting two padded jeweler's clamps to hold one of Embra Silvertree's hairs stretched taut in front of him. "I shall set him the task of restoring Beirldoun's eyes before evening."

Markoun nodded. "Forgive me, Lord, but I cannot help but wonder why we're meddling in Adeln when they obviously don't welcome even scrying from afar?"

Had he been a little less in awe of the baron, and so less apprehensive about the consequences of daring such a question, the youngest Silvertree wizard might finally have noticed the eye peering from a spy hole behind the baron . . . an eye that had spent much time watching the ruler of Silvertree and his Dark Three in recent weeks. But he wasn't.

The Baron of Silvertree lifted up a goblet from the table as if he'd never seen it before, sipped from it, and then told it, "The need to wonder aloud, and know things that concern them not, are failings that seem to afflict all wizards," Faerod Silvertree drawled, "those loyal to me regrettably included."

"Forgive me, Lord, I-I—"

The baron held up a hand. "Enough; you have asked, and so you shall hear . . . a little. It can hardly come as news to a studious mage that the baronies all up and down the Silverflow are rising to war—war that will come, once 'tis expected, as night follows day. Hireswords eat too much, and their loyalty comes at too high a price, for any of us to let them go unused for more than a season at most. Someone will strike at someone else, and all the Vale will erupt. I'll see to it, if no one else does."

Faerod Silvertree gave his youngest wizard a wintry smile and said, "You've no need to know who in my judgment will do what; that's a game open only to those who try to hold land in the Vale. It matters little, in any event, for since Blackgult fell to me and I was able to seize all it held, the rest of the rulers of the Vale have been doomed. Aglirta shall rise again, and I shall be its king . . . though a lot fewer folk will be around to see it, once the war to come—and the specific slayings it'll be prudent for me to carry out, thereafter—are done."

It seemed to be Markoun's day to dwell dangerously. He found himself boldly asking, "But surely, Lord, every baron with armaragors and hireswords enough might, in private, say the same words you've just uttered? How can all of you be right?"

The baron merely smiled, and Markoun nervously rushed to fill the lengthening silence. "Or is it all up to the battlefield and the whim of the Three?"

The baron's smile did not change. "I think you've seen something of how well prepared Silvertree is for war to come. Not merely you three, and my alliances, and an army larger and better than all others in the Vale, but the granaries."

"Granaries? Yes, but—"

The baron stroked the head of his favorite maid, who was nuzzling at his codpiece. "Ah," he said, "you see, but you do not see. Learn, then: when we ride to war, the warriors of Silvertree will fight with torch and oil-

jug every bit as enthusiastically as they ply their swords
and loose their crossbows."

Markoun's eyes narrowed. "To burn and destroy?
Forgive me, Lord, but that's something I've never understood . . . how does harming and despoiling what
you conquer gain you anything? Won't the Silvertree
warriors who die in battle have thrown their lives away
for . . . nothing?"

Faerod Silvertree smiled down at a surging sea of
heads, as all six of his maids sought to reach where the
others had not. "A ruler must take a longer view of
things than those he rules," he explained. "So should
you—a wizard—if you expect to flourish. In your mind,
you see only the fires and the deaths and the wailing and
think only of plunder as slaves or as stuff of gold that
you can snatch up in your hands and bear off in triumph.
Learn another way of thinking of things, Yarynd."

"Ah . . . what other way?"

"Thus," the baron said smugly. "The devastation
well-prepared Silvertree will wreak on its foes—including those neighbors who think themselves my allies but who are going to be revealed as faithless
traitors, once swords are out—will plunge them into
starvation in the hard winter ahead. A few weak survivors will make poor farmers in the season beyond,
whereupon conquering them—as they face a bleak harvest and another winter—will be simple. I shall hold
feasts in every town and village my forces occupy.
Those who eat at my table will thereafter be loyal to
me—in the war I shall wage next, to conquer new lands
and fill my granaries again."

Markoun stared openmouthed at his employer, the
blood slowly draining from his face. His mouth
worked, but for the moment he could think of no words
to say. It was so cunning, so utterly, horribly . . .

"Brilliant, is it not?" Faerod Silvertree said jovially,
waving his maidens away and reaching for a decanter
of wine. "You must learn to think thus, and be shocked

by unfolding plots no more. Our Spellmaster saw every step of it at the same time I did, when we went up against Blackgult." He nodded his head again in the direction of Ingryl Ambelter.

Markoun looked to the Spellmaster and saw that Ingryl had turned away from the flickering radiances of the spell he was crafting to favor Markoun with a smile. It as a bland and unreadable smile—and it did not reach Ingryl Ambelter's eyes.

Embra's still and silent body was shaken by a sudden spasm, and Craer shouted in alarm. Sarasper and Hawkril came crashing back through the trees from the riverbank, where the healer had been restoring something of the warrior's strength.

By the time they reached the dell with its dying fire, the Lady Silvertree was awake at last, and sitting up with her fingers over her eyes, shaking away the procurer's attempts to hold her still.

"My eyes, Craer!" she was hissing. "They burn! They *burn!*"

"The flames on the boat? Can you see?" the procurer asked, cradling her shoulders as she shook herself and restlessly tried to rise.

"Yes, yes, but—the pain! Just now, out of nowhere! Ah! Ah, it eases. . . . "

Hawkril looked grimly at Sarasper. "Can we have a little healing?"

The older man was frowning, his eyes narrowed. "If 'twill do any good . . . this seems to me more like a spell from afar. Lady? Can you see?"

Embra snatched her hands away and glared at him. *"Yes,"* she snarled. "Open or shut, my eyes feel like hot coals in my head! Graul and bebolt! It *has* to be some magic sent by my father's mages!"

Hawkril loomed over her like an attentive mountain. "Should Sarasper try to banish i—"

"If it goes on and on until I can't take it," Embra snarled, "yes. I'll need to sleep, for one thing. But . . . not yet."

She growled, shook herself all over, and said suddenly, "I've been in the river . . . the boat. By the Three!" She looked wildly around. "All of you— whole? Unhurt?"

"Just as you see us. Everything else . . . boat, crew, all of our carryings . . . gone," Hawkril growled. "We've been arguing about where we go now."

Embra smiled thinly. "Away."

Sarasper said gently, "My fear was that the quest would be forgotten in the haste to flee the hand of your father, but Craer and Hawkril hold to another view. 'Tis only fair, Lady, to hear your thoughts. . . . "

The sorceress turned her head. "We do owe Sarasper our aid," she reminded the men of Blackgult. "If we are to be any better than my father, our promises must mean something."

"Neither of us want to forget our promises," Craer said smoothly, "but we daren't chase after them and do nothing else, or whenever the fancy takes him your father can cry news of a Dwaer and hold out his hand to snatch us when we come running."

Embra nodded. "That's—aaaahhh!"

The three men leaned forward as one. "Lady?"

Embra's hands were at her eyes again. "No, no," she murmured weakly. "The pain is gone." She lifted her head again. "Magic," she confirmed, looking at Sarasper. "You see why we must do more than chase enchanted Stones, no matter how much I'd like to hold one when next I must face my father's mages?"

The healer nodded, face somber, but the sorceress was already turning to Craer and Hawkril again. "Yet think, both of you: we might well be able to help our friend gain a Stone easily if we act the moment we have any hint of where one might lie."

As they nodded, another thought struck her. "How far are we from Sirlptar?"

Everyone looked at Hawkril, who rumbled, "We went on the rocks on the west side of the Gullet, the narrowing below Glarondpool, and are a bend below that now—a day or two of steady travel, if we meet with no delays, out from the Glittering City."

Embra's eyes narrowed. "In which direction does it lie—exactly?"

Hawkril pointed through the trees, and a trace of a smile touched his lips. "There. Exactly."

Embra nodded and said briskly, "Our disguises are gone; we'd best hasten. Gather around and touch me, all of you. Fingers to my bare skin, and firmly—my shoulders, not my face or hands."

"What casting?" Craer asked sharply. "We're a team, remember? Magic need not—must not—be your solitary mystery, kept from us."

"A spelljump," the Lady of Jewels replied with a nod of apology, "to the top of yonder ridge, where I can see bare ground enough."

The three men looked at each other. "Agreed," Sarasper said after a moment, and extended his hand to her neck. Impatiently she tugged the lacings of the tunic loose and pulled it down to lay bare one shoulder. "Here," she said. "I know some of you would rather get your fingers around my throat, but . . ."

With grins the men of the Four gathered around her. When they were all touching her, she held up a glowing mirror from the Silent House, spoke some words over it, and watched it fade away between her fingers like bubbling smoke.

There was an instant in which the world seemed to be falling away under their boots, and a confused rushing was all around them, like beer hurling itself from spigot into tankard. Then, abruptly, the trees around them changed. They were on the ridge, a little way closer to Sirlptar, on the bare shoulder of rock they'd seen from beside the river, with trees standing thick and dark before them.

The Lady Silvertree trembled, broke free of the hands on her, and staggered away to fall on her knees, white-faced. As they watched, she was loudly and noisily sick, her shoulders shaking with sudden weariness, and then started to crawl laboriously to her feet, wiping her mouth with the back of her hand.

Behind her back, the three men of the Four exchanged somber looks.

They did so to the accompaniment of the loud snarl of an arrow that came hissing out of the trees to strike, quivering, in a tree trunk beside Craer's nose.

10

In the Glittering City

The arrow busily burying itself in the tree had been no warning shot.

Others followed, hissing forth from the trees in a deadly cloud as the Four cursed and sprinted away along the ridge—all except for Embra, who was still on her knees, retching.

Not an arrow found its mark, and there was cursing in the trees. "Out and at them!" someone roared. "They must have food!"

"Not the woman—leave her!" someone else insisted. "She'll be our body slave!"

"How by all the holy Three could all of you *miss?*" a third someone snarled.

"Same way you did," came a laconic reply, as men in motley armor, with swords and clubs raised and ready in their hands, trotted out onto the ridge and leered down at Embra.

"A pretty lass!"

"Hoa—they're coming back! Snatch her!"

Eager hands reached out, only to break fingers on something unseen that barred their way like a shield— the hasty conjuring that had driven the arrows wide and was now weakening Embra with each passing moment.

As the outlaws snarled astonished curses, she swayed on her hands and knees, face white to the lips . . . and started the slow sag into unconsciousness.

Craer had seen the failed grabs and led Hawkril in a wide arc around the fallen sorceress, while Sarasper felt his way carefully toward her from behind.

"For Blackgult!" Hawkril thundered, swinging his blade, and one of the outlaws looked startled.

"Wha— why, that's . . ."

A blade laid open the man's neck. He staggered and fell, managing to gasp, ". . . us!" before he died.

Craer bounded over him, into the trees. "Attack us, would you?" he cried, stabbing and then racing around a tree to stab at someone else. "Ruin our stealthy approach to the Glittering City, hey? Well, pay the price, fools!" He stabbed a third time, and someone gurgled in reply.

"And dead men," Hawkril added gravely, hacking through a raised hand to slice open the throat behind it. On all sides there were crashings and cursing as the agile procurer swung around trees, kicked faces here and knees there, and danced among blades that never seemed quite swift enough to catch up with him.

"Who sent you?" he asked one man, as he drove his sword through the outlaw into a tree beyond.

The man coughed forth blood, sagged forward as Craer dragged his blade free, and moaned, "No one! Back from the wars . . . starving . . ."

"Well, so are we," the procurer snarled. "Go dine on Silvertree's soldiers, dogs!"

"You seem unusually agitated, friend," Hawkril observed, as he chopped aside branches to engage three outlaws. "Questions, orders—you sound like a swordmaster!"

"I *feel* like a swordmaster," Craer snarled, "surrounded by idiots! Can't these thickskulls go attack someone else?"

"Are we leaving any to mount such attacks?"

Hawkril inquired mildly, sending one opponent crashing back through a dead tree and in the same movement bringing his blade around to take out the throat of another.

It was at that moment they heard Embra's scream.

"No," Craer answered savagely, as he spun around and raced back through the trees. "Not a one!"

Sarasper put a hand on Embra's cheek from behind. Sargh, but she felt cold! He slipped one finger into her mouth and went to his knees beside her. Her shielding sighed away into nothingness as he did so, and he hissed a hasty curse and poured some of his own vitality into her. It wasn't bones knit or wounds banished she needed . . . it was the force of life itself restored to her, energy that each spell she worked was stealing from her. A weakness new to her, on the night they'd met. A wizard's curse, perhaps? Well, it almost had to be.

Embra moaned, under him. Sarasper felt weak and empty himself, now. Shuddering, he sank down atop her shoulders, smelling the sweet spice of her hair. Some guardian he was. Oh, to have strength to stand again! How could the lass *do* this, day after day? She must have the will of an angry dragon!

He heard the panting first and then the thud of running feet. Sarasper rolled over and saw a wild-eyed outlaw racing from the trees, sword out. "Least I'll . . ." the man gasped angrily, swerving toward the healer, ". . . get you!"

A sword stabbed down viciously. Sarasper kicked and twisted, and the blade sliced along his ribs as it slid into the stony ground beside him. The healer winced at the icy fire in his side and grabbed at the man's sword wrist. When the blade was snatched back out of the turf, the old healer was hauled up with it. He kicked out his heels, twisted, and the startled outlaw went over Sarasper's head with a cry. They rolled together across the rocks, and from somewhere near at hand Embra screamed.

"Bebolt and *blast* you!" the outlaw gasped. "We just wanted . . . food!"

"And our lives," Sarasper told him grimly, as he found the hilt of his belt knife at last, and drove it almost delicately into the man's left eye. "And our lives!"

The man stiffened under him, and then went limp. As Sarasper rolled away, gasping, he heard the thunder of a new pair of booted feet. These were much lighter and faster. "Craer?" he called.

"At your service," the procurer chuckled, "seeing as how you and Embra have taken care of things so well here."

The old healer rolled over and stared up at the cloudless blue sky. "Delnbone," he gasped, "if you and Grimthews have finished your merry butchery in the trees, I need some of your blood."

"You, too? That's what all of these dead men were after," Craer told him, kneeling down beside him, "and we weren't very gentle with them. Knowing that, answer right carefully: what do *you* want it for?"

"Keeping our lady sorceress alive," Sarasper grunted, before he passed out.

"By the Three!" Hawkril gasped, his face going pale. "I feel like . . . someone's torn out my insides and left me nothing!"

"That's what the Lady Silvertree's been feeling like with every spell she's cast," Sarasper said gruffly. "Now lie still sensibly, like she's doing. Just a moment more, and she'll have life enough to spelljump us again, away from here. Craer thinks those outlaws may have friends we haven't met, yet."

"Your thoughts, healer, always cheer me," the armaragor growled, and let the world fall away into darkness. . . .

* * *

"Not much of a map, is it?" one of the warriors grunted.

"You haven't gone out exploring to improve it yet, have you?" Rivryn replied crisply, lifting his head to glare at the man, who stepped back, muttering. Silence fell again, as they all stared at the scratches on the shield of a warrior who'd never need a shield again, now.

It was crude, yes, and only a small corner of the ruins of Indraevyn, but it was enough for them to see what stood where under all the trees and undergrowth. They were fairly certain, now, that their immediate surroundings were free of both lurking terrors (such as whatever had slain Nynter) and of promising surviving buildings to explore—though anything might be buried under fallen stones, or overgrown, or in hidden cellars underground.

"Less than promising," another Ornentarn warrior murmured. "Have we l—"

His words died away unspoken as the sentinel outside whistled two notes, and Rivryn's head snapped up. "All of them back," he reported a moment later, and the atmosphere of the room suddenly seemed less tense.

They came into the room in a weary line of ready-armed warriors, back from their "long ramble." In their midst was the older and more powerful of the two mages. Huldaerus, the Master of Bats, leaned down with a drawn dagger to carefully mark three new buildings on the shield. "These were the most promising sites we found," he announced to the silent room, then turned his head to look at the other wizard in the group. "Take you some warriors and have a look at the first— this one." His dagger tapped the shield.

"While you sit here safely guzzling wine, I suppose," Phalagh replied, looking up.

Huldaerus shrugged. "*I* went into danger," he said, waving a hand at the open doorway and the ruins beyond, "and now it's your turn. We dare not risk both of us at once—and so court the greater risk of leaving these good swordsmen mageless in this most dangerous of backwaters."

"No," Phalagh observed, rising with a sigh. "I suppose we dare not." He looked around at the faces of many not-quite-grinning warriors, and asked, "Which of you accompanied the Lord Wizard Huldaerus into these three ruins?"

Several warriors raised reluctant hands. Phalagh smiled. "Good—then you can now lead *me* into them."

There was a long silence before the first warrior shouldered out the door, and the others slowly began to follow. Phalagh ignored their growls of resentment, gave the room a tight smile, and strode out after them.

As the scrape of their boots on the rocks died away, Huldaerus looked at the map, and spoke to the nearest warrior without looking up. "Despite what happened to Lord Master Nynter," he said, "we've been here overlong without facing an attack. I need guards posted, in pairs, here and *here*. . . ."

"Once more," Sarasper said soothingly, his arms warm and gentle around a shivering Embra. "Just once more, and we're there."

"But this shouldn't be *happening* to me," Embra sobbed. "It's as if working magic is making me sick!"

Sarasper drew back her tunic to lay bare her shoulders, and Hawkril and Craer reached out grimly together to put their hands on her.

The Lady of Jewels steadied herself, drew in a deep breath, and held up another knickknack from her dwindling supply. She murmured something, made a complicated gesture with her free hand—and the world around the Four changed suddenly.

They stood now on a rocky knoll, with tilled fields on all sides of them—and the walls of Sirlptar in the distance. "I can see the gates," Craer murmured, more to lift Embra's spirits than for any other reason.

They stood together, the three ignoring Embra's feeble attempts to shake them free as Sarasper worked a magic of his own, stealing more energy from all three of them to strengthen the sorceress.

Craer gasped at the sudden weak emptiness in his guts. "Could this be the curse of the Silent House on the blood of Silvertree?" he asked.

"Or something cast by her father's mages?" Hawkril rumbled. Silence was the only reply to both questions.

Set free at last, Embra turned to face them, white to the lips, and snarled, "The same guises as in Adeln?"

Three nods gave her answer, and she dug out almost the last of the little magics from Silvertree House, in trembling hands, and set to work, touching Hawkril first—the others nodded in approval—then Craer, and then Sarasper. She fell limply against him before she could do any more, and started to slide toward the ground.

Wordlessly Hawkril extended his cloak. Sarasper and Craer wrapped the Lady of Jewels so as to conceal her face, the armaragor lifted her into his arms, and they set off toward the gates of the Glittering City.

Laughter rang off a ceiling in Castle Silvertree. "I can see through both eyes again!" Markoun Yarynd announced triumphantly to the baron, "and more than that: I've just seen, through farscrying, four folk enter Sirlptar—a tall warrior, a short man, and two others, one of them bundled up and being carried!"

Faerod Silvertree smiled. "Our little band of four fools," he purred. "Ingryl, alert my men there. It's time, and past time, for the slaughter of these three men my daughter's acquired. She'll be much more biddable when stripped of them and alone again."

"Done, Lord Baron," Ingryl murmured, turning back to his corner to work the necessary magics.

"'Twere best if the shielding and listening spells

were settled on Embra before the blood of her new-found play fellows starts to flow," the baron continued silkily. "See to it, won't you, Ingryl?"

"Indeed," the greatest of his wizards replied, without turning. "Klamantle has been working hard to ensure my success in such matters."

At this barbed comment Klamantle went red, and then white. He'd thought that the mental orders he'd just magically given his own personal agents in Sirlp-tar—to capture the mysterious third man of the four, for questioning—were his own secret. The accursed Spell-master must have woven some trickery into the spells that had just restored Klamantle's eyes to be able to read so much.

Fighting to make his face smooth and impassive again, he called up a mind-shielding spell, whispered its casting over the implements on his worktable, furiously wished Ingryl dead . . . and started to wonder just how to bring that death about.

The gate guards merely looked bored as the three men and their bundle entered; perhaps scores of women wrapped up in cloaks were carried into Sirlptar every day. All three conscious members of the Four had seen the crowded, narrow streets before. They patiently shoved their ways along the lanes, through the busy throngs of folk, in the shadows of the ever-present over-hanging balconies, enduring the smells and the din. The Glittering City seemed, if possible, more crowded and frenetic than ever, with many armed men—obvious outlanders among them—shouldering through the thick press of crowds and insistently calling vendors.

Hawkril caught sight of a banner and shook his head. "Bah," he said over his shoulder, as he started to clear a road for the others with his bulk, "you'd think the mas-ter bards would choose some quieter place for their Moot."

"Castle Silvertree, for instance?" Craer murmured in arch reply, but the noises around them were so loud that Hawkril heard him not. By unspoken agreement the three were heading for one of the oldest and shabbiest houses of accommodations in Sirlptar, one that welcomed armsmen more than others: the Wavefyre Inn. To fighting-men it had the attractions of good food, reasonable prices, never being quite full, and—for those who knew—of having many side entrances and back ways out. This was the inevitable result of years of success under proprietors who disposed of easy-stolen riches by purchasing the building next door, and then the one beyond that, breaking through walls to string everything together and leaving the ground floors rented to shopkeepers.

There was, however, just one "proper" entrance. As they mounted its worn steps, Sarasper said suddenly, "I hope someone has coins enough for our stay. I've a few oddments from Silvertree House, but explaining such things attracts far more attention than I'm fond of."

"Have no fears," Craer murmured almost jauntily. "Hawkril will provide."

The armaragor turned and gaped at him. "I *what*?" Swiftly scowling eyebrows drew together. "With what?"

"With this, Tall and Menacing," the procurer replied smoothly, plucking a gold coin from the cuff of the armaragor's boot and a handful more from under the knuckle plates of Hawkril's right gauntlet, and displaying them with a flourish.

Hawkril's jaw dropped—and then his lips quirked into a smile. "I was richer than I knew," he told the door of the inn, as he booted it open and turned to shield Embra from its return swing. "Perhaps our favorite procurer will enlighten me as to how long I've been carrying around such epicene wealth."

"Since Adeln," Craer replied merrily. "I couldn't risk being caught with them in my possession at the tavern I was stealing them in—and there you were, sitting like a patient mountain beside me, draining tankards like a horse at a water trough."

"While there *you* were," the armaragor replied, "stealing coins like Craer in any tavern I might name."

"No names, Tall and Mighty," the procurer said warningly, as they arrived at the inn desk together. "We're romantically involved, remember?"

"I was forgetting that, yes," Hawkril said heavily. "Help me remember, O ardent lord of my dreams, won't you?"

"By the Three," Sarasper muttered to the armaragor, "he does get going, doesn't he?"

"He always gets good rooms, though," Hawkril murmured. "Watch."

The procurer leaned close over the desk and murmured dark warnings to the stiff-faced clerks, tossed a few gold coins carelessly into their laps, accepted some looks of new respect, and was done.

"Act haughty and mysterious," he said out of the side of his mouth, as they went to the stairs. "We're high-ranking baronial agents, securing a private room for a *very* discreet meeting with certain high priests—and foreign envoys."

"Don't embellish," Hawkril grunted. "The only out-landers we know where to find hereabouts are lasses who remove overmuch of their clothing and dance in taverns."

"*That's* why I included them," Craer replied archly. "After all, one never knows, does one?"

"Sounds like you've already chosen your baronial motto to me," the armaragor grunted. "Now there's just this small matter of acquiring a barony . . ."

Three stairs rose out of the lobby. The southernmost, curving up the left wall, was the darkest and least used. With four loose keys in his fist, Craer led the way up two flights, to a small landing where a third flight ascended and two doors faced each other. He applied his key to the door on the right with an air of mischief, shrugged when it rattled in the lock but failed to open the door, and turned to the door on the left—the clearly marked door of the room they'd rented.

"Displayed enough cleverness yet?" Hawkril grunted. "This bundle grows no lighter as the hours pass!"

"Complaints, always complaints," the procurer murmured, as he peered out windows and pulled open doors in swift succession, his drawn sword in hand. At last he turned to face them and announced with a sigh, "It will serve."

"I'm glad of that," Hawkril replied in dry tones, "seeing as I've put the lass into this bed already."

For all his dash and dazzle, the procurer had missed seeing the door across the landing open a finger's width for a few moments and someone peer across the landing as the Four entered their room.

The someone was a man possessed of a weathered face, a short and close-trimmed beard, and a pleasant expression. He wore trail leathers of the sort favored by bards—and vagabonds. One eyebrow rose in surprised recognition ere he pulled his door closed again and was joined by a thoughtful frown as he shot the bolt.

The Lady Silvertree played at disguise the way most mages did: all folk enspelled together saw each other's true seeming, not the disguise provided by the magic for others to look upon. Her three sword-companions were obviously unaware that her magic had failed, and their true appearances were visible to every interested eye in Sirlptar. The Glittering City had far too many such eyes for the watcher's liking; he hoped the four who'd come all this way from the Silent House weren't going to learn a bloodily expensive lesson for their slip. And was the Lady Embra just asleep, or had some harm befallen her? That could well shatter her spells—and men unfamiliar with magic might not even realize this.

Behind his closed door, the bearded man had a sudden thought—or came to a decision. He spun around in haste and strode away.

Behind another closed door, Craer was checking the readiness of knives up this sleeve and that, and saying firmly, "The master bards are still meeting, Hawk. Your height makes you too easily recognized and remembered—so you must bide here, guarding Embra, and not show his face or hers outside yon door. All of the barons are sure to have spies and agents at work in the city right now."

Hawkril nodded, growling reluctantly, "I'll do so, but I'm setting a price: mind you bring me back a roast kleggard and a bottle of wine, at least, when you return."

He sat down on the largest chair in the room and laid his naked war sword ready across his knees as Craer and Sarasper made their promises. The procurer looked at the warrior settled into his chair and said, "Very impressive—but you've got to get up and bar the door behind us—the bar's in yon closet."

"Clever, aren't you?" Hawkril grunted, as he went to the closet.

As the procurer and the healer went out, they heard the bar rattle down into place. They traded grins as they clattered down the stairs and threaded their ways through the crowded Wavefyre common room to the street. "Bloody Droppa's Window?" Craer asked, not noticing a man in one corner of the room stare hard at him, then draw back and swiftly go elsewhere.

"It's still there?" Sarasper responded in delight. "Then of course!"

Sirlptar was a maze of hurrying people, rumbling carts, shouts and curses, and trotting dogs. The noisy, muddy streets were awash in a thousand smells, most of them particularly strong in the alleys and back passages Craer ducked down and hurried along, with Sarasper following trustingly in his wake.

As they descended toward the harbor, the streets

grew narrow and dirtier, and the alleyways more littered with all manner of rotting filth. It was a relief to the healer when they turned into a half-remembered street overhung with dripping washing, and slowed. Ahead, a shifting group of men were gathered around an unadorned window, in the side of a crumbling building that had probably begun its career as a warehouse.

The smells rolling out of that window, amid streamers of steam and smoke, made mouths water and throats tighten. Roast kleggard, horse, and what must be a mixed-fowl stew mingled with the seemingly perpetual stink of overscorched boar that both men's memories carried about the Window. The familiar crumbling clay pots and dirty sacks taken from grain hauling use because of holes, were also in evidence as customer after customer trotted away from the window laden with steaming supper.

When it was their turn, Craer ordered enough for six hungry armsmen with the muttered comment to Sarasper, "He eats for three, and we've got to keep her strength up, hey?" The healer was staggering under a hot, gravy-soaked sack when they made their own retreat from the Window. The procurer took one look at Sarasper's face and said, "I know an even shorter way. Come!"

They ducked into an alley that was so dark and narrow that it seemed almost like a tunnel. Almost immediately Craer bent low with his dagger and slashed a trip cord. Turning his head to the left, he snarled, "I've magic to burn you with!"

The empty threat seemed to work. Hastening in his wake, Sarasper saw eyes ducking away from a dark opening and almost missed seeing the procurer duck through another opening, into what seemed more a sewer than an alley. They splashed through filth for only a few steps before Craer turned sharply again, plunging into darkness.

"Slow *down!*" the healer panted.

"Daren't!" the procurer called back happily, as they mounted a slippery, stinking flight of stone steps that seemed to be climbing a rough dirt hillside of impromptu graves—some of them yawning open, waiting—under the floor of a building held above their hurrying heads by pillars crisscrossed with fading messages scrawled in fire ash.

"Death to all barons" was burned across "Death to all wizards," and there were names and cryptic symbols; Sarasper hadn't time to notice more before they reached another tunnellike passage, low under the overhanging building, where they had to scuttle along bent double. A dart hissed out of the darkness to strike, quivering, in a rotting wooden beam that was sagging down from the building; rats scurried toward it, in case it was something to eat.

Craer snarled, "My curse will find you!" but did not slow down to do so; panting, the healer caught up to him just as the passage ended on the lip of a stinking pit choked with kitchen offal, spoiled food, and human waste. The procurer ignored a forlorn figure stirring the fly-swarming mess with a stick in hopes of finding something, and ran along the edge of the midden to another slimy set of stone steps.

Sarasper rolled his eyes and followed. Their way led through several more noisome passages and stairs that the healer would have termed near-sewers had Craer tarried long enough to listen, and skirted a dozen or more open middens, before the procurer was forced to halt for a little local traffic.

It occurred when a gasping Sarasper judged they'd climbed a little more than half the way back up to the Wavefyre (which stood two streets over on the seaward side of the ridge that southern Sirlptar was built on), when they came to a space where refuse abounded and five twisting back lanes met.

Two men rose from behind mounds of rotting, rat-infested waste when the procurer and the healer were crossing the moot. Men with leather armor under their rags, who bore long, well-used knives in their hands, and wore unpleasant smiles.

"Give, friend, and live," one of them directed Sarasper, beckoning for the still-steaming sack.

"You've been to the Window," the other purred, hefting his knives menacingly. "Yield the sack."

Craer plucked up a handful of slimy, fly-haloed fruit and threw it almost casually into the face of the nearest man, then tripped him as he staggered back, shouting.

The second man rushed forward to stab and hack at the procurer, snarling curses, but Craer lured him back into a refuse mound and then sprang all around him slashing—until the slipping, sliding knife man was streaming blood from half a dozen gashes and was starting to gasp and go pale.

Then Craer plucked up a length of rusting pipe from the rubble and swung it in a great arc from his knees right around until he'd turned, shoulders and all, to cleave air. Somewhere in the midst of that swing he struck the man's arm, and a knife went clanging and whirling away. The man staggered, clutching at his hand—and the backswing of the pipe met the side of his head. He fell on his face, in silence.

The other man was snarling vicious curses as he wiped streaming eyes, but Craer smiled at him across the steaming sack and warned, "Back off, friend, and live."

The man glared at the grinning procurer, eyed the food and the knife that had appeared like spell's work in Craer's hand—and was now poised for throwing—and then ducked away down an alley.

"By the Three!" Sarasper gasped. "That was . . . too . . . cl— Craer? *Craer!*"

The procurer uncurled out of a nearby window with three bottles of wine splayed in one hand and grinned at his comrade. "Look what just fell into my hands! Folk are *so* careless about where they leave things! Can I keep them?"

"For about an hour, I'd say," the healer replied in very dry tones, jerking his head in an insistent "move on!" gesture. "Try to leave a little for the rest of us to drink, eh?"

They hastened up streets that were more flights of steps than anything else, and plunged into one of the gatherings where merchants met to trade odd ends of goods, settle debts, and plan future prosperity. Snatches of excited talk came to their hurrying ears as they scuttled around and between grandly gesticulating men.

"Well, *I* say that we'll have war again, and soon! Just yester—"

"Can't be, Nolos; even wizards can't be in two castles at once. If las—"

"—mages coming from all over Darsar, I've heard, to some ruin far upriver. Something about the Sleeping King—p'raps they've found his tomb, all full of magic! Wouldn't th—"

"That Silvertree, now: I've heard he's planning how to seize the city itself! Aye, right here, and he'll tear down most of Helder Street to build himself a soaring castle atop everything! Won't *that* be—"

Behind two fat and bearded perfume dealers, two men in long cloaks stiffened at the sight of the hurrying pair and abandoned the comfortable pillar they were lounging against to move in the same direction as the supper bundle. As they went, they clasped sword hilts to keep scabbarded blades from knocking into the oblivious merchants crowded around.

"Aglirta doesn't need *that* sort of king! Armsmen torching cottages by night, and slave-chaining up everyone who so much as looks back at them—I don't *think* so! We'll end up as bad as—"

* * *

It was a long way from Castle Silvertree, but Daerentar Jalith and Lharondar Laernsar had no difficulty remembering the baron's blunt orders. Their constantly tingling bodies reminded them with each step they took and every twitch their limbs made—spasms that were unpleasantly new to them and had begun to foster in them the beginning of respect for wizards. If working magic was like this, no wonder most mages were right bastards.

Daerentar's head snapped around. Was that—? *Yes.*

He clapped a hand on Lharondar's arm, and pointed, using only his head. A moment later, the two spell-bearing warriors were moving carefully through the crowd after the agile little procurer and the old man trudging along with the sack. Two fools whose fates mattered not a whit—but who couldn't be cut down until they led the way to the Lady Silvertree.

They crossed Arn Lane, and then Belzimurr's Way, turning up a nameless alley that crested the ridge and dropped down into Stamner's Street. It was in the alley that it became obvious to the baron's best blades that others were following the renegade pair. Well, no wonder. Kidnapped or no, if the Lady of Jewels could be turned against her father, any baron of the Vale would dearly love to have her spells bent to his causes.

The procurer and the old man with the sack slowed as they came to the gates of the Wavefyre Inn horseyard. Hard against its posts stood a small knot of men—three bards, including the well-known Rhaerandul of the Lute, standing listening to a youngish, handsome man in black robes adorned with runes that meant the man was either a powerful mage . . . or wanted all who looked upon him to think he was.

"Who—?" one of the cloaked warriors asked a merchant who'd tarried to listen, too.

"A mage of Elmerna, staying yon," the merchant muttered, inclining his head at the inn. "Jaerinsturn, he's called." A second jerk of his head indicated that his own words were done, and the words of the mage should now be heeded.

"... it must have been a mage sitting in the front chamber of the House of the Raised Hand, or someone he commanded," Jaerinsturn was saying grimly. "I was there; perhaps thirty of us heard, perhaps more. Yezund set forth his entire deduction—I don't think I can recall the entire spread of his argument, but we all heard the conclusion clearly enough: Candalath, the Stone of Life, lies now in the ruined city of Indraevyn. For speaking thus, Yezund died; none of us knew that he entertained any foes nor feuds—nor anything much at all. He wielded no power, his manner was not unpleasant, he owed no monies, either here or back in Elmerna . . . someone wanted him dead so their rush to seize the Stone of Life would not meet failure because Yezund, armed with whatever secrets he hadn't yet babbled, got to the Worldstone first."

"The Dwaerindim, power to set the world afire, power to raise it up," one of the bards breathed a few lyrics of a ballad, and the others nodded.

"I've just heard something more," another of the bards said then, in a deep, mellifluous voice. "Ghonkul at the House of Tomes over on Claremmon Street is a friend of mine. He tells me only three of their books even mention Indraevyn, only one of those was ever rented—and that, somehow, all three tomes have been stolen during these last two days!"

Craer tugged at Sarasper's arm, and they ducked around the group and went into the yard.

Several other listeners, moving at more idle paces, followed.

"Food?" Hawkril grunted, as he set the bar against the wall and held the door wide.

"Of course," Craer said excitedly, as he and Sarasper bustled into the room. "Warriors think of nothing else."

"That's because someone has to think of the practical," the burly armaragor growled, "while all of you oh-so-clever sorts are thinking all manner of useless witticisms and pranks and suchlike. I'm not blind, Craer— you're bursting with more of it right now."

"With *news*, Hawk," the procurer corrected, almost happily. "Listen: there's a mage from Elmerna down at the gates, telling everyone who stops—and three bards at least have—that the wizard Yezund declared that Candalath, the Stone of Life, is in the ruined city of Indraevyn! Yezund was murdered for saying so! Ther—"

Hawkril firmly closed and barred the door again, and so the three conscious members of the Four never saw the door across the landing abruptly swing open. Had they been standing watching, they'd have seen a pleasant-looking man in trail-leathers, who sported a short, neat beard, stride out onto the landing while a pair of very odd objects descended to the floor inside his room.

Those objects were floating, obviously magical silvery spheres, their surfaces shimmering rainbows of iridescence wherever they reflected back the dim stair lanterns. They were fading in both size and brightness as they sank floorward, but scenes sparkling in their depths were still clearly visible. One held a view of the inside of the Band of Four's room (complete with faint echoes of Craer's taletelling), and the innards of the other showed the bottom of the flight of stairs their owner was now standing at the head of. In the darkening scene in the sphere, several fighting-men were mounting the lowest steps, blades half drawn and held ready. The bearded man descended to the topmost step and stopped with his hands on both stair rails, blocking the way.

Moments later, he heard the expected thud of boots whose owners had opted for haste over stealth, and the stair was suddenly boiling with warriors.

The foremost saw the man in leathers, squinted menacingly up the stairs, and brandished two long and gleaming feet of sharp steel before snarling, "Get out of the way!"

The figure at the head of the stairs gave him a wintry smile and replied calmly, "No, I think not. Your better course would be to turn around and depart this house— for good."

The squinting man looked both astonished and delighted, and there were wolfish smiles on other faces down the stairs, too, as blades in plenty promptly sang out of scabbards. There was some shuffling among the leading warriors, so that three could stand abreast on the stairs and menace this lone, unarmed man who barred their way.

The man gave them a patient smile. Eyes narrowed as some of the warriors wondered if they faced a wizard—or a half-wit—but they extended their swords in glittering array and advanced a step up the stair . . . and then another. Swords drew back a little for the thrusts that would come with their next step, and some warriors in the second rank extended their blades over the shoulders of the foremost warriors, all of them bent on carving up the lone man who opposed them.

That lone man bent over to meet their advance, smiled broadly, and spat something into their midst— something that burst into a cloud of spreading greenish vapor. There were startled shouts, and then coughing, and steel rang against the steps and railings as warriors scrambled to move—and then reeled, or stumbled, and fell where they stood. A breath later, and they were all sliding back down the steps in a limp flood marked by echoing crashings of armor upon steps and stairposts and other armor.

The man in leathers calmly picked his way among the fallen, plucking up daggers here and swords there. Wherever he found buckles he could wrest away from their belts, he took them too—men whose breeches won't stay up are seldom eager to swagger into a fight. When his steely armfuls grew too heavy, the man in leathers tossed them, in their own series of small clangs and crashings, down the laundry chute, whose door opened onto a landing. When every weapon he could see was stripped from the senseless warriors, he applied the toes of his boots to their limp bodies, rolling them into boneless journeys down the next flight of stairs. Then he sprang back up the steps in a few uncannily quiet bounds and slipped back into his room.

In the brief instant before his door closed again, anyone who'd stood on the empty landing would have seen the two silver spheres brighten and begin to rise from the floor again.

On the other side of the closed and barred door across that landing, a sleepy-eyed Embra was pulling herself up to a sitting position against her pillows as Craer enthusiastically finished his tale: ". . . so it seems the Three have practically handed us one of the Dwaerindim—on the heels of meeting Sarasper, look you! Can there be any doubt what we must do next?"

There had been a time—as recently as four days ago—when Hawkril would unhesitatingly have followed Craer wherever the procurer's quick wits and slick tongue led them. Now, however, his eyes flickered in the midst of enthusiastically agreeing, with one bite gone from the gravy-dripping roast kleggard in his hand . . . and he looked to the wan-eyed, tangle-haired woman on the bed.

Embra licked dry lips, and the room fell suddenly silent. She looked around at the three men awaiting her words, and a smile flickered for a moment about her lips. "I had forty servants," she said in a voice raw from disuse, "but now I have three friends. Much better."

She sat up and seemed to gain both strength and excitement together. "I can spelljump us all to about a mile distant from Indraevyn."

Sarasper lifted one busy eyebrow. "You can? How is it that you know any locale deep in the Loaurimm Forest?"

The Lady of Jewels gave him a weak smile. "You're a nasty, suspicious old man, Sarasper. One of my tutors liked to go swimming in waters more warm and placid than the Coiling, and in years gone by we often practiced spelljumping to Lake Lassabra, called by some—"

"'The Sheet of Mists,'" Hawkril interrupted, causing three heads to turn his way in surprise. The armaragor looked back at them and shrugged. "There's a ballad," he explained rather apologetically.

"Lady Embra," Sarasper said then, "are you sure you should try such a thing? Every spell you work seems to bring you a stride closer to death."

"Aye," Craer agreed. "Shouldn't y—"

Embra held up one hand in an imperious "heed me" gesture and followed it with a long look and the words, "Think, friends, how many spells I might have to cast if we trudge and fight all the long and winding way upriver, *through* Silvertree—only to find that one of the countless other mages who's heard Yezund's tale by now jumped to the ruin long since, found the Stone of Life, and is off raising an army of loyal walking dead or suchlike with it."

"Sargh, *yes!*" Craer burst out, at about the same time as Hawkril muttered, "Graul," under his breath. The three men looked at each other, and with the next moment, the room erupted into a whirlwind of repacking and slinging packs and crowding together, punctuated by Hawkril's loud complaint that he'd had just *one* swallow of what looked to be a gods'-blessed good hot meal, and he'll never—

A raw, feminine scream of pain echoed through the middle floor of the Wavefyre Inn—a scream that abruptly cut off, leaving empty silence behind. There came a soft footfall outside the room whence that cry had erupted, a discreet knock, an attempt to quietly open its barred door, and then a small, silvery twinkle of light at the keyhole. A miniature eyeball floated out of that light, drifted briefly about the room peering hither and yon, and then withdrew with a satisfied air.

Hard on the heels of its disappearance came a sudden uproar from below, as the common room erupted in tumult. Out of the din came shouts, the ring of drawn steel, and the thunder of hurrying, running boots with heavy men in them.

Men who had awakened bewildered and shamefaced on the stairs not long ago were back, fresh weapons in their hands and new allies at their sides—hard-faced ruffians who shouldered aside angry inn patrons and staff alike to begin a breakneck, crashing race up the stairs. Most waved drawn swords, but a few carried large cutters' axes, to deal with any barred doors that might stand ahead.

Where their way had been barred before, the stairs and landing beyond were empty. One door opening off it stood open, the room beyond empty and dark. The other was closed and barred.

Men snarled, other men shouldered to the front, and a rain of heavy ax-blows fell upon the door, biting deeply. Again the axes fell, and again, before the first splinters fell away and impatient hands were thrust through the rents in the door to snatch up the bar inside, and let it topple away harmlessly.

Armed men burst into the room in a snarling, menacing flood and darted to every corner, closet, and chamber beyond. Of the four people they were seeking, not one was to be found—Lharondar's curses rang off the walls—but the air was heavy with the rich smells of hot roast and dripping, and in their raging midst stood a bed still warm and hollowed from the body that was no longer lying in it . . . a body whose spicy perfume at least one of the furious swordsmen had smelled before: the mystic scent of the sorceress Lady Embra Silvertree, as he was helping her down from a horse after a ride through the forest on Silvertree Isle.

11

Crowded Shores and Ruins

*I*n Castle Silvertree, three mages stiffened in unison. "That was her!" Markoun gasped.

"Your daughter, Lord Baron," Spellmaster Ambelter said gravely, "is in Sirlptar, at a place I don't recognize—an inn . . . which stands on the seaward flank of Southsnout Ridge."

"Get there," the baron snapped as he sat bolt upright in the chair he'd been lounging in, his eyes lighting like two flames of fury. "Get there *now,* and slay her companions. Bring her back here at once." He rose like a black whirlwind, snatched a whip down off the wall, and stalked out of the room, cracking it savagely in the air.

The three mages exchanged looks. Then Klamantle and Markoun darted to the tray on the table in front of the baron's vacant chair. Snatching aside its glass dome, they plucked strands of the Lady Embra's hair from the small and untidy pile it guarded and hurried to the balcony.

Ingryl hastened along in their wake but found no room left on the balcony to stand and work magic. He watched the younger mages conjure giant-size nightwyrms, leap astride them, and flap away. In their wake, he strode out onto the balcony and waved his hands in frantic spellcasting gestures—until the racing nightwyrms had dwindled out of sight in the bright sky downriver.

Then the Spellmaster let his hands fall, went to the small glass forest of decanters on the sideboard, and unhurriedly poured himself a drink.

"Fools," he told the room with a smile, and sipped at his glass.

"Hmmph; clumsily poisoned," he said consideringly a moment later, rolling the liquid around in his mouth. "Makes it burn a bit."

Ingryl shrugged, swallowed, and poured himself more.

On the shore of Lake Lassabra, in the early hours after noon, Embra Silvertree was on her knees, gasping and shuddering in pain. The bright sun had driven the mists that normally cloaked its placid waters away, leaving it a sheet of still blue amid the encircling trees. Trees that might hide any number of sorcerous foes.

Sarasper was kneeling beside the Lady of Jewels, awkwardly cradling her shaking shoulders. "Has working magic always hurt—*drained*—you like this?"

Tears flew as she shook her head . . . and convulsions wracked her again.

A blue-and-white glow occurred about Sarasper's fingers as he called up magic that would drain some of his own life energy into the woman in his arms. It passed out of him silently, leaving him feeling weak and sick. Hands trembling, he almost lost his hold on Embra's suddenly heavier body—as she collapsed with a gasp, head lolling in senselessness.

Sarasper let her down onto the ground as gently as his weak arms allowed, sighed, and looked up grimly at the procurer and the armaragor. Craer and Hawkril were licking their fingers after devouring the meal from

the Window—the *entire* meal, the shares that should
have been Sarasper's and Embra's included—in gob-
bling haste.

Just now, Sarasper was too weary to care. "If this
goes on," he told them quietly, "we may need this Stone
of Life just to provide her magic enough, every day, to
keep her alive."

"So she stops using magic," Hawkril rumbled flatly.
"Completely. Right now, while we go looking for this
Stone—that is, if it's anything more than a wizard's
wild tale."

"Someone believed that wizard well enough to kill
him for it," Craer said quietly, "and burn down his
house, no doubt to cover the signs of their ransacking
it."

"She needs shelter," Sarasper said sharply, looking
around at the unbroken line of trees. "Where, exactly, is
this ruined library from here?"

"In an abandoned city, Indraevyn by name, about a
mile away, Embra said," Craer replied. "In which direction, I know not, but—"

"I'll wager it's where yon war band is heading,"
Hawkril said calmly, pointing. A little way around the
curving lakeshore—not all that far away—a line of men
in armor, interspersed with a few in robes with shields
strapped to their backs and breasts, were coming into
view through the reeds and bushes, walking cautiously.
The armaragor saw their heads turn to regard the Four
and slowly drew his sword.

"If we tarry here overlong, they'll get to this city
first," Craer snapped. "Come *on!*"

"I suspect the ruins are crawling with eagerly searching wizards already," Sarasper said, watching the procurer almost dance with mounting impatience, "and we
have a burden to care for, no?"

"Wake her," Craer replied, not unkindly. "We haven't
time to wait. All it takes is one mage who knows what
he's doing to get his hands on this Stone before we do,

and we'll be just a few more twisted corpses in the huge pile of victims who dared stand in his way."

"Oh, there's no need to wait that long to become twisted corpses," Hawkril rumbled casually—and suddenly turned with the speed of a striking snake and lunged, thrusting his blade deep into the thick green wall of a crow's-apple bush. There was a shriek of startled pain, and the shrubs around erupted with the thud of rushing feet, a volley of curses, and charging hide-cloaked figures.

Hawkril fell back hastily, his sword dark and wet with blood, and Sarasper snapped out a few strange words and tossed a token he'd plucked from somewhere in the breast of his tunic into the air. Craer saw that it was a triangle made of three interwoven, miniature swords in the instant before it vanished in a flare of magical radiance—but he barely saw that brief shower of light give birth to a trio of floating, spectral longswords as he sprang to meet their attackers, with sword and dagger drawn.

There were eight in all, he judged, and none of them had been in the band they'd seen walking along the shore. These men wore the worn hides and mottled, drab-hued cloaks, tunics, and ragged breeches of foresters—but they stumbled and swayed off balance as they ran, like armsmen used to weapons practice in courtyards, not men at ease among stumps and soft mosses underfoot. Moreover, as Sarasper's conjured swords flashed through the air to hack and parry, slashed jerkins revealed the dark gleam of armor beneath.

Hawkril tripped one foe, put his blade into the throat of another, danced back to chop at the neck of the man he'd tripped, and then rushed forward to lock blades with, and hurl aside, a third false forester.

He'd fought as frantically before. On the Isles, yes, but when he was younger, too . . . in that hollow full of treacherous priestesses, for one. . . .

* * *

As he fought his way to stand over his baron at last, the Golden Griffon stared up at him with darkening, failing eyes. There was blood on Ezendor Blackgult's rueful lips.

"You . . . right, Hawk," the man he loved more than all the world struggled to say,

". . . but too late . . ."

Hawkril ruined the baron's agonized speech by blowing the second, brighter horn from his belt, as hard as he could, as he swung his blade in another great circle.

A priest tried to tackle his knees, and the armaragor clubbed the man's nose into oblivion with the horn before tossing it into another holy face; its job was done.

The singing in the air that marked the collapse of the spell shield across the entire hollow came an instant later—and Hawkril had the healing vial out and to his lord's lips in the instant after that. Then he tore away his codpiece, snatched out the second vial, slapped it into the baron's hand, and turned to stand astride the Golden Griffon and keep him alive for the next few frantic minutes until the other armaragors arrived.

Or until the spells of the furious priestesses of the Huntress claimed the lives of everyone in the hollow. There was a flash and a roar, and limp holy bodies were hurled in all directions. Hawkril cursed loud and long; he'd given orders that were very blunt and even more clear that the horn-helmed women were to be cut down the moment the spell shield was raised—but someone had failed to get far enough, or been distracted by leather-clad beauty, or—

A second flash spattered the hulking armaragor with blood and dirt and ploughed a huge trench in the soil that stabbed at the moaning baron—but just failed to reach him.

These priestesses obviously didn't care how many fellow holy exalted clergy of the Lady they slew. Hawkril saw one of them caught in a ring of armaragors, glaring at him from afar—and then there was a different sort of flash, and the world became a place of white mist, sparks, and muffled sound, where Hawkril stood over his fallen master, and the priestess hovered above them both, with no one else to be seen. From somewhere outside, a sword stabbed into the mists and melted away into smoke as it came, until a bladeless hilt was drawn back.

The priestess had a sword, however, and she swooped down at Hawkril and stabbed at his face. Hawkril saw what she was about, and instead of ducking away he caught her blade with his own, forced them both past his nose, and brought his parry far to the left, overbalancing, so that she tumbled helplessly past the baron instead of getting a clear thrust at him.

The meeting of their blades gave birth to swarms of swirling sparks, and Hawkril surged through them to meet her next dive with a parry that bound their blades together. Nose to nose they struggled, and the furious priestess snarled, "You risk being damned by the Lady, warrior! I have only to name you before the Lady! Stand aside—you were forbidden to enter the hollow!"

"How so?" Hawkril roared back. "My Lord the baron agreed to attend a parley alone and unarmed! I attended a battle, as I am trained to do—aiding one man, who stood alone against the treachery of eighty! Who are you to forbid or to damn?"

"I have but to say the words," the priestess purred as they spun around each other, blades locked together, muscles straining against magic, "and your life will no longer be worth living."

"Loyalty makes life worth living, priestess," Hawkril blazed back. "And keeping one's word, and standing by comrades. Priests and gods may fail to help, or be revealed in deceit and corruption, but swordbrothers dare not cross each other. We prefer to die rather than fail each other!"

He was shouting now, as her surging magic forced him back. "Gods fail," he bellowed at her, "but honest men prevail!"

"A pretty speech," the priestess sneered, as Hawkril's blade exploded in a shower of sparks, and her own sword darted at him, "but none can withstand a true servant of the Huntress!"

An armored hand took her by the throat, then, and tightened.

"I think it's been some time," Baron Blackgult remarked cheerfully, "since you've been a true servant of the Huntress." His fingers closed, the priestess sobbed forth blood and fell on her face on the trampled ground, and the mists and sparks melted away together.

The dying priestess thrashed briefly and lay still. Hawkril snatched up her blade to defend his baron— and then they stood together in silence, Blackgult and Anharu, and looked across a field of butchery. There was no one left to fight.

Here and there men of Blackgult raised bloody swords in salute. The hollow was awash in the blood of Sharaden worshipers.

The Golden Griffon put his arm around the shoulders of his armaragor—he had to reach up to do it—and said thickly, "Most loyal Anharu, I live because of you. If ever you stand in similar need, I'll return the favor, or submit myself willingly to the damnation of the Lady these unholy ones were so swift to invoke. I bind myself in this!"

His voice dropped, he gasped for air, and he added, "And now, Hawkril, let's find something copious to drink!"

"Lord," Hawkril murmured, as they staggered across the fallen together, feeling the smart of their wounds in *earnest now,* "*you always boldly snatch at wisdom. Behold your latest great idea.*"

On a battlefield bereft of priestesses but holding no less blood and desperation, Craer leaped high into the air to kick an enemy face, and then shoved the staggering man back into the reach of Sarasper's whirling spellblades. He saw two foresters desperately parrying the darting swords—but the man he'd introduced to them had no blade up and ready to fend off steel. A leaping spellblade made short and bloody work of the man's face; as he gurgled and fell, the conjured sword that had slain him started to fade away.

By then, the procurer had grown tired of trading slashing parries with a false forester who was taller, stronger—and angrier. The man seemed to like launching huge backhand slashes, so Craer lured the man into one with a feigned stagger that became a somersault forward under the forester's sweeping blade.

He landed hip to hip with the man, but another foe— the man Hawkril had hurled aside—was temptingly close, staggering and facing away from Craer. The procurer leaped, thrust his dagger into the man's throat, and dragged it back and to the right, tearing open the man's neck and turning him into the path of the man who liked to slash so enthusiastically. Halting or turning aside slashes, it was immediately and bloodily apparent, was something the tall false forester needed rather more practice at.

Craer was already spinning away, his dagger trailing a bright arc of blood, to confront two more foes—a pair of foresters who were advancing on him in careful, menacing unison.

Somewhere to his right, Hawkril had trotted carefully around the dancing spellblades to reach the two foresters struggling against the flying fangs, and was now slashing enthusiastically at their faces, seeking to distract them from their parries. One of them was a little too slow in frantically batting away one of the swooping swords—and the armaragor's blade slid into his throat.

He choked, gagged, and spewed forth a rush of blood, and was still staggering vainly toward Hawkril, eyes darkening, when his brother forester moaned in fear and fled . . . straight at Craer.

Hawkril cried a warning, and the procurer obligingly faded out of the way, allowing the terrified man to blunder right into the heart of the careful attack being launched by his two fellows.

The spellblades raced after the man as Sarasper rose to his feet, letting Embra sag against his shins, to direct his spell at the last few foresters.

Hawkril felled the dying forester with a backhand slash as he broke into a lumbering run after the spellblades. The other foresters were backing away in the face of this magical menace, and Hawkril had little stomach for long, gasping chases through the trees—into who-but-the-Three knew what ambushes or encampments. So he hurled his blade, sidearm, at forester ankles. It found only one pair—but that man obligingly crashed to the ground, and the whirling spellblades settled on him in a bloody storm.

The fleeing forester never slowed to stand with his fellows but plunged on into the trees now, and Craer saw the danger an escaped foe could bring down on them.

"Take care of this!" he shouted to Hawkril, and bounded after the man, the crashings of his running feet in the leaves fading swiftly into the distance.

The last forester was backing away, swinging his blade in a defensive wall to keep Hawkril and the last spellblade at bay. Patiently the hulking armaragor and the flying sword pressed the man, driving him in retreat around trees and up slopes, deadwood, and stumps.

As the spellblade moved out of sight, Sarasper grew

increasingly pale and clutched at his temples with fingers that soon became steely claws. The healer trembled, blundered to his knees, and then collapsed with a gasp, sweating profusely; somewhere in the forest his awareness sank into a yellow fog of bedazement as his last spellblade dissolved. He'd sent it voyaging farther than many a worker of spells, but there were no prizes for such things, and he had one more task to do, to cling to life. . . .

On hands and knees, almost overwhelmed by weakness and waves of utter exhaustion, Sarasper crawled back to where Embra lay.

"Lady," he murmured, when he got there. "Lady Silvertree! Lady Embra, hear me!" Falling on his face beside her with a groan, the aging healer reached out and slapped her cheeks gently, calling out her name over and over with what little energy he had left. He must revive her before fainting himself, lest the other war band from the lakeshore should come upon them, and find two senseless, helpless victims, suitable slaying for but a single careless dagger thrust each. . . .

On a hillock between two gigantic gnarled trees, the looping, thrusting spellblade shimmered and was gone. The forester barked out a single guffaw of triumph—in the instant before Hawkril smashed their blades together, used his grander size and weight to force both locked weapons upward, and charged forward until their bodies met and the armaragor could bear them both to the ground.

They landed hard, and the breath whooshed out of the grunting, writhing forester, but this was to the death, and two strong sets of hands grappled each other and snatched at sheathed daggers with equal enthusiasm. Hawkril had chosen his ground well: two moss-covered stones small enough to use lay near at hand, where he'd espied them before making his takedown. He plucked one up as they twisted and strained against each other and brought it down with vicious force. The first blow

mashed the dagger-holding fingers of his foe, and the
forester's nose broke under the second. Armaragors
won no victories with gallantry—and to true fighting
men, with no courtiers' ransoms to claim, victory meant
life, and so was everything.

The forester flinched, blinded by his own blood, and
Hawkril backhanded the gurgling man across the face,
wrested away the man's sword, and snatched up his
own blade to bring its pommel crashing down on the
forester's temple. His foe sagged back, senseless.

The armaragor retrieved all the weapons he could
see, hoisted his foe onto his shoulder, and brought him,
dangling, back to Sarasper and Embra.

He found them both sprawled unconscious on the
ground and dropped his burden none too gently in his
haste to make sure neither the healer nor the sorceress
lacked breath or sported wounds that he could see. He
was relieved to find that they both seemed peacefully
asleep.

"Fine guardian you are," he grumbled to the gently
snoring Sarasper, and set about making his foe helpless.
An indecently thorough search for weapons yielded a
needle knife from the forester's boot and another that
had been hidden down the back of his sword scabbard.
These were foresters' weapons?

Shaking his head, Hawkril removed the man's boots
and belt, wrapped the belt around one hairy ankle, and
then used it, by way of a tree limb and the other ankle,
to hang the man upside down. Something fell out of the
man's clothing to sway and dangle below his head on a
thong.

Hawkril made a face. If that was the man's purse, he
didn't work for a generous master. He plucked it away
from around the man's ears, laid it on the ground, and
stripped away the thong to tie the man's thumbs and
smallest fingers together, at full stretch over the
forester's head.

All of these false foresters, it seemed, were wearing—under cloaks and tunics that had probably come from true foresters they'd slain—leather coats pierced with many rings that held odd plates of salvaged armor to them. Hawkril yanked his captive's tunic and armor coat down over the man's head. He looked at the dangling man for a moment, then nodded and emptied the purse out onto a rock.

"Hardly worth it," Craer commented, as he reappeared through the trees, wearing a satisfied look. "A few copper blestrans, one silverstar, and—hmm: a badge of Cardassa. Well, that saves us the time of questioning this fellow—this lot must be Baron Cardassa's attempt to seize the Stone . . . or part of it; I suspect a wizard or two lurking about somewhere."

Hawkril looked at his dangling captive again, and then at Embra and Sarasper. "And now?" he asked, gesturing at them, himself, and the procurer.

Craer shrugged. "Indraevyn must lie *that* way, if the war band we saw yonder was heading for it. The best thing we can do is get away from here—off *that* way—and fast, in case they come around the end of the lake and decide to just butcher us. From there, we can strike out thus, and hopefully circle around to come at the ruins from another way."

"All too good a way to get lost," Hawkril said slowly.

"Preferable to walking into an attack by armed folk expecting us?" Craer returned. "I think not."

"And if we miss the ruins entirely, and blunder around in this forest? It stretches for miles; 'endless,' they call it," Hawkril growled.

The procurer shrugged again. "If we go not overfar," he said in a low voice, "and keep quiet before dusk, the fires and sounds made by these others will at least tell us where *they* are—and some of them must be in or at the ruins by now. After we've gone a little way, we'll try to wake Embra. Now—when I signal by waving this

sword, bring Embra and then Sarasper to me, as quietly
as you can."

Craer took up the sword Hawkril had seized from his
captive and moved off through the trees, heading away
from the lake. When he and the armaragor could only
just see each other through green gloom and tangled
trunks, he made sweeping circles with the blade.

Hawkril obediently scooped up Embra, carried her to
Craer, and returned for Sarasper. The bound captive still
dangled unconscious, but the man's handful of coins
had vanished from the rock where he'd dumped them
out. The armaragor's mouth quirked onto a smile;
Craer, no doubt.

The procurer had laid the sword on the ground pointing in the direction the war band they'd seen earlier had
been heading, and was now at work trying to gently
awaken Embra. Craer was whispering her name, touching the cold metal coins he'd acquired from the rock to
her cheek, forehead, and the back of her hand, and
stroking her wrists and chin gently but repeatedly.
Frowning, Hawkril leaned near, watching—as, at last,
the eyes of the sorceress flickered open. She was white
to the lips, and looked dazed as she stared around, not
seeming to recognize her companions.

"Can you walk?" Craer asked gently.

The Lady of Jewels frowned—a puzzled frown that
suddenly deepened into irritation. "Of course I can
walk, procurer," she snapped. "I'm weary, not addled or
crippled!"

She brushed aside his hands, stood up—and
promptly fell over.

"Is this some sort of high style practiced in the court
of Silvertree?" Craer teased, as his swift arms caught
the sorceress and kept her standing. "Some intricate
courtesy above mere commoners?"

"Craer," Embra and Hawkril said in heartfelt unison,
"closebelt thy tongue." Their eyes met in shared startle-

ment at having inadvertently felt the same sentiment at the same time. Hawkril grunted, shuffled his feet, and looked away.

Embra impatiently pulled free of the procurer's grasp, took a few strides to have room enough to twirl about with hands on hips, and snapped, "Of *course* I can walk, Craer—what's the point of all these games?"

Craer held up his hand in a gesture that at once both warded wrath and requested patience and used his other arm to point through the trees. "If where we left the lake lies yon, Lady, how judge you lies ruined Indraevyn from it?"

The sorceress frowned and then pointed. "About a mile in that direction."

The procurer quickly crouched and turned the sword on the ground to point exactly as Embra was. Then he looked up from it and told her, "You and I walk as far as we can and still remain where Hawkril can see us. He gestures to us to move this way, or that, until we're in line with the sword. Then I lay *my* blade down to point at where he's walking from, and we stay still as he carries Sarasper and the sword to us. When he reaches us, we do it all over again; I take the sword he brings in place of my own, and so on. Thus we walk more or less in the direction we intend. We've moved far enough from the water that we should go past the ruin, so as to come up to it on the far side."

"Where foes may be fewer, though we'd still best beware guards," Embra agreed, nodding in admiration of the forester's trick he'd described. "I fear half the mages in Aglirta, and more besides, are hurrying here to snatch the stone, if they can."

Craer nodded. "Have you any idea what's harming you when you use magic?"

Embra lifted her slender shoulders in a shrug. "A curse, perhaps. The work of Father's mages, almost certainly."

"Will killing them end the curse?" Hawkril rumbled.

They both turned to look at him in surprise for a moment before Embra nodded slowly. "It would, yes, I believe it would—if all who had a hand in its casting were slain."

He gave her a slow and silent nod in return, before turning to Craer and gesturing to him to begin moving where the swords pointed. As the procurer and the sorceress moved off through the forest together, all three conscious members of the Four wore thoughtful looks.

They spent the afternoon proceeding as Craer had directed. It was some time before Sarasper regained wakefulness, though his face was creased with a head pain, and he stumbled weakly instead of striding. Once they heard a brief commotion of battle—cries, the clash of steel, and an echoing spell blast—but during all that quiet journey they saw no living thing larger than a slinking tree cat.

The day wore on, and the time came when they must make a turn, and they did so, halting only when Embra lifted a hand and said softly, "Indraevyn must lie there, and stretching that way, before us."

Craer and Hawkril looked to their weapons; Embra felt around her person for the remaining enchanted House knickknacks she'd need to power any spells she might have to cast.

"It would be best," Sarasper murmured warningly, at her elbow, "if you cast no magic that is not desperately needful."

She looked back at him. "It would," she agreed gravely. "See to it, then, that my need is not desperate."

The healer grinned and spread his hands in an open, helpless gesture. They shrugged in unison, then started toward the ruins, moving as stealthily as possible. Craer took the lead, making hand signals as to how and when the others should follow.

They hadn't been creeping forward for long when a sudden flash of light occurred above the trees ahead. On its heels came screams of pain mingled with shouts of alarm and anger.

The Four looked at each other.

Craer silently signaled the advance.

12

Uneasy Mastery of Magic

*O*ut of the bright and clear blue sky over the Glittering City, on an afternoon not soon to be forgotten in Sirlptar, two black, bat-winged, and serpentine monsters swooped down. Miniature dragons, they seemed, with men riding their backs.

As folk who glanced up cried out and pointed, older and longer-bearded ones looked, and saw—and ducked into doorways, to seek cellars in haste. Nightwyrms out of ballads and tale-tellers' legends these might be, yes, but to them that didn't mean happy endings and romantic moments as heroes grandly saved the day—they knew what nightwyrms could do. They also knew what sort of men would dare to ride them.

Horns that had not sounded for many a year awoke into frantic life, bellowing brokenly over the rooftops, calling on Sirl archers and mages to drop whatever affairs presently pressed them, and leap to the defense of their city.

They did not have to reach a watchtower to see why the alarum had been raised.

Over the oldest and wealthiest streets of Sirlptar the sinuous and splendid wyrms of the air banked, gliding along the ridge like black ghosts while the robed men astride them worked with strands of hair feverish magic . . . magic that did not go well.

As the wind of his wyrm's glide tossed back his hair and cooled his cheeks, Klamantle finished his spell and used its risen power with his customary care. He'd been careful to phrase his incantation to "feel" the Lady Embra within—and a goodly way beneath—the entire city, and all river and land now within his sight.

Yet the spell found nothing.

Markoun raised a similarly baffled and angry face from his own casting, and their eyes met in shared fury and frustration as the two wyrms flashed past each other and circled under the frustrated guidance of their creators, for a parley that both already knew the opening and sole concern of: the Lady Silvertree was not to be found anywhere in or near Sirlptar.

"Our fury will be nothing to the baron's," Klamantle told his fellow mage grimly.

The younger mage flashed his teeth in a smile too fearful to be pleasant and shouted back, "Only if we fail!" He bent low over the neck of his conjured mount and, as it turned into a savage dive, began to murmur words Klamantle knew all too well.

Tiny whirlwinds of flame spun out from Markoun's fingertips, slashing through the air like arrows streaming one after the other.

Arrows of flickering fire that streaked down into the many-gabled roof of the Wavefyre Inn.

The building shuddered, and many shingles spun into the air, trailing flames. There were shouts and screams, and Markoun smiled tightly as he followed his fiery darts down in a deadly plunge.

With easy grace he pulled his mount out of its dive at the last possible moment and leaned out to almost nonchalantly hurl a Fist of Fury down through that shattered and blazing roof as he swept over the inn. Most of its uppermost story erupted into the air in his wake.

Klamantle watched, shrugged, and sent a Woodmelt

spell of his own into the Wavefyre, to hasten its collapse onto the heads of folk within. That at least would send Markoun's reckless flames down into the heart of the Wavefyre, rather than dancing over rooftops to raze half Sirlptar.

Floorboards and pillars alike melted away and slumped, and screams rose among the crackle and rising roar of flames. Markoun snarled another firespell, uncaring of the destruction he might cause—and most of the next floor down was blasted into flaming wreckage. Men shrouded in flames could be seen staggering vainly about amid collapsing floors and toppling walls, seeking a way out that they would never find in time. Raw-throated wailing accompanied patron after desperate patron in frantic leaps to the street, where they lay dashed and broken on the unyielding cobbles. Behind them, among the milling many who'd streamed out of the common room to stand aghast and stare, drinks still clutched in their hands, the Wavefyre Inn went up like a wind-whipped bonfire.

Sobbing for air, Daerentar Jalith and Lharondar Laernsar clawed at a door already darkening with rippling flame and died together in the hungry smoke with their curses choking them. They were only paces away from a hasty magic that was keeping a column of air free of fire and smoke, but it might as well have been a broad barony distant. Seconds after they'd fallen, the door that had resisted them collapsed over their bodies in a shower of sparks.

At the bottom of that column stood a mage aflame with his own fury: Jaerinsturn of Elmerna, his spellbook between his feet and his arms raised to hurl death back at whoever had done this. He saw nightwyrms circling in the sky, and in a trembling voice he fashioned the strongest ravening spellblast his mastery could encompass. It snarled out from his thin lips and shaking hands—and a diving nightwyrm became so much black roiling smoke, spilling its robed rider out of the sky.

"Aid!" Klamantle shouted, clawing at air that would not hold him. "Markoun! A rescue!"

The younger mage swept past, their eyes met—and the nightwyrm flapped on, trailing Markoun's cold laughter.

Dark Olym take him! As the cobbles rushed up to meet him, Klamantle desired only that he could whisk himself away from here, to a safe hideawa—

By the Three! *Yes!*

Klamantle mouthed three words he'd almost forgotten—and the world changed around him, whirling away mere instants before he would have struck the ground, and whirling him back into utter darkness. Dank, dust-filled darkness, a smell he knew—and did not know. What was that . . . musk?

There was a grunting sound very close by. The mage turned and in frantic haste made the air glow with light, revealing a boar, perhaps six paces away, hooves slipping as it began a charge!

Klamantle shouted the simple spell that births flames for campfires and hurled it down a tusked throat before diving aside. Crumbling tomes of his own long-ago making tumbled around him as he rolled, the boar growled its way past, and flames erupted with a dull, wet booming.

A hoof struck the wall and rebounded past the dazed wizard, dust rolled up like stormclouds, and a little silence fell over Klamantle's hideaway.

He crouched on hands and knees, blinking into the gloom, for what seemed like a long time, listening and just gathering his wits. He'd prepared this little hideaway when? Twenty years ago? That long?

Long enough for something to find and roll aside the boulders that held the door shut and for a boar to lair here. Long enough for his simple novice spell writings to crumble, even before he'd worked magic in the little cavern to blow the boar apart.

He should find his way to the entrance and see if

there'd been changes outside—in the abandoned, over-grown village wherein his little cave had once been a root cellar . . . or in the fallen barony of Tarlagar around it. Soon.

The last echoes of the tumult faded beyond hearing, and Klamantle shrugged, clambered upright, and started around familiar rough stone walls, picking what fragments of cooked boar he could find off the stones. It'd been months since he'd tasted good cooked boar, without all of the strange, sweet sauces the baron liked to smother it with, and knowing the temper of the master of Silvertree, it might be a long time before certain wizards tasted decent meals again.

Wait! Hadn't he—yes, here! Up the little fissure, feel up and back—the thong was still there! He plucked and pulled, gently, until the tiny, crumbling leather bag fell out into his cupped hand and yielded up the dull, fire-spoiled ruby he'd enspelled so long ago. Probably the only thing of worth left here, beyond healing potions: the proud achievements of a sweating year of castings and mistakes and endless recastings . . . a scrying gem. *His* scrying gem. Klamantle found a tiny pedestal table he'd forgotten existed, dragged it over to a cold stone seat set into the wall, and set down his gem on it.

Sitting down to stare into ruby depths, he thought of the burning inn in Sirlptar. Flames roaring up, smoke rolling up into a long, greasy plume over the ridge that rose into the tallest turreted houses in the Glittering City . . . there. There in the ruby deep: a tiny, gleaming scene growing steadily larger, nearer . . .

The nightwyrm convulsed in agony, almost spilling Markoun Yarynd from his perch.

The youngest of the Dark Three wizards of Silvertree clawed at glassy black scales to keep from falling to a tumbling, helpless death, recovered himself with a desperate snarl, and turned to look back with the sweat of fear running off him like a rainstorm.

Markoun's eyes were wide and staring, and he was shaking in rage and terror. If his fingers had slipped . . .

He shuddered and then wheeled his dragonlike mount savagely around. Twice the nightwyrm turned in the sky over the Glittering City before its rider regained enough control over himself to work magic again. Futile arrows leaped up at him in some places, falling far short, and the flashes of spells too slow and too timidly aimed shook the sky in other places.

Markoun ducked his head away from the magics and thanked the Three that the city seemed to be so empty of mages at the moment. When the nightwyrm responded to him again, his first, snarling act was to hurl a handful of fire back down at the wizard standing in the heart of the inferno. The only one who'd touched them with his spells, smashing Klamantle's spell-spun wyrm out of the sky. Thankfully, his second strike had missed Markoun, though not by much.

It was a spell not known in Silvertree. Who *was* that mage down there, alone amid the flames?

Had the Silvertree wench run to this stranger? Had he hidden or transformed or spelljumped her away out of a whim or to draw Baron Silvertree into battle?

Or was it just the laughter of the Three that he'd been staying at this inn right now?

Then the young wizard's mind came to the most important of his string of questions: It didn't really matter now, did it?

If Markoun didn't claim that wizard down there was to blame for Embra Silvertree's escape—after destroying him utterly in what must look like a city-shaking battle, the hide that would pay the price of Silvertree fury would be one that answered to the name of Yarynd.

As horns blared again in the city below, something purple suddenly burst in the air close by to his right.

Markoun flinched and set his wyrm tumbling away without waiting to see if it had been hit. Even the mightiest battle-spell couldn't harm what it couldn't hit. . . .

He had to destroy this stranger-mage, the inn, and a lot more besides. Perhaps if he whisked aloft those barrels of cooking oil from three streets over, caused them to hang above the inn, and then tore them apart. . . .

At his thought the nightwyrm climbed, its powerful wings stroking the air like the oars of a racing boat, that obsidian back undulating with the power of its wingbeats. From somewhere among the taller houses on the ridge another spell streaked out, tracing a slow green arc across the sky . . . and falling short.

Arrows sought him, a few wingbeats farther on, but a sharp bank and slip to one side, and they clawed emptiness and fell. Chuckling in delight and rising battle-rage, Markoun clung to his perch and cast the spell that would snatch aloft the barrels. It worked as smoothly as a bard's ballad; he urged his mount away only just in time.

Behind his nightwyrm's curling tail, the air erupted into a ear-shattering torrent of flames that the gods themselves might have been proud of. Markoun couldn't even hear his own shouted laughter as he turned his mount from the height of its frantic race out of harm's way, looked back, and waved his fist in exultation.

Jaerinsturn of Elmerna, the Wavefyre Inn, and several surrounding buildings of fair Sirlptar vanished as one, in the heart of a blast that hurled citizens into the air like rag dolls, splattered them against walls like so much rotten fruit, and smote the ears of everyone else in the Glittering City with a ringing, muffled tumult that would take hours to pass.

The nightwyrm bucked and shuddered in the roiling air, but Markoun held his seat with a grim smile, waiting for smoke and dust to clear enough to be sure that no sly adventurers would be creeping out of inn cellars with tales of reckless wyrm-riding mages.

Something streaked up out of the city to burst nearby; the nightwyrm recoiled in the air and almost fell over into a wild tumble.

Another spell soared up from another street—and another; Sirlptar seemed full of angry mages, all seeking revenge for the disturbance on the man in the air.

Markoun raised a hasty shielding, and almost immediately a scattering of midair stars told him that it had been tested . . . by a bearded man in leathers standing in an alley not far from where the inn had been. A man in the gaudy robes favored in far Carraglas peered sharply at the bearded man—and then joined him in hurling spells into the sky. When they began to arrive all around the twisting, thrashing nightwyrm, Markoun was suddenly too busy for spellscrying anyone on the ground . . . any one, for instance, of the score or more of mages now hurling destruction into the sky.

The nightwyrm shuddered underneath him as fire burst out of empty air not so far away—and Markoun decided a return to Silvertree was now more than increasingly attractive. It was urgent.

In the heart of the ruby, Klamantle saw his younger colleague wrestle his dark and scaly mount around to streak upriver, as spells burst in the air all around. He'd never seen so much magic hurled at once . . . but then, he'd never seen a mage reckless and stupid enough to invite such a display.

Reckless and stupid enough to strike at a busy inn in the heart of a bustling city that was bound to be acrawl with wizards, at the bright height of day and in full sight of all, parading around the sky on a conjured nightwyrm. And now Markoun was *flying away,* not even paying the price for his folly!

Disgusted, Klamantle stared hard at the gem and

thought of his own worktable in Castle Silvertree. Its dark expanse just so, the little brazier there, the row of clay jars along the back . . . and suddenly he was looking at them all, Sirlptar and bright-bursting spells gone. He turned the view in the gem away from his worktable, to look across the spell-hurling chamber.

The Baron was sitting in his customary seat at the table—but Ingryl Ambelter was sitting at his side. Elbow to elbow, they were, like two close friends, their heads bent in close converse . . . plotting.

A trio of hand-high figurines stood on the polished wood between them, little statues of deftly carved wood. The baron gestured at one of them, and the Spellmaster took it up into his hand. It was a very lifelike miniature of Embra Silvertree. The glows of unleashed, building magic were already flickering around Ambelter's fingers as he raised it in front of his face.

Its removal let Klamantle Beirldoun get a clear look at the other two miniatures on the table. He blinked, and then blinked again but had no trouble in recognizing himself and Markoun Yarynd!

Cold fear shivered through the mage in the cave, and he found himself blinking at the gem, shoulders back against the cold stone wall and sweat running down his jaw.

So the jaws had drawn close. Well, he'd always known they could, more or less at the whim of the Spellmaster or the ruler of Silvertree. 'Twould it be best to flee far from Aglirta, right now? Or pretend he knew nothing and walk back into the waiting deathtrap?

Klamantle sat in the darkness for a long time before he admitted to himself that he had no real choice; Ingryl, if not the baron, was sure to have some magical way of readily tracing and tormenting him.

He sighed, returned the gem to its hiding place, and looked around his hideaway. Scoop the crumbling books behind some stones to keep casual searchers from becoming enthusiastic, leave what was left of the boar to the flies, and . . . no, there was nothing he wanted to take from here.

Wearily, Klamantle Beirldoun strode to the entrance, seeking enough open ground to conjure another nightwyrm and get home. As he shouldered his way out into the forest, he never saw the motionless man watching from behind the tree right beside the entrance to his hideaway. A man clad all in leathers, who never lost a grim but gentle smile.

Markoun was unable to keep the smile from his face, even with most of his magic gone and his mount collapsing under him. The hail of spells that had forced him away from Sirlptar was still eating away at his nightwyrm, forcing him to stay over the wide but winding river—better a ducking than a bone-shattering fall onto rocks or into the ever-present trees . . . of lands that had no cause to love Silvertree mages.

Ah, but what a bright battle it had been! To rend that inn like a handful of rotten kindling and scorch a dozen mages or more . . .

Markoun found himself grinning again, as the nightwyrm's scales became smoke beneath him, and he was suddenly tumbling through the air.

The River Coiling was cold—kisses of the Three, 'twas cold!—and Markoun found himself gasping for air as he struggled to the nearest bank. His fingers were numb already; it took him three tries to claw himself up the rocks and ashore, dripping.

His probable reception from the baron, of course, would be even colder. Markoun looked upriver until he found a landmark he knew, shook river water from his fingers, and cast a spelljump.

An instant after the Silvertree mage vanished, an arrow hissed through the spot where he'd stood. In its wake came a shouted oath of disgust from the archer of Adeln who'd shot it.

* * *

The Priest of the Serpent smiled as the kneeling woman gasped. "Sssuch venom slays all who serve not the Ssserpent," he told her. "Rise, sssister, and join in the most sacred service in all Darsar."

Almost hungrily the woman kissed the scaly snout of the serpent. The fangs that had bitten her breast gnawed at her mouth as tenderly as any human lover, and the snake seemed almost to purr as her limbs started to twitch and tremble, and foam gathered at the place where their mouths met. The Priest's smile broadened.

"Dusk's not far off now," Craer murmured, as the Band of Four crouched together in a fern-filled hollow. They'd been quiet enough that birds hadn't stopped calling and whirring overhead—and they'd still seen no sign of men or tall stone buildings for men to lurk in.

"Are we lost?" Sarasper asked doubtfully, looking around at the unbroken trees of Loaurimm Forest.

"You're never lost," Hawkril growled next to his ear. "You're always 'right here'—where you don't want to be. Old soldiers' joke."

The healer gave him an exasperated look. "Well then, Clevertongue—where's Indraevyn?"

"Right here around us," Craer murmured, spreading his hand in a gesture that indicated the sweep of forest all around.

"Oh, *surely*," Sarasper said in disbelief. "Where're the buildings—inside these trees?"

Hawkril touched the older man's arm, and pointed. "See yon? And there?" The armaragor was indicating what looked like a mound of vines tangled around shrubs, with the leafless skeleton of a fallen, long-dead tree draped across all.

"I see only forest," the healer told him.

"And we see overgrown lumps of stone—suspiciously numerous and steep-sided," Craer replied. "Behold ruined Indraevyn."

Sarasper looked stunned. "If it's all like this," he said grimly, "we should have brought lit torches in plenty—and a hired hundred of farmers with good shovels. There'll be no wizards mincing grandly in to pluck up Dwaerindim in *this*."

"All the better," Embra put in, looking skyward. "Dusk is coming down soon."

"We'd best camp back at the hollow with the stream," Craer suggested, "and venture forward in earnest on the morrow. But there's a little time left, and we've been managing stealth well enough thus far. . . . "

"Forward the Four," Embra murmured. "To do what?"

"Scout a bit," the procurer said, "so we don't end up trying to cross any bare ridges or open places in the bright sun, under the nose of a sentinel."

"Lead on," Sarasper directed, and the procurer did, leading them cautiously up a little valley. There was a ridge at its head, and they clambered cautiously up its vine-cloaked slope together—only to come to a sudden, still halt.

A grisly warning hung in front of them. Someone had seized a warrior and tied him head downward, spread-eagled in midair by ropes at his wrists and ankles stretched tight to four trees—and some prowling forest predator had come along and eaten away his head.

Hawkril's mouth tightened. "That forester I left, back by the lake . . ." he murmured.

"We daren't go back now," Craer told him. "At least you left him alive, where most would have slain him out of hand." He lifted his head slowly, just a trifle, and then let out a soundless sigh of satisfaction and lowered himself down again just as achingly slowly.

"Companions in this crazed quest," he announced in a murmur, "I must ask you to keep your heads down as you hear this news: over that height, I could see four or five large stone buildings—crumbling, to be sure, but buildings nonetheless. There's also a very good chance that someone has seen *us,* so I want all of you to get back to the stream-hollow now, as quickly as you quietly can."

"While you? . . ." Embra asked.

"Climb this tree and tarry for a bit," the procurer told her, "to watch our back trail, and make sure no one follows you. Mages wouldn't even have to risk themselves to send death to our camp . . . all the snoring night long."

Embra shuddered at the thought and sank back down the slope. Hawkril quickly moved to take the lead, lifting a hand to salute Craer, who returned it and swarmed up his chosen tree.

"No, healer: no fire," the armaragor growled. "Ever heard of beacons? This forest is alive with wizards and priests and battle-hungry warriors, and even the most stupid of them can move toward a fire."

"It's not dark yet," Sarasper muttered. "I can get us some hot herb brew and have the fire out before full dark."

"Ever heard of smoke?" Hawkril snarled. "At least a few of them can smell, too." The armaragor looked over at the sorceress, found her gone, and lifted his head sharply. Turning, as if sniffing a scent only he could smell, he spun around to glare across the hollow.

"Lady Embra," he snapped, "what are you doing?"

The sorceress had her back turned to them both. They saw her stiffen at his question, but she did not reply or turn around.

Sarasper and Hawkril exchanged glances. Hawkril's face darkened, and he took two quick strides toward the Lady of Jewels, feeling for the hilt of his sword. Her

arms, he now saw, were moving slowly, almost lazily—
but they were shaping gestures in the air in front of her.

"Embra!" he barked. "What are you *doing?*"

The sorceress said nothing, but there was suddenly
movement in the dusk-darkening air above her. Hawkril
stared, openmouthed.

Dark shadows and semisolid wings and a tail swept
and coiled above the Lady Silvertree, shimmering
darkly . . . and growing ever more solid.

Abruptly, a black-scaled, sinuous thing faded into
full being above the dark-haired sorceress. She held her
hands up to it as if in supplication, as it flapped batlike
wings and writhed in the air, tossing two cruel-jawed
heads and raking the air with talons longer than a man's
forearm. It hung over her like a canopy, facing the astonished and furious armaragor, and it did not look hesitant or friendly.

Then the Lady of Jewels turned her head. Her eyes
stared straight out into the gathering night above
Hawkril's head, seeing nothing—as blank as if she
were a statue. "Nightwyrm," she commanded tone-
lessly, *"fly!"*

The miniature dragon-thing boiled across the hollow
like a storm breeze—but the armaragor was already
bounding to meet it, his drawn sword flashing out in a
savage chop that sheared off one squalling head.

A black eellike body thrashed in eerie silence, twisting back and away in the air with dark blood spraying
from the great wound Hawkril had dealt it.

Its barbed tail lashed out, smashing a great splintered
gouge in the side of a tree—and giving Hawkril time to
dive aside, and the healer time to throw himself face-
down behind its groaning, sagging branches.

Writhing in agony, the conjured nightwyrm flung itself from side to side in the air, as if to shake itself free
of the pain. Hawkril snatched out a dagger, in case its
next strike should tear his sword free of his hand, and

dodged and darted beneath it, seeing the right place to stand and meet it. He noticed Sarasper up and running again but could spare no time to see where he was going—or what the Lady of Jewels was doing now.

Spellcasting, yes—he could hear new mumblings from her, a sort of chant—but she was somewhere behind him, and before he dared look for her, he had to take care of this hunting wyrm.

When it came down at last, in a long, curving plunge preceded by snapping teeth, he was ready.

Hawkril lunged under its scaly bulk, twisted up to slash with his dagger along the edge of its mouth, and left the steel buried hilt deep in the angle of those cruel jaws.

As the wyrm turned away from the fresh pain, thrashing, the warrior sprang forward and got one arm hooked around the bloody, curling stump of neck from which he'd severed its other head. His grip held, even when its frantically flapping batwings plucked him aloft—and with a snarl, Hawkril sworded its remaining head again and again, ignoring the thrusts of its snout and its wriggling attempts to bite him or slash him with its teeth. He went on hacking until he'd slashed that head to ribbons, and he was rolling in forest leaves drenched with dark blood and half crushed beneath a heavy, wildly whipping body of black scales and quivering agonies. Still eerily silent, it died.

Hawkril rose, saw no fresh spell menacing him, and let out his rage on what was left of the nightwyrm. He was not gentle in his butchery. By the time he'd dismembered the dragon-thing, he was drenched in its dark blood, and his eyes blazed like twin coals.

He stalked toward the sorceress, who had somehow ended up on her knees with her wrists held behind her by a grim-faced Sarasper.

Their eyes met. He'd never seen a woman's eyes so large and dark before. She shook her head a little but said nothing.

Embra's face was pale, and tears had left two bright tracks down her cheeks. Her lips trembled as Hawkril loomed up over her.

He took her by the throat and hauled her to her feet, and he was not gentle about it. "Well, wench?" he growled. *"Why?"*

"I—I—," Embra said, and choked. Her next word was a sob; wordlessly she shook her head, fresh tears bursting forth.

"She was under compulsion," Sarasper said quietly. "Some spell sent by her father's mages, no doubt. She's said the wyrm was meant to kill us."

Hawkril nodded curtly and took Embra's chin between two of his fingers. Almost delicately he shook her head swiftly back and forth until she stared at him dazedly, tears abated.

"So what, Lady Silvertree," he asked coldly, "are we to do with you? Are we to trust you or . . . ?"

Embra's eyes held shame, and pleading, and a vast weariness as they looked up into his. "Kill me," she whispered, her lips trembling.

"Slay me now, swiftly, before they come into my head again . . . or I start pleading. Oh, Hawkril, I am so sorry! I—slay me! *Please!*"

The armaragor's face was cold and as unyielding as a war helm as he nodded, drew in a deep and reluctant breath, lifted her chin with his thumb to lay bare her throat, and drew back his bloody war sword.

Craer stayed in the tree until the light of the risen moon outshone the last afterglow of the dying day. No one came skulking through the forest in any direction.

The procurer had just begun the climb down when, glancing back at the ruins one last time, he found himself looking into the calm, dark eyes of a wizard watching him from the heart of the ruins.

At least, he judged the man to be a mage. Who else

wears robes and does sentinel duty by standing on empty air seventy feet or so off the ground?

Stifling a curse, Craer went down the tree in frantic haste, clawing the bark for handholds in the night gloom. His landing was noisier than he liked, and he dodged a good six paces in a false side foray before slipping toward the hollow. Should they all move on immediately? No, trying to blunder around in the deep forest now, all four of them, would make so much noise that 'twas wiser to stay still. Had Hawk heard anyone else moving nearby, though? Hawk—

—had the Lady of Jewels by the throat. Sarasper stood watching, the dark coils of some slain serpent-monster lay all around, and Hawk's war sword was drawing back for—for—

"Hawk, have your wits fallen right out of your *head?*" Craer was too aghast to keep his voice down or his words prudent; his shout cracked across the hollow like a pine bough shattering in a fire.

"Gods above, man," he added furiously, striding across the slaughtered nightwyrm as if it wasn't there, "has some spell got ahold of you? Put down that sword!"

The armaragor stared at his friend in dumbfounded silence. He'd never seen the spiderlike little procurer this angry—not even the first time some long-dead idiot had called Craer "Longfingers," a name the procurer still, twenty summers later, wasn't fond of. Hawk blinked—and his sword halted, right where it was.

Craer marched right up to him and grabbed Hawkril's sword arm by the wrist. "I said *drop it!*"

Hawkril shook his head, let fall his sword, and reached out a hand toward the procurer's face, as if in wonder. "She tried to kill us, Craer. . . ."

"Spell-thralled by one of the Silvertree mages, no doubt," the procurer snapped. "So your brilliant response to this is to butcher her, just as they're trying to do to us, hey? So tell me, Hawk: have we *joined* Silvertree's army, after all this? Or has he put a spell on you to make you do his bidding . . . is that it? Just how long do you think we'll last against those same three mages without her, hey? Did you think of that, yet? Or were you going to wait until you'd cut her head off, and start doing your thinking *then?*"

Craer was almost shrieking his words now, spraying spittle with every sentence, his face white and his eyes glittering. Embra's eyes were still closed, and Sarasper came around to stand before her, watching her intently. Her throat moved in a tremulous swallow, and her tongue flicked out over dry lips, but she neither moved nor spoke.

"Craer . . . ?" The armaragor's rumble held an almost pleading tone.

The procurer shouldered past him to take Embra by the elbows—he could not reach her shoulders—and sit her down. "Idiot," he snapped over his shoulder at Hawkril, and then turned his head to look at Sarasper and asked calmly, "Good healer, would you stand watch right now? I need you to go a few paces away from our noise and listen hard, *that* way in particular. Someone—or some*thing*—may have heard us."

Without waiting for a reply, the procurer leaned forward to the sorceress until their foreheads were almost touching, and asked gently, "Embra? Lady Embra? What happened?"

Faerod Silvertree's daughter raised agonized eyes to him, tried to frame words, and then burst into sobs and threw her arms around him. The procurer held her tight and waited for her weeping to subside, hearing Hawkril move restlessly behind him. One of the sounds was the scrape of the armaragor's sword being grounded in mossy soil.

It was some time before Embra recovered herself enough to gasp out so much that the three men understood the dreadful compulsion that had seized her, when through mists in her mind she saw the Spellmaster sitting at a gleaming table in her father's favorite chamber in Castle Silvertree with a wooden figurine in his hands . . . under her father's cold smile, as the magic took hold. . . .

"No more tears, now," Craer snapped, and raised his eyes to Sarasper, who'd drifted back to hear the sorceress.

"Is there any way to break this magic?" the old man asked carefully. Embra was gulping in deep, shuddering breaths, her face hidden behind tangled hair, but she managed to draw up her shoulders and then drop them, in an exaggerated shrug.

The three men traded grim glances, and then Sarasper bent again and asked, "If that wood doll he's using was destroyed, what then?"

"T-that would work, yes," Embra gulped. "Until Ambelter made another. He'd need to craft a new figurine, himself, and bind to it something of me—probably hairs from my hairbrush, if they haven't used them all to work their seeking spells by now."

"Can we, say, burn that thing from here—with your magic, if I—if we all help?"

Embra closed her eyes and seemed to shrink. They saw her shiver before she said very quietly, "There is a way. It will . . . kill me."

"How so?"

"I have to set myself afire . . . and as I char, hold the link to the thing of wood back in the Castle, so that it burns, too."

"What if we three healed you as you burned? Would we heal the doll, too, or can you hold that back?"

Embra opened her eyes and looked at him sharply, sudden hope leaping in her face. "That—that would work, yes!"

"Then we'll do that," the healer said quietly. "Disrobe, everyone—and get all metal far away from us. Hawkril, don't forget your bracers. *All* metal must go."

"Our clothes?" the armaragor growled, his hands already on a buckle.

"Unless you want them burned to ash," Sarasper said almost cheerfully. "I'll be needing to draw on both of you, if we're to keep our Lady alive. Don't strew things; I want bundles we can snatch and run with, if we have to. She'll probably do her share of screaming, once we begin."

"Right," Craer said, almost briskly, and then looked at Hawkril. Slowly Sarasper and Embra turned their heads to regard the armaragor, too.

Hawkril Anharu growled something wordless, deep in his throat, before he stepped forward and laid a gentle hand on Embra's shoulder.

She put her fingers over it and stroked it, biting her lip to hold back fresh tears, and he gave her an awkward pat before taking his hand away.

"I *hate* magic," Hawkril told all Darsar then, looking up at the night sky as if he expected a reply.

There was a brief sputtering that surprised all three men, and then Embra Silvertree was crying and laughing at the same time, struggling to frame the words, "I've said that, myself, more than once!"

Three men exchanged slim ghosts of smiles and turned away to disrobe.

It was not long before the hollow was lit by eerie flames—fire that rose raggedly from the bucking body of a beautiful woman who arched and shrieked in agony, her ankles hooked under a smoldering fallen tree and her wrists held firmly by an old and bony man upon whose face pain danced and twitched. A large man and a small one held to the old man's arms, and they trembled and cursed softly, but did not draw away.

More than once the large man growled, "I *hate* magic!" but the dark and silent trees standing all around made no reply.

Above a glossy tabletop, deft fingers suddenly convulsed and flew apart. Flames burst into being between them, and the wooden figurine at their heart seemed to smile coldly at Ingryl Ambelter for an instant, before it slumped into ash in the fierce conflagration.

"Serpent in the Shadows!" the shocked Spellmaster hissed. "She has *that* much power?"

Baron Faerod Silvertree smiled faintly and spread his hands. "Well, now, Ingryl . . . she *is* my daughter."

13

Things Become Crowded

The doors of the chamber boomed with a cold and very final sound under the firm hands of armsmen who kept their faces carefully impassive as they shut themselves out.

"Stand just there," Baron Faerod Silvertree told his two younger wizards, in the same gentle voice he'd used when greeting them. His eyes, however, were wintry, and Spellmaster Ingryl was standing close behind him with wands just visible poking out of both sleeves, and a cold and silent smile on his face.

Klamantle and Markoun moved to the indicated spot in similar silence, not looking at each other, and the ruler of Silvertree put his fingertips together almost like a priest choosing gentle words of prayer.

"I thought you wizards of passable skill when I employed you," the baron began, his voice still silky, "and more than that: I considered you men of good judgment. That is something all too rare among mages . . . rarer, it seems, than I'd thought."

He reached for a goblet in slow elegance, sipped, and added, "You stand revealed as a pair of reckless, destructive fools—whose continued lives have become matters of consideration, not accepted certainties. Have you any idea just how many of my Sirl investments you've burned or blasted to dust this evening?"

Markoun licked dry lips, and said, "Lord, I—"

"Be still," the baron almost whispered. "Speak not. Hear instead my orders: exhibit no shred of disloyalty, and perform no act of independence, but abide here in this room until given leave to walk elsewhere—and use every scrap of magic you have mastery over to return *my daughter, the mortar of my fortress!*"

"Lord," Markoun protested, "I want y—"

"Did I, young fool of a mage," the baron asked, "or did I not command your silence just now? Is my authority such a light and trifling thing to you?"

Paling, Markoun opened his mouth and then shut it again and shook his head.

The baron nodded slowly. "Better," he snapped. "Yet I think it's time for a little bald reminder. Relics belonging to all three of my *most loyal* mages—and vials of blood, recall you?—lie hidden around this castle in such profusion that I enjoy complete control over Ingryl, Klamantle, and Markoun. If a relic and so much as a drop of that blood touch each other, the mage from whom both were derived will forthwith experience a long, slow doom. A death of howling, convulsing agony, if my memory of another foolish wizard still serves me. Now get to work."

The eye watching from the carving might have judged Klamantle and Markoun both chastened and fearful as they hastened to their worktables—but if that eye had chanced to intercept either of the glances those mages threw in the direction of Spellmaster Ingryl, the judgment might well have been altered, to "murderous."

Sarasper. The voice in his head was back.

The healer drew in a deep breath. Keeping watch here in the deep woods was largely a matter of still wakefulness spent listening to chirruping insects—or rather, to sudden silences in their songs. *Sarasper, have you forgotten me?"*

The sharply listening singing in his head built quickly into impatience. *No, Old Oak,* the healer replied.

Well and good, for there is a task.

Sarasper smiled into the night. *Of course.*

Less mockery, mortal, and more awe would become thee rather better.

The healer spread empty hands. *I am what I am. How can I serve thee?*

The sorceress Embra Silvertree lies under a curse. Remove it.

Without guidance, Sarasper thought, *I cannot even begin.*

A beginning is all you can hope to accomplish this night. Hear me and heed.

Old Oak, command me, Sarasper responded, and then did with his hands and his energy what the pictures and whispers in his mind showed him.

Hours passed as he labored, sweat running down his face like a spring racing over rocks. Craer and then Hawkril in turn stood watch, while still the old healer sat with his fingertips hovering over Embra's brow. By unspoken agreement, they never wakened the sorceress to take her turn on watch.

It seemed to Sarasper that destroying the curse, once they found the bright threads of enchantment in the dreaming mind beneath his fingers, should be a simple thing . . . but the voice in his mind guided him into shifting this thread and altering that one, in an endless and ever-more-complex web of rootings and twistings. Near dawn, with Hawkril listening intently to something that prowled nearby but never actually approached their hollow, the exhausted healer could not help but think that all of this tinkering with the curse was doing little more than hiding it from the one who'd cast it, burying it more deeply in Embra's mind . . . and making it answer a new and different master.

And what need would Old Oak have of a curse that made one human sorceress pay with a shred of her life for every spell she worked?

As if that thought had been a trigger, a scene unfolded in Sarasper's mind, of a door in a curving, crumbling stone wall. It faded into another scene, a domed circular building, long disused and partially overgrown with clinging vines, its walls matching those of the first scene. *The library of the wizard Ehrluth. Seek within for the Stone.*

And then the scene seemed to recede down a long, dark tunnel, and Sarasper was falling away from it, down, down into black and waiting oblivion. . . .

"Longfingers," some men called him. "Little Lord Spider" he was to others; "that rat" he'd been to a few. But never before this night, Craer Delnbone reflected, as the strange restless, swelling feeling that had awakened him swept over him like a warm breeze, sweeping his dark armor of mockery aside for a while, had he been called "savior."

And by a sorceress of noble blood at that, a woman of power and such beauty that gazing on her left his mouth dry, even when she was shorn of garments, with her hair atangle and her face pinched with pain. Ahem; that'd be better put: *especially* shorn of garments.

When the rage left Hawkril, even the burly armaragor had wrapped Craer in a fierce embrace and whispered his thanks. "I almost killed her," he quavered in the procurer's ear. "Thank the Three you got back here in time."

The warrior had pulled back then, and stared at Craer with real fear in his eyes, before asking roughly, "If I'd killed her, what would we have done then?"

The procurer had shrugged, not knowing what to answer.

"What would you have told us to do?" Hawkril persisted, still looking stricken.

Craer opened his mouth, shut it again without saying anything, looked around at the night mists drifting through the trees, and shook his head.

"The mists don't answer," he'd told the armaragor bitterly. "They never have."

Surprisingly, both Embra and Sarasper had nodded at his words, as if they understood.

Craer stared at the moon now, feeling the old dark nightmare rise within him, until it spilled over, and he was back on the reeking docks, on the day his youth was swept away forever. . . .

"Aye, he gave us a few fists," Jack-a-Blade grunted, nudging the senseless, naked man with his boot. "But he went down for all that—and not much damaged, neither. When he wakes, you'll find he still has a jaw and his wits. A fair tally scribe, too."

"Reads and writes—or just counts and marks?"

"Reads and writes. His woman does, too."

"What? What did they do, again?"

"Ran a warehouse for the Star Sails," Jack-a-Blade said, and the young boy crouched in the rafters could hear the chuckle in his voice.

"Ah." The slaver was not a slow man. "One that recently and mysteriously burned, eh?"

"Now that you mention it," Jack-a-Blade said slowly, in a broad impersonation of a surprised man, "I do believe that the couple who betrayed the Sails and burned their warehouse after emptying it of several wagonloads of valuables might just be this same Phorthas and Shierindra Delnbone."

"I can't sell or use openly what a large merchant

house searches for," the bald-headed slaver said flatly. "That drives the price down."

"Read and write," Jack-a-Blade murmured. "Who'd want to let them go?"

"Letters aren't as rare a skill as you think," the slaver said, crossing forearms that were thicker and hairier than Jack-a-Blade's thighs. "And they're not all that big, or young, or fair to look upon."

He waved a hand at the woman, lying still in her chains. If he'd purchased her, he'd have used his boot, but there were rules. Both men knew by the way she tensed and caught her breath that she was awake, but neither would say a word if she didn't scream or try to wriggle away. And both men judged this Shierindra Delnbone too sensible for that, even if her bared body didn't stir the loins at first glance.

Like her husband on the rough wooden floor beside her, she lay on her back, with the backs of her wrists chained together at her throat, under the slave hood, and her ankles manacled well apart to the drag bar. The drag pad under her shoulders wasn't yet laced down her back to that bar, but it would be before she was moved. Both men standing over the scrawny, flat-breasted woman knew that she was going to be bought and sold, and soon; the slaver had made no move for the door, and Jack-a-Blade hadn't suggested one.

"Granted," the port pirate agreed, "so I'll only ask ten drethar. Each."

The slaver snorted. "Six drethar for the pair would be a little less outrageous," he said, not quite keeping a snarl out of his voice. Crossbowmen behind sliding panels in every wall of a room earn a man a little respect—but not that much.

Jack-a-Blade's fingers, of the hand that was behind his back, crooked in a certain sign, and those panels slid open. Noisily. The boy in the rafters, crouched above the bright flickering of the candle-lamp, shivered soundlessly.

The slaver didn't bother to stiffen or turn his head. "Perhaps my judgment was hasty. Say, five drethar for the pair."

The port pirate acquired the very faintest of smiles, and said, "Eight drethar. Each, of course."

The slaver smiled more broadly and took a casual stride toward the door. "I can sail into forty ports and take my pick of the unwanted. Perhaps when these two are older and their teeth have fallen out, the price will have come down enough that I'll be able to afford them. Unless, of course, you can find someone else to take them off your hands. A word of friendly advice: don't offer them to the Sails. They have keen noses."

Jack-a-Blade hadn't risen to hold more real power than the local baron by being stupid. "Perhaps I meant to say six drethar each," he said smoothly.

The slaver stopped, turned slowly, and stooped to wave cheerily at the nearest open panel. "Perhaps you did," he agreed, "and perhaps you meant to say five drethar each—but perhaps I might go back up to six if you throw in the boy."

"The boy?"

The slaver nodded. "Their son. The little spider who scrambles all over the cargoes doing the tallies for them—ah, I meant 'scrambled,' of course." He smiled again. "Slavers watch warehouses, you see."

Jack-a-Blade tossed his head in an indication of futility and growled, "No one's seen that lad since the fire."

The slaver raised an eyebrow. "Oh? You don't look up very often?"

The port pirate frowned. "Don't? Eh?" He spun around and stared up into the rafters—and for just one horrified moment, Jack-a-Blade and Craer Delnbone stared into each other's eyes.

Then the knife in the boy's hand slashed out, shearing through the candles of the lamp hanging beside him on its chain, and in the sudden, curse-filled darkness

Craer extended that knife down like a spear and followed it, pitching forward into the emptiness above Jack-a-Blade's upturned face.

His blade struck something solid with force enough to numb his arm right up to the shoulder, and sliced as he fell past. The port pirate cried out—a raw shriek of pain laced with a wet bubbling. Craer was already crashing to the unseen floor, gasping to find breath or a groan of his own, when the sharp cracks of many firing crossbows almost deafened him.

The sharper cracks and splinterings of the quarrels striking walls and glancing off couldn't entirely drown out the wet thuddings of bolts finding homes in bodies. Groans much larger and more frantic than Craer could have uttered did, however, drown out the small sound he made next.

Everywhere men were cursing and booted feet were hurrying and stumbling and doors were crashing open—and the chain of the lamp was rattling as it fell to its full length, a few feet off the floor; someone must have pulled out its peg in hopes of getting it relit. Someone who hadn't counted on the slavers' men bursting into Jack-a-Blade's warehouse with swords drawn and fury in their hearts.

Craer heard the crash and sing of steel meeting steel, the coughs and screams and sobs of men being stabbed in the darkness, and confused flashes of light as lanterns were lit and then smashed, or doors to distant rooms opened and then smashed shut again. One flash told him no one was standing in the slaving room anymore, and that something studded with crossbow quarrels was trying to, and that the lamp chain was . . . there!

He sprang forward in the dark, found its hot, grimy metal with fingers that trembled with fear, and swarmed up it in frantic haste, as men died in the darkness all around him. The rafters above could take him out into

*the night before he joined their ranks, if he could
only . . .*

A boy crouched on a rooftop in the damp river mists
and trembled, too drained to sob any more. Wisps of
smoke still rose from the ashes of the second warehouse
to burn in as many days, but the men with buckets had
rubbed their backs and grunted and gone wearily off in
search of ale, or at least a place to lie down in a port
free of Jack-a-Blade.

Craer looked down at where the bones of his parents
must lie and whispered their names in despair. In an alleyway below, there was a sudden skirling of swords as
someone disagreed with someone else about who
should succeed Jack-a-Blade as the real power in this
barony. The boy whom some called the Spider listened,
uncaring. When life is in ruins and revenge over with
and done—so sudden, and so empty—what is left?

Too puny to stand up to anyone in a fight, too small
to carry on the docks, and knowing no other life but the
docks . . . no one would want such a boy. No one would
trust such a boy, what with his scrambling along
rooftops, hiding, and pranks. A thief, a worthless
vagabond . . . an orphan. Left alone to die.

Craer Delnbone lifted his head from the rough
shakes of the roof and asked the uncaring mists fear-
fully, "What do I do now?"

He waited, but the mists chose not to answer.

"See who it is, Sarintha," the baron said, and as her long
hair brushed along his bare body on her silent way off
the bed, he did something to the bedpost beside him
and drew forth a wand from it. If any of the other
women entwined around him in the bed in that bright
dawn noticed that he'd trained it on the door—and, of

necessity, squarely on Sarintha's shapely back, as she drew on a silk robe that concealed nothing and went, as he'd bid—they said nothing.

"The Spellmaster," she called in the huskily musical voice that had first attracted the baron to her charms, and let the little circle of armor plate in the door fall back into place while she awaited his reply.

Faerod Silvertree allowed one eyebrow to lift loftily before he said calmly—as if dawn visits from the most powerful of his mages occurred every morning—"Show him in, and get you speedily to the baths, all of you. No tarrying to listen, mind . . . unless, of course, any of you believe your beauty would be improved by the loss of your ears to a hot iron."

One hastily suppressed squeal was his only reply, amid a flurry of slitherings and pillow clamberings and pale bodies bobbing away across the floor furs. Sarintha was the last, rising from kneeling by the door she'd opened to close it again, then sprinting for the archway into the baths.

Spellmaster Ingryl Ambelter almost turned to watch her go—almost. His shoulders quivered as he quelled the movement, and his baron almost smiled at that. Almost.

"Yes, Ingryl?" he asked, instead, not bothering to cover himself . . . or the wand in his hand, resting on a pillow and aimed rock-steady at his most powerful wizard.

A wizard who seemed weary this morning. "I've news I know you'll want to hear, Lord," Ingryl replied, "won for you through great, night-long magical striving. The Lady Embra and her three companions are at the ruins of lost Indraevyn, in the Loaurimm Forest, seeking one of the Dwaerindim. Ambitious mages from all over Aglirta, and beyond, are there, too, pursuing the same prize. The place is both a deathtrap—and a golden opportunity to seize magical greatness for Silvertree."

"If we gain one of the legendary Dwaer, you mean?"

Ingryl nodded.

"And your plan for gaining it?"

The Spellmaster echoed the baron's almost-smile. "I believe the Baron of Silvertree would be tactically astute to immediately order his mages Klamantle and Markoun thence, carrying touch-delivery shielding and listening spells for the Lady Embra, with their most pressing orders being to get to her and deliver those shields first, before and above all else. If they fell into battle with other explorers of ruins, thereafter, and we were to observe and guide them through my spells . . ."

"The Baron of Silvertree's beliefs concur with yours in this matter," Faerod Silvertree told him. "When this is done, and Embra safely back in thrall or spellchains, shall I lend you, say, four of my love-chamber girls for a night?"

The Spellmaster did look quickly over at the archway that led to the baths, this time, but his face was as carefully impassive as one of the baron's own armsmen when he looked back at his master and replied, "That would please me, Lord. Please do."

Morning brought death to Indraevyn in earnest. From where the silent man lay, sprawled atop a creeper-shrouded tower, he could see a conjured spellstalker crushing armsmen with its fists, the mage who controlled it crouched in a thicket unaware that three armaragors were creeping up behind him with naked daggers in their hands; at least two separate spellbattles between rival mages at opposite ends of the ruins; and something that looked like a man-size scaly rock lizard in battle leathers, with a lion's head, leading a grim band of fighting men up against a cluster of armaragors who were serving as bodyguards to a frightened bonfire wizard.

The silent man watched and listened to screams and bloody deaths as the sun climbed the sky. Wizards certainly seemed to know many nasty ways to slay . . . but sword swingers were always happy to repay the damage when magic ran out or they could catch a mage alone or unguarded. Well, let them slay tirelessly and with enthusiasm, doing Luthtuth's work for him.

The servant creatures summoned by mages, in particular, he'd be happy to see others destroy for him. Bodyguards and even veteran armaragors he could handle, but the procurer some knew as Luthtuth and others called Velvetfoot had no love for magic, and even less for the creatures it could call, and those who wielded it. So he lay still, fire smoldering within him, and watched vicious confusion reign below, spell-battles erupt and be resolved, and men die by the dozens. The dying, wounded, and those who merely blundered off alone would be his prey once darkness came again.

"An agile, lurking strangler who likes to strike from above," a patron had once described him. Luthtuth had smiled then, and he smiled now, his body wound about with a shifting armor of trip-cords, strangle-wires, and climbing lines that would come into their own once darkness fell. If he should be attacked before then, his weapons would be the few enspelled "smoke eggs" he carried, the sack of daggers he could throw with deadly accuracy, and his wits.

His current patron was a masked and secretive mage who claimed to be from far Renshoun. His task was to seek and bring back to the Masked One the four stones called the Dwaerindim, for "if used together in certain rituals, they'll serve to awaken, free, and call forth the Serpent in the Shadows, age-old foe of the Sleeping King."

This aim bothered Luthtuth not a whit; mages are always chasing some unattainable, crazed thing beyond their powers. So long as they pay first, and in full, let them destroy themselves in all sorts of spectacular and clever ways, and leave Darsar that much safer for all the rest of the not-quite-so-clever folk to enjoy.

His own clever plan was to gain this Stone, hire someone to make a replica of it and someone else to deliver that replica, and take advantage of the resulting fury of his employer to call in some known foes of the wizard to settle old scores. Luthtuth would hide and watch, just as he was doing now; if the opportunity presented itself, he'd ransack the Masked One's lair; if not, he'd merely slip away . . . one Worldstone richer.

A leaning stone tower off to their left suddenly burst into rock shards with a roar. "By the Three, but there seem to be a lot of wizards on the loose today," Sarasper muttered.

"Am I not enough for you?" Embra Silvertree whispered teasingly, as the Four crouched together under a tilted slab of stone.

"Now there's a line to quote back at her, once she's Queen Embra of the Vale," Craer muttered to the other two men. Then he pointed ahead. "Could that be the top of your domed library, Old and Wise?"

Sarasper squinted. "It could be, Small and Annoying. Let's get closer, shall we?"

Closer proved to be a tangle of bushes, the stone rubble of a fallen building, and a little open space between that and a series of crumbling half-walls, with the circular domed building rising almost untouched beyond. Craer slipped calmly from one wall to the next, until he saw a door in the library wall. He turned his head. "There 'tis, m—"

"*Down!*" Embra cried, and he fell on his face without hesitation. Something sizzled past low overhead, and the procurer rolled sideways until he was behind what was left of a stout stone wall.

"Who's trying to kill us now?" he asked the armaragor behind him calmly.

Hawkril was lying on his side behind another partial wall, and spread empty hands. "I know not. Some mage or other—looks young, and has scepters—long metal ones, like the one old Mellovran Spellshards used to wave around, when we were young—in both hands."

Part of the armaragor's wall exploded into purple flames, and he flinched, backed away, and asked, "See?"

"If you hadn't been so quick to roast my best warriors," the Baron Silvertree told his two younger mages, "this task would not now be yours. So put away those scowls, take up the shielding spells, and bestow them on my daughter without delay." He leaned forward in his seat, and asked silkily, "Or is there something else—terribly pressing—you wish to tell me at this time?"

Klamantle looked up at the familiar ceiling of this chamber in Castle Silvertree and said nothing, but Markoun, after darting several glances at his fellow mage, burst out, "Lord, both of us are less than enthused with the act of riding a conjured nightwyrm down into a cauldron of battling mages, but Klamantle has a plan."

The baron quirked an eyebrow. "One that has robbed him of his powers of speech, perhaps?"

Klamantle brought his eyes down from the ceiling, his face smooth and blank, and said, "I happen to have once visited Lake Lassabra, Lord. I can spelljump us both thither, and from there we can approach the ruined city with stealth enough to hope to accomplish our task."

The baron's eyes turned to meet those of his Spellmaster and collected an almost imperceptible nod. He extended his hand toward the mages' worktables. "Apply yourselves, then, and let us see victory therefrom."

When two robed backs were turned, the Spellmaster approached the baron's table and set down a cloth with something inside it: two palm-size glass globes. Ingryl let the fold of cloth he'd peeled back drop back into place over them and murmured, "In these, we shall see as if staring out of their belt buckles."

The baron nodded and wordlessly reached for a decanter.

When the mages departed and the globes glimmered to life, rising a few inches off the table, the first thing to be seen in the depths was the shore of a lake ringed by trees.

The second—the baron stiffened and leaned forward in his seat—was a hail of arrows, leaping from the nearest of those trees!

Stones erupted into dust and smoke, and Sarasper fell on his face with a gasp. "It's no use," he panted, across the little open space between them—ground that it would mean instant death to try to cross. "He knows exactly where we have to get to, and until those scepters run out of magic, he can blast the ground we have to traverse as he wills!"

"How long does it take scepters to run out?" Craer snapped.

"Centuries," Embra told him, with the ghost of a smile. Sarcastically the procurer echoed it, and then peered around the edge of the wall again. A scepter spat, the ground erupted in a line of racing flames, and Craer sniffed at it and pulled his head in again, spinning smoothly around on his haunches to face Hawkril and Embra.

"He's behind that stub of wall on the left," the procurer told them. "Have you some sort of blasting spell, Lady?"

"I do," Embra confirmed, eyes narrowing. "Why?"

"Because I'll need you to strike him down right after I do this," the procurer replied, scrambling to his feet, "and right before I need the healer!"

And he put his head down and sprinted around the end of the wall that was sheltering them, straight out into the open and running hard for the library door.

Sarasper gaped at the running figure, and then shouted, "No! Come back, you dung-witted purse picker! *Come back!*"

He leaped up from his own sheltering wall and took two running steps after the procurer—just in time to have all Darsar erupt in front of his face as a scepter blasted Craer Delnbone off his feet and hurled him through the air like a child's rag doll.

14

Borrowing Privileges

C raer!" Embra screamed, leaping to her feet. Beside her, Hawkril sobbed. Fists balled and shaking, she turned to face the hulking armaragor just as he spun around and lumbered toward the end of their wall. "No!" she cried. "No!"

He put his head down and did not slow. Desperately the Lady Silvertree flung herself to the ground in front of his ankles.

Her ribs took a heavy blow, her sky was darkened by fast-descending warrior, and Hawkril Anharu crashed to the ground, chin bouncing, as purple fire spat again, scorching the stones a few feet in front of him. Something small out of that inferno struck the armaragor's cheek, and Embra, winded and floundering under a pair of large and heavy shins, distinctly heard flesh sizzle, followed by Hawkril's soft curse.

"Hawk," she gasped. "Hawkril, *listen!*"

A rising growl of fury was her reply—and boots that weren't at all gentle scraped and scrabbled around her as the armaragor gained his knees and turned with frightening speed to catch hold of her by the fabric covering one shoulder. Hot eyes glared into hers. *"What?"*

Embra panted for breath, suddenly awed by the warrior's strength, and gasped out, "If you rush out there, he *can't* miss you! How will that help Craer?"

"Lady," the armaragor snarled, "Craer Delnbone is my oldest friend in the worl—"

"And perhaps he'll remain so," the sorceress snapped, "if you can keep him alive. To do that, we need Sarasper unharmed. To manage that, we need that guard gone." She clasped slim fingers to his shoulders and shook him with all her strength; she fluttered like a leaf in a gale, but he held firm. She shouted into his face anyway. *"Listen to me!"*

The armaragor blinked at her and then barked simply, "Talk."

"I need you to rise up, but then get right down again, once he fires the scepter. I'll need that time to see him and finish my spell. If the Three stand with us, that should shatter his shield."

"Shield? My swor—"

"Not that sort of shield. The spell I sent at him struck something—a spell of his, a barrier—and so did the little stone Craer threw to ruin his aim. That mage is standing behind a wall of magic."

Fire spat again, they heard Sarasper sob from somewhere in the spreading smoke, and earth and gravel spattered the other side of the wall they were crouching behind.

Hawkril's head snapped around to peer in the direction of the unseen guard for a moment, then he looked straight back into Embra's eyes and snarled, "Lead, then. Tell me when you're ready for me to do this little dance." He hefted the heavy war sword in his hand meaningfully, face still hard, and something in his eyes made Embra shiver.

She drew in a deep breath, turned herself to face the wall and the guard beyond, closed her hand around another of her dwindling store of knickknacks, and said softly, "Do it now."

A stone rolled as the armaragor moved, rocking his

shoulders to make it look like he was rushing forward
when no scepter spat fire in the first moment. Then purple fire roared out once more, and Embra shot up to
peer through the smoke as the air beside her sizzled.
There!

She fancied that distant eyes met hers, just for a moment, as she calmly and precisely spoke the last words
of the spell—and lightnings of black tinged with purple
flashed out of her hands, wrestling at the air as they
leaped forward through the smokes in a spectacular
crawling that arched up and over a suddenly staggering
figure.

Beside her, there was sudden movement, something
whipped through the air, almost singing as it went—
and Hawkril stood watching grimly as his hurled blade
cut through spark-strewn air, end over end.

Steel spun about a throat, and a scepter exploded in a
whirling wash of light. Hands spasmed in pain—and in
a sudden burst of purple fury, the second scepter exploded, hurling stony rubble and small cantles of wizard in all directions.

Hawkril didn't wait for the gruesome rain to settle.
He had a dagger out and was lumbering around the end
of the wall even before Embra could swallow at the
sight of a ragged torso toppling out of sight. She drew
in a deep, shuddering breath and ran after him.

Somewhere ahead, Sarasper was sobbing weakly.
They caught sight of him, staggering dazedly through
the smoke, and he looked up at them with pleading eyes
and mumbled, "I can't find him."

There was a small sound from the smokes above, and
even as Hawkril whipped back his knife for a throw,
stones clattered down, followed by a small, limp, and
familiar body. Its boneless fall smashed the healer flat
to the littered ground, a bare three strides away from the
armaragor.

Hawkril covered that distance in one long lunge,
plucked up Craer's body as if the procurer was a child's

rag doll, caught hold of a bruised jaw, and stared into the little man's bloody, unconscious face. Then he turned his head and peered keenly, for all the world like a falcon glaring down at prey, into the face of the moaning healer . . . just as Sarasper's head lolled back, his eyes rolled to their whites, and his discomfort fell silent.

"Alive, both of them," Hawkril said gravely to Embra, as she knelt beside him, panting from her hard run over broken, smoke-shrouded ground. "This is probably not a good time to enter yon portal."

She smiled almost impishly at him. "So what're we waiting for?"

After a startled moment, he grinned wolfishly back.

"Horns!" Klamantle swore, breaking into a clumsy run that ended in a stumble and sprawl. Arrows hummed past him and on out over the waters of Lake Lassabra.

Markoun stiffened as a shaft cut bloodily along one of his arms, and whatever magic he'd been struggling to hurl collapsed into a gout of winking, swift-dying lights.

Klamantle snarled out something through the dirt on his face, and without trying to rise lifted both of his arms like gliding wings. They tingled as they poured forth thousands of racing blades, glittering needles of force that hissed out in a silvery cloud.

A dozen or more archers shrieked or shouted in vain alarm ere they died, and when the spell-fangs had all boiled away into smoke and the twitching bodies had slumped down amid shredded leaves, Klamantle rose, wiped himself off, and gave Markoun a disgusted look. "My best battle spell, gone already," he growled.

Markoun looked up from the healing vial he'd just sipped a careful few drops from, and shrugged. The gesture made him wince and clutch at his half-healed arm. "At least we're alive to see you cast your second-best battle spell."

The older wizard's face split in a wide, mirthless mockery of a smile. "Most amusing," he snapped. "Let's get away from this shore before someone else sees us. Come!"

"Yes, master," the younger mage muttered, dropping his voice below audibility on the second word. He followed Klamantle across blood-drenched ground. "Who were these men anyw—*what're* you *doing?*"

"Collecting weapons," Klamantle said, lips tight with revulsion as he bent to his second gory bundle and tugged at a scabbard still under a spray of fountaining blood. "With swords and knives enough, we can turn a whirldance spell into a wall of slicing swords. Besides, 'tis always wise to seize what you can't borrow. Hasten!"

"Indeed," Markoun almost snarled, bending to take up a sword that spasming hands had thankfully hurled a good distance from its owner. If haste good Klamantle desired, haste he would get. He glanced up at the thick forest around and shuddered. If dark found them still creeping around this, getting stabbed at by arrows shot by unseen lurking foes, then he was all for a running charge into the ruins, and to the Three's dung midden with stealth and slow, cautious advances!

"Faster," Klamantle grunted, from somewhere ahead. Markoun didn't bother to look up, but merely waggled his fingers in an appropriately rude gesture.

The top of a wall nearby suddenly exploded in flames, and from somewhere in the distance in quite another direction, a short, choked-off scream rang out. Embra looked up at the armaragor bending grimly over her, his scorched and bloody war sword back in his hand, and said, "T-this is going to be dangerous."

Hawkril glanced around as the clash of steel arose from behind a building on their left, and the burning wall slumped to the ground, a limp dark-robed body tumbling amid its rubble. "This concerns me," he replied, not bothering to smile. "Deeply."

Embra smiled for him, and shook her head in warm mirth as she bent to her task in the armaragor's protective shadow. She rose from her knees to place knick-knacks on two foreheads, clapped her hands over them and leaned forward into an all-fours position, and looked up at Hawkril. "Now."

The armaragor nodded expressionlessly, and she felt surprisingly gentle hands plucking at her tunic, dragging it out of her belt to lay bare her back. The great war sword was planted in the turf bare inches from her cheek, and she felt rather than saw him take out his knife again. There was a tap on her back. "Here?"

"Y-yes," she told the ground in front of her, and caught at her lip. There was a sudden coldness, a wet trickling, and growing pain as Hawkril carefully took the enchanted curio she'd given him and pressed it into the bleeding cut he'd made. Trembling, Embra said, "If it'll stay, stand back now."

"Back," the armaragor agreed, and she heard the scrape of one of his boots, moving away. The sorceress drew in a deep breath, felt the pain growing, and murmured the incantation.

Her back exploded with fire, as she'd known it would, and through the sudden, stinging sweat her world suddenly became a small boy frantically climbing a chain out of a dark room of death, a howling pack of war dogs racing nearer . . . and her father smiling down at her chained nakedness and spilling a lazy handful of gemstones onto it. "My little Lady of Jewels," he drawled, "what will you become?" His dark laughter rolled over her then, deafeningly, and left Embra blinking in a sudden chill. Wisps of spell-smoke were rising from under her fingers—fingers tensed over foreheads that had suddenly risen bolt upright, and belonged to faces now frowning at her in bafflement.

"Don't pull away," she pleaded, and poured her pain into them, urging it down trembling arms as she drew in the racing tide of magic from the vanished knick-knacks and sent it raging down into them. Almost immediately she felt Sarasper steering the flow, twisting and tugging at it as he sighed out relief and satisfaction. Cool healing flooded all three of them, and its intense pleasure made them gasp, sigh, and shudder in unison.

"If you're all *quite* finished," Hawkril growled from somewhere near at hand and yet a world away, "we'd best get on and into yon library. Folk—and mages, too—are trying to kill each other a mite too energetically."

Craer sprang up, all trace of harm gone, and chuckled. "When did you become so talkative, Tall and Mighty?"

"When I saw how far it took you in life," Hawkril growled, as they trotted through the last wisps of smoke to the library door.

It was an oval twice as tall as even the massive armaragor, and its stone surface had once been sculpted to present some sort of elaborate face or scene to the world. Unfortunately, years of weather had cracked and worn most of that impressiveness away; it was impossible now to say for certain what the door had looked like or proclaimed.

"Looks like a tomb," Hawkril grunted.

Craer lifted an eyebrow. "A tomb for words?" he commented archly—and then, not bothering about traps or stealth, swung wide the door, and darted in.

It must have been counterweighted and finely carved indeed; the huge slab of stone pivoted easily and without a sound. The procurer had ducked into the gloom within crouching low, and Hawkril knew his first act, if what was within allowed it, would have been to spring sideways, out of the way of the door. Probably to the right.

"Duck low and go left," he grunted to Sarasper and Embra. "Nothing clever."

The armaragor went last, casting a quick look around at the various battles raging in the ruins. Had the door banged closed behind him a single breath later than it did, he'd have seen two wizards staggering along through the rubble toward him, their robes held up like aprons before them around ungainly bundles of weaponry.

"Swords are bebolten *heavy*," Markoun snarled, stumbling for the sixty-third time. "Can't we just drop them?"

"No," Klamantle snapped, his eyes on the door ahead. *"Hurry."* A moment later he caught his foot on a loose stone and fell headlong with a mighty crash.

"Yes," he amended grimly, staggering to his feet without any of his scavenged weapons before Markoun could open his mouth to say anything. "We'll have to move quietly in there, I'll be bound."

Markoun shrugged, grinned, and let his own weapons spill out onto the ground in a rushing clatter. Bound would be a good state for Klamantle—bound and gagged, even better. That thought carried him right to the door, and Klamantle's gentle opening of it and gesture for him to enter.

Enter yawning darkness whence the Lady Silvertree and her three armed companions had gone, only moments ago. Markoun swallowed, came to a sudden halt—and earned himself a hard look from Klamantle.

He smiled, shrugged, and stepped into the waiting darkness. Ready to hurl deadly magic? Of course. As always. Might I have a target, please?

* * *

"Spread out and keep low and quiet—but stray not far," Craer murmured in their ears and watched as they did his bidding. Crouching silent and motionless in the gloom, the Band of Four peered around.

It was like a vast, dark cavern, low overhead where they stood, and rising to dusty, cobwebbed heights ahead. Craer held out his hands for silence, and the Four kept as quiet as they could, Sarasper jamming two fingers up his nostrils to quell a sneeze.

Dust and the reek of mold were everywhere. This must be the library of the dead wizard Ehrluth, unless there'd been other domed libraries in Indraevyn of old. On all sides of the crouching adventurers were bookshelves . . . empty bookshelves.

Dark, smooth spans of fluted wood, their runs broken by stone columns. Curving, concentric circles of shelves, pierced by straight aisles that radiated from a circle of bare tiles under the center of the dome—where six pillars of faintly glowing air stretched from floor to the high ceiling—to many sets of outer doors. Closed, dusty, dark. Yet somehow aware, waiting. Something small—a pebble?—fell or clattered, very faintly, in the distance; the sound echoed around the dome. Indeed, they were not alone.

This might just be *their* waiting tomb, a deathtrap to swallow them all with ease. The Four exchanged glances and then began to silently point at things in the gloom that seemed most interesting . . . or ominous.

Those central pillars of light seemed too soft to be sunlight, throwing too little illumination outside their confines. There were lesser glows in the vast chamber, too—glows that *moved*. Slowly and silently, undulating or creeping along and down some of the shelves. Craer raised one hand in a "stay here" gesture, and then pointed at Hawkril and the door they'd come through, reminding the armaragor to be ready for other arrivals. An instant later, the procurer crept around the corner of a shelf like a supple spider and moved to where he could get a better look at the nearest glow.

It seemed to be some sort of man-length caterpillar, or furry snake—a long, fuzzy segmented body, gleaming pale white, shot through with wandering pink veins. It looked *raw,* like a grave maggot or a shellfish torn out of its shell.

Craer stared at the thing as it traveled patiently down a shelf, its head—if it was a head—waggling about in an obscene, silent questing after . . . what?

Flesh? Paper? Leaves? The more he looked at it, the more it looked like a caterpillar; the most monstrous such thing he'd ever seen. Craer moved a few paces closer—and then crouched down, swiftly drew back, and went scuttling back the way he'd come.

Embra almost put her dagger into his face when he reappeared suddenly around the corner of the shelf. She let out an indrawn breath in a trembling sigh of relief, and he gave her a grin and tapped her shoulder with a few fingers in silent reassurance.

His words took that feeling away again. "Man in leathers, atop the shelves yon," he murmured. "Saw me looking."

Sarasper drew a knife and Embra took another knick-knack into her hand; Hawkril already held steel in both hands and was looking and listening intently, head questing from the door behind them to the gloom all around.

The ceiling hung close above the tops of the tall bookshelves around them but soared up to form the dome nearer to the center. Their eyes were getting more used to the gloom, now, and by unspoken agreement they began to move forward, half crouched and as quietly as possible.

Fist-size spiders and what looked like centipedes the length of farm carts scuttled or perambulated silently across the floor ahead as they went . . . and under the shelves, where the darkness was deepest, there were many small pairs of watching eyes. They were white, glowing orbs, not the eyes of rats or mice. Ahead of them a crack as wide as a man's hand wandered across the floor . . . and at some time in the past, something that left a white trail of slime, now long since dried, had crawled into or out of the fissure. The trail went wandering off through the shelves, through thick spiderwebs—and unpleasant-looking solid lumps hanging here and there in those webs. A few of the webs were quivering, as if something unseen, somewhere else, was plucking at them or struggling in their grip.

Embra decided she really didn't ever want to have to lie down in the library to try to sleep—at the very thought her skin seemed to *crawl* from slimy, or scaly, or just coldly foreign touches, all over—and she wasn't the only one to have that thought, just then.

Watching for men in leathers, snakes, and worse, the Four moved cautiously forward, toward the center of the dome.

It was a vast, open area, those shafts its only brightness. In the light of their eerily serene glow, the stone vault could be seen curving up unbroken, pierced by no windows. As the four companions advanced, the glows of the shafts showed them that the inside of the dome was encircled by a balcony above where they were now. It ran above the ranks of shelves, all around the circle, an empty ring with an ornately carved inner railing. Scrolling leaves, and soaring bird shapes, entwined with what looked like ribbons or sashes and snarling lion faces . . . all of stone, and obscured by thick coatings of dust. Many doors opened off the balcony, and a handful stood open. Now that they were nearer, faint light could be seen through these open doors— illuminating clouds of gently drifting dust. Three spiral stairs of slender stone, spaced around the central circle, reached from its tiles to pierce the inner balcony rail.

The open center of the dome held only dust, cobwebs, small scatterings of rubble, and here and there small heaps of dark, dried unpleasantness where a bird or small scuttling creature had met its end, and there rotted.

Soaring darkness; a tomb waiting here in the green wilderness above the baronies of Aglirta. A tomb wizards and their guards seemed to be converging on, only to find the secrets they sought gone, Ehrluth's library long ago . . .

"Plundered," Embra murmured, staring all around with wondering eyes. "How many books were there in all this hall, I wonder?"

Craer touched her wrist and put a finger to his lips warningly. As if in reply to her question, there was a scrape of an uncautious boot on stone somewhere in the shelves well around to their right—and then, off to the left, a sudden, startlingly loud commotion of steel, snarled curses, a gasp, and a heavy thud . . . and then silence.

The procurer leaned close to Sarasper and Embra and murmured, "We move one row back, and then along one aisle away from here; follow Hawk."

He moved his hands in a sign to the armaragor, and they moved, creeping along in careful stealth. Somewhere else a door opened, and sunlight flooded briefly into the room. "By the Three—," someone said, startlingly loud, and someone else urgently shushed the first someone.

Urgently, but not swiftly enough. A bow twanged, there was a wet thump, and an unseen man gasped, choked, and crashed to the floor, his armor ringing. Another arrow hummed; another man fell.

"Stars and shards!" someone else snarled, voice high with the fury born of fear, and then chanted something that could only be an incantation.

Light bloomed in the dusty, midair heart of the dome—high, bright, and sudden. The Band of Four found themselves blinking at each other. They had just reached the new aisle, and could see that the outer door it ran to was blocked by the twisted, stunted tangle of a tree trying to grow past the ceiling. The flagstones of the floor had been heaved up at crazy angles by its hungrily coiling roots, and as they peered at what lay before them, something small, dark, and long-tailed among the roots scurried under a shelf, out of the light.

The next aisle over must be blocked, too—much of the room above it had fallen long ago, collapsing down onto those library shelves in a large and untidy fall of stone. Stone ceiling tiles hung down, bulged and discolored, like some sort of gigantic, petrified infection. The arc of shelf leading in that direction was dark with the ashes of a long-ago fire that had been small but fierce. Hawkril and Craer exchanged glances, and the procurer led the way up their new aisle, two rows closer to the center.

Here there were still tomes on the shelves. Embra made a little eager sound and tried to push past the procurer—but the blade of his slim sword barred her way, and even as she pressed against it, hissing her frustration at him, she saw that the books were in truth books no more, but a quivering flood of fleshy brown and black mushrooms, their spores drifting around them in a lazy, ale-hued cloud.

The Lady of Jewels made another small sound, this one of disgust and dejection. A moment later, she almost jumped out of her skin when Hawkril's large and heavy hand descended without warning on her shoulder.

"If it's books you want," his deep growl said almost lovingly into her ear, "look into yon shafts of light—up high off the floor here, mind."

Embra moved to where she could see past a tangle of cobwebs, and looked . . . and saw. Inside each of the six glowing columns of enchanted air, hanging high out of reach of normal-size folk standing on the floor, floated an open book of massive size. "Oh," she gasped, and started forward without thinking.

Hawkril's gripping hand and Craer's raised sword reached her at about the same time—which was also when something swooped in the central darkness, there came a flash, and a figure in robes tumbled out of the high gloom, plunged past the books in their lighted shafts, and struck the floor with an ominous thud and cracking sound.

The Silvertree sorceress swallowed in the firm grasp of the Blackgult men. Together they saw another mage come into view, darting through the air like a gigantic, wingless wasp. He peered down at one book, hanging in the light, and reached for it.

His grasping hand seemed to pass right through it. Even as he frowned down at it in astonishment, crossbows snapped from three places among the shelves on the far side of the dome. Quarrels sped, a transfixed body jerked with a grunt, flung up its arms wildly, and slumped down, sinking swiftly out of sight.

"By the Three," Embra murmured, shaking herself as if emerging from an unpleasant dream. Another of the glowing caterpillar-things slunk slowly into view along shelves to their right; shelves that were empty of all but heaps of pulp dripping with mold. It had fleshy horns on its head, which curled and uncurled in constant, almost lazy motion as it undulated along. When it saw them, it reared up, as if to survey them, and then suddenly turned and slid from view, its body passing along the shelf in an impossibly long procession of palely glowing segments. The Lady of Jewels stared at those sagging heaps of discolored pulp. "What's written, I wond—"

There was a thump on their right, very close by, and a swift, light metallic grating or scraping. The Four barely had time to stiffen before two plate-armored figures, as tall and as broad of shoulder as Hawkril, burst around the end of a shelf. Their faces were hidden in full war helms, but their intentions were clear enough. They thrust forward the long and heavy swords in their hands as they came, jabbing the air viciously and charging swiftly enough that the air they were lancing could not help but soon contain one or more of the Band of Four.

Hawkril hesitated not an instant but shouldered through his fellows to meet the warriors. He drove those stabbing blades aside with ringing blows of his own war sword, and in an instant the aisle was a crashing confusion of grunting men, clashing steel, and hulking warriors spinning and darting about like dancers at a revel.

"A deadly sort of revel," Sarasper murmured aloud, as that thought struck him, and Embra jostled him hard into a shelf.

"Old man, how can I loose a spell if you're—" she hissed, and then spun around with a little scream of alarm.

The tentacles that slapped and tore at her midriff were flailing the air in front of the healer's face by then, and he swore and backhanded them away from his throat, feeling the numbness of life-seeking magic where they touched his skin.

Beyond the tentacles that coiled and glided in search of their deaths stood their source: a tousle-haired young man in wizards' robes, the badge of Ornentar on his shoulder and excitement flaming in his snapping brown eyes. From his extended hand, surrounded by a roiling glow of fresh magic, the writing tentacles ran. He laughed softly as the tentacles came at Sarasper and Embra in a flailing forest and said, "Die, whoever you are—*die!*"

A tentacle slapped around one of Embra's wrists, and she shrieked and tried to pull away. Sarasper saw another of the rubbery things reaching for her face or throat and lifted his dagger to stab awkwardly at it, wishing he . . .

A head lolled over the edge of a bookshelf, followed by a limp, dangling arm. Blood dripped from its finger-tips as it swung gently, back and forth—and that grisly movement had barely caught Embra's eyes when a swift shadow sprang out of the darkness above the corpse, a familiar, hurtling silhouette that plunged feet-first into the aisle, kicking the tentacle-mage's head sideways into a shelf.

Bones cracked, blood flew, and the mage's stare be-came glassy before he slid down the shelves, his head leaving a dark and bloody trail in its wake. Craer landed, plucked something like a cluster of fused gems from the man's belt—a cluster in whose depths small lights were winking, ever-faster—and peered at it.

"Aleglarma," he read aloud, and those inner lights burst into flames, racing to meet each other in the lam-bent depths. The procurer straightened and threw the egg of gems in one smooth movement, hurling it over the heads of Hawkril and his two foes into the central, open area.

"No! You *fool!*" Embra screamed. "It'll . . ."

The fury of the sun seemed to burst momentarily at the base of the six light shafts, and the entire building rocked and boomed around them as the Four were flung off their feet. The two armored warriors tumbled help-lessly down the aisle, through their midst.

When the shaking and shuddering stopped, Hawkril was on his back amid the drifting dust, with a warrior atop him. Embra rushed forward with a scream, tearing at the man's helm with her bare hands, but Craer was swifter. He drove a dagger to the hilt into the man's neck, and then peeled him away from the armaragor, grunting with the effort.

He needn't have bothered. The man hung heavy and limp, and dark liquids rushed out of him as they lifted him a little off Hawkril's chest—enough to see that the entire length of their friend's war sword was buried in the man's belly, where an armor plate had fallen away, and must have run up inside his body to his throat.

"Hawkril?" Embra asked, her voice not entirely steady. "Are you—"

"Hurt?" the armaragor growled. "Don't think so. The blast impaled the bastard on my blade . . . wrist still numb . . ."

There was a steely sound behind them, and the procurer and the sorceress whirled around—in time to see Sarasper calmly drive his knife hilt-deep through one eyehole of the helmed warrior who lay in a dazed and helpless heap beside the healer.

A vast silence fell in the library then . . . a stillness broken only by the grunts and scrapings of Hawkril finding his feet again and feeling gingerly along his ribs. Embra took one hesitant step toward the center of the library, and then another.

"Wonders of the Three!" she breathed in delighted awe. Where she'd expected to see only ashes and dark smoke, the shafts of light—with their floating books—stood as before, apparently untouched.

The Lady Silvertree turned and found Craer at her elbow. "We—are we alone here?" she asked, almost fiercely.

"No, L—Embra," the procurer replied. "That lurker I saw, and at least one more mage . . . probably more than that, besides; they're all still here, somewhere."

"I've *got* to get a look at those books," the sorceress told him. "But how?"

"Can't you fly up there, with a spell?"

"Of course. It's bows I'm worried about, and—"

"Worry about the bolts and arrows," Hawkril rumbled in her ear. "Never the bows."

"Funny, funny man," she told him out of the side of her mouth, and took a stride forward, and then another. Her companions didn't try to stop her this time.

"Can you raise a shield, like that mage outside?" Craer asked.

Embra put her knuckles to her mouth. "Yes, but any wizard can destroy such a magic," she said slowly, "and I can't fend off dozens of crossbow bolts. I don't know about getting into those columns of light and keeping my spells active, either. How? . . ."

"Just do it," Craer urged her, "but don't stop and hover—dart this way and that, swoop, drop suddenly, and never stay still. If someone fires at you, fly away, but try to mark where the shot came from and then get above it—*high* above it. We'll run there and see if we can't silence the bowman."

Embra looked at him, fires of excitement rising in her eyes, and then plunged both hands almost greedily into her bodice, brought out two rather battered-looking knickknacks, and hissed incantations in furious haste. A small, wet sound in the next row made Hawkril dart around the corner, where he found a sagging warrior pinned to the shelves with a heavy war quarrel, a dark ribbon of blood spreading out from the man's twitching feet. The dying man had been there for some time, by the looks of all that spilled blood. Hawkril shot glances up and down the aisle but could see no foe to be wary of.

He was just turning back into the row where the Four had fought the warriors when Embra rose into the air, glided along the tops of the shelves with the toes of her boots almost touching the weathered wood, and then reached the curving wall of the dome and soared up along it.

No arrows reached for her, and they could hear no sound in the dark, dead library but their own breathing.

"I hope the lass isn't chasing a trap," Hawkril muttered. "You saw that wizard's hand pass through the tome? Those books aren't even *here*."

"It's only in bards' tales that folk cast mighty spells and spend bags upon bags of gold to build traps every-

where," Craer murmured back. "The books lie open—
'tis some sort of message intended for mages."

"Or passing pigeons," the armaragor grunted. "If
that's not too much of a stretch, outside a bard's tale,
that is."

"Funny, funny man," Craer told Hawkril out of the
side of his mouth, in devastating mimicry of Embra's
tones.

The armaragor grimaced and then stiffened as the
Lady of Jewels swooped out of the great arc of the
dome, curling around its far surface where runes were
written. She peered at them narrowly, slowing in her
glide, and then soared again. The men of the Four
tensed, straining to hear the rattle of a windlass or the
thrum of a bowstring, but the library seemed eerily
quiet.

Embra plunged into view again, now clearly curling
around the columns of faintly glowing air. She slowed,
peered, and then circled away, coming back to the same
book again, and then tossed her hair back and soared up
into the dark heights of the vault again. Craer nodded
approvingly.

*"Then did the Golden Griffon rage . . . At his forever
foe enthroned . . . in the splendor of a nest new and
strong raised,"* Embra Silvertree murmured to herself,
the dusty air whistling past her shoulders. "His foe
would be a Silvertree and the nest Silvertree House, if
the writing is old, or Castle Silvertree if 'tis recent.
Probably 'tis old . . ."

She bit her lip and plunged down out of the heights
once more, peering at the dark arcs of shelving as she
descended, seeking bows and men in armor and eyes
glaring her way.

Embra thought she saw movement, back in the dark
reaches well away from her companions, but when she
peered again, she saw nothing but empty shelves and
drifting mold spores.

The book she'd glanced at before showed her the

same words. That was good. She swept past it and slowed at the next one, murmuring its words under her breath as she scanned them: *"The place of fallen majesty, its master and namesake now gone, with all his strivings, to a pearl upon the fast Silverflow, an upthrust prow of shields for to cleave the winter waves."* Well, that was clear enough: the pearl was Silvertree Isle, and the place of fallen majesty Silvertree House. If these were clues to the whereabouts of a Dwaer, they were clearly pointing to the Silent House.

Perhaps the third b—

The world around her exploded in a burst of varicolored light, shaking the vast dome above her with a sound like rolling thunder. Amid the roaring, dust rained down, and out of flickering, pulsing afterblasts below her raced long, snakelike necks with needle-toothed, snapping jaws.

Too breathless to scream, Embra was snatched away from them by blasts of tortured air that felt like the blows of large, wildly swung fists. She was cartwheeling through the air, spinning helplessly through shafts of light and phantom books—well, that was one thing learned: touching a shaft, or even a book, robbed a mage of no magic!—with those snaking, impossibly long necks twisting up after her, climbing nearer . . . and nearer . . . and she was feeling sick again, weak and empty and . . .

Whenever the snakelike spell-things touched one of the glowing shafts, they boiled away into it and were gone, Embra saw. Her wild spinning was slowing now as she approached the curving wall of the dome and met roiling air rebounding off it. The dome above her was still ringing like a bell, but through its din she could now hear shouts and the high clang of swords meeting in anger. A shout rose above the rest, soaring up to her ears as she struggled to gain control of her flight: "For Ornentar! For *victory!*"

By the Three, did warriors bellowing war cries ever realize just how foolish they sounded?

Embra shook her head and plunged down through thinning smokes, past snapping jaws that veered and swooped at her too slowly to find their mark, toward the shelves where heavily armored warriors were hacking at Craer and Hawkril, who stood back to back with old Sarasper dancing between them, tiny lightnings flickering between his fingers as he held some spell she didn't recognize ready . . . to heal? To harm?

Beyond and behind the warriors stood two men in robes—men with cruel faces and cold eyes. One stood with hands raised, sweat glistening on his forehead, and the ripples of intense concentration playing across his jaws. Jaws, like those that snapped and swooped at her . . .

The other mage was older, and from his jowls to his wintry brows he reeked of power. His eyes were on her, and his lips were moving. From his fingertips dark wisps of smoke or shadow were curling, welling up as they escaped from his grasp, into dark and flapping things that squeaked and cut the air like shards of black glass. They were . . . bats.

Embra frowned, even as she hurled herself sideways in the air to escape whatever doom this cold-eyed man was weaving. Hadn't Spellmaster Ambelter—her lips curled in revulsion at the mere remembrance of his face—once disparagingly mentioned a downriver wizard who styled himself the Master of Bats?

Bats were circling the cold-eyed wizard's arms and over his head now, a score of them or more, and Embra applied herself to climbing away from him and getting to where the shafts of light would stand between them. She was going to make it, she was . . .

Caught like a leaf in a gale, hurled away again too stunned to shriek, as the world exploded in blinding brightness that seared her eyes and rang in her ears and smacked her against curving stone that threw her away again into emptiness. . . .

Was her arm broken? Her hip shattered? Or . . . were they just numbed past feeling? She tried to turn her head and look at herself and had a confused sight of red threads of blood trailing like ribbons behind her, through a white and ever-present glow.

Something struck her, hard—something smooth and solid—and she crashed along it until she came to rest, half through something . . . it was such a relief to just slip away. . . .

Craer sprang up, kicked a gleaming helm squarely between the eyes, and had time for a glance up and across the dome as his opponent staggered back. Embra was half sitting, half sagging among the carvings along the ornate balcony rail, a trickle of blood falling from her open mouth. She was moving slowly, her head lolling . . .

"She's alive!" the procurer howled. "She lives!"

Hawkril's answer was a roar of approval, and his blade shrieked it protest as he drove in half through a breastplate. There was a muffled cry from within the helm, armored shoulders shook, and Hawkril moved with the reeling warrior, driving his sword in low under the man's arm—into a second warrior, who'd been trying to reach past the first. There was a roar of pain.

Hawkril twisted his sword, clinging to it with both hands to keep custody of it as one warrior flailed about in agony, and the other backed away. With a wet wrenching, the second armsman tore free of the steel that had thrust into the chainmail at his crotch, and staggered away, hunched over and groaning.

Craer parried a vicious sword cut, but its force drove the procurer to his knees. His Ornentarn attacker bounded forward to stand over Craer, so as to hack him to the floor. Sarasper snatched a handful of moldering mushrooms from the nearest shelf and hurled it into the man's face, up under the helm. The shuddering sneeze was immediate. The old healer gritted his teeth, tried to ignore a second armsman trying to reach past the first with his sword—and drove his dagger firmly up under the edge of the sneezing man's helm, jabbing again . . . and again. . . .

There was a sudden flash of light from behind him, and the healer spun around. "Hawkril?" he cried in wild, rising fear, trying to peer into blinding white-starred smoke. "Hawk?"

"I live," the armaragor growled. "Guard thyself!"

The healer spun around again, raising his dagger in a frantic parry—and the warrior lumbering past him ignored it and its wielder in his haste to get at Hawkril.

The hulking armaragor grinned, beckoned the Ornentarn with a wave of one large hand, and brought his blade up. Whereupon the world exploded again behind him.

A mage was flung helplessly out of that tumult, his flailing body sweeping the legs of an Ornentarn warrior out from under him. They crashed into a bookshelf together with bone-shattering force, and it shuddered, swayed, and started to topple.

Beyond the blast, shelves were crashing down, ponderous and inexorable, rolling thunders rising from their ruin. The ceiling above the shelves was shuddering as dust and stone blocks rained down together, crashing and rolling.

"Silvertree!" a coldly triumphant voice called, from the far side of the echoing chaos—and in the wake of that war cry something bright stabbed out, a lance of light that lasted for but a breath and then was gone. Its brilliance faded more slowly in the eyes of those who'd seen it. Where it struck, an Ornentarn warrior crashed onto his face, smoke rising from his armor.

Bats were flying wildly everywhere, and the mage who stood where they clustered thickest turned to face this new threat. He said one cold word as he traced a symbol in the air before him—and the smoke rolled away, as if swept by an unseen hand, to lay bare a scene of splintered and twisted devastation.

Shelves lay like so much storm-felled timber, with broken bodies of fighting-men draped here and there among the broken spars. Beyond the ruin stood two mages, smiling slightly as they stared at the mage among his bats . . . and the second wizard, struggling to his feet barely a sword's reach in front of a narrow-eyed Hawkril.

"Silvertree?" the mage of bats sneered. "You look far too young even to be allowed to launder mage robes in that dark barony."

The older of the two Silvertree mages lifted a scornful eyebrow. "The courtesy of Huldaerus, Master of Bats, is legendary—and now I see the reality is no less. A pity your tongue outstrips both your judgment and powers." He raised a hand as if in salute . . . or to unleash a spell. "Klamantle and Markoun of Silvertree, here to hand you doom."

"Fine words," Huldaerus purred. "Can you make them more?" He did not lift his hands, but from the rings on his fingers dark lightnings spat, snarling across the open space of shattered shelves at the Silvertree mages.

Halfway there the dark bolts struck an unseen shielding, clawed along it, and then expired in swirling black sparks. Klamantle acquired a stiff smile and brought his upraised hand down.

A stone block larger than a man obediently tore itself out of the ceiling right above Huldaerus and crashed down—but the body that was smashed to the floor beneath it wore the armor of a warrior, and the wizard of the bats suddenly stood some distance away along the shelves, where an Ornentarn warrior had raised a sword but a moment before.

The Master of Bats barely had time to twist his lips

into a scornful smile before Markoun of Silvertree raised his hand and hurled a raging sphere of flames at Huldaerus. The Ornentarn mage lost his smile and ducked around the end of a shelf with rather more haste than dignity. Markoun's magic burst with a roar—a roar that was immediately echoed by the flames it birthed, as they tore hungrily along deserted shelves.

"Impressive," the other Ornentarn mage commented, raising an eyebrow. "Phalagh, by the way, at your service."

Hawkril swung his war sword even faster than the Silvertree mages could snarl spells, but his blade passed right through the smiling Phalagh as if the mage had been made of smoke.

Phalagh gave him a tight smile, murmured, "Await my revenge, thickskull," and stepped through the shelf he'd been leaning against, out of sight.

An instant later, that entire course of shelves vanished into whirling splinters with a roar. Klamantle stood at one end of it with the hands that had cast that rending spell still raised, peering through the dust, but Phalagh's laugh came back to them from somewhere in the dark shelves beyond. Shelf after shelf crumpled and sighed into nothingness in the distance, more and more slowly as the spell spent itself.

A last shelf groaned and fell, and the wizard Huldaerus stood revealed, trying a small and ordinary door in a wall none of them had seen before—a wall that stood amid the shelves, enclosing a wedge-shaped room. The mage glanced up at them, face tightening in anger, and hissed something. When he touched the door next, it vanished in a gout of smoke, and Huldaerus darted into the space beyond.

As Markoun raised his hand again, an Ornentarn warrior sprinted after the wizard of the bats.

"Ehrluth's spell chamber?" the younger Silvertree mage asked, his eyes narrowing.

"Whatever it may be," Klamantle replied, "he enters

to win time to work magics against us—or to seek new weapons to slay us with. Come!"

The room Huldaerus hurled himself into was dark and dusty, but it sang with the echoes of countless forgotten, long-cast spells, their jangling rising anew as the mighty magics of the spell-battle flooded in on the heels of the hurrying mage. This was Ehrluth's spell chamber—and if the Three were kind, it just might hold some spell or scepter that he could hurl against these Silvertree mages.

His bats squeaked around him, telling him that the room stood empty, and Huldaerus made candles of his own fingers to peer at the walls for runes or storage holes or handles. Nothing. Curses of the Three, had he raced into a trap?

He turned and wove the strongest shielding he knew with shaking fingers, almost humming in his haste, and barely had time to curse the Ornentarn warrior who blundered into the room with drawn sword and wild eyes before the older of the two Silvertree mages could be seen beyond the door, weaving a spell of doom.

Huldaerus cloaked himself in his shielding and stood tall and still, feeling every curve of his shaping, tracing its web in search of weaknesses that might mean his death, and finding . . . nothing. He found that nothing just as the room screamed around him, exploding into amber fire tinged with green and purple, a magical conflagration that broke like a wave over the Ornentarn warrior still blundering along the walls.

The warrior screamed once, a wet and bubbling sound that quavered to the floor along with his body. His flesh and bone melted together into a sort of red jelly that slumped across the floor, leaving his armor behind as an empty, rocking shell of armor plates. All around the room, bats turned to dark and shapeless globs, and splashed and pattered like broken eggs on the floor in a short, wet rain.

The Master of Bats tasted real fear for the first time

in long years, turned on his heel from that horror, and rushed for the door, hoping his shielding could hold off the flesh-drinking fire long enough for him to escape.

Of course, he was running right into whatever those mages wanted to hurl at him—and they knew it. He shaped bats in feverish haste as he ran, feeling them wriggle along his flanks and crawl near his throat. If he fell, and but a single bat of his desire flapped safely away, Huldaerus could rise again. . . .

Long and cold years might pass then before he had his revenge. But have it he would, oh, yes. . . .

The younger mage was, of course, too impatient. He stepped into view before Huldaerus had quite reached the doorway. A ruby circle appeared in the air above his palm, red radiance that burst into a thin, bright, ravening ray that seared the very air. The Master of Bats, racing too fast to stop or veer, simply flung himself on his face—and the floor opened up beneath him.

Red fire exploded harmlessly above his head as the Ornentarn mage tumbled down a stone-lined pit, a trap that Ehrluth must have placed under the very threshold of his spell chamber, a—no, not a trap.

It was a bone pit, a body disposal for creatures slain by spells, and . . .

He was crashing through their remains, bones crumbling to acrid dust all around him as he plunged and rolled and came to a crashing, breathless halt atop some loose stones that had fallen from the pit walls.

Dazedly, Huldaerus heaved himself upright, wincing at his bruises and still struggling for breath. He must climb out, or be truly trapped to face the next spell—as if he were standing at the bottom of a bottle held in the gloating hands of his foes.

He'd fallen only about twenty feet or so, and the walls of the pit were all large, rounded, loose stones stacked carelessly together, offering easy purchase everywhere for fingers and boots. The Master of Bats let two of his little creations spring out of the neck of his robes and flap upward, and then he set his teeth and followed them, surging up swiftly. He was going to make it, he was . . .

Gasping as he set his hand on a smallish stone, and raw power shocked through his arm! Power that numbed and surged and . . . he was lying on his back amid swirling bone dust again, back at the bottom of the pit.

Huldaerus shook his head to clear it, barely knowing where he was. Such power! Could it be? Well, whatever it was, he needed it now, more than he'd ever needed raw, untried magic before.

He started to climb again, slipping in his haste, looked up—and saw the younger Silvertree mage smiling down at him.

Snarling in fear and desperation, the Master of Bats clawed his way upward, crying in a desperate ploy, "It's eating me! It's got me! Come no closer! Save yourself!"

Markoun laughed aloud—and Huldaerus of Ornentar tore the small, round, dun-colored stone out of the wall. Fingers bleeding, he held it up . . . and the Silvertree mage stopped laughing.

And then, with a leaping heart, Huldaerus was certain. He was holding the Stone of Life!

His hand swept up, trailing fires, and he exulted. Then he called on its power, and as the leaping warmth flooded through him, he hurled a spell he'd dared not use before. He knew he held power incarnate, one of the Dwaer that could reshape all Darsar.

A moment later, Markoun Yarynd knew it, too.

15

To Stand Upon A Stone

The fires raining down on the Master of Bats should have crisped him on the spot. The very stones he clung to cracked and burst in the heat, showering him with hot shards.

"Too late, young idiot," Huldaerus told his foe exultantly, standing unscathed in the heart of the inferno.

As the roaring flames boiled away, their hurler stared down at him, gulping in disbelief—an emotion echoed in the raised eyebrows of the older Silvertree mage as he came to stand beside the first and look into the pit . . . and swiftly lost his air of bored unconcern. Both wizards hastened to send down deadly magics.

Huldaerus did nothing as lightnings crashed and fires roiled and lances of pure force stabbed around him. He laughed triumphantly, even as stones around him melted, slumping and flowing, and the pit grew deeper. He stood patiently as stones crumbled, flames roared, and deadly gases raged around him, until at last the onslaught died away.

In the sudden stillness, Huldaerus decided it was time to raise a sardonic eyebrow of his own.

Only the younger mage was still poised above the pit. The sneering face of the older Silvertree mage was gone; its owner had fled. Huldaerus looked up at the young fool who'd used his last few battle-spells in vain and now stood with smoke curling away from empty hands, looking down at his own death with dark despair in his eyes.

Looking down at the Master of Bats.

Huldaerus gave his foe a gentle smile and, almost delicately, sent killing flames up at him in a steady, inexorable roar. His smile did not waver, nor his fires lessen, until Markoun Yarynd had become small embedded pieces of flesh sizzling in the ceiling above the pit.

Huldaerus watched scorched stone creak and shimmer as it cooled, ignoring the sounds of battle above. He was too busy exulting at so narrowly escaping death and at the sheer power he now commanded.

At length he chuckled and lifted a hand to burn footholds in the dripping stone beside him. Well, now, it seemed Ornentar might prove the mightiest barony in all the Vale, after all. A quick clamber up, a rallying of the helmheads, and then . . .

The removal of Phalagh, who was all too quick to see things and apt to succeed in wresting the Stone away from his colleague, a mage he hated and feared . . . a mage who, bats and all, still had to sleep sometime.

Huldaerus shaped gauntlets out of the air to keep his hands from burning on the searing stones, and climbed. Halfway up, the rich stink of smoldering leather reminded him to do the same for his feet. By the Three, there was no end to the spells he could spin with this power!

As the Master of Bats clambered out of the pit, he feigned weariness—and was pleased to see Phalagh run to his aid. Feigned? Well, no, he *was* tired. Huldaerus shook his head as the world started to spin. All that crafting and guiding of spells . . . the Stone might power them without stint or faltering, but his were the wits that still had to frame each magic. . . .

His fellow Ornentarn was bending anxiously over

him now. Huldaerus looked up, smiled tightly, and cast a fleshripper spell right into Phalagh's startled face. It was a magic that tore apart its caster as well as its victim, usually employed only by doomed mages desperate to fell a foe as they died.

Phalagh didn't even have time to scream. His glistening remains were still spattering down into the pit when the Stone of Life finished restoring its bearer, and Huldaerus completed his many-times-interrupted rise back into the library.

He did not have to look far to find his warriors. Ornentar helms turned toward him to receive his orders.

"Kill everyone," he told them, waving his hand casually at the shelves around. "Scour out this place; leave none living."

Obediently they turned and lumbered away to do that. The Master of Bats watched them go, smiling faintly. Now, if *he* ruled all the Vale, what sort of land would he desire his kingdom to be? Hmm?

The slaughter took a long time, and two more Ornentarn fell. The last one took an armored giant from Brostos with him, grunts of furious effort twisting into gargling sobs of agony as they drove their blades repeatedly through each other. When the Ornentarn warriors strode up to the shafts of light where Huldaerus was standing, there were only three of them left.

"The hall is cleansed?" Huldaerus asked.

A helm shook in a reluctant "no," and a scarred gauntlet rose and pointed down an aisle. "The sorceress lives and has rejoined her companions."

"Kill them for me," Huldaerus said mildly. "Or have you seen fit to change my orders?"

"No, Lord," the warriors assured him hastily, and stalked off to deal death. They'd gone perhaps halfway down the aisle when a bright blade stabbed at them out of one of the rows; when they charged thence to give battle, a bookshelf was thrust over on them, crushing one Ornentarn.

The man's high, shrill scream brought a scowl to the face of the Master of Bats, who plucked up a piece of wood from the nearest fallen shelf. Touching it to the Stone, he closed his eyes and murmured something.

When he opened them, all wood in the part of the library he was facing melted away, leaving his two warriors facing four adventurers across a bare stone floor.

Four bedraggled adventurers. One was a mountain of an armaragor, eyes bleak and battle-calm, shoulders and arms as broad and as mighty as many a castle door—but the others were but wisps: one was old, one was little larger than a boy, and one of them was a dazed, limping woman. As the Ornentarn stalked forward, Huldaerus smiled grimly, awaiting butchery to come.

But it was one of his own warriors who came crashing down on his back, after an agile procurer had rolled hard into the man's legs—and the other who retreated in fear before the armaragor's shrewdly swung blade.

The Master of Bats snarled. Hefting the Stone, he worked a spell to make many whirling axes appear out of the air to race and spin through the area. The fully armored warriors of Ornentar should suffer little, but as for their foes . . .

He'd barely drawn breath for a grim chuckle when his conjured weapons, fading into view, flashed and fell and were no more. His spell was broken.

Beyond the flashing swords of the fighting men, the young woman stood glaring at him, no longer dazed. Then her lips twisted in a smile that promised doom.

Huldaerus gave her a sneer in answer and lifted the Stone, causing blue fires to play about it to show her what she faced. A moment later, the tiles beneath his feet abruptly heaved upward, as if punched by a huge rock fist—and he landed hard on his own backside. The smile on the face of the sorceress widened.

Huldaerus snarled, lifted the Stone over his head without bothering to rise, and willed forth bolts of lightning to lash and tame this arrogant woman.

Armored figures staggered in the sudden blue-white cracklings, but he hadn't even managed to spit out a curse at his own stupidity when the lightnings died away, and the groans of his warriors became gasps and grunts—and the clash of blades began anew.

"Horns of the Lady!" Huldaerus snarled. "Die, sorceress! *Die!*"

And he reached down deep into the Stone and called forth the strongest slaying spell he knew. He'd have a headache to outsing bards soon, and weariness to overmaster wakefulness, but if it slew this woman and let him walk free of Indraevyn with a Dwaer stone, 'twould be worth it. . . .

Like a black and vengeful ghost his cloud of slaying left him, rippling as it rose, and he saw his foe's face go pale as she recognized it.

Huldaerus smiled. Fitting, 'twas, that she'd know her doom just before it took her. The Silvertree mage, then Phalagh, now this one . . . he was going to enjoy destroying wizards up and down the Vale this season, until none but the Master of Bats could hurl a spell from Sirlptar and the sea to the singing headwaters in the wastes, wherever they might lie. He'd . . .

Embra thought furiously, watching death come for her. She had no effective counterspell. The only way to end a death shroud is with a death—either of the caster or the target. So all she had to do now was slay an accomplished wizard who commanded the endless power of a Worldstone.

She smirked bitterly. Simplicity itself for the legendary Lady of Jewels, no?

Embra retreated from the swordplay to buy herself a few more breaths to think of a way out of this. Patiently the drifting death shroud followed, looming up large and dark, opening out to receive her. . . .

She stumbled against a fallen ceiling stone and almost fell. Wait—*that was it!*

Bending over to wrap her arms around the block with one of the last few knickknacks caught between two of her fingers, she strained to lift the stone block an inch off the floor, gasped out a spelljump incantation—

—and was suddenly straining in the air, with Huldaerus just beneath her boots. She let go of the block and arched upward, seeking to climb empty air.

The Master of Bats had time to look up as the block came down—but no time to gasp. It smashed him to the floor, driving his head deep into tiles far harder than flesh or bone. His hands, however, were moving. . . .

Embra came down kicking at them. One out-flung forearm cracked like dry kindling as she landed on it, bouncing and gasping in pain. His other hand spasmed open in agony—and the faintly glowing, awakened Worldstone fell out of it. The dark wall of the death shroud faded away.

The Lady of Jewels rolled over, groaning from her landing, and snatched up the round and reassuringly heavy Dwaer.

The Ornentarn warriors had broken off their losing battle with Hawk and Craer to thunder toward her, blades raised. Sinister helms glared down, promising her swift, sharp death.

Embra kept rolling, found her feet, and raced across the rubble-strewn floor toward one of the stairs. Wind whistled near her shoulder as a blade didn't quite catch her, and then Craer yelled as he always did when throwing something heavy. There was a curse and a heavy thumping close behind her—as her running feet found the first step.

Hugging the Stone to her breast with one hand and snatching at the stair rail with the other, Embra burst up those steps like a storm wind, hearing the scrape of pursuing boots only on her last turn around the rising coil. She came out onto the curving balcony gasping for breath and staring at doors . . . closed doors.

There! One stood open, and she made for it. She had to win time to collect her wits and call on the Stone before a sword cut her open and ended all striving.

The room beyond the door was dimly lit by three tall windows and held a tangle of decaying chairs around a grand table that had collapsed long ago. Embra spun around, shoved the door shut—and discovered that its latch bar had rusted away. There was no way to secure it closed.

Hissing a curse, she hurried to a window. At least she could leap out if that swordsman got to h—

The library around her shuddered as if struck by a giant's fist, and the ceiling came down in rolling thunder. Shouting in alarm, Embra threw herself desperately out the window as stone blocks poured down and the dust rolled up.

The Stone let her fly, and even hover. She swooped up from what would have been a nasty landing on tumbled rubble in a rising arc that brought her almost nose to nose with Klamantle Beirldoun, as he stood perched on the crumbling summit of another building, his trembling hands spread in the exhausted aftermath of trying to bring down the dome of the library. His face went white as he saw the Stone in her hands.

"Yes," Embra snarled, as she flew past. "So you should fear, pawn of my father! So you should fear!"

And she turned in a tight bank, seeking a perch to slay wizards from.

The din was deafening, and the very floor shook under their boots as stones crashed down all around the dome, smashing away parts of the balcony rail. Dust rose like smoke from a wind-whipped fire. In the quaking gloom, no one saw three black bats flit up from the body of the Master of Bats—or the stones hurtling down that smashed one of them back to the floor. The wizard's remaining hand twitched once, as if trying to grasp something that wasn't there, and then was still. Dust started to fall on it as the thunderous clamor slowly died away. In the distant shadows, two bats flapped furiously away, seeking the forest beyond this shattered, doomed place.

"Hawkril?" a voice husked, and then broke off to cough. "Craer?"

Something moved elsewhere in the gloom, an agile shadow that slid a dagger into an Ornentarn throat, and then glided down a spiral stair.

"Hawkril?" the voice came again, sharp with alarm. "Where *are* you?"

The warrior of Ornentar who'd begun to move slowly toward that voice, sword raised to slay, suddenly staggered, twisted over backward under the cruel force of a choking arm—and then stiffened as a dagger slid into an eye slit of his helm. The shadow bounded away even before the warrior crashed onto a heap of fallen stones—and when Hawkril came stumbling past a moment later, peering this way and that for Sarasper or a foe, the shadow was gone amid the swirling dust.

It rose up again to scale a bookshelf, outlined for a moment against the steady, unchanged glow of the columns of light, and the only person to notice it saw it steal along the lofty wood like a prowling cat, drawing nearer to an unsuspecting Hawkril Anharu . . . and nearer . . .

A knife flashed as the shadow sprang, fingers reaching for an unprotected throat, steel ready to slash an unhelmed face.

A second shadow hurtled out of the dust, boots spread to smash aside a knife arm and drive a heel solidly into the side of a head. The two shadows met, twisted—and crashed to the floor, bouncing and rolling apart.

The armaragor spun around. "Craer?" he called, trotting forward. He recognized that slim, agile figure.

But two short and slender bodies rose in the dust, and two knives flashed. Hawkril slowed, peering over his raised sword, seeking to know his friend.

A steel ball flashed at Craer's temple. He ducked away and sensed rather than saw the thin cord trailing behind it—the cord that tugged at his arm as the ball spun in a curve. The procurer who'd thrown it pulled hard, seeking to haul Craer into his raised dagger.

Craer planted one foot and lunged in the direction he was being pulled in, bringing his dagger up with both hands to fend off that stabbing blade as he plunged past it, kicking hard at where an unseen belly must be. His boot touched something that was fading away, and a faint chuckle came to his ears as the waxed cord dropped across Craer's throat—and tightened.

The procurer threw himself onto his back and kicked out wildly with both feet, hoping to hurl himself out of his foe's reach before his shoulders struck the floor—and out of the darkness overhead a hulking body reached out a war sword over him, stabbing at his foe.

"Little dancing man," Hawkril growled. "Who are you?"

The answer that came out of the gloom was delivered with soft amusement. "Luthtuth am I, and your death this day."

Someone snorted, not far away, and Sarasper's unmistakable voice complained, "How many times have I heard such claims? How churlish! Not even 'You must die because my master decrees it!' or 'Know that the price of your doom is six golden sarcrowns, and he who paid it is—'! These younglings have no style, no respect for the rules and rightness of things!"

Luthtuth replied silkily, "I dislike babblers. Be then the first to fall!"

Sarasper snorted again, and as the shadow sprang at him, the old man was gone, and a longfangs scuttled away through the drifting dust. In the distance they heard him shout, "Embra? We need you!"

The voice could not be mistaken, nor its cry ignored. The Lady Silvertree sighed and turned reluctantly from the pleasurable job of chasing and slaying Klamantle to swoop back through a window into the library. It took but two thoughts to banish dust and make the air glow brightly as she went. Framing magics was tiring, yes, despite the coursing power of the Stone—but she was being drained no more, and by the Three it felt good to work spells unafraid!

Rubble lay everywhere, and among it her three companions—Sarasper halfway up one of the stairs—and a stranger. A slim, crouching man who by garb and manner was probably another procurer. There was a knife in his hand, and he was headed toward Sarasper.

"Shall I slay this one?" she called, slowing.

"And rob me of the pleasure?" Craer called back. "Oh, all right!"

She shook her head at his mock dejection and hurled lightnings at the stranger—but the man vaulted over some crumpled shelving and was gone down a dark opening to unknown spaces beneath.

Embra frowned. "I'm reluctant to go down there," she told her companions, hovering above them. "Why not gather up on the balcony? From there we can see him approach if he returns."

"What?" Craer croaked, rubbing at his throat. "You've got this precious Stone everyone's after—let's begone, before all the *rest* of the wizards and outlaws in Darsar get here!"

"Soon, soon," Embra told him. "There's something I must do first!" She turned and flew to the glowing shafts.

Behind her, Hawkril and Craer groaned.

* * *

Ingryl Ambelter lifted his eyes from the scene that flickered in the depths of a glass globe up at the baron, raising his eyebrows in a silent question.

Faerod Silvertree smiled. "Treachery and young mages go hand in hand; when I deal with those young in sorcery, I expect no less. Wherefore I feel no loss nor loyalty when I must spend the life of such a mage. Klamantle has reached his final usefulness to us. Use him, by all means."

The Spellmaster nodded, turned with a grim smile, and murmured into the sphere, "Fleeing so soon, Klamantle? Ah, be brave!"

His fingers moved briefly, and he saw Klamantle stiffen as that magic reached him. The flying mage froze in midair, only his twisting, trembling face betraying a frantic struggle against its grip—and then turned, firmly under the Spellmaster's control, to fly back at the dome.

There was stark terror in Klamantle's eyes as he hurtled to his doom.

The Lady of Jewels hovered above the open books, quoting aloud. "Then did the Golden Griffon . . . ," she muttered, moving restlessly in the air, her brow furrowed in thought.

Her face changed as something new occurred to her, and she deliberately brought the Stone in her hand into one of the shafts of light.

Nothing happened, and after a moment she thrust it into the next shaft of light, and watched nothing befall there, either. Shrugging, Embra went back to reading.

And gasped aloud, face growing pale. What she'd done with the Stone had made the writing on one page change.

If ye have but two Dwaerindim, the Sleeping King

*can be awakened thus: touch ye the two stones together,
and say aloud . . .*

Embra read the few lines over and over again, trying
to burn them into her memory beyond all forgetting.
She was almost done when the writing flickered under
her gaze—and she was staring at what she'd read there
earlier: cryptic clues as to the whereabouts of the
Dwaer. Clues that she could make sense of readily
enough, but that seemed, well, *wrong.*

"These point to Silvertree House," she said aloud at
last, shaking her head. "But I must be wrong, or this a
ruse—this Stone *was* right there, in yon pit."

As if her words were a cue, a bright flash and a deafening roar smote the Four, crashing into the dome on
waves of flooding sunlight—as part of the dome was
blasted down from above. Huge shards of stone hurtled
down, dashing the sorceress to the floor but tumbling
through books that hung untouched, intangible, and
oblivious.

Shouting in alarm, the three men ran forward as one,
seeking Embra.

They barely noticed something small and spiderlike
land just behind their hurrying boots. Something that
was bloody beneath the dust, and twitched slightly, like
a tired spider. It was a man's right hand. Until very recently, it had belonged to the wizard Klamantle Beirldoun.

Faerod Silvertree was not a slow-witted man, but he
seldom allowed more than malice to master his face and
voice. He had kept silent, pretending ignorance, waiting
and watching as all of his Dark Three wizards had unfolded their own separate treacheries. How best to use
their misdeeds?

One tool was now shattered; it was time to temper
another. "You made him a living spellblast," he murmured. "Rather wasteful, don't you think?"

Ingryl Ambelter shook his head violently. "My Lord," he snapped, "believe me when I say Silvertree could no longer afford his ambitions. Markoun was merely blindly and ineptly greedy; Klamantle was an active and capable danger. He laid a curse on your daughter that brought this whole affair about, causing her to flee the castle in open disloyalty to you and work all the trouble and mischief you've seen since. Klamantle was behind it all."

The baron's eyes narrowed. "And my Spellmaster caught him not?"

"Lord," his last and mightiest mage snarled, "I'll gladly discuss all this later. Right now I must work a magic on the healer."

"Your 'Voice of the God'?"

"The same," Ingryl Ambelter snapped, settling his nose against the glass globe. Laying two fingers of either hand atop it, he muttered a few soft words. The baron watched for a moment, not quite smiling, and then bent his attention to his own globe. As he peered into its familiar glow, a thought struck him: what would be left of him if his willful Spellmaster decided to make a certain glass globe burst apart?

In the depths of the glass there was frantic activity. Hawkril and Craer raked stony rubble from Embra's crumpled body in feverish haste, tossing it so wildly aside that Sarasper was moved to circle widely around them, and come at her from another way.

Sarasper, it is time.

Old Oak?

You know me, Sarasper. Now heed: seize the Stone. Take it into your hand and bear it away, smiting with its fires all who seek to gainsay thee. Take it. Now. I command thee.

Sarasper whimpered then, staring wide-eyed at Embra Silvertree's sprawled form. Craer looked up at the sound, eyes narrowing, and the healer waved his hands as if to brush that glance away.

"No," Sarasper moaned, "not my friends. Not to betray, to harm. . . ."

A wave of well-nigh-irresistable coercion washed over him. *Betray me not. Seize the Stone. Seize the STONE! Take it NOW!*

The old healer shuddered and staggered forward, snarling. "Craer! Hawkril! Stop me! Stop me from what I must do!"

"What's he gibbering about *now?*" Hawkril growled, as he ran careful fingertips over Embra's head and back, seeking out broken bones and the sticky wetness where blood welled and—thank the Three!—finding nothing. Yet.

"A spell on him, I think," Craer said, feeling around in the rubble for a stone that would fit his hand without taking his eyes from Sarasper, who was now sobbing and protesting incoherently. "I don't think a man can hurl spells while fighting a spell sent by another . . . but what if he stops fighting?"

As the procurer and the armaragor exchanged grim glances, a shadow stole forward with swift, gliding strides, to pause on a balcony not far above the four adventurers.

"Luthtuth comes creeping back," the figure whispered soundlessly to itself, and smiled. "Luthtuth always comes creeping back."

The baron pushed the candelabra across the polished tabletop, into easy reach. Ingryl thrust one hand into its flames, hissing as he drew in its heat, the pain its searing brought—and fed them to the distant Sarasper. "Now," he said, his voice as deep and yawning as a fresh grave, "healer, you *are* mine."

And in the dusty, rubble-strewn wreckage of the library of Ehrluth, in a ruined city half Aglirta away from where the Spellmaster sat hunched in growing pain, Sarasper Codelmer's distorted voice fell silent, his eyes blazed with sudden fire, and he strode purposefully toward Embra.

Craer and Hawkril sprang up as one, charging at the older man—and Ingryl Ambelter gasped, "Now! By the Three and all the love of the Lady for dark weavings, *now!*"

The flames under his fingers flared to scorch the ceiling and sent the baron wincing back, a hand shielding his eyes—and then went out. The Spellmaster reeled and fell back in his chair shuddering and trembling uncontrollably, his face lined with sudden exhaustion.

And across the miles, through the spell-link, his lightnings cracked out of Sarasper's body, lashing the procurer and the armaragor with purple fire.

They were hurled away, end over end. Hawkril struggled to shout in pain but managed only squeaks and the whistling of trembling lungs—in the instant before they crashed among the fallen stones.

Purple fire howled on across the room, crackling among the clouds of dust and racing up spiral stairs to make the balcony rail erupt in a racing line of blue, snapping sparks. The shadowy figure crouching at that rail trembled uncontrollably, doubled up in pain—and slowly toppled off the balcony, crashing heavily onto splintered shelves below.

Sarasper reached for the Stone. He'd stumbled across loose rubble and fallen on his knees, and uncaring, had crawled on and up Embra's motionless body until now his hand was almost on the Dwaer.

Luthtuth rose out of the wreckage of the shelves, shaking off pain, and stared across empty space at the Stone he'd come so far to seize. Too much empty space to cross in time.

The old man's fingers touched the Stone, and it winked once, mockingly.

Luthtuth turned, a shadow once more, and sprang into the darkness, running awkwardly but swiftly, stumbling only once. Fleeing to await a better time. Again.

The healer lifted the Stone, and Embra's limp hand came up with it, dragging it out of his hand. Sarasper reached for it again, his hand closing around the smooth, heavy . . .

Something struck the old man aside and senseless with one brisk, shrewd blow.

Another hand closed on the Stone of Life. A hand that belonged to a bearded man who wore trail leathers. He had a pleasant face, and the Dwaer lit it with a soft, warm glow as the man touched the Worldstone to Embra—who stirred under its touch, the bruises and lines of pain receding from her face—and then to Sarasper, where it made the blazing light abruptly fade from his open, staring eyes.

The man put the Stone into Embra's hand, closed her fingers around it, and slipped away. He did not go into the shadows whence the shadowy procurer had fled.

There was a little silence in the library before a slender figure suddenly sat up, dust and small stones falling from her limbs, blinked, and looked around.

The six books still floated serenely above Embra Silvertree, and her three companions lay sprawled on all sides. As she stared at them, another tiny piece of the riven dome high above her crumbled and fell, plunging down a very long way to the floor. Its sudden shattering awoke rolling echoes.

Somewhere in the ruins nearby, a wolf howled—and from farther off, other wolves answered. The Lady Embra Silvertree shivered and scrambled to her feet. Her injuries and her weariness were gone, and instead she felt a rising, insistent tingling. She looked down. In her hands, the Stone had begun to glow. . . .

16

Live by the Spell . . .

Screams split the air in a guarded chamber in Castle Silvertree.

Ingryl Ambelter arched back in his chair as lightnings leaked from his eyes and mouth, shrieking his agony. The chair burst into flames beneath him, shuddered, and was ashes before it struck the floor. He never felt himself crashing down with it, never saw the baron flung senseless into a stately ebon-wood sideboard or the glass globes melt into teardrops that arced across the room to splat and sizzle against distant walls—and he never noticed his safe-spell claiming the lives of the only two guards bold enough to burst into the room with swords drawn.

When the lightning died away, it left behind no sound but sizzling.

Somehow the Spellmaster reeled to his feet and staggered across the room. He went to no guarded door, but to a dark green statue of a forever-staring sorceress that stood where a side wall met the outer wall, and muttered a word to it.

The staring sorceress obediently sank into the floor, plinth and all. Ingryl shouldered through the low opening thus revealed, and gasped his way down the dark and cramped passage beyond.

White-faced and sweating, the Spellmaster staggered along through chill, damp stone to the spell-locked closet he'd hoped not to have to visit for years yet. Never again would he doubt the power of the Dwaerindim or dare to stand against them. His hold over Sarasper had been snapped in an instant, broken with such a backlash that he was still burning, inside . . . and if he didn't get to what lay within the closet soon . . .

The House of the Tall Sword was the grandest inn of the Glittering City. It rose like a castle, its dark stone walls as thick as a wagon and crowned with battlements—and men paid handsomely for the use of its fortified, defensible upper rooms. Many a plot had been hatched therein, many a coup planned—and many a meeting in the "Upper House" had ended with blood on the floor and a body or two discreetly dumped down the midden chute.

The Chamber of the Falcon was smaller than some upper rooms and was given to cold drafts. Despite the dark and heavy tapestries that cloaked its walls, it saw less use than some House chambers—and by tradition, its door stood always open. For years, in fact, the thick oaken door that should have barred passage to the room had been missing.

That door floated somewhere on the winds, bards said, with the body of a dead king pinned to it by many swords—and no one dared replace it for fear of what spell-chaos might ensue when the spell that had sent the door forth was broken.

But then, bards said a lot of things.

Right now, the room was crowded with nervous men in robes and suspicious, grim-faced men in armor, their hands never far from the hilts of their weapons. A bard could have identified them as lesser mages from all over Aglirta and the grim-faced warriors, their baronial escorts. Many eyes strayed often to that missing door—as if their owners expected some foe to suddenly appear in fire and risen spellglow, to menace them all.

". . . and they've gone to this ruined city in the forest, too?" one mage snapped.

Another shrugged. "Gone in any event, this month past. Grave times are upon us, I fear."

"You fear, you fear, Andraevus—you're always fearing something," one of the warriors snarled. "Be a little more specific, will ye?"

Andraevus replied coldly, "I shall. Hearken: worrisome times have come to Aglirta. Powerful mages are missing, and there are dark rumors—of wizards being slain, dragons being bred in the wilds to feast on folk who venture there, the ancient Serpent in the Shadows rising . . . and the Baron Silvertree trying to make himself ruler of all Aglirta with fell magics, seizing the fabled Dwaerindim to smash any armies sent against him."

In the still silence that followed his grim words, Andraevus looked hard at the warrior who'd snarled at him and asked, "Specific enough to fear, Andrar?"

"Dragons bred? I'd like to watch a witch try *that*! Their tails'd flatten her into mead in half a breath!" a voice rang out, and suddenly the scoffing was in full, loud sway around the table—scoffing that slowly died away into silence as men looked at each other, and the stink of fear again ruled the crowded room.

"Many of us here are accomplished at talking, and talking, and then talking longer," the warrior Andrar said heavily, carefully not looking at any of the mages, "but we are gathered here—and that alone imperils many of us—to try to agree on something . . . anything . . . we can *do*."

He looked around, bushy eyebrows raised, and growled, "No suggestions, mages of the Vale? Well, we *do* make history here today, then."

As the din of sneers and shouts arose, Andrar stepped back again against the wall, collecting more than a few half-grins from other warriors standing in their places around the room. It looked to be a long and noisy council. . . .

"Well said, Andrar," Ingryl Ambelter said sardonically, leaning back at ease in his chair with the scrying-sphere gleaming in front of him. It had taken more than a little magic, but he was fully recovered. The thorn wand floated ready, black and menacing, above the table to his right, where a guard lay hooded, bound and helpless, his bared chest rising and falling rapidly in fear.

The Spellmaster of Silvertree commanded magic enough to shatter shieldings and force his way into almost any spellguarded chamber in Aglirta, but the gods were smiling on him at last. By incredible happenstance these bonfire wizards had chosen the House of the Tall Sword for their council, out of all the inns in the Vale. More than that, they'd met in the Chamber of the Falcon—the very doorless chamber where on Ingryl Ambelter, fledgling but cunning mage, had long ago set up a portal to aid him in controlled spelljumps, so he could visit Sirlptar whenever he chose.

That meant he'd been able to steal past wards upon wards undetected and could reach out at any time now to hand them their doom. It was clear enough that none of them commanded a Dwaer or had any secret scheme or powerful magic at the ready. The council would, therefore, soon become tiresome. It was time.

Ingryl smiled, said softly and gently, "Now," and waved his hands in a last spell-gesture. A tiny blue flame began to leap and lick up and down the dagger on the table in front of him.

The Spellmaster took it up, plunged it with a sudden, grunting effort into the heart of the man on the table, and as the guard's body convulsed and arched in the spasm of a life's passing, he plucked forth the dagger again and touched it to the thorn wand.

Blue flames whirled around the wand in a sudden rising fury, and the wand cracked, blackened, and crumbled to dust.

In the Chamber of the Falcon a weird ball of coiling and sputtering fire burst into sudden being above the table—and then raced around it in a widening spiral. Men shouted, toppled chairs in their haste to rise, and snatched out swords or wands or scepters. Rings winked like scattered stars on fingers all around the chamber.

Blue and hungry were the flames that raced around the seated circle of mages, burning away one head after another. Fearful warriors threw themselves at the doorway after one look at the stump-necked, spasming torsos the rolling fire left in its wake. . . .

Ingryl smiled at what he saw in the scrying-sphere. Spellmasters should never indulge overmuch in gloating, but . . .

A door that no one but Ingryl should have been able to open banged behind him. The Spellmaster of Silvertree whirled around, his hand closing again on the dagger.

"Put that down," Baron Faerod Silvertree said with terrible gentleness, over the blasting wand he held aimed and ready, "or lose the hand that holds it, mage."

The smile frozen on his face, Ingryl let the dagger

fall. The baron cast a glance at the dead guard, whose blood was starting to drip steadily from the edge of the table now, but the cold, calm expression on his face did not change.

"My patience is at an end, Ingryl. My daughter is still out of our hands, and your deeds have cost the barony two of its mages. Spellmaster, your own life is forfeit if you fail to deliver a Dwaer safely, without magical traps or coercions bound to it, into my hands—soon."

Silence fell as cold eyes met. After it had stretched for too long a time the baron added, "Never forget those vials of blood. I've only to shatter one to burst your heart."

Ingryl nodded soberly. "I will succeed in my present task, Lord," he said grimly.

Faerod Silvertree flashed a mirthless smile, raised the wand in what might have been a salute, and strode out of the room, exuding menacing grace and exultant power.

When he was gone, Ingryl looked at the open door, shrugged, and then smiled. He'd long since subverted the baron's magical hold by switching his own heart's blood with that of an innocent mage elsewhere. As he quietly closed the door, his smile grew broader. This was going to be fun.

Embra Silvertree let the Stone rest on her knees, stared up at the riven dome above her, and drew in a long, tremulous breath. What would happen now, if she lost this wonderful, deadly thing—and was left powerless to undo blunders and wounds to herself and her companions?

"Solve the worries of the world later, lass," Hawkril Anharu rumbled, close beside her. "We must be moving; Indraevyn is full of hungry human wolves."

Embra smiled and nodded. She trusted the armaragor. More than that . . . she loved him. She loved and respected all of these men. Feelings born such a short time ago, but none the less for that. Together, the Four would stand against all Darsar could hurl at them.

She shook her head at such grand thoughts of doom, sighed, tossed back her hair, and agreed briskly, "Yes. Let's go."

It was long past time to leave this shattered library, with its ghosts and fresh corpses alike shrouded in new dust. They moved without further word or ceremony, Craer at the fore all peering and stalking grace, intent on seeing that lurking shadow-man before he saw them, and Hawkril bringing up the rear, peering back warily over his ready war sword to ensure that nothing was following or rearing up to spit one last deadly magic at their backs.

When they were gone, the library of Ehrluth knew a single moment of stillness before a hitherto blank stone wall opened, and the man in leathers stepped out of the darkness behind it. He took one step amid rubble and the next into air, striding smoothly up through the empty air to the books floating in their shafts of light.

Reaching into those steady glows, he turned the pages of all the tomes, touching them where the hands of Embra and the others had passed vainly through, until all six displayed different writings.

The man stood on nothing reading them for a moment, nodded as if satisfied, and went down to the wall again, leaving the open books hanging in the air like so many white birds frozen forever in flight.

Suddenly they were standing on a slate-and-pitch roof with empty laundry racks all around them and a seabird eyeing them suspiciously before it waddled a little farther away. The smell of the sea was strong, and a city fell away on all sides. Craer stared around suspiciously. "I should know this place," he said, and looked to Embra. "So where are we?"

"Urngallond. The roof of The Lion Looks Seaward, a luxurious inn," the Lady of Jewels replied. Hawkril eloquently raised his eyebrows, and she added, "One must spelljump to a known place. I once stayed here, when my father had business yonder in the Coinhalls."

"He let you leave the barony?" Sarasper asked, looking down over roofs to where the forest of tall masts in the harbor began and gulls wheeled and shrieked. The open sea lay like a gray line beyond headlands cloaked in old, tall, many-balconied buildings.

"I was an infant then," Embra told him. "All I knew how to do was watch things."

"A superior sort of infant," Hawkril growled, and jerked his thumb at Craer. "All *he* knew how to do was snatch things."

His voice acquired sharp alarm as the sorceress strode toward him. "What're you doing?"

"Healing all hurts," Embra told him crisply, touching the Stone to his cheek. He seemed to shimmer before their eyes, growing at once shorter and fatter. "Oh, and making you look like an old, fat merchant."

Sarasper and Craer stared at a bulbous nose, dangling jowls, and a pout that would have served a whole household of petulant folk—and burst into laughter.

"A little less mirth," the armaragor growled at them. "You're next."

The old healer looked gravely into Embra's eyes as she drove away the pains in his back and arms and made him an overly rouged trader in purple silks, and asked, "Casting magic . . . is your pain all gone?"

The Lady Silvertree gave him a quick smile. "Yes," she murmured, and beckoned to Craer. "Little man," she said in a voice of doom, "it's time."

"I seem to recall a lady saying just those words to me, once before," Craer remarked slyly. "Now, was it in Sirlptar? Or—"

"'Twas in some place where you had to lay down

coins, I'll warrant—or where she got a good look at all of you," Hawkril grunted.

His eyes widened as Embra turned and he got a good look at all of *her.* A bewhiskered and sneering man in well-worn vest and breeches stood squinting back at the armaragor from under a broad sun hat.

"Rundrar the trader can shuffle off elsewhere after we take rooms," she explained crisply, in a voice that wasn't far off a man's. "Then he can send in his lady partner to deal with you three."

There was a chorus of welcoming chuckles and explanations, which she quelled with a rather withering glance.

"Just acting like merchants, Lady," Craer explained with a quick smile. "I—"

"What's this 'Lady' talk? It's Rundrar, remember," she growled. "Rundrar the Bold!"

The three merchants coughed at her. "Oh, *well* . . . 'the Bold,' eh?" the procurer replied. "Uh-ha."

"Rundrar always shares a suite with his friends on the road," Embra added rather grimly, "just so you don't go ordering me separate chambers or something similarly suspicious." She sighed and added, "Though I suppose I'm being overly wary. Even if some scrying mage finds us here, hired slayers can't ride up to the inn without being seen."

The three men exchanged rather more sober glances before Craer laid a hand on Embra's arm and said in low tones, "Think you slayers jingle about with scab-barded blades thrusting out from their armor in all directions and scars all over their faces? Lady, know this: It is so pitifully easy to kill a man. One knife-throw, one shove—even one well-placed broken goblet."

Embra sighed. "I was hoping to forget about all that for a few days. I want to test this Stone, and then give it to Sarasper."

"Ah," the healer said hesitantly, "perhaps that

wouldn't be such a good idea just yet. You wield it so well. . . ."

Craer shot him a look. "A god demanded you undertake this quest, and perhaps it's not such a good idea, now? D'you habitually try to outdeal gods, or is a grave looking particularly welcoming just now?"

Even through his florid, warty disguise Sarasper looked uncomfortable. "I-I don't trust myself with such power, that's all."

The armaragor's heavy hand came down on his shoulder. "We none of us love what life hands us, all the time—but there's no one listening, I find, when you give complaints to the Three. If you don't like what befalls, it seems, that's just too flootin' bad!"

"Friends," said the healer in a small voice, "I'm just a lot more . . . tired than I thought I'd be. I've hidden and skulked and grown patient for too long. Give me some time."

The procurer clapped his arm. "Well, *that's* easily done. I'd rather leave saving all Darsar from doom to someone else for a month or more, too, and go where every passing man with a tankard *isn't* a mighty mage trying to slay me in slow, utter agony just to gain a lump of rock."

Sarasper nodded as they went down the old and groaning roof stairs. "It'll probably be best if we lie low and use spells to scry out the land for a goodly time before we try to gain another Dwaerindim."

"For that matter," Embra agreed, "I'll be happier if we stay well clear of Aglirta while it's full of armies whelming and wizards swarming like angry bees around a cracked hive."

And she said not a word more until they were settled into their rooms, with a large, full tub of hot petal-scented water to soak in, and cold wine to share. Then she calmly kicked off her boots, dropped her clothes and her magical disguise together, picked up a wine flask, and asked, "Well? What are you all waiting for?"

Wisely the three men said nothing—but none of them failed to notice that, bare as she was, Embra had the Stone of Life tucked securely under one arm.

"Well?" Baron Ithclammert Cardassa sat back in his ornate chair of office and regarded his two advisers with a thin, unfriendly smile. "I'm waiting. Have either of you any *other* brilliant deductions as to the whereabouts of Dwaerindim?"

Baerethos and Ubunter squirmed under the baron's cold, watchful gaze. News of spell-battles in the wilds was all over Cardassa, and more: priests of the Three up and down the Vale had just proclaimed from their altars that a Dwaer Stone had been found and called upon.

The three men facing each other across the grandest table in Cardassa knew something else: that the baron's two best war blades had gone to great expense to hire wizards near the places Baerethos and Ubunter had said a Stone would be found. Exhaustive searches had followed—and found not the slightest trace of anything.

The two advisers darted glances at each other, found scant comfort in the view, and looked away, Baerethos regarding his own reflection in the mirror-polished table and Ubunter raising his eyes to the nearest flame-winged crow of Cardassa, of many adorning that lofty hall. Neither looked at the cortahars in gleaming armor stationed along the walls.

"As I'm sure you both know, trusted advisers," the baron added in tones that were silken but not a shade warmer, "I've hired a new House Wizard for Cardassa in recent days. You may also have suspected that he's been doing much farscrying for me. Almost all of it has been to observe both of the searcher wizards, often and at great length. He has seen nothing—yes, nothing—to suggest that either mage has secretly found a Stone. Nor have they since gone anywhere, including back to the locations you were so knowledgeable about, and searched for one on their own."

Baron Cardassa drummed his fingertips gently on the tabletop in front of him, then picked up his goblet. "All of this has cost the coffers of Cardassa precisely sixty-two thousand, three hundred and twelve gold thelvers to date," he announced softly. "Have my two most trusted and capable advisers any ideas as to how they might be able to make up these losses before next spring? At that time, should any monies still be owing, their less-than-capable carcasses will be sold to the slavers of the far south to gain back at least a few coins."

Ubunter and Baerethos exchanged looks again, found as little comfort in each other and in shared dismay as before, and slumped dejectedly in their chairs.

Ithclammert Cardassa set down his goblet, swallowed, and ordered curtly, "Start thinking." He made a signal, and two cortahars left the wall, jerked the old men to their feet, and marched them out of the baron's presence.

The little glass sphere rose out of its box, spinning gently as it chimed. Ingryl smiled at it. A thing of beauty, all his own. . . .

As the scene he was seeking obediently swam into its depths, all candles and sighs and bodies moving on the great bed, the Spellmaster murmured an incantation.

The crack of a whip curled up from the sphere, and then a sob. It was time. Oh, yes. It was past time.

The whip snapped again, and there was a ragged cry. Tearful protests followed, and Ingryl Ambelter leaned forward to better see his magic unfold.

Sarintha was the first, as she lay weeping under her baron's lash, her unbound hands clawing the sleeping-furs above her head. Abruptly they caught and tugged fur with her every jerk and clutch. Faerod Silvertree was displeased with her, and the aftertaste of his wine, and his mages living and dead, and his daughter, and because the woman under his lash didn't break and beg.

And so he laid her back open, and went on flogging, as blood flowed, Sarintha wailed into the furs, and the other lovechamber girls shrank back in fear, hating their cruel master. He was sure to turn to one of them when Sarintha fell senseless and silent. Already she looked more like a slab of meat in the kitchens than a lass meant to excite and give pleasure. The baron snarled down at her as if he was a raging lion rending a kill with his claws and not a naked, aroused man.

The furs caught in Sarintha's lengthening nails, then fell away, sliced free. One of the girls reached to scratch herself, and gasped. Her long-nailed fingers were now impossibly long, and stretching still more, turning to— to talons!

She choked back a shriek and looked at the others. One of them was staring down at her spread hands in horror, as they grew visibly: a foot long . . . and more. . . .

Sarintha rolled over, pleading—to no avail. The blood-soaked whip rained down on her breast and flank as Baron Silvertree shouted at her. Then, with a snarl, he clubbed her across the face with the gilded butt of his weapon.

Sarintha's eyes blazed, and she reached out, catching hold of the whip. Screaming in fury, the baron tore it free, not noticing how much of it was left behind, and lifted both hands to punch at her breasts, and drive her down broken on the bed. She must submit! She would surrender! She w—

The first slash of her talons raked across both of his uplifted arms, and he screamed at the sudden, burning pain and clutched his bleeding limbs to his body. As Faerod Silvertree stared at her in disbelief, the second slash laid open his belly.

He shrank back, howling in pain—and the bleeding

thing rose and roared out her pain and rage in a snarl of her own—as she went for his throat.

Frantically Silvertree fended her off, rolling away on the bed, but her claws cut away one of his nipples and a long strip of flesh with it—and by then, with shrieks of fury, all of the baron's lovechamber girls were charging across the room at him with long, rending talons raised.

The baron cursed them and ordered them back as he fell out of bed in his haste to back away, regained his feet barely in time to win free of clawing and clinging talons, and backed away across the room, kicking and punching viciously to keep them at a distance.

Terror made him smash his bedchamber pretties with all his strength, and more than one fell senseless, but bubbling rage was banishing wide-eyed fear in the faces of the rest. Their claws tore and slashed at their master, slitting skin to ribbons and slicing away his very fingers as he fought.

In the end Faerod Silvertree could think only of fleeing. He staggered and kicked and tore his way across the room, his feet leaving a bloody trail as cruel claws tore away flesh and hair and even genitals. Gasping and shuddering, the baron fell through the curtains, rolled out onto the balcony beyond the women sobbing, groaning, and clawing beneath him, and fetched up hard against its parapet, fighting desperately.

A shrewd slash laid open his side, robbing one arm of all strength and twisting him around—and with a long, wailing scream of bewildered pain and despair, Baron Faerod Silvertree plunged down, down into the cold and waiting waters below.

The River Coiling received him with a splash—and reaching talons found him no more.

As Ingryl Ambelter's harsh laughter arose in front of a spinning sphere, sobbing women sank down on their knees in horror in the blood-smeared bedchamber, trailing gory talons as long as short swords and weeping at what they'd become.

* * *

A stone wall slid open with a deep rumbling in the darkness, and a man in trail leathers stepped out of the hidden passage and walked quietly across a many-pillared hall in the Silent House, toward a distant glimmer of light. He descended a short flight of steps, ducked through a low archway—and then stiffened as something slapped him across the face. Something fanged and hissing.

The man struck it away from his brow and half turned to pull the Stone of War from its sling in the breast of his leathers—whereupon he stiffened again, looked down in disbelief at the point of the spear protruding from his belly, and slowly sank to his knees.

He clawed out the Stone as he fell on his face, but it was hooked away from him by the bloody spear, even before hissing rose loudly on all sides . . . and a score of serpents glided in to feed.

The Priest of the Serpent reached down and took the Stone of War into his hand. Power! Ah, yes, fairly throbbing under his hand. Ready. . . .

Looking down at the corpse, half hidden under wriggling, striking snakes, he smiled and observed, "It seems Koglaur can fall, after all." Then he turned his back and walked away, heading for the waiting glimmer of light.

When he came out into that candlelit room, he held up the Stone of War in triumph, and there was a roar of approval from the shadows. Cowled figures pressed forward around him, straining to touch the Stone. He laughed and strode to the dark star of tiles that marked the center of the chamber, raising a hand for silence.

And they gave it to him. "Faithful of the Ssserpent," he cried into it, his voice louder and more excited than they'd ever heard it before, "I need your service now!"

Their roar of reply rang off the ceiling, and he smiled and held up his hand again. When they were silent, he held the Stone aloft in his other hand, and caused it to glow with white fire.

"Great is this Worldstone, and its power now serves us," he intoned, "but the Stone of Life is in the hands of another. We must have it. We *shall* have it! We *can* have it, if you but aid me now!"

The roar was of assent this time, and the Priest of the Serpent cried, "If you would serve the Ssserpent henceforth, disrobe, kiss your snakes, and dance to the song of the Stone—now!"

The Stone flashed once with a hungry ruby radiance, then throbbed like the boom of a drum so deep it made the ears tingle. Once more, and again, slightly faster. Again. Faster and faster—and with the hand that wasn't holding the Stone on high, the priest threw back his cowl and signaled his most senior priestesses.

Their sashes flew, their robes swirled away, and they began to dance, passing from his right side in front of him to his left, and on, circling him, their snakes coiling excitedly around their arms.

Other, lesser worshipers, snakes coiling along their limbs, hastened to join the throbbing, quickening dance, as the Stone flashed again and again.

At each flash the lashing, slithering serpents drew back their heads and then struck, sinking their fangs into the bared flesh that carried them, and the dancers wept and sobbed and wailed, raising their hands to the Stone. The priest laughed in exultation and stared up at the Dwaer he held, feeling it reaching across the miles to wherever the Stone of Life was tugging at it . . . bringing it home.

The dancers were whirling in a frenzy now, the snakes biting repeatedly. The song of the Stone rose louder, and the dance of the circling clergy moved with it, then started to change. Quickening limbs jerked stiffly, bare bodies became deep amber and then deepened to a dusky purple, staring eyes glittered golden, and mouths began to foam as venom surged through veins. Only the sweeping, rising power of the magic kept the faithful on their feet.

A door opened in Castle Silvertree, and a man in rich robes strode into a blood-smeared room.

One of the women lying dejectedly against the end of the bed looked up through weary eyes. "You," she said, a thread of contempt in her exhausted whisper. "I knew you'd find your way here before long."

Ingryl Ambelter spread his hands with a smile. "And I've not disappointed you." His gaze roved around the chamber, meeting many reddened, empty eyes, and he added, "As Spellmaster of Silvertree—as *ruler* of Silvertree—I offer you a choice."

He waited, but the watching women gave him only sullen silence. The Spellmaster's friendly demeanor shrank to a half smile. "If you serve me in all matters, as you did the baron, I'll banish those talons and make you normal again."

Sarintha stiffened and rose off the bed, holding out her talons like daggers before her. Her bare body was black with blood, not all of it her own, and with every step she left a bloody footprint on the furs underfoot.

"Serve the magic that made us this way?" she hissed, eyes glittering. "Serve the only man even Silvertree feared?" She launched herself into a sudden dash at him. *"Never!"*

As Sarintha reached for him in savage anger, curving claws raking, Ingryl Ambelter calmly stood his ground, and fire roared out of his hands.

He blasted the leaping woman to ashes and bones not two strides from his nose, and watched all that had been Sarintha clatter and sigh to the furs, trailing smoke.

Then he lifted his head to smile again at the rest of the bedchamber girls. The survivors. Standing there with the last wisps of flame curling up from his palms, he gently repeated his offer.

Slowly, eyes downcast, a slender woman with a magnificent mane of flowing black hair crossed the room and knelt at his feet submissively, carefully holding her talons behind her and away from him. He felt the soft brush of her lips on his boot, and smiled.

After a moment, another of the baron's girls padded across the floor to kneel beside the first . . . and then another. There followed a general move toward the Spellmaster, and he threw back his head and laughed in exultation.

As the last woman knelt at his feet and bent her head to kiss his boots, Ingryl made a grand gesture—and one of the baron's coronets rose from its jaunty perch on a bedpost and floated across the room to the wizard's head.

As it settled about his brows, he felt gentle kisses on his boots and his legs, and laughed again—never noticing that for every kiss that landed, a dozen or more tears fell. But then, it's not in the nature of most wizards to care overmuch about the desires and feelings of others. The crown of Silvertree rode well on Ingryl Ambelter.

Unheeded, the tears pattered onto the bloody furs.

The song of the Stone of War shook the Silent House as the dancers moved ever faster. The priest at their heart felt power, dark and mighty, rising within him.

There came a flash outside the circle, a radiance the Priest of the Serpent wasn't expecting. He frowned at it, peering to see. Perha— there was another!

When the second mysterious glow died, the priest saw that a headless man he didn't recognize was jerking and shuffling along in the dance, a tattered bat circling him. The man ahead of him was a warrior in the armor of Ornentar, head lolling loosely over a slit and gaping throat. There came another flash, and another, bringing two more warriors to join the circle of dying, foam-mouthed clergy.

The Priest of the Serpent gaped at them for a few moments and then shrugged and gave himself over to the awe and power of the ritual, accepting that the floating clouds of bloody bones and fragments that appeared next, bobbing and swaying in time with the rest of the dancers, had once been living men.

It wasn't the end that either Markoun or Klamantle had anticipated for themselves, but, then, few mortals of Darsar get to choose the time or manner of their passing.

As the torn bodies of bards and headless, scorched wizards joined the outermost ring of dancers, the delighted priest laughed aloud, and the ritual roared on. . . .

A small, translucent castle of flasks and bottles stood on a certain marble floor in Urngallond. Beyond their gleaming spires was the lip of a tub inset in the floor, where four heads leaned back at ease, and there was much merriment.

"Gods!" Craer gasped, nearly dropping his half-full bottle into the warm, scented bathwater. "I'm as hard as a hammer!"

"Hah!" Sarasper snapped, swiping the wine out of the procurer's hand. "No more dallying with lady sorceresses for you!"

"Well," Hawkril rumbled, "I never thought I'd end up bathing with a lady wizard in water that's more wine and Craer's bladder juice than water! Hand me another of those, will you? Embra?"

The Lady Silvertree had fallen silent.

"Embra?" the armaragor asked roughly. "Is something amiss?"

The sorceress turned a grim face to him and then looked back down into the water—where the three men, getting themselves upright with sudden urgency, could see a glimmering glow.

"Lady?" Sarasper asked, "What's happening? *Tell us!*"

Embra's eyes were large and dark with apprehension as she lifted her head to look at him, wet hair trailing back over her shoulders. "Magic," she murmured, "tugging at the Stone."

Even as the words left her lips, the glowing Stone rose up like a giant mushroom shedding dew, making the bathwater bulge. Then it burst free of the water entirely, its glow blazing whiter and brighter as it ascended.

The Lady Silvertree clung to it, her wet fingers wrapped around it going white with the strength of her grip, and whispered a prayer to the Three.

The three men watched apprehensively as the Stone rose slowly and silently straight up into the air with the sorceress clinging to it, until she was hanging upright and dripping in midair, her dripping feet a hand's span above the water, and more. . . .

Hawkril reached out one large and hesitant hand to grasp at her ankles, rumbling, "Lady Embra? Should I? . . ."

The sorceress flung her head around to look back at him down the glistening length of her body, the Stone now at full stretch above her head. "I—," she began, in tones of obvious bewilderment—and then the Stone suddenly brightened.

They saw wisps of steam drifting from her slender fingers like smoke as its heat banished the water on her skin. Then there was a sudden roar, and the Stone burst into green-and-golden flame.

Embra cried out in pain. The men below her, scrambling up with shouts of alarm, saw her fingers, locked to the Stone, begin to char.

17

No Stone Unburned

The sizzle of burning flesh was loud enough to be heard over the splashings of three men clambering out of the tub to reach for the sorceress hanging from the Stone of Life.

"Don't *touch* me!" she screamed at them, through tears of pain. "Get back!"

Flames roiled up from around her blackened fingers, and Embra wept, her trembling lips barely able to grasp out, "S-show me the cause of this!"

The Dwaer flashed, and suddenly a scene hung in the air beside the naked sorceress: a room where a cowled man held another Stone on high as many folk danced around him. They seemed almost drunken, reeling with their heads lolling, but their limbs jerked with wild speed. The innermost dancers were naked save for flailing and thrashing snakes coiled around their bodies; the outer dancers wore all manner of garb, but looked decidedly . . .

"Sweet kisses of the Three!" Hawkril gasped. "They're all dead!"

The song of the Stone was deafening now, and the Priest of the Serpent sang worldlessly along with it, borne along in utter triumph. There came, suddenly, a deeper boom than before—and the song died away almost to a whisper.

Above his head, the Stone of War erupted in red and then black pulsing flames, fire that did not sear the priest's hand. He gazed up at the fiery tongues in delight and wonder as they spat outward . . . and seemed to cause ripplings through the slowing ranks of dancers.

He looked to see what those ripplings might be and saw that they were waves of change wrought by the Stone. Scales were appearing on the bodies of priests and priestesses, and the tongues lolling beneath those dark, dead eyes were suddenly long, forked, red, and darting.

The priest laughed aloud, glorying in power—and he was still laughing when the dancing corpse of the wizard Jaerinsturn, its face and breast still blackened and blistered from the fires of his death in Sirlptar, shuffled up behind the serpent-man, drew a massive bone club from under scorched robes, and dashed the back of the priest's scaly head in, so hard that the brains met the serpent-man's nose.

With a sniveling, bubbling sigh, the priest fell dead to the floor, the flames dying away from the Stone in his hand like a snuffed candle.

Somewhere in a seacoast inn, flames died around another Stone, and Embra Silvertree gasped in relief as she fell back into the tub with a mighty splash.

Not caring where the waters went or how many wine bottles were swept to ruin, she sobbingly called on the Dwaer to heal what little was left of her fingers and tried not to let go of the precious thing in her shudders.

Three men plunged back into the pool to hold her and murmur comforts. She smiled tremulously up at them through glistening tears.

* * *

There were thuds and thumpings in the Silent House as dancers slumped to the floor in a lifeless ring. Snakes glided swiftly away, heading for shadows.

None slithered toward the center of the ring, to menace the only being left standing in all that chamber. The dead wizard lowered the club that had slain the priest and turned away—and as he did so, the burned face of Jaerinsturn melted away into a featureless, fleshy mask.

As the faceless man picked his way through the circle of the dead, his face slowly began to acquire the features of someone else. . . .

Lying in the cooling waters of the tub in Urngallond, Embra went white.

"What is it, lass?" Hawkril asked quickly, one large and hairy arm tightening protectively around her shoulders.

The sorceress looked at him and then back at the scene hanging in the air above them. "There was a book in my father's library," she said, voice trembling. "An old history; large and embossed, with locks and latches I loved to work and fondle. . . . Yet the pages, within— I was always scared of the tale they told. Something about 'The Faceless shall deliver thee . . .'"

"The Koglaur," Sarasper whispered. "Those who walk among us, weaving a design we know not, always watching . . . even in the temples of Forefather Oak, we were taught to fear them, for they serve none of the Three, and speak not of their intentions, even under magical urging."

"So who are they?" Craer hissed. Embra and Sarasper shrugged in unison.

The Four stared up at the scene floating above them and saw the Koglaur striding through the Silent House to the room that held the hacked and scarred Throne of

Silvertree. He set the Stone of War upon its seat, murmured something over it, and then slipped out a hitherto-secret door, leaving the Dwaer sitting there.

Sarasper cleared his throat. "We must get it at onc—"

The air beside the throne shimmered and became a smiling Ingryl Ambelter, with a crown of Silvertree on his head. The wizard extended a finger, and lightnings briefly played between it and the Stone. When they died away, he shook his head and scooped up the Stone. "You Watchers are fools," he told the empty room scornfully, and vanished back into swiftly dying shimmerings.

With that the scrying-scene collapsed, leaving the Four blinking up at the ceiling of their room at the inn.

"Where's he gone?" Sarasper asked sharply.

Embra closed her eyes, and the Stone in her hands glowed once. When she opened them again, it was to reply calmly, "He's in Castle Silvertree."

Craer caught at her arm. "The Stone can *trace* folk? Why, we—"

Embra shook her head. "No, I called on the Stone to power my own perceptions. They trained me to be the 'Living Castle' of Silvertree; I can *feel* things through its very stones, and influence—in, I fear, too small ways—how the castle itself behaves." She sighed and sank back down into the tub until the waters touched her chin.

"Hand me a bottle, one of you, and then get dressed and packed," she announced wearily. "If we don't finish yon mage now, he'll finish us later this night, when sleep takes us."

Three men scrambled grimly to do her bidding. When the evening wine server rang his gong outside the locked door and then used his passkey to let himself in for the collection of empty wine flasks and to serve the bedtime hot nut-cider, he was astonished to find the palatial rooms empty except for a tub of cold water, a forest of empty wine bottles, and a scattering of gold coins across the unused beds.

The Band of Four were suddenly standing in a chamber Craer and Hawkril had seen before—a room hung with many gowns. Through gauzy curtains they could see warm, moving glows in the next room. A trio of glass lamps made to resemble floral blossoms were floating there about the shoulders of a man sitting at a table studying an open book.

"Ingryl Ambelter is my father's Spellmaster," Embra breathed in their ears. "He just might be the most powerful wizard in all Aglirta. Keep *very* quiet."

"What's he doing *here?*" Craer whispered back.

"I always had the best lighting," Embra said, as they watched the lamps drift. "Prettying myself, you know." She touched her companions, drew their heads together, and added, "Make ready, now. The moment he starts hurling spells, I want all of you touching me—at all times. It's the only way I can call on the Stone to protect you."

And she raised her hands and brought into being a bolt of lightning, following it an instant later by another. As their flaring birth made Ingryl's head jerk up, Craer threw a dagger at the wizard's face, as hard and as fast as he knew how.

Ingryl waved two fingers in greeting, smiling a wintry smile—and both the bolts and the dagger struck an unseen spellshield. The lightnings crackled right back at the Four, and Embra shouted, *"Remember—hold to me!"*

The snarling bolts struck, crashed blindingly around the Four, and swirled away again, leaving behind only numb tinglings. They saw the Spellmaster smile more broadly as a spell left his nimble fingers.

The air grew shadowy, half-seen fangs, mouths that

gaped and snapped. Craer ducked away from one and caught back hold of Embra's sleeve just in time, as she shouted warningly and the jaws swept down on the procurer, passing through each other in their haste to savage him.

Embra waved an arm and the half-seen fangs were gone, swept away in a sudden wash of white radiance that scattered like dying stars across the space between the two mages.

Ingryl clutched the Stone of War to his chest, book and all forgotten as he backed away from the table, fumbling a scepter from his belt with his free hand.

Embra's mouth tightened. She called on the Stone of Life and her years of spell-servitude to awaken her control of the Living Castle once more, her will rushing along well-worn links and enchantments and half-sleeping warding magics . . . and as the scepter rose to aim, a flood of painted tiles tore free of the ceiling and came crashing down on the Spellmaster, battering his arm back down to his side.

"You've got to advance on him, lass!" Hawkril roared, by her ear. "It's the only way our blades can reach him! Walk with us while working your spells!"

And he stepped forward. Frowning and nodding, Embra took a step forward to stay with him, and then another. Like a plodding turtle, the Four advanced together through a whirling storm of spells.

Tapestries battered the Spellmaster, and more tiles, smashing aside his scepter time and again as leaping lightnings snarled and spat between the Stones glowing on two breasts. The men of the Four reached for Ingryl Ambelter with their weapons as they came, and the angry snarling of lightnings rose ever louder in their ears.

Ingryl retreated, back through a door curtain and across a room until he passed through another curtain, moving from the garden side of Embra's chambers into the rooms overlooking the river. When his hip met the dark-polished table where her father had always met with her, the Spellmaster smiled for just an instant, and the Lady of Jewels wondered just what doom he was seeing for them.

An instant later, she saw—too late. There was another scepter lying on that table. The wizard made no move to try to snatch it up; he simply tapped it with the scepter he held, despite the whirling storm of tiles and tapestries she was hurling at him, and triggered the magic he already wielded.

The Stone of War flashed as it kept the Spellmaster from harm—and an instant later, the castle all around them exploded.

The sound smote their ears like a hammer, deafening the Four so that what happened next seemed to befall in something of a peaceful hush. All was blinding brightness, and hurtling through the air, striking unseen things very hard—and then being half buried in rubble.

The death of two scepters, one in his hand, should have torn Ingryl Ambelter apart. Instead it reduced most of the Lady Silvertree's riverside apartments to rubble, hurled the Band of Four back the length of a room, and then flung them in all directions.

Desperately Embra caused what was left of the walls and sconces and tapestry rails to rain down on the last of her father's mages, but through their battering Ingryl cast a spell as fast as a striking snake.

Out of his hands roared the purple fire that turns flesh and bone to jelly—straight at the only one of the Four still standing: the staggering Hawkril, doggedly launching himself into a charge.

Embra frantically called on her Stone to work a spelljump on the armaragor—and managed to snatch a startled Hawkril out of the room onto its adjoining balcony, an instant before Ingryl's deadly fire would have swept him out of Darsar forever.

Something else flashed across the room then, bounding and somersaulting amid the dust and rubble: Craer Delnbone, with a dagger in his mouth and death in his eyes. He'd seen his oldest friend charge the wizard and disappear; Hawkril Anharu had to be avenged.

Ingryl was clambering free of the wrack Embra had pelted him with—the only things her control of the castle could reach in that room, a control lost once they'd been torn free of the walls and hurled. He barely had time to snap out a flamefist spell.

The procurer ducked away, rolled, kicked a shattered chair up into the path of the pursuing spell-flames, bounded into the air, and when he came down somersaulted again and launched himself into a dropkick that caught Ingryl low in the belly, hurling the Spellmaster back through the Lady Silvertree's largest oval standing mirror.

Amid its singing shards Ingryl lost a lot of blood, bouncing hard as the frame spun around and collapsed on top of him, and as one elbow struck the floor, he lost his grip on the Stone of War.

Craer bounded after it, but Ingryl didn't have to rise to aim one hand along the floor and gasp the word that smashed the procurer across the room in a web of flames.

Craer screamed and fell. The Spellmaster laughed and flung aside the mirror frame to get up and finish off the procurer with the last flamefist.

Embra called on her Stone and her failing control of the castle once more. The scorched carpet underneath both Spellmaster and procurer reared up wildly, spilling both men into the air. Flames caught one of Craer's hands but spent the rest of their fury on walls and carpet as Ingryl was dashed face-first into the floor, spitting curses—and as she'd served the armaragor, Embra also aided Craer, plucking the sorely wounded procurer out onto the river balcony.

There was a grunt of triumph, then, that made both mages turn their heads. Sarasper Codelmer was rising to his feet with the Stone of War clutched firmly in his hands. Anger twisted his face as he turned and glared at the Spellmaster.

Then he came to a swaying halt, his eyes blazing.

Sarasper, I am Old Oak. I command thee. Blast this woman and the two men out on the balcony, with all the fires the Stone can hurl. Blast them all. I command thee! I am Old Oak. STRIKE NOW!

Lying on his side on the crumpled carpet, Ingryl Ambelter let his "god" voice fall silent as he willed Sarasper to turn—and raised both of his own hands and hurled a dozen firelances at Embra Silvertree.

Only her Stone could shield her against so many seeking deaths. As Embra called on it, Sarasper turned again, and the Stone in the healer's hands spat red and black ravening fire at her.

Desperately Embra dropped the shield she was raising, and out of its chaos whirled herself and Sarasper out onto the balcony, spinning the healer around once more to send the war fire of the Stone out over the river, away from them all.

It melted the very stones of the floor as it went, cutting cleanly through floorboards, pillars, furniture and all in a dark slash of disintegration that took her breath away. What in all Darsar could stand against *that?*

The war fire swept out into the empty sky, and Ingryl snarled another spell: a simple enchantment bonfire wizards use, a noose of force that lasted for only the instants needed to trip the legs of a warrior . . . or an aging healer with the most potent weapon in all Darsar in his hands.

As Sarasper toppled, the war fire lashed upward—and a turret of the castle directly above him exploded into huge shards of stone and started to fall. Ingryl kept the noose to the very end, rolling the old man over and over. War fire sheared through the balcony beneath the healer, cutting it away from Castle Silvertree.

As it started to fall, and the shattered turret thundered

down the fortress wall after it, the Living Castle poured its pain into Embra—pain such as she'd never known before.

She screamed out her agony, clinging to just enough wits in its red roaring to bend all the power she and the Stone in her bleeding hands had left into thrusting the falling turret sideways to veer in *through* her shattered rooms, right at the Spellmaster now rolling across the carpet toward the safety of an open doorway.

The turret crashed into her chambers in a scouring flood of tumbling stone, rushing across the carpet as a grinding, shrieking chaos of shattered rock.

Ingryl's dying scream didn't last long. Two stones ground him to liquid between them in an instant, in their thundering haste to roll the width of the castle and see the gardens for themselves. They made it, too.

No one stood watching. Embra Silvertree was shuddering and arching uncontrollably, her raw, throat-stripping scream echoing from end to end of Silvertree Isle, as the broken balcony, the Band of Four, and both Dwaerindim crashed down into the river below.

The Silverflow swallowed them, and but for a brief glimmer of radiance under its fast-rushing waters as awed armsmen rushed along the battlements from the other end of Castle Silvertree, no more was seen in the Coiling but tortured waves tossed up by the slow rain of falling stones.

He'd heard the voice coming out of the darkness before.

"Flaeros Delcamper," it greeted him warmly. "Come and sit over tankards and talk to an old lion."

Flaeros of Ragalar flushed with pleasure as the three arrogant bards he'd been trying to impress all night gasped, and one of them murmured, "You *know* Inderos Stormharp?"

He nodded pleasantly to them as he swirled away to

where Stormharp was sitting. "Of course," he replied gently. "Don't you?"

The darkness gave him a chuckle. "Your blades are as keen as they are gentle, youngling. So, now: tell me what Sirlptar knows of the battle at Castle Silvertree."

Flaeros sat down. "My thanks, sir, for your interest and for this tankard." He interpreted the dismissive wave of a hand correctly, and without further ado added, "Sir, they speak of nothing else. The Lady's Tower, if I'm calling it right, lies open to the stars this night, that whole end of the castle riven. They say the baron is dead or missing, and all the Dark Three—his mages, that is, but of course you know that, my pardon—too."

The old, lion-maned bard chuckled. "Slowly, slowly, lad . . . unless of course a lady or a challenge waits for you, and I'm keeping you from it!"

"No, no," Flaeros replied, with an embarrassed laugh. "Nothing so grand, I'm afraid. Just . . . nerves. It's all so exciting. Some bargemen saw the Lady of Jewels, you see—"

"Yes?" Stormharp asked sharply.

"Uh, ah, yes, Lady Embra Silvertree herself. She was seen to destroy a turret of the castle, and a balcony that she and others were standing on, sending it crashing down into the river. Neither she, nor her mysterious companions, nor the baron and his mages have been seen in the days since."

"She still lives," the old bard told the table softly, seeming for a moment to have forgotten Flaeros was there. "I'd be able to tell if she died."

Sometimes it seemed to Flaeros Delcamper that he stood like a fencepost while important folk galloped by, rushing past before he could even learn their names, let alone understand their hastes. Hesitantly he clutched the reassuring, heavy coldness of his tankard and asked, "Ah—why?"

"Hmm?"

Flaeros never knew, later, how he dared to ask that question, with one old eye staring at him across the table like a hawk who's just realized that helpless prey is sitting right under one of its talons. "You'd know if she died—how so?"

The hawklike gaze dropped, and Stormharp said, "I was one of the four commoners used in a spell cast on Embra Silvertree when she was but an infant. 'Anchors,' her father's wizard called us, then; I heard later that the magic, which had to do with stone, as I recall, and calling to us through it, was part of something mages call a 'Living Castle.' I've never been able to get any of them to explain that or even to admit those words mean anything. But perhaps it's just that I never had cartloads of coins enough to go with my questions, if you catch my meaning."

Flaeros nodded, and they sipped from their tankards in companionable silence. The young bard glanced around, but could see only a few figures, sitting at other tables—none close, though the three bards were looking longingly in their direction—in the gloom of this shadowy back leg of the taproom.

"Ah, Flaeros," the old bard said then, as much hesitation in his voice as Flaeros had felt earlier, "have you ever heard the tale of why Blackgult and Silvertree, rivals down long years, became in latter days such, ah, deadly foes?"

"No," the young bard said eagerly. "Please, tell me! This is one of those things that everyone seems to think all folk know—and shouldn't speak of. Please!"

"Well," the old bard said from behind his tankard, "I just haven't the stomach for all the grand phrases and trappings, right now—so to say it simply: the man they called the Golden Griffon was well favored and caught the eye of many a lady. Ah—in short, he fathered Embra Silvertree. When Faerod Silvertree guessed this, he slew his wife, enspelled his daughter into virtual slavery, and raised war on Baron Blackgult."

"By the Three," Flaeros said in awe. "All that bloodshed and strife because two nobles couldn't control their loins."

A silence followed his words, and as it grew longer and deeper the young bard swallowed, a sudden fear rising in him that perhaps he'd angered the great Inderos Stormharp.

The old man's tankard was set solidly down on the table between them, ringing empty, and the cold feeling in Flaeros grew.

He sat frozen, watching an old hand cupped over the tankard as a long, silent time passed. Then the hand went away, and he heard the bard sigh and murmur, "Ah, but she was beautiful."

An old lion rose then, stalking as if he'd once been a fighting man and a graceful, handsome dancer to boot, waved to him in silent farewell, and strode away across the darkened room.

Flaeros let his own hand fall from the wave he'd given in return, then half rose from his seat with a gasp as the old bard ducked out a door, turning his head a trifle.

"Inderos Stormharp" was really—Baron Blackgult!

By the Three! When he tol—

His eyes fell on a face visible by a curtain not far away—a face that was watching him intently, studying Flaeros Delcamper as if a bard's each breath, pimple, and every stray glance betrayed many secrets.

He'd never seen this watcher before, but something about the man made Flaeros swallow and sit down again quickly. It was hard to say what seemed so dangerous; the man had nondescript looks, wore the trail leathers of a forester, and offered the world a close-cropped beard and a pleasant expression.

Nevertheless, Flaeros almost dropped his tankard in

his haste to pick it up, as he tried *very* hard to look young and uncomprehending, reminding himself that he was still both of those things, though perhaps not as much now as he had been just an hour ago. His life might well depend on his apparent innocence.

Wherefore he hoped he was succeeding in looking foolish. As a bard, he *should* be able to. After all, it was something most courtiers managed every day.

The murmuring that had soothed her for so long became the fluid gurgle of rushing waters, sweeping her back to sudden dark terror and remembered pain.

"No," she cried, into the endless darkness. "I can't save them! I love them all, and *I can't save them!*"

With a shriek she sat upright, staring at nothing, still asleep. A man frowned at that. Her first moans had awakened him from his doze on blankets where he'd been lying beside her for days, waiting for her to rouse.

"Is she awake?" a voice called gently and excitedly across the riverside cavern, but the hulking man on his knees beside her made a sharp gesture for silence, and the voice did not come again.

"Lady," he said, his deep voice so low it was almost a whisper. "Lass, come back to us. We're all here . . . you saved us all."

The staring, unseeing lady trembled all over, suddenly. For the first time in days her white-clenched grip on the Stone loosened, and it rolled out of her grasp.

Hawkril calmly caught it before it rolled into the water, and hefted it in his hand.

Embra seemed to sigh, and he almost tossed the Stone away in his haste to catch her as she sagged, and lower her gently—ever so gently—back down onto the blankets. He cast a look back across the cavern to where the other two men were talking in low tones and then shrugged. Let them see, and tease.

The armaragor bent forward with infinite care, and

kissed the pale-skinned, sleeping lady full on the lips. For a moment she lay slackjawed, and then, slowly, responded, molding her lips to his and lifting herself against him, as if offering herself.

A slender hand rose to trace his stubbled jaw and then patted his cheek and pushed him gently away. A smile crossed parted lips, Embra Silvertree's head fell to one side, and she slept. In peace, now, still smiling, her hands no longer claws around a stone that could reshape the world.

Suddenly reminded of the power he held in his lap, Hawkril Anharu juggled it gingerly, quelled a wild urge to just hurl it into the waters rushing past, and then cradled it to him. Something seemed to thrum and awaken in it, whispering to him, showing him endless, rousing power. . . .

"No!" he hissed, speaking to it as if it were a disobedient child. He held it in both hands and shook it. "I've a sword and my strength, and that's enough. Let clever folk play with you—and get burned for their troubles."

The Stone seemed to murmur in his ear, at first soothingly and reassuringly, and then inexorably and repeatedly, like a war drum driving armies on, until Hawkril was bent over it, straining to hear.

"Hawk? Hawk, what're you up to?" Craer asked sharply. He found his feet with easy grace and started across the cavern. Sarasper, too, was watching Hawkril in sudden apprehension.

The armaragor looked around at them like a guilty child caught stealing sweets and growled, "Nothing. Ah—nothing."

And then, with Craer Delnbone still six strides away and unable to do more than watch, Hawkril reached out with the Stone in his hand, like a small child experimenting, and touched it to a second Dwaer: the Stone of War, sitting on the blankets Sarasper had left some hours ago.

The Dwaerindim sang, and a sudden radiance appeared around them.

"Hawk!" Craer snarled in alarm. The armaragor hastily pulled the Stone Embra had carried for so long back to his breast, away from the other Dwaer.

The radiance stretched to follow it, brightening into an arc between them that arched and rose . . .

"Sarasper?" the procurer called urgently over his shoulder. "We may need a spell!"

The glow became man-high, and acquired colors . . . hues that shifted like threads in a rich fabric around the edges of its bland brightness. In her slumber, Embra made a small, disturbed sound.

Abruptly the radiance became a scene hanging in the air, like the scrying-scenes Embra had called out of the Stone. It was a view of someone none of them had ever seen before.

A man in gleaming black armor, all smooth and supple curves trimmed with silver, sitting in a vaulted room upon a throne made of flames, his head bent on his breast in slumber.

"The Sleeping King!" Sarasper gasped.

"Gods, yes!" Craer echoed, his voice hoarse with excitement. "The king!"

"He's real!" Hawkril added, in a trembling voice. His heart lifted in hope—as if all the rosy things he'd been told as a child about the Three providing for Darsar were true.

"Shaerith melbratha immuae krontor," Embra Silvertree snapped from where she lay, her words seeming to echo across the cavern. "Arise, Kelgrael! Awaken, Snowsar! Return to your throne, for Aglirta has need of thee! *Shaerith melbratha immuae krontor!*"

Her words echoed and rolled around them like thunder . . . and the eyes of the enthroned figure opened. His pupils kindled into twin flames, just as in all the tales.

"The king! The king!" they shouted together. The

figure seemed to see them and smile—and then, quickly, started to fade.

"He's going!" Hawkril hissed desperately. "What shall we do?"

"Kneel to him," a sleepy Embra muttered from behind them, "and then go and find him."

"But where?" Craer snapped, as radiance and king faded entirely away together.

"I know that room," Sarasper whispered, all of the color gone from his face. "It's in Silvertree House. Embra must not accompany us—or she'll perish, to be sure: the curse of the Silent House."

"And how is it you know *that?*" Hawkril rumbled in astonishment.

"Something Baron Blackgult once said," the old healer said wonderingly. "I never knew what it meant until now."

They heard Embra gasp behind them, and whirled around, reaching for weapons.

The sorceress was stretching out her hand to the Stone of War—and her fingers were passing through it, as though it was but an illusion. It was pulsing with faint flashes of light, and with every flash its image grew more ghostly, fainter . . . and fainter . . .

"What's happening?" Craer snapped, his dagger in his hand. "Embra?"

"It's taking itself away," the Lady of Jewels said slowly. "Just as the writings said it would, if used thus. Going somewhere else."

"Writings? What writings?" The procurer seemed suddenly furious. "Does everyone know all the secrets of Aglirta but me?"

As the Stone of War faded entirely away, Hawkril laid a large and steadying hand on his friend's shoulder. They all looked at the Stone of Life; Embra was clutching it against her breast with both hands, as if fearing to lose it, too.

"Everyone feels like that betimes, Longfingers," the armaragor said roughly. "We just have to get up and go on. Just now, there's a king waiting for us—think of that! It's not every Aglirtan who gets to be the first to greet a king who's slept for a thousand years!"

Craer blinked at him, suddenly abashed. "You want *me* to greet him?"

"I thought you'd want the first chance to dip into his pouches and pockets," Hawkril said in dry tones. "You being the procurer . . . and the desperate one of us two, remember?"

And for once—just once in his swift, eventful life—Craer Delnbone could think of nothing to say.

Raurdro Muthtathen had never much liked this muddy little patch at the bottom of his river pasture. He'd failed to see why it remained so wet, with a stream either side of the field and no trees hereabouts with roots to hold the damp . . . and failed all over again right now, as he reached out with a hoe and a dark expression to uproot a tangle of muck weed.

And to stare astonished at the round, hand-size stone that appeared in midair with a brief, silent flash of light, right in front of him, and fell into the mud beside his hoe with a loud *plop.*

Raurdro reached down to pluck it out and hurl it to the stonepile back over his left shoulder, looking to the sky but seeing no playful bird or anything else that might have dropped or hurled it. Disbelievingly, he hefted the stone in his hand.

It was warm and made his palm tingle . . . almost as if it was *alive,* thrumming with its own inner energy. The astonished farmer stared down at it, his wits just beginning to tell him to throw it away, hard and fast, before . . .

The shimmering in the air behind him became the full-blown arrival of a gray-scaled woman in wine-dark robes. Her forked tongue darted at the farmer's back as she brought her hands up from her sides, in twin throws.

Her loud hiss brought Raurdro lurching around to face her—in time for his nose and cheek to take the wide-stretched fangs of the flying snake the serpent-priestess had launched from her left hand. The other snake swerved and darted over to sink its fangs into the wrist of the hand that held the strange stone.

And as Raurdro gurgled, stiffened, and took a step back—the last step he would ever take—the priestess pounced with the speed of a striking snake, snatching the Stone of War from his hand.

"Have my thanksss, dead man," she hissed, as the shimmerings started to take her away again. Her snakes darted hastily into the radiance so as not to be left behind, as a cold breeze arose out of nowhere to blow across a pasture in Ornentar . . . a breeze that ruffled the hair of the purple-faced, foam-lipped farmer who lay on his back, staring forever at a blue and cloudless sky.

Epilogue

Sunlight gleamed on a tabard that flamed with its own sun—the symbol of the Risen King of Aglirta. The wearer of the tabard would have topped six feet in height had he been standing on the ground. He was sitting in a saddle almost as high as that, on the largest and most magnificent horse the graveyard had seen for many a century. He wore a plumed hat, gauntlets as heavy and impressive as those of any fighting baron, and a coldly formal expression. Only his eyes betrayed his rising anger. They were like two tiny suns straining to join the competition.

"One does not," the herald on the horse said severely, "ignore a summons from the Risen King of Aglirta."

The old man standing in front of the Silent House squinted up at him. "I'm not ignoring it. I'm refusing it." He started to turn away, then looked back and said, "You're probably too young to appreciate the difference."

He turned away again and added without turning. "Your tabard's torn down your right side, did you know?"

The herald's face went scarlet. "I—ah—sir! Goodman Sarasper! The king calls you to *court!*"

The old man turned around again, a certain sharpness around his eyes. "Old I may be, but there's as yet—thank the Three—nothing whatsoever wrong with my *ears*. I heard you, and I hear you now. You have done your office—and have my leave to depart. Or are you too young to heed hints, yet?"

The air in front of Sarasper shimmered, barring the old man's way back into the Silent House. The emptiness blossomed with many winking lights, fading and falling like tiny stars as they shaped a tall, slender figure clad all in black, sleek shoulders and a glistening fall of silver-mounted jewels, and . . .

The herald sat in his saddle gaping openmouthed as the air gave forth the Lady of Jewels, standing in the old healer's way and smiling faintly. She lifted her eyes to the herald, gave him a smile, and then pointed him firmly back the way he'd come.

Without another word, he bowed his head, turned his horse, and went. It is not the business of heralds—even Voices of the Risen King—to argue with sorceresses cloaked in all their power.

"Embra," the healer growled, squinting at her with more eagerness and favor than he allowed his voice to tell the world he felt, "are you as reluctant to stand before the River Throne as I am?"

"Of course," the head of House Silvertree replied. "Which is why we're going there together—each one dragging the other along. I don't want to be the Baroness Silvertree, trusted by none, and be named a traitor whenever my father and his mages reappear. Barons and tersepts in plenty are just itching to ride here and settle their grudges against anyone wearing the name of Silvertree . . . and they'll use swords to do it."

She smiled affectionately at the old man, tousled his hair with her spread fingers, and asked, "And why are *you* so reluctant to answer the royal summons?"

Sarasper gave her a dark look. "Too many soldiers for my liking. Most barons want a healer in chains, as their own hidden healing machine—perhaps this king does, too."

The Lady Silvertree pursed her lips and nodded her head slowly. "I don't think he's that way, but I see your peril . . . who's to know until it's too late?"

Sarasper nodded gloomily and clapped a hand against one vine-cloaked wall of the Silent House. "Here, at least, I have passages to hide in and dark places to run to," he growled. "Over yon . . ."

He jerked his head toward the river, and the island there. Castle Silvertree it had been, all his life, but Flowfoam Isle it had been when there was a king in Aglirta before, and Flowfoam Isle it was again now. The Risen King's court. Aglimmer with a hundred lamps at dusk every night, and the Silverflow busy with boats at all hours. Sarasper shrugged to show Embra what little he thought of his chances of escaping it, if King Snowstar should desire him to remain—and she nodded soberly.

"Where have you dwelt, this month and more?" he asked suddenly. "Is there aught left of your own castle, 'tother end of the isle? Or were you judged too dangerous to be that near his High Mightiness?"

Embra's face split into a sudden smile. "There are lodges here and there among the gardens; I've been quite happy to move into one of the smallest and most secluded. As to the court—yes, it *was* amazing how many righteous lordlings rose up out of nowhere to demand me out of my lands and away."

She leaned against a mossy headstone of some long-forgotten ancestor and added serenely, "I told them all to go and talk to the king—and warned them that if anything befell me, the walking statues would awaken and tear apart the entire isle, themselves, king, and all, and there'd be no one alive to stop them."

Sarasper's dry laugh turned into a wheeze, and worse. He was still coughing, face in a rueful smile and leaning on the wall for support, when an all-too-famil-

iar voice asked, "Is this a private moment of passion?
Or may I have the next dance?"

"Craer!" Embra cried, only a breath or two behind
Sarasper's croak of "Little thief! Welcome!"

"I'm here, too," Hawkril rumbled, stepping into view
around the corner of the Silent House. A moment later,
he'd swept the Lady Silvertree off her feet in a surprisingly gentle bearhug, his greeting a deep and purring
roar.

Embra was surprised to find her eyes wet with tears.
"Put me down, you lumbering bear!" she cried, more
amused than upset. There seemed to be backslapping
and sly tradings of jests occurring near at hand, where
the procurer and the healer stood. She delivered a few
playful blows to the armaragor's head and shoulders,
found warm lips seeking hers . . . and found their touch
good.

It was in fact quite some time, and she'd delivered
herself of several moans with her lips still locked on
those of Hawkril Anharu, when a comical chorus of
loud and oh-so-casual throat clearings brought her back
to noticing Sarasper and Craer—and their raised eyebrows.

"Why, Craer," she observed, without a hint of embar-
rassment, "you're all over silks and furs! Whence this
finery?"

The procurer pointed down toward the river. "Court.
King. Ladies to impress. No longer do I look good in a
dress."

"Shall we?" Hawkril rumbled, waving his own hand
toward the water. "The herald gave me to understand
that there's a boat waiting for us."

"Ah," Sarasper said a little grimly, "did he also promise that it would be waiting to bring us back again, at
our pleasure?"

"No, O Suspicious Skulker," the procurer said, "he
did not. By the Three, Sarasper, set aside your mistrust
for one night at least! There's a king in Aglirta again,

set there by *our* hands . . . do you think he means to murder us, by way of thanks?"

"You're expecting a lordship?" the healer asked dryly, looking the magnificently garbed procurer up and down. "For Hawkril, too?"

"Why, yes," Craer replied seriously. "A title, a keep each to call our own, and retirement there forthwith to indulge in a little hunting, a little drinking, a little— pray pardon, Embra—wenching . . ."

"Lord Delnbone," Sarasper said softly, "would you mind drawing back your right sleeve?"

The procurer gave him a brittle smile, and did so. Two knives gleamed in a double forearm sheath there, ready to be plucked and thrown in an instant.

The healer nodded, not quite smiling. "And the other sleeve?"

Craer displayed another pair of knives and then bent, unbidden, to touch the hilts of knives in both boots, as well as the one they could all see at his belt. None of his three companions doubted he had others, carried in places of rather better concealment.

"Trust in our new king strong and surging, eh?" Sarasper asked innocently. "Lordships for all, eh?"

"Sarasper," Craer told him in tones of gaiety, "I said I was expecting a lordship. I didn't say I'd lost my senses."

"Ah," the old man replied. "Well. I *was* intimating you had, and still am."

"Nothing changes much between us," Hawkril observed. "Shall we to the boat?"

They moved forward without hesitation, together.

"Leave us," the Risen King commanded, in a voice that rolled to the corners of the room, sharp with sudden command. Courtiers and trumpeters and guardsmen alike blinked, hesitating.

"But your Majesty," the officious steward who'd

found most—but by no means all—of Craer's knives protested, "these folk come armed! With weapons and spells! Who knows wha—"

"It would grieve me to grow accustomed, so early in the resumption of my reign, to having to repeat my orders," King Snowsar said mildly, allowing his eyes to flash just once as he strode forward to loom over the suddenly pale courtier.

The room emptied in a rush that owed more to haste than dignity. The steward actually uttered a squeak as he turned and bolted.

The Band of Four kept their faces carefully impassive. The king directed silent looks at Craer and Hawkril, then nodded at the doors. The two turned to make sure the known ways out of the room were secured and relatively free of folk pressed against them to listen, and Embra glided forward to murmur, "Lord and King, there is a secret passage behind that tapestry, and spy holes above us here. Might I suggest we use the way behind your throne, and repair to a chamber I know to be rather more secure?"

The corners of the king's mouth twitched. "And have them tearing apart the castle looking for me?"

Sarasper shrugged. "It'll give them something useful to do."

The king's mirth built into a roar of laughter. When he could speak again, he turned to the Lady of Jewels and said, "I know I can trust you. Lead us to your secret place."

Embra bowed her head and did so. The secret place proved to be a small, ornately paneled room crowded with a small table and some large, comfortable chairs. The king's brows rose in pleased surprise at the sight; Embra gave him a grin and said, "As I'm sure you've already discovered, the Silvertrees made a few changes to your castle. I hope this one, at least, meets with your approval."

"My lady, it does," the king told her.

She turned and did something to a panel. It slid aside to reveal a window overlooking a long avenue of trees into the gardens. Outside, all was green and beautiful. They heard the King of all Aglirta gasp in pleasure.

He leaned forward to admire the view, spreading his hands flat on the table, and Embra calmly sat in the nearest chair and put her delicately booted feet up.

Her three companions eyed her, then shrugged and found themselves comfortable seating, too. The king seemed unsurprised at their dispositions when he turned around again.

He gathered their gazes with his own and said simply, "Have my thanks. Neither I nor Aglirta can ever properly repay you. I had hoped to shower you with land and gifts, bring out the best Silvertree vintages, and spend a month talking with you, getting to know my kingdom again. But that's not to be; that month is time none of us has."

"A task for us, then, not a revel," Craer murmured.

The king nodded. "This is not," he added quietly, "a time for celebration."

He started to pace in the tiny room, restlessly, looking up to its ceiling and seeing not gloom and shadows but something in his memory. "Two nights ago, I dreamed of the missing Stones."

"Shall we go and round them up for you?" Craer asked. "A grand quest for the King's Champions?"

The Risen King shook his head, his eyes large and dark. "The dream changed, Craer."

He seemed to stand taller, looming over the Four. "The people cry out in joy for their king restored—at least for now—and the barons cry out with them. Yet not a one of my loyal barons has joy in his eyes when he comes here . . . and all of them have men skulking here and there, answering only to them, sniffing out ways to make the River Throne weak or even topple me from it to make room for their own masters. I am besieged here among the silks and gold, one man encir-

cled by wolves. The River Throne will fall if I leave it
unwarmed for as much as twenty days, and I have no
army that is not beholden first to this baron or that. As
you just saw, I find myself cloaked around and about by
glib-tongued men whom I know not, who seek to raise
themselves by clinging to me and speaking in my
name . . . I dare not leave this island to do what must be
done."

The procurer raised an eyebrow. "And that would
be?"

"Find the unfriends who aren't here," Embra Silvertree murmured. "The ones who keep hidden, biding
their time and building their power—because they now
hold other Dwaer stones."

The king nodded slowly. "You freed me, never knowing why I slept." He leaned forward and asked in a low
voice, "What were you told would happen when I
awakened?"

"The king will rise," Sarasper replied, in mellifluous
mockery of the voice of a sage, "to restore peace and
bounty to the land."

King Kelgrael nodded. "And yet that was never my
task. In a time when the realm was strong and needed
no king, I agreed to sleep, to await the time when I
would be needed to fight a great foe of Aglirta. By freeing me, you—"

"Oh, no!" Embra gasped. "Three save us, no!"

The King of Aglirta nodded grimly. "You awakened
that foe, too. Others less than friendly to Aglirta were
alerted, too. Some of the Stones have fallen into cruel
hands."

As he spoke, the Dwaer riding in Embra's bodice
flashed, lighting up her throat with an eerie glow. As
they stared at it, Sarasper said grimly, "Someone is using another Dwaer to seek this one."

The Lady of Jewels nodded and passed her hand over
the Stone. The radiance was suddenly gone, the room
shadowed once more.

"My father lives, I do not doubt that," Embra murmured. "I would be unsurprised to meet with one or more of his mages alive again, too."

The king nodded. "I did not mean to accuse you, Lady, or impugn your loyalty. Aglirta has many enemies, not all of them risen since I first left my throne, and they grew to like lawlessness. They are gathering now, wolves beginning to circle."

Something dark and swift flapped its wings past the window just then, causing everyone to start and snatch at weapons. A bat glared red-eyed at them for a moment as it fluttered, circling once before flitting from view.

"That was less than natural," Hawkril growled. The Four exchanged glances, and in grim unison they drew their weapons.

"Have you noticed, any of you," Craer asked bitterly, "that the work of heroes is *never* finished?"

"Until death finishes everything for them," the old healer told him quietly. "I wonder how many barons' spies are waiting for us to leave this room right now?"

The king nodded grimly and undid the lacings of the pouch at his hip. "Lady Embra, I have gathered here what you'll need to cast a spell that carries you all away together, against that very peril."

"Your Majesty is too thoughtful," Embra murmured, not raising her eyes.

Kelgrael Snowsar sighed. "You, too, Embra Silvertree? Have I *no* friends in all the Vale?"

"I did not mean that," the sorceress said quickly, lifting pleading eyes to meet his gaze. "I hope you never have cause to doubt us, Lord of Aglirta."

"The name is Kelgrael," the king said quietly. "And I hope, in time to come, to name you all Lords and Ladies of Aglirta. I desire this almost as much as I desire the gods to keep an Aglirta safe and standing for all of us to enjoy, as we grow old."

"Sounds like a childrens' fireside tale to me," the armaragor rumbled, and the king nodded grimly.

"Aye," he said, as he slapped purses heavy with shifting coins into their palms, "I fear it does. Go and write me a brighter one to stand with it."

The Adventures of
the Band of Four continue in

The
VACANT
THRONE

T he old minstrel shook his head. " 'Tis hard to believe, lad," he said, "even for such as us. Legends come to life—four vagabond adventurers, one of them the Lady of Jewels with her spells swirling around her like fire, rousing the Lost King back to us."

Flaeros Delcamper nodded, "I know, but it *did* befall just as I've said! I stood in the throne room on Flowfoam Isle and saw the barons kneel to the Risen King!"

His voice was rising, he knew, but Flaeros cared not. He was home in Ragalar, in the tankard-hung back room of The Old Lion, and the man across the table had been house minstrel to the Delcampers for near a century, and tutor to Flaeros since he'd been a boy.

Old Baergin smiled and shook his head again in disbelief, even though all Darsar had heard by now that the King had returned to Aglirta, and a shining future of peace and prosperity could well be opening up.

The hands that had guided the fumbling fingers of Flaeros on their first tentative pluckings at harp-strings set down their tankard, and their owner asked softly, "So what of these famous Four now, lad? What was the last you saw of them?"

Flaeros took a generous swig from his own tankard

A lowly band of four adventurers, thrown together by circumstance and adversity, must recover the legendary Dwaerindim stones to restore peace to the land and save themselves from a fate far worse than death.

"The Kingless Land . . . supercharged action and attention to detail that will undoubtedly satisfy Greenwood's core audience. There's more than enough arcane magic, pumped-up swordplay, and gory injury for the most dedicated gamer."   *—Quill and Quire*

". . . A new world of magic and bold deeds . . . a graceful tale of high fantasy."   *—Library Journal*

"Agreeably entertaining all the way."   *—Booklist*

"Energetic."   *—Kirkus Reviews*

Tor Books by Ed Greenwood

The Kingless Land
The Vacant Throne
A Dragon's Ascension
The Dragon's Doom

The Silent House